I0788223

OUT OF THE DARK

By: H.E. Willis

Dedication

To all my friends, family, and readers who critiqued, encouraged, and inspired. I couldn't have done this without you.

Chapter 1

Spring was too beautiful to spend indoors, especially that day. So, acting on impulse, Astrid paused just outside the longhouse door, and Hjordis, the house thrall, promptly ran into her from behind. Astrid blushed. Hjordis huffed, took the bowl of raw chicken from Astrid's hands, and swept inside. Astrid sighed. She'd annoyed everyone at home that day by being distracted by the outdoors. Well, she could enjoy it now, being alone.

A cool breeze swept by, playing with her two braids. The sun warmed her face and neck. Honey-sweet flowers bloomed in the pasture. Spring had been here for the past month, yet she never tired of it. The warmth meant household work could be done out-of-doors, a relief after the constant confined quarters of the smoky longhouse during the winter, and that made any work pleasant, even processing a chicken.

But spring meant raids, and raids meant young men had to leave, including her brother Sven. Whenever she could, Astrid went up to her favorite hill in the woods to pray for his safe return. Engaging in a raid was one thing, but leading it was quite another.

Work kept her home so far today, and she had no choice but to press down the growing desire and continue on until it drove her wild. The thought of the hill wouldn't leave. Something was different that day—she'd felt it as soon as her feet hit the floor that morning.

The inside of the smoky one-room longhouse was almost dark compared to the glaring afternoon sun. Light beaming through the front and back doors was just sufficient to illuminate the oblong fire pit in the middle and the laden shelves against the back wall. The three curtained-off rooms to the right would have blended with the brown plastered walls if the light had been any less, as would have the bench stretching from the nearest room to the front wall.

At one end of the fire pit, Mother was stirring a bubbling stew pot, and Hjordis was laying kindling into the fire, and at the other end, sweet-smelling flatbread cooked over live coals. Baby Snorri played with blocks to the left, near the door, and Sven's wife, Swanhild, sewed in her corner.

Hjordis finished her task and whisked away out the back door.

"Check the bread, please, Astrid," said Mother, glancing up and moving to the table. She picked up a knife and grabbed a turnip.

"Yes, Mother." Gingerly, Astrid used her fingertips to lift a piece. Its underside was golden-brown, so she set it down on its top side, flipped the others, and squatted down, leaning her elbows on the warm hearth. "They're nearly done."

"Good." Mother paused briefly to wipe gray hair from her forehead and tuck it under her headscarf. She took up a handful of chopped onions and tossed them into the pot first; they hissed as they hit the hot broth. Then she added the rest of the vegetables and gave the soup another stir. A brothy, onion-rich aroma rose, and Astrid's stomach rumbled.

"I'm going to the cellar," said Mother. "There is more dough that needs to be cooked, and make sure nothing burns on the bottom of the pot."

"I will."

Mother nodded and went behind the table to the loaded shelves, taking down a woven basket and settling it on her hip.

"Are you certain you don't want my help?" asked Swanhild from her corner. Purple smudged the skin under her eyes, and her shoulders sagged. Her round cheekbones, soft jaw, and round eyes were softer than ever because of the gentle shadows wrapping around her. The folds of her kirtle, created by her posture, only emphasized her large, round middle. Only four months remained before the baby's arrival.

"No," Mother snapped. More gently, "You did enough this morning. No arguing, rest. And stay there while I'm gone." She squeezed her daughter-in-law's shoulder and left.

Astrid watched her go and immediately regretted it. There was the bright green of the wood again. An itch formed between her shoulder blades; she squirmed and turned her back to the outdoors. Keeping the door open was finally permitted after the bitter cold that had kept them inside so long, but it only made today more difficult.

"Did you get in trouble again?" she asked Swanhild, grabbing the lump of dough on the tabletop and rolling it into a log.

Swanhild groaned. "I'm not as tired as I look, but she insists I rest whether I need it or not."

"You're not known for resting," Astrid teased. She cut the dough into rounds, shaped them, and plopped them onto a tray. "But I know you don't like being idle. Mending isn't idle, you know."

Swanhild shifted the jerkin in her lap and smiled her slow, blooming smile that must have won Sven's heart. "True, but she could have allowed me to watch the bread."

The bread pieces over the coals were done. Astrid stacked the round loaves on a plate and put the dough in their place, then settled down to watch them bubble and rise.

Snorri made a beeline to the door, crawling as fast as his legs and hands could go, but Swanhild, who was sitting nearby, caught him by his tunic as he passed by, picked him up, and set him back among his blocks, where he screamed and tried to get to the door again. Swanhild slapped his bare legs, told him to stay, and set him down again. This time, he didn't try to run away again, but pouted. "Watching him isn't idle, either," Astrid laughed, turning over the bread.

Chubby hands rested on her forearm, and Snorri pulled himself to his feet. His legs wobbled, but he smiled at his success and reached for the pan. Astrid grabbed her brother's hand and turned him around.

"No, Snorri. It'll burn you. Hot. Let's go play with your blocks."

Snorri tottered, and she caught his other hand. He eagerly walked back to his toys near the wall and plopped down among them. Grabbing one, he jabbered and held it up to Astrid, who couldn't resist. She took it and sat beside him as he began stacking the others. She added hers to the tower and straightened the rest. When the last one had been placed, the tower came tumbling down.

Astrid laughed at Snorri's rapture and looked to see if Swanhild enjoyed it as much as she, but Swanhild looked past her and cried, "The bread!"

Smoke tingled her nostrils. In a shot of panic, Astrid leapt to her feet and lifted a piece. The underside was black. She groaned and moved the burnt bread to the plate with the others.

Mother entered with a jar of sour goat's cheese (called skyr) and a small bag of dried fruit and stopped, sniffing. She looked at Astrid, who turned away to hide her burning cheeks and waited for a rebuke with tingling cold in her legs. This was not the first time today she'd been forgetful.

However, Mother merely shook her head in her tired and displeased way, making Astrid wish for the rebuke instead. Mother set her items on the table, then squatted by the pot, stirred it, took up a piece of chicken between her fingers, and, while blowing on it to keep her fingers from being burned, split it down the middle to see how far along it had cooked. She tossed it back in and wiped her hands on her smokkr. As she did so, she glanced up at the hanging cloak Sven had left behind, possibly forgotten, and sighed.

Poor Mother. She'd objected strongly to his leading a raid, but Father had talked her into agreeing to it. Their supplies from the meagre harvest wouldn't last long enough until crops and gardens began producing, he argued, and a raid was a perfect opportunity for Sven to show his capability for leadership. Although Mother eventually agreed to let him go, she was loath to do so. Astrid understood how she felt. Sven couldn't go off raiding and trading; he had to stay at home, where he was meant to be. If only coming of age didn't result in leaving and changes and empty chairs at the table. She shuddered.

All that remained was to let the meal cook. Mother joined Swanhild and picked up a bit of sewing, and Hjordis stayed outside to tend the garden.

Astrid remained where she was by the cooling bread pan, hesitating. Now was her chance, if it would ever come. She cleared her throat.

"Mother, can I go to the hill until the meal?"

Mother shot her a glance. She bit her thread, set the fabric aside and, taking up a stocking that needed darning, said coolly, "You usually do not return when needed." Her brown, calloused hand whipped the white bone needle through the worn heel.

"I'll be fast, I promise! Just for a moment!"

Mother nodded toward the door. "Very well, run along."

This is how the chickens must feel when released after a long storm. Astrid jumped up, giddy with excitement. "Thank you! I'll be back soon." She hastily kissed Mother's cheek before rushing out the door.

Freedom, at last! And naught but the woods before her. She broke into a run across the bare ground from the house to the woods and slowed only when she reached the path.

It was a thin, wandering path that she and Sven had visited daily from the earliest days of their childhood. It led through an old, memory-rich wood where no troubles remained as big as they were elsewhere. Elves must have lived there long ago, and the wood remembered them, holding their sense of wonder and peace for generations. She breathed it in. The air had an earthy, leafy smell of dew and rain mixed with the souls of flowers from springs past.

The path led her up and up, until it came to an end at the very top of a grassy hill on which a spreading oak grew. She skipped to the tree and wrapped her arms around its cool, rough trunk. Before her, the hill dropped into a cliff at the bottom of which bushes and young trees grew. The space in front was open, revealing the western sky with its curling clouds layered all the way to the ocean line. Today, the waves rose high, were crowned with foam, and crashed back down into the deep blue. Somewhere on the water was her brother with his ships sailing homeward. At least, she hoped he was.

She grasped her Mjolnir pendant and prayed aloud. "Odin, All-Father, give my brother victory. Thor, god of thunder and of the people, bring him safely home to me. I thank you for driving away the storms that had gathered for some time and ask you to keep the ocean clear for his return."

A gust of salty wind blew from the ocean, whipping through her hair and ruffling her eyelashes.

She closed her eyes to better relish it: the spring wind. With it came green in the trees and green in the grass, blues and purples and oranges in the flowers, driving away the dead brown, cold gray, and endless white of winter.

Another year had come and gone, and another had taken its place. She was now fifteen years old, past the marriage age of most girls. Perhaps the raid wasn't so terrible after all, for it bought but a little more time to remain home, with all the young men gone. Her stomach trembled, and she pressed a hand to it. Then she shook her head. Thinking of this would only spoil the moment. Father had always said all parts of life must be thought upon, but she didn't want to. Not right now.

She held the tree tightly with one hand and reached out as far over the cliff as she could with the other. A thrill shot all the way to her toes. None of her friends let her do it, but now she could do it as many times as she wanted without them interfering.

She drew back and sat on the edge of the cliff, letting her legs dangle over the edge. The sun was delightfully warm, and the breeze had died down to a steady caress. She leaned her head against the tree trunk and watched the sparkling waves until her eyes hurt. Above the waves, wind-torn clouds flew by like white clover.

"That one's like a fox skin," she murmured, "and that one's like Father's beard, bushy and long. Pity he keeps it shorter than he used to. Oh, and that one looks like Sven's knife. Dear Sven! How I miss him!" She sighed, plucked a blade of grass, and twisted it into a ring that fit nicely on her finger. If only he'd come soon. If the gods were kind and remembered her faithfulness to them, they would send him home safely.

But if she must marry, would that be kind of them? One of her friends had already married and borne a child, and by the looks of the young man hanging around Borgny's house, she was next. They were all growing up faster than she liked. She wasn't ready to leave her family. Yet, when the time came, she must.

She shook her head, closed her eyes as another breeze brushed her cheeks, and sang a few lines from the Volsung Saga.

Alone, abroad,

She sat in the evening,

Of many things

She fell a-talking.

No lack in her life

She wotted of now—

The breeze passed, and Astrid opened her eyes again—and stared. There was something on the ocean. Squinting, she made out five somethings— there were sails—they were longboats. As they came closer, the blue and yellow stripes on the sails grew visible. Excitement ran through her. They belonged to her island.

She scrambled up and ran back down the hill. Her feet flew across the bare ground, past the well, chicken coop, around a flock of protesting chickens and curious goats, to the longhouse.

Checking her speed by grabbing the doorway, she stopped, panting, and called. None but Hjordis was inside.

The house thrall shifted her mending and said, "We received news that boats have been sighted. The others have gone to the wharf."

"Thank you," Astrid answered, turning. The goats had followed her, and her knees collided with their round sides and sent her sprawling over them.

They bleated at her and scattered while she picked herself up and rushed down the footpath to the wharf.

She lived on the very edge of the village, where houses were spread out and separated by each family's fields. As she passed between them, they shrank in size, and longhouses moved closer. Eventually, the fields disappeared altogether and were replaced by backyard gardens enclosed by low picket fences, and the footpath merged into a dirt road. Another well was located here. Coops were smaller, and animal shacks were built into the houses. As she neared the wharfs, more villagers hurried alongside her, thickening until she was forced to a walk.

There were men, women, and children pressing and shoving and carrying a swift current to the wharves. They spoke in excited snatches: "They're here, our raiders are here!" There were smells of sweat and grain and smoke, of cattle, manure, and dirt, of onion and beets and bread. Many eyes shone and necks stretched to see above the crowd. Astrid was jostled from this side and that, stepped on by feet both big and small.

The hard-packed dirt road gave way to wooden planks from old boats, and the villagers spread out along the wharf. At last, she could breathe. She sucked in fishy ocean air and searched for her family. So many people dazzled her eyes, but to her relief, several crates were nearby. She stood atop one. Now she could see everyone! There was Father, waving from the edge of the wharf. She waved back. He shouted something, but even his big voice couldn't be heard above everyone else.

When the coast was clear around the crate, she jumped down and forced her way through until she bumped against Father's muscular back. Beside him stood Mother, who held Snorri, and Swanhild.

Father turned around and wrapped his arm around her shoulders, pressing her to his chest. His heart was pounding like a drum for a festive dance. "Your brother's returning," he said, his deep voice vibrating her cheek.

"I know." With her head still against him, she looked out at the nearing boats. His jerkin muffled her voice. "I saw them from the hill."

"Eh? What's that?"

Father bent his head down, and Astrid repeated herself.

"Ah," he said with a chuckle, "that's a good lookout." He tickled her face with his beard. "Were you a good girl today?"

She squirmed when she remembered the burned bread, but forced a laugh. Father meant it as a jest, although not two years ago, he said it to keep her from shirking her responsibilities.

"I hope so," she answered with a sideways look at Mother, who glanced her way and gave a nervous smile. Mother's thumbs worked the inside of her fingers, rubbing over and over, and muscles moved in her temple as she clenched her jaw. The same fear that haunted her now settled on Astrid, and she shivered. They couldn't have waited this long just to find out he'd never come back.

"Oh, Thor, no," she breathed.

Father's arms tightened around her.

The longboats neared; the sail was reefed, the boats were slowed, and oars splashed the water. Several men stood in the prows, waving proudly while the villagers shouted until Astrid's ears rang. She cheered, her throat sore.

The head boat pulled alongside them, and a rope was thrown to men who caught it, pulled the boat the rest of the way in, and tied it securely to a post. In the prow of the boat, a familiar figure signaled thanks and turned to grin and wave. It was Sven, happiness radiating from him. He was browner than ever, a dark scab ran along his cheek, his beard was a little longer,' he'd been through water and war, joy and sorrow, but he was still good ol' Sven.

He leapt onto the wharf, and Mother ran weeping into his arms. He held her tight, squishing Snorri between them, and whispered in her ear. Whatever he said must have been drowned out by Snorri's howl of protest, but Sven only laughed, took Snorri and tossed him until the little boy crowed with delight, then handed him to Mother and turned to embrace Swanhild.

"You're home!" Swanhild cried as she flung her arms around his neck.

Sven kissed her. "Are you any better than when I left?"

Swanhild laid a hand on her swollen stomach and rested her head on his chest. "Better now that you're here."

Astrid found herself blinking away tears. Why? She loved it when Sven and Swanhild showed their affection to each other, but this time, it brought an ache to her chest, something she hadn't felt for a long while. Was this longing? How could this be, when marriage would only take her from her family? She tried her best to smile when Sven looked her way.

He released Swanhild and tweaked one of Astrid's braids. "What have you gotten into since I left, little troublemaker?"

Astrid made a face just before he engulfed her in a hug. "Nothing, without you here to get me going."

Sven laughed and slapped her shoulder in his old way, but there was something amiss about his eyes. They looked down and seemed a little… occupied. Like something was on his mind, but he flashed a grin and said, "How about the hill after the meal?"

"I'd like that."

It was Father's turn now. They embraced, and Father shook Sven's hand heartily.

"Let's go now," said Mother, settling Snorri on her hip. "Hjordis is waiting with the evening meal."

As Astrid turned to go, she caught sight of another familiar figure. Isar. He jumped from the boat and nodded at her, one side of his mouth curved upward. In two of his big strides, he reached her before she could turn away.

"Heil, mær," he said warmly.

The warmest of tones couldn't fool her. She stiffened, returned the greeting for civility's sake, and marched to where her family was talking with some villagers, clenching her hands and muttering under her breath.

How dare he, after all those childhood years of tormenting her—calling her names, tweaking her hair (something only family or very close friends could do), laughing at her. If the verbal torment hadn't been enough, he left her alone in the woods when she was only six summers old. Sven and his friends had gone to the woods after sunset, and after much imploring, Astrid convinced Mother to let her go along with the condition that she stayed with at least one of the others. Somehow, she found herself alone with Isar, who told her to wait where she was while he looked around for Sven and never came back. She stayed put patiently until the eerie darkness of the wood put her into a panic. She ran around screaming and crying for Sven and finally found him. Isar was rebuked the following day, but wasn't punished severely enough.

How could he dismiss all of that and give a greeting of goodwill like they were close friends? He'd better not be starting it all up again, at his age. They were too old for such behavior.

Astrid put these things out of her mind when they reached the longhouse. It would have been difficult, if not impossible, for the most bitter brooder not to cheer up at least a little with all the laughing, story-exchanging, excitement at home that day. All worry was forgotten. The cause could have been served before the king, and the burnt bread could have been honey cakes. The creases on Mother's forehead smoothed away and were replaced by crinkling crow's feet around her eyes. Father let out his hearty, booming laughs. Swanhild stirred from Sven's shoulder only to spoon the skause in her mouth. Astrid had to sit on her hands to keep from grabbing her brother's. Even Hjordis and the other thralls eating at the bench were smiling.

"Tell us about the raid," Astrid begged.

Sven looked over Swanhild's head. "Not until I hear about things here. Has it been peaceful, Father?"

"Peaceful enough," said Father, raising his spoon to his lips and blowing briefly on the skause.

"Danes bothering you again?"

"Hmm? Oh, no, not yet. Their boats have been spotted near the island, though. Seems they're biding their time. Holskuldr won't rest until he tries to add us to his domain."

"Now that we're back, he doesn't stand a chance!" said Sven, raising his cup. "By Thor—" He stopped, and stuttered, "W-we're too much for him."

His gaze fell to his plate, and he stuffed a big piece of bread into his mouth.

Father grunted. "Besides that, the crops have sprouted, and the livestock is doing well. We have two new calves and six piglets, all healthy and growing fast. Now, how was the raid?"

"It went as smooth as can be expected," said Sven, keeping his eyes on his plate. He raised them momentarily—was there grief in them? "We sailed a few days before we arrived at the village. We pulled up a distance down the shore and went through the woods. The villagers couldn't organize well enough to retaliate thanks to our surprise. We quickly overpowered them and took our spoil. On our way back, a storm hit our boats and drove us far off course. Nothing was lost, however, and after an extra week of rowing, the island was spotted. Navigating from there was easy."

Mother sighed with relief.

"Anyone lost?" Father asked.

"None. Several showed great courage and character, Isar, son of Ragnar, most notably. Not only did he show valiant courage in battle, but he also kept his head during the storm." Sven glanced her way, and Astrid shrank back. Why had he singled out Isar?

Father raised a cup and made a toast. "To Sven, sped by the gods safely home. Freyja prosper you, my son."

Everyone raised their cups. "To Sven!"

They clinked, and there was a round of laugher. But, as Astrid looked over her cup while she drank, Sven set his down, licked his lips, and kept his eyes on his plate.

Swanhild leaned toward him and whispered, "What is it, darling? Are you ill?"

Sven glanced at his wife, smiled, and nuzzled her red hair. "Tis nothing. It will pass." Then louder, with a wink toward Astrid, "If Astrid's finished, Father, I promised to go with her to the hill after the meal."

Father chuckled and rose from his seat. "Then you'd better keep your promise. Off with you."

Astrid jumped up and danced out the door behind her brother. Once outside, she grabbed his hand and said, "It's good to have you home!" Sven looked down at her, frowning slightly, and said nothing. She felt like she'd been slapped. She dropped his hand, but he didn't make any sign that he noticed.

At the top of the hill, they seated themselves at the tree with her against it and him beside her. His brows settled over his eyes, and he stared off over the ocean. Astrid looked him over, from his light brown, shaggy hair to his big hands pressed against the ground. The big hands with the sun-bleached hair on top. Sven looked her way and attempted a smile. He played with one of her braids.

"You look troubled," she said.

All feigned happiness left, leaving him tired and worn. A haunted look came into his face. "What I tell you, I trust you not to tell anyone, not even Swanhild." He paused and studied the ocean.

Weight settled over her. Sitting up, she shuffled behind him, caught a lock of hair, and began to braid it as he liked her to do. It wasn't like him to be so grave. She waited for him to speak, braiding the same lock of hair over and over, tugging a little during the third time as his hair snarled.

He sighed. "Astrid, I've been a coward."

The words struck her like a thunderbolt. She laid a hand on his shoulder and opened her mouth to say it wasn't possible, that he must be mistaken, but he went on.

"No, it is true. When we entered the village, people fled. All but one: a feeble old man in a plain brown tunic. A monk, I think. He fell to his knees and shielded himself. His eyes, looking out from between his fingers, showed fear, then courage and… a reprimand. I couldn't move. My companions continued on. Ages seemed to pass. He lowered his hands and studied me. He frowned, then slowly, quietly, he said, 'My son, even now, search your heart. It is dead. But my God can make it alive again.'

"I found myself trembling and suddenly able to move. I rushed by him." Sven paused, and his chest heaved. "Later, after taking our spoil from the village, I chanced to go by that place again. The monk was dead." He swept a hand over his eyes. "Astrid, what has come over me? At the sight of him, I nearly dropped the chest I carried. How weak I've been! To mourn the death of one killed in a raid! But… his words have not left me. My heart is dead, feels dead. The days spent holed up with the spoil were maddening. The spoil doesn't give me the pleasure I thought it would; it only reminds me of that old man. The old man's words, his courage, wouldn't give me a moment of peace. It's led to—oh—such things I shouldn't think about." He clamped his lips shut.

"Like what?" she pressed.

A sigh. "The gods. Why we believe in them, why they're the way they are."

The anguish in his face hurt and frightened Astrid. A lump rose in her throat. She swallowed and crooned, braiding his hair again, "It will pass. Hasn't Father always said those monks are just religious? Good works and prayers and such."

"But what would make an old man like that not fear me? And how could he make me afraid? I could have killed him then and there! I should have!" A sudden movement jerked his hair from her fingers. He pummeled the ground beside them. Under his breath, he added, "Would have saved me from this."

No words came. She opened her mouth, closed it again, and swallowed. Sven tore up handfuls of grass and threw it over the cliff, then clawed dirt over the edge. In panic, she grabbed his hand and pressed it down to make him stop.

"Don't anger the gods more than you already have! This is why the storms came." Slowly, she straightened and let him go. "What do you think now?"

Sven rubbed his wrist on his temple. "I don't know. But the emptiness won't leave. What am I missing? What does he have that we don't? A different god, yes, but is that enough?" He fell silent, then shook himself. With a trembling breath, he straightened and forced a smile. "I didn't mean to come home in this way. But I needed to get it out, and I knew you'd understand better than anybody. You always have."

Again, she was silent. She ran her fingers over Sven's hand, but he pulled away and rubbed his temple again as if it ached. Until now, she's always understood. All their lives, they went on adventures together, hiked the woods together, shared their deepest secrets that otherwise would have smothered them. Now, she tried to understand and failed utterly. How could he doubt everything he'd known? The raid really was a bad idea.

Pushing her two braids behind her, Astrid climbed to her feet and tried her best to smile. Now wasn't the time to tell him of her own troubles. "Let's go back. Mother might need me."

Chapter 2

What did the monk know that they did not? That was the question that kept Astrid up that night. He'd shown uncommon courage, for someone like him. Or, more than she would expect. She was inclined to say it was because he wasn't as bright as the others, but that couldn't explain his behavior. A person with a dull mind might react the way he did, yet his words showed this was not the case. There was something more.

She knew little about monks. She'd seen a few from the Isle of the Angles before, when they came once a few years ago. They wore simple brown tunics, belts and shoes. They stood on the wharf, just disembarked, while villagers gathered to stare not only because of their strange looks, but also because they spoke of the Christian God in the people's own language. Father soon came to them and dismissed them gruffly but not unkindly.

"Take your saints and acts of penance to another place and be gone," he said. "We do not need them here!" Mother ignored them and so did Sven—until now.

She shuddered. He'd turn the gods' wrath upon the village if he continued in his questioning. How could he doubt, when Odin himself created the very ground he stood on? The gods upheld order against the opposing force of chaos, creating peace in the world as long as the people continued to serve them. If they turned to the Christian God, would that peace disappear? On the other hand, if the Christian God was one of them, what part did He play? Perhaps he upheld order when the other gods had to fight against other forces.

Her sleep was plagued with dreams. Dreams of Sven tossing away his sword and crying out. Battle cries would drown him out, and a dark mass would sweep him away. Each time she awakened and fell asleep again, the dream returned. Each time, there was nothing she could do to save him.

The next morning, she was awakened by light shining around the curtains of her room. She groaned and pulled her blanket over her head. The night had left her unrested. She started to drift to sleep again, but the clank of a pot jolted her awake. With a sigh, she stretched and rolled out of bed. She pulled her kirtle and smokkr over her head, pinned the smokkr straps in place with her turtle brooches, and, after slipping on her shoes, she pushed aside the curtain sectioning her room from the rest of the house.

"Good morning, love," Mother said breathlessly as she hurried by with a heaping tray of sliced meat. "We left the wash water on the table for you." She whisked away to the many pots and trays in the fire pit.

"Good morning," Astrid called after her. She rolled up her sleeves, pulled a sopping cloth from the wooden bowl, and washed her face and hands. After drying off with another cloth, she carried the bowl outside and poured the water over the tiny green shoots in the garden beds.

She put the bowl away inside, took a basket from the shelf, and went past the garden to the chicken coop, where Swanhild was letting out the birds. A score of chickens rushed out and gathered in a cluster to peck furiously at kitchen scraps, their heads bobbing up and down.

Swanhild laughed and opened the coop's side door, where one could climb in and collect the eggs. "I never get tired of watching them," she said, glancing at the chickens again. She reached for the basket, but Astrid pulled it back.

"I'll get the eggs this time. You're too big to get in there now, with the baby and all." A teasing note entered her voice, and she grinned. Shrugging, Swanhild laughed again and shooed her away. Astrid pulled herself up by the square door frame and scrambled inside the coop.

After the meal, Astrid stole a few moments of solitude in the woods. How quiet it was under the green canopy! Nothing hurried here, unlike her busy home. Leaves unfurled in their own time and buds formed slowly, then opened overnight. Grass didn't change after a week's time. Birds sang as if their work was their joy. Here, she could breathe. And she did, deeply, and let it out slow as the sheltered breeze. In the solitude, the night's vigil came to mind.

And Sven's doubts.

The sun broke from the clouds, and beams shifted through the treetops. She reached up and felt the warm light on her hand. As a child, she often wondered what it would be like to ride on a sunbeam up to the sky and join Sòl in her chariot, guiding the sun. Now, she wished she could.

She held her skirts aside and stepped between bushes, then paused again. As much as she wanted to stay here, she must return home. There were garden beds to weed and clothes to mend; there was fire to tend, food to prepare, and crockery to wash. Her energy drained, and her shoulders slumped at the thought. If only she'd slept better! Could it be a punishment for entertaining Sven's questions?

She took the long way home. Down the other side of the hill to the warm, sandy beaches. Here, Astrid took off her boots and walked bare-footed, enjoying the grit of the sand between her toes. Memories of her childhood flew by: building sand-villages with her friends, wading into the water and splashing each other until everyone was soaked, venturing out with Sven on a little wooden flat. Then there was the time they tipped into the water, all because of a rock she'd hit!

Those were the good days, when there was nothing to puzzle through, when it was easy to please the gods, when her only duties were to obey her parents and work when they needed her.

A sense of urgency came over her, and she broke into a run. She'd been gone too long. Waves rushed up the beach and chased her, hitting her feet with a splash that sprayed foam onto the back of her neck. It was refreshing, just what she needed. She'd dunk her whole head in the water if she could, but she'd never hear the end of it from Mother. Her already-wet hem wouldn't escape notice, as it was.

At the sound of men's voices, she stopped, dried her feet off with her sleeve, and put her shoes back on. It wasn't so pleasant to walk with sand trapped in the damp leather, but she'd done it before.

The wharf was as busy as ever. The fishermen had just come in with their catches, and merchants were unloading their wares. Many women were there, their own items of fabric, baskets of food, and rolls of furs tucked firmly in their arms. In exchange, they'd get fish, leather, pots, pottery, spices from other lands, and maybe even silk. Village craftsmen were there, too, some holding jewels to the sun to look for impurities, and others searching for the perfect material for their work. Men had also gathered to make their own trades.

Astrid searched for an old merchant friend of hers, Wulfstan, but his boat wasn't with the rest. He'd return any day now from his trading voyage with plenty of wares, if it pleased Njord, god of wealth. Turning homeward, she forced her way through the bustling wharf and found herself face to face with a young man she recognized as one of Sven's childhood companions and as one who accompanied him on the raid.

"Sæl, mær," he said with a smile, "I wish you much happiness. He's a good man."

He was gone before she could say anything. She stared after him, stunned, trying to piece together what he said. Sven was a good man, but… sæl, "blessed"? For what? Had he heard something she had not?

"Wait! What do you mean?"

But he was gone, swallowed up by the swarms on the wharf. She ran after him in vain. She could not find him again.

She pressed her arms against her quivering middle and hid her face from everyone passing by. His congratulations could only be for the marriage. Who would have asked? Had she already been asked for? She pushed her way out of the wharf and ran down the road. Turning a corner, she nearly ran into a group of men with field tools in their hands, on the way to the fields behind the village. Astrid shied and smoothed down her hair as they greeted her.

"Good morning, Mær!"

"Good morning, Karls," she mumbled. She flattened against a wall while they passed, then fled.

At the doorway of her house, she paused briefly, collected herself, and went in. Mother was at her loom in the corner, weaving blue wool into soft fabric. No one else was inside. Astrid sat cross-legged on a mat in the corner near the door and picked up the kirtle Swanhild had worked on the other day. It was nearly finished. Once the collar was completed, Sven could wear it instead of his old, mended one.

Mother looked up suddenly. "Astrid, go help Swanhild in the garden. She wouldn't wait for you. Where were you for so long?"

Astrid's hand faltered, and the collar slipped out of place. She shifted it carefully, not daring to look at Mother. "I was in the woods. Just for a short time."

"Hmph. Tasks won't complete themselves when left alone. Go help Swanhild, now."

"Yes, Mother." She wove the needle securely at the collar and folded the kirtle up. There was no doubt someone had spoken to her parents. She wanted to ask her and get it off her mind, but she dared not. If it were true, the rest of the day would be unbearable. But what was more unbearable: living in anticipation or living with confirmation? Unable to decide, she quietly went out the back door to the garden.

Sure enough, Swanhild was squatting beside a garden bed with a stick in her hand and a bag by her side. Sweat glazed her neck and dampened her head covering. She looked up and gave a tired smile. Dirt was smeared across her cheek.

"Good of you to join me," she said kindly, as Astrid knelt beside her. Swanhild handed her the stick.

"Sorry I took so long," Astrid mumbled, running the stick through the soil to make a little trench. "I didn't know you'd work out here. You should have waited."

The tired smile came back tenderly. Swanhild sprinkled seeds in the trench and gently covered them up again. "Don't feel sorry. I like working alone. It's quiet and peaceful." She dipped her hand in the bag again and sprinkled more seeds into the soil.

"What are these?"

"Carrots. Down a few rows are peas. I've gathered branches to make a trellis for them, but that'll have to wait until we're done here."

Astrid brushed excess dirt from her stick and shuffled down the bed to make more rows, nearly tripping over two buckets full to the brim. "Did Sven get the water for you?"

Delightful crow's feet formed at the corners of Swanhild's eyes. "No, I got it myself."

"Swanhild!"

Her sister-in-law laughed. "Since no one was around to help, I got away with it."

"But you're with child! Where was Hjordis, or the field thralls?"

"All working."

Astrid groaned, but had to laugh when Swanhild winked. Independence was something they both had in common. And in spite of her quiet ways, Swanhild had a strong will of her own.

At the sound of footsteps behind them, Astrid turned. Sven was coming toward them with a field tool over his shoulder and muddy shoes on his feet.

"How goes the planting?" he asked.

Swanhild rose to greet him, and he pulled her to him briefly to plant a kiss on her forehead.

"It's going well," she said. "This bed is almost done, leaving only one more."

"Glad to hear it." With a grin at Astrid, he said, "Is Astrid being a good help?"

"Very. It's going faster with her here."

Astrid couldn't help breaking in, "Swanhild's been naughty again."

Sven's eyebrows rose in mock horror. "Oho! What did she do this time?"

"Drew two buckets of water by herself."

"That is serious!" Sven's brows now shot down, and his mouth downturned. He hooked his arm around Swanhild and nuzzled her hair. She laughed and pushed against his chest, but he held her more firmly. "You're not going anywhere!" He gave her a quick kiss and let her go. "See you both soon. Don't do anything too hard for you, alright?"

"If you say so," said Swanhild with something between a laugh and a sigh.

Astrid, feeling a sudden rush of tears, turned to the bed she was working in. There was that strange ache in her chest again. It was as though she missed something, missed it terribly, and didn't know what it was or how to get it back. She thought of when

Sven said he felt empty. Now she understood what he meant. Was it his doubts that made her feel empty, or was it their shown affection? It *couldn't* be that!

Swanhild knelt by her side again, sprinkling seeds in the rows. Astrid kept her face turned away, but even still, Swanhild asked, "Are you alright?"

Astrid took a breath. "Yes."

The weight of Swanhild's gaze fell on her. "Is something on your mind?"

She would understand, if anyone could. "Do you ever want something, but don't know what it is?"

Swanhild nodded. "Many times, but especially while Sven was gone. It left me with an aching yearning here." Her fingertips touched the center of her chest, right where Astrid's felt empty. "Does this sound right?"

Astrid ran her fingers through the warm topsoil, then stuck her finger deep into the coolness underneath. She nodded slowly, yet hesitated. "Maybe it's just… anxiety, perhaps. Home isn't what it used to be."

Swanhild covered a row of seeds with one smooth swipe of her hand. "Sven's been preoccupied, although he won't tell me with what. You probably sense it."

Astrid squirmed when she remembered the promise she'd made not to tell.

Swanhild glanced her way. "It's not that, is it?"

"No..." With a weak hand, she dropped seeds in another row, then tucked her hand under her arm. "Something's going to change. I can sense it. Someone wished me congratulations today." Her voice sank. "I think it was for a marriage arrangement." She took a shaking breath and looked into Swanhild's round sea-blue eyes, which begged her to continue. "But it isn't exactly what is giving me the... aching yearning, as you put it."

Gently, Swanhild laid a hand on top of Astrid's. She looked over the garden bed for a moment before meeting her eyes again. "We must let go of old ways to find joy in change." She covered the exposed row of seeds, patting down the soil, and waited.

With a start, Astrid snatched up her stick and ran it through the soil to create another row. She cringed at Swanhild's words and tried to convince herself they were not right. Her efforts failed. They didn't answer the ache, but they did, however, target the resistance she'd felt against the oncoming change.

"Astrid!" Mother called from the doorway, jolting her out of her thoughts. "I need your help."

Astrid sighed and stood, wiping dirt from her hands with her smokkr. "Coming."

Swanhild caught the cuff of her sleeve. "You can talk to me whenever you need."

"Thank you."

The morning faded into the afternoon, which passed so quickly that Astrid found herself making the evening meal. She flipped slices of fish in the pan and piled more hot coals beneath it.

"We're out of water," said Mother, crouching beside her to tend the fire.

"Would you like me to draw more?"

"Yes, please. The bucket's on the shelf."

Astrid stood and stretched her cramped legs. She hobbled to the shelves and took the bucket from the top shelf. Its old metal handle was cold and rough in her hand.

Outside, she breathed deep and walked the short distance to the well. She set the longhouse bucket aside, threw back the wood cover, and tossed the well bucket down. Doing so reminded her of the many times items were dropped down the well, on purpose by naughty children, as well as by accident. Father eventually tired of the frequent fishing he or others had to do, and built the cover for the well. Nothing had fallen down it since.

The bucket hit the water with a plunk, and when it filled, she drew it up. With both buckets balancing on the ledge, she paused. It was too beautiful and fresh a day for her to go back inside right away. A light breeze stirred dirt on the road and plucked at her skirt. The sky was brilliant blue, with nought a cloud in sight. Karls—village men, women, and children—worked outside. There was Sven with a bundle of tools on his shoulder, and Father right behind him, heading toward the house. Two men stopped them and spoke with them. Thane Ragnar and—Isar? She gripped the buckets. Too late! They both slipped from her grasp and fell into the well. The one on the rope was easy to retrieve, but her own was quite another matter.

Father looked her way and spoke to the others, who left. Then, he started slowly toward her.

Astrid shrank against the wall and pretended not to see him. She leaned over the well's mouth and looked down into the black water, too far down for the sun to reach. Faintly, she could see the bucket floating.

Gravel ground beneath Father's boots. He stopped right behind her. "Astrid."

Holding her breath, she turned and faced him. Lines were set across his forehead, and under his thick beard, his mouth was set in a straight line. The stones of the well wall scraped against her hand. Her legs shook, but she attempted a smile.

"I dropped something in the well. Do you think you could get it out for me?"

"Wha—" Father glanced past her.

"It slipped," she offered.

"The bucket can wait."

"Mother needs it."

A sigh rumbled deep in his throat. "Stay here."

He left, shoulders straight and back stiff, and Astrid's stomach fluttered again. She crossed her arms and pressed them over her middle.

What the young man said at the docks that morning hit her like a thunderbolt. Isar had asked, and Father had agreed.

Father exited the house with a hook and cord, but also with Mother, whose face was carved with anxious expectation. Sparks danced in her eyes as her parents approached.

Father set the cord and hook on the well's ledge and stood beside Astrid while Mother watched.

"Shouldn't we be cooking..." Astrid mumbled.

"Swanhild and Hjordis are taking care of it," said Mother. She looked at Father.

"Now that Sven and the others have returned," he said, "we cannot put it off any longer. Isar has asked permission to court you for marriage, and I have agreed. What do you say?"

What *could* she say? Words fled, and the thoughts and reasons in her mind suddenly made no sense. She couldn't communicate them if she tried. Once or twice, she opened her mouth without success before she could speak again.

"I can't."

Father's frown deepened.

"Isar and I, we haven't... gotten along well."

"That trick he played on you happened long ago," replied Mother, crossing her arms. "Has anything happened since then?"

Yes. There had been teasing and hair-tweaking, and many times he'd left her in tears of anger and sadness. She said nothing.

Mother sounded impatient. "Has anything happened since you were children?"

He'd ignored her for three blissful years, but twelve wasn't exactly a child, was it? "Not for a while," she said slowly.

"Then there's no reason for you to object," said Mother, more gently this time. "Our hope was for you to settle down comfortably, with sufficient means to be cared for."

"What better alliance could you make?" added Father. Only the faintest of frowns remained. "Isar has distinguished himself as a man of valor and honor, both at sea and in a raid. His father is of high standing, and his family is well-respected. It would bring us great joy to know you were in such good hands." He looked now as he did when he waited for her to recite sagas back to him. With all her heart, she wished not to let him down, but how could she not this time?

"Besides," he continued, "it's not as though you would marry right away. Courtship lasts four months at most."

All at once, her composure began to fall apart. Four months was too soon. Panic pressed just behind her face, her eyes misted, and she fought to keep her voice steady. "I cannot leave you. Sven is home, Swanhild's baby will be born during harvest—" Her voice broke.

"Now, child..." Mother reached out, but Astrid stepped back.

She choked, "Why can't I marry for love?"

"Is there anyone else?" Mother said drily. Astrid couldn't answer, for there was none.

Father laid his arm across her shoulders and held her there, though she stiffened at his touch. "Love may determine some unions, but not everyone. I married your mother because it was my duty, and love soon followed. You will never know, though you will hopefully understand one day, all the nights we spent seeking Odin's guidance concerning you. Now, Isar has asked for you. If he were some scoundrel, I would not let him anywhere near you. Do not meddle with fate." He removed his arm from her shoulders.

If this was her destiny, the gods would bless her if she obeyed. By disobeying, she might bring disaster upon her family. And how could she ignore the pleading look in her father's eyes?

She took a deep breath. "I'll do it."

Mother sighed as if she'd been holding it the entire time, and Father smiled and nodded.

"This is for the best," he said. "You will see."

Astrid hoped he was right.

He bent and took up the hook and cord and, once they were tied together, lowered the hook into the well. She'd forgotten all about the dropped bucket.

It was drawn out and safely set on the ground, filled to the brim and soaked. Father picked it up and gestured toward the house. "Isar and the thane are with Sven, awaiting your answer." He handed the bucket to Mother and led the way. Astrid couldn't move until Mother prodded her forward with a hand at the small of her back.

The bucket, hook, and cord were left at the door, and they rounded the house to the garden beds, where Isar, his father, and Sven turned to face them. With one last prodding, Mother stepped away from her.

Astrid sent a word of prayer for courage to Thor and lifted her eyes. Isar met hers, searching, and he waited, standing tall and straight. She straightened like him and clenched her hands. "I accept your request of courtship."

Isar bowed with a smile. "I am honored."

After shaking both Isar's and the thane's hands, Father invited them to join their meal and settle the terms of the marriage. They accepted, and everyone filed through the back door to the table. Blindly, Astrid followed, thinking, what had she done?

Swanhild met her as she entered. "I'm happy for you," she whispered.

Astrid shrank away and looked past her to the others taking their seats. This could not be happening. Any moment, she'd awake and find it a dream. The walls were closing in on her, and the hot, smoky, stuffy air was suffocating.

"Come, Astrid, Swanhild," Father called.

Swallowing, she crossed the room and took her seat between Mother and Sven, across from Isar. She glanced at Father at the head of the table, but he was too busy conversing with the thane to notice her.

She couldn't eat a bite. She pushed her food around and nibbled on some dried fruit and a cake, but the broiled fish caught in her throat.

The conversation sounded like a curtain muffled everyone. She couldn't understand them, but didn't care. She was married to Isar, and that was all that mattered. One detail she did catch was, the ceremony would be held after harvest. Four months away.

There was the scraping of wood as her family stood and cleared the table. Her plate was taken away, and she stared at the tabletop, trying to keep calm. Father's deep voice boomed. He left with Isar and Thane Ragnar, and the door shut.

"You may go," murmured Mother, with a hand on her shoulder. "Hjordis and I will wash the dishes."

With a shake, Astrid pushed her stool back. Gripping the table, she pulled herself up. She stumbled to the front door, groped for the latch, and yanked the door open.

Chapter 3

Cool air smacked her face, and sunlight blinded her. Upward she climbed, stumbling, falling, scraping her hands. Higher and higher the ground sloped. Then, at last, the top. Astrid flung her arms around the tree, her tree, and pressed her hot cheek against its cold, rough bark.

She'd agreed for Father's sake. He relied on her. She couldn't go back.

Unless Isar was more unbearable than she thought.

She sat with her back against the tree, closed her eyes, and felt her strength give way after being strained for so long. Now, she was tired. Exhausted.

"Freya," she murmured, "I cannot do this." If it were possible to change her fate by prayer, she would have prayed until her mouth dried, voice cracked, and throat split. As it was, all she could do was hope happiness would come as Swanhild said it would.

A cold shadow fell over her. She opened her eyes. Sven stood, tall and silent, between her and the sunlight, looking over the ocean. He settled down beside her and looked her way.

She lowered her eyelids and tilted her head down. He had the uncanny ability to guess her mood, but he must not guess it now. He must not know the anger that flamed in her chest at his appearance. All this time, he'd known but said nothing of warning.

"It isn't that bad, sister," he said, voice low.

"You don't know," growled Astrid. "You married someone you loved." She lifted her eyes and let him see her anger, but he didn't back down.

"It's a great opportunity. You'll lead a comfortable life, as Father wanted. Thane Ragnar is a high-standing member of the council, and his family is wealthy and greatly respected."

"Isar ridicules me!"

Sven's gaze flickered away, then met hers squarely. "That's in the past. If he mistreats you, you are free to come back home. But marriage is a serious thing, and he knows it. He'll behave."

Astrid scowled.

Sven leaned forward and whispered, "Have I ever let you down?"

Astrid shook her head, and her anger melted away. "Never."

A smile came to his face. "Even when you're married, you can still confide in me. Just like I confide in you."

"When you're married." She shivered. This was getting unbearable.

She took a breath. "Have you thought more about the monk?"

Sven leaned back with a sigh and swept his hand over his eyes. His jaw tightened. Fingering the grass beside him, he looked at the trees below the cliff. He sighed again. "All the time."

"What do you think about it?"

"About what?"

"What did he have that we don't? About the emptiness?"

A pause. "I don't know." A blade ripped up, and he shook it over the cliff.

Astrid watched him throw several more down, biting her lip. Her questions came back. "Sven?"

"Yes?"

"What do you believe about the gods? I mean, is the Christian God real, too?"

No answer.

"It would be best if we put this out of our minds. Your doubts already caused a storm to throw you off course. Let's stop before something worse happens."

Sven fisted the grass he'd just rooted up. "I tried." He paused, then threw it over the cliff. Then he was still. "Alright," he said slowly.

Astrid let out a breath, but it sounded like one of Mother's sighs.

Four months later, Astrid stuffed the last onion in the last hemp sack, tied it shut with a cord, and hoisted it onto her hip. She glanced at the sinking sun as she took up the other sack. Just a little longer, then the meal! Food and rest. At least she wasn't in the fields, where she'd spread grain flat with a splintery rake, her back bent for half the day.

Behind the garden, the cellar door, simply a wooden flat closing the hole in the ground, was open. She descended the ladder into the musty interior and set the onion sacks against the wall with the other sacks and boxes of food. Hardly any of the hard-packed dirt walls of the cellar were visible. Carrots, peas, beets, and cabbage had all done well. The hogs and cows were harvested, their meat dried and salted and packed in boxes. There was also plenty of skyr to last the winter. Most of the barley was stored away, as well, and took up all the room in the back of the cellar, pushing the rest toward the ladder. The extra barley would go in the barn for livestock.

Two weeks remained for the harvest. And afterwards...

Astrid tucked loose hair under her headscarf and ascended the ladder. One could face the future better in daylight.

Two more weeks, and she'd be torn from her family. Two more weeks, and she'd be chained to that horrid Isar. He'd made himself agreeable these last four months, so much so that she felt guilty for hating him. He was separating her from her family, she must remember, and he ridiculed her during childhood. It was a relief to hate him, and oh, how she did!

Yet she couldn't find fault with any of his conduct during the summer. He came over often, lent help to Father and Sven, talked to her when he met her, and ate the evening meal once in a while with her family. No, there was one thing with which she found fault: he stayed once after the meal. Astrid treasured evenings with her family, when she'd get out her lyre and Sven his flute, and Father, Swanhild, and Mother told sagas or sang songs. It was a sacred time that no one, especially Isar, could participate in.

Pressing her lips together, Astrid squatted by the bed of herbs and slashed at the plants. There was no doubt about it, she'd grown used to Isar. How could she forget his taunts and rude remarks? And now he was taking her from her family. Someone else would have done it, but since it was him, she could hate him for it.

She gathered the small, cut branches into a bundle and tied them. Later, all the herbs would be hung from the rafters to dry.

"Astrid!" Mother called from a corner of the house, shading her eyes with a hand. "Run and tell Father the evening meal's ready."

"Yes, Mother." Astrid tied another bundle up, tucked the shears in her belt, and went off.

Their fields were beyond the chicken coop and enclosed with a low woven fence, and grey silhouettes of the workers were visible from the house. The golden sunlight glowed fire-red on the barley and on the workers' fair hair. At the edge of the field, she inhaled deeply the sweet scent of fallen grain, which tickled her nose, but it was a good smell. Then the wind changed direction and blew a draft from the livestock's meadow. That was not a good smell. She scrunched up her nose and swung a leg over the fence.

Drying barley crackled under her feet, dust stirred, and the smell of the grain was overpowering, catching in her throat and making her cough.

Ahead, the harvesters swung their scythes and barley fell with a swish. Behind them, rakers spread the grain out. Sven and Father were with the harvesters; she couldn't get to them because of the danger of the many swinging blades, and so stood where she was, wondering if she should shout or wait for them to notice her.

Thank goodness, Father straightened, ran his hand over his forehead, and saw her. He spoke to a fellow harvester, who stopped briefly to let him through. Father tossed his scythe aside and put an arm around her shoulders.

"Work going well at home?" he asked.

"Yes. Mother says the meal is ready."

Father grunted and called to Sven, and the workers around them stopped. The sun sank behind the forest, plunging them into shadows.

"Quitting time," said Karl, looking at the sky. The others nodded and said the same.

"See you tomorrow, Jarl," they said to Father.

"The gods keep you," he replied. "Good work, Karls."

The workers finished their tasks and left one by one. Father and Sven started homeward. And Astrid turned to follow when someone called her name.

She looked over her shoulder. Isar was crossing the field, rake in hand, with settled brows and firm mouth. Astrid's stomach soured, and she clasped her sweaty hands together.

Isar slowed and planted each step so eddies of grain dust swirled about him; he kept his eyes down, and his empty hand was curled in a fist. He stopped, set the handle end of the rake on the ground and leaned the toothed side against his shoulder, and finally looked up. His eyes were piercing. Astrid clasped her hands tighter.

"The four months are ended," he said quietly, still looking her in the eye.

Astrid swallowed. "Excuse me, but I must help Mother." She crossed the field and its fence and wished she could run to the shelter of her home.

"Astrid, wait," Isar called.

She kept walking, stiffly. "Whatever you have to say, you can say it with the others, can't you?"

"No, I cannot."

Isar stepped in front of her and held his hand up. "Listen. If you still despise me, I can't blame you. But could you give me a second chance?"

She mustn't let the remorse in his voice win her over. Straightening, she said coolly, "What is your point?"

He shifted his weight while holding his gaze. "Courtship has ended. Will you marry me?"

She winced. "It's—it's still the harvest. Mother and Father need me."

"If it changes anything, I will keep helping in the fields."

He expected her—everyone expected her—to say yes, but she choked on the word. The hope in his face was confusing; she'd never seen him like this, so eager and hopeful and was he trembling? His half-hidden hand shook. She looked away. She mustn't let his emotions sway hers.

But they were. To her horror, she felt herself thinking it wouldn't be so bad, and she searched frantically for something to keep herself hardened against him. None came, however, and it left her helpless. But she still couldn't say the horrible words.

She blew out a breath. Think of Father.

She couldn't.

Coward.

Involuntarily, she glanced up at him and was caught by his deep blue eyes, his thick dark brows, the scruff of a beard softening his sharp chin. He'd shifted closer to her and had a white-knuckled grip on the rake.

"Will you?"

Her hands were shaking. Clenching them, she struggled with the words in her throat. "Yes—I will."

His grip on the rake loosened. A smile spread over his face, and he extended a hand. "Shall we go together?"

She stared at his hand, then brushed past him without a word. Again, the itch to run, but giving in would bring to light what had best remain in the dark, unknown. It was impossible to determine how much he, striding upright with arms swinging freely, had guessed already.

At last, the cool shade of the house... and the inquiring eyes of her family rested on her. She met Father's and said in a low voice, "Isar has come to speak to you."

Isar pushed through the doorway and bowed his head toward Father. "Your daughter has agreed to hold the marriage ceremony."

Father's beard lifted as he smiled and nodded. He added a stool to the table and motioned to it, saying, "Come, and we'll settle it now if that is your wish."

Astrid leaned against the doorway.

"I am honoured, Jarl," said Isar. Chairs scraped.

"Astrid, sit," Mother commanded in a whisper as she whisked past and shut the door.

Somehow, Astrid dragged her shaking legs to the stool beside Sven, who reached for her hand under the table and squeezed it. She couldn't make herself squeeze him back.

A dish clinked. Mother set before her a plate of roasted meat, fried beets, onions, cabbage, and goat cheese. And beside it, a bowl of skyr and berries.

Astrid picked a berry from the sky and popped it into her mouth. Sweet and sour. Mostly sour. She stared at the creamy white against the brown and red, the smoothness of the carved bowl, the shininess of the blackberries. Her stomach dropped like a stone, and all the sweetness in her mouth turned bitter. She looked away.

"Eat something," Sven whispered.

She shook her head. "Can't."

He shrugged and stuffed his mouth with fried cabbage.

"...nothing would keep us from holding it next Frigg's day," Father was saying. "The early harvest should be finished before then."

A shiver slithered down Astrid's spine. Five days. Her throat burned, and she feared she'd get sick.

"If not, Jarl, I am fully willing and able to lend a hand," said Isar.

Father grunted. "As for the other agreements, do they still agree with you?"

"Yes, Jarl, but if you desire to make any changes, what is that between us?"

She bit her lip. Isar was laying it on thick. Bile travelled up her throat. She gagged and choked it down.

"Astrid?" Mother whispered, her forehead creased.

"I'm fine," Astrid answered. But Mother's gaze remained on her. With a shaking hand, Astrid picked up her cheese and nibbled on it. Mother turned her attention back to Snorri, who was trying everything on her plate and spitting it out again.

Astrid's nausea grew worse. Anything would do to distract from it. What about Sven's doubts? Were they the same? With all the work and activity, she had hardly given them a thought. She welcomed them heartily now.

Sven must be crazy. The gods were as real as anyone in the room, as real as Isar. Astrid wrapped her fingers around her Mjolnir pendant. Thor was the protector and helper of the people, a hero, a blesser of crops. None could do without him, but here Sven was, questioning not only him but the other gods also.

Chairs scraped again, and Sven squeezed her shoulder. Isar was leaving. Astrid scrambled to her feet and found herself staring into Isar's face.

"On Frigg's day, Astrid. Sæl." He waited a moment as if waiting for her to say something, but she didn't. Isar shook Father's and Sven's hands, nodded to Mother and Swanhild, and left.

Everyone else gathered around the table again to finish the meal, but Astrid remained rooted where she was. Five days to prepare for the biggest change in her life, five more days to spend in her family's house. Her eyes stung.

Swanhild touched her shoulder and offered a smile.

Astrid swallowed and, without hesitation, flung her arms around Swanhild. She pressed her cheek against hers and whispered in Swanhild's ear, "I love you."

Swanhild pressed Astrid to her chest. "I love you, too. We all do." She let her go and prodded her to the table.

When she saw the food again, bile shot up her throat. She clasped her hand over her mouth and swallowed hard, gagging. "Excuse me," she croaked. And fled.

At the top of the hill, Astrid lay with her back against the tree, eyes closed, focusing on her breathing. Her mouth was dry and sour with vomit, and her lips stung. She licked them again and ran her sleeve across her mouth. Five days were not nearly enough time. They'd pass quickly with all the planning and preparation. Cooking had to be done, sewing perhaps.

Sven appeared over the top of the hill, settled down beside her, and sat cross-legged. "What's bothering you?"

Astrid flung her hands up in exasperation. "Don't you know?"

Sven looked away for a moment, jaw settled, then pinned her with a stare. "Is it marriage that bothers you, or is it Isar?"

Astrid opened her mouth to give a retort, then closed it. With a sigh, she hung her head. For the first time, she couldn't tell him exactly how she felt. Not because he wouldn't understand, but because she didn't understand herself. So she muttered, "I guess it's Isar."

"What about him? He's matured greatly since you were children."

"Then why does he act so—so entitled?"

"Your imagination, sister. He's a passionate young man, well-mannered, maybe a little prideful, but pride is good to an extent. Too much makes people foolhardy, but he doesn't have too much. You misunderstand him, that's all."

She struck the ground. "Then why does he always look at me like 'you're mine'? And what he said to Father was a bit much. He's not as good as you make him out to be."

He sighed and rubbed an eyebrow. "As I said, you still think of him as if he's nine years old. You need to let go of what you think he's like. He's different."

She glared. "Prove it."

Sven's voice rose a little. "How can I prove it when you see things your way?" He blew out a breath. "Just trust me. Once you get to know him more, you'll see his true nature." With another breath, a sigh this time, Sven looked away, beyond the woods and to the sea.

She swallowed, then whispered, "Sven?"

He continued to watch the ocean. "What?"

"I… I'm sorry."

He turned toward her.

Astrid bit her lip. "I'll try, really. You've been right before." She met his gaze for a moment, but guilt seized her, and she dropped her eyes.

After a pause, Sven said, "That's more like you. Are you ready to go back?"

She nodded and scrambled to her feet. Usually, Sven led the way back, but he remained standing, staring out at the sea with his body tense with attention. Sidling up to him, she squinted and, as far as she could see, the ocean was calm and empty.

"What did you see?"

Sven shook himself. "Nothing. Do you see something?"

"No."

With one last look, Sven turned to the path down the hill. "Nothing to worry about."

In the evening, Astrid sat on her bed, combing out her hair for the night and listening to the lullaby Mother was singing to Snorri. The same lullaby she'd sung to Astrid and, before Astrid, to Sven.

Astrid braided her hair and tied it off, then peeked out of her room. Father came in, closed the front door behind him, and stoked the fire. The white hair at his temples shone in the darkness, and hot coals burned red. A string of smoke rose and disappeared as he placed thick pieces of wood over the coals. Father stood and wiped his hands on his jerkin. Sven came inside and spoke to him in low tones, and Father nodded slowly.

"Post a lookout on each side of the shore. Better safe than sorry," he whispered. Sven left, and Father looked around, his majestic face tired and worn. When he saw Astrid, his beard widened with a smile, and he sauntered toward her.

Taking her face in his big, rough hands, he kissed her forehead. "Good night, my little girl."

Astrid reached as far as she could around his big middle and squeezed hard. "Good night, Father. Love you."

Father hugged her to himself, and his peppered red beard tickled her face. "Love you, too. I'm proud of you. Life is full of hard decisions. You've done well."

"Thank you, Father."

He released her and ducked into his room. Astrid took another look at the main room, soaking in every detail. Very soon, she'd leave, and this would no longer be her home. Her chin trembled, but she clenched her jaw and retreated within her curtained room.

Mother's lullaby hushed, and there was a murmur and a chuckle. The lullaby started up again in a hum. Astrid scrambled into her bed and closed her eyes. She'd hardly lain still when her curtain rustled and Mother's light steps, calm and slow, crossed the dirt floor. Astrid sensed her coming to the bed and bent down. Mother's warm hand rested on her forehead like a blessing, and the hum of the lullaby took shape.

Sleep, love, the sun has set.

Hear the breeze, ocean waves,

Close your eyes, rest on me

Feel my arms 'round you,

Sleep 'til dawning light

Mother straightened, and her hand left Astrid's forehead. Astrid peeked through one eye as Mother went to the curtain and paused with a hand on the curtain to look back. A smile hovered over her usually pressed lips. With a sigh, she left.

Alone, Astrid opened her eyes. Although the air inside her room was stuffy and warm, she shivered. The thoughts that'd plagued her all day came crowding back: marriage, and Sven's doubts. Her head hurt. Astrid rubbed her temple and turned onto her side. She'd never fall asleep at this rate.

The next room was Sven and Swanhild's. Faint giggling and whispering came from it. From her parent's room came a whimper from Snorri and a croon from Mother. Father chuckled. Sounds died away, and the house was quiet. A few footsteps from the thralls settling into their beds, then silence.

Outside, wind rustled the fallen grain in the fields and the leaves on the trees. A bird chirped and was answered from far away. A shout from the village, then silence again. If Astrid strained hard enough, she could hear the ocean's surf thundering on the rocks at the beach.

Astrid opened her eyes for a moment. She hadn't visited the ocean that day. No wonder she felt like she would fly into pieces. First thing tomorrow, if she could get away early enough, she'd go to the ocean. It always understood her moods. It laughed when she laughed, cried when she cried, and was angry when she was. No matter where she went or what happened to her, she would always have a friend.

Chapter 4

Astrid awoke to the harsh blast of a horn. She'd heard it before, but never in such earnest as now. In the next moment, someone pounded on their door. Astrid stumbled to her feet and looked out from the curtain as Father opened the door and a man rushed in. The burning lamp held by a thrall cast red light on the man's creased forehead and widened eyes.

"What is it?" Father barked.

"Attackers coming from the south. Seven longboats fully loaded."

Father strapped on his sword, took up his battle axe, and threw his cloak around his shoulders. Mother ran toward him, and he kissed her before following the man out the door with Sven behind him. Swanhild huddled just inside her room, shaking like a leaf in a winter wind. A gust blew through the open doorway and chilled Astrid's face and hands. The lamp blew out.

Mother relit the lamp and poked Astrid back in her room. "Get dressed quickly." She snapped the curtain in place.

With shaking hands, Astrid pulled on her red kirtle and smokkr, hooked on her brooches and necklaces.

"We're being raided!" Swanhild cried, sobbing. "I'll never see Sven again!" Mother spoke softly and quickly to calm her, but Swanhild continued crying the same words, more and more hysterically. Astrid tied her belt with shaking hands. Swanhild was never like this before.

The door opened again, and Mother called, "Swanhild, come back! Come back! Oh dear, she doesn't hear me. The village isn't safe. Hjordis, run after her. Astrid! What is taking you so long?"

Astrid crammed her shoes on and rushed out. Mother pressed Snorri into her arms and cupped her shoulders. Her vision whirled as Mother hurried her into the cold night air. Mother was taking her to the cellar just outside the house. Clashing metal, battle horns, and blood-curdling cries battered her head.

Mother lifted the cellar's grass-covered door and hurried her down. Astrid stumbled down the cellar steps, clutching the baby and feeling along the packed-dirt wall. Darkness closed in. Mother followed, set a lamp on a crate, and took Astrid's face in her hands. She kissed her forehead and cheeks and stroked Snorri, who'd fallen asleep again.

"Keep him safe. The gods keep you, love," whispered Mother. Then she was gone. The cellar door closed, and the only light came from the lamp. Its small flame quivered as a draft blew through the cellar.

There was a scream above them, and Snorri jolted awake. He wailed.

"No, no, no—hush!" Astrid rocked him and placed her hand over his mouth to quiet his cries. As his wails increased, so did the commotion outside. Footsteps thundered overhead, and yelled and clashes grew louder. She blew out the lamp, cowered against the wall, and buried her head in the folds of Snorri's blanket. No need to bother hushing him now; he couldn't have been heard above the noise. It sounded as if all Helheim had broken loose.

Thor, protect them.

The battle thundered and clattered—then, silence. An empty silence. Astrid stretched her cramped limbs and froze when Snorri, who'd cried himself to sleep, sighed. He puckered his lips and was still. She moved again, but this time a victory shout stopped her. It wracked her body and sent shivers down her spine. It was not the shout of triumphant defenders, but the vicious cry of triumphant attackers.

A red glow filtered through the cracks of the cellar door, and at the sound of crackling wood, the back of her neck crinkled. She carefully set Snorri down and crept up the ladder. Pausing at the top, she pressed her palm against the wood and eased the door up just enough to peek out.

In front of her, a building—her home—was in flames. Gathered around it were tall, crude men. The center man stood taller than the rest, and the fire gleamed red on his chain mail and sword. Someone ran up and knelt before him, holding an object in both hands.

"Their leader's sword, Jarl."

The jarl took the object and held it up: Father's sword. It reflected the red light back onto the jarl's white-blond hair, braided, thick beard, and green-yellow eyes.

"Gather the villagers and keep them under guard. We will hold a feast for Odin!"

Another shout split her ears.

Astrid dropped the door and leaned against the ladder, trembling from head to foot. Father used his sword only in the greatest need and would never part with it, unless... unless...

Choking, she felt her way down the ladder, collapsed against the wall, and clenched her jaw against the sob rising in her chest. A hot tear ran down her cheek. Wiping it away, she drew her knees to her chest and lay her head on them.

Father was gone... Mother, Swanhild, Sven...Isar... gone. The thralls, too, were gone. She and Snorri were alone. Alone. She squeezed her knees and let the sobs come, let them shake her, but silently. If only she were in the woods, where she could cry freely! There, no one would hear.

A whimper from Snorri startled her. She scooped him up and held him against her chest. His whimper turned into a whine. He was hungry. Scrambling up, she carried him to the ghoul-like shadows of crates and bags, but could distinguish nothing. He must wait until sunrise, if it would ever come. The night was so dark it felt like Sól had been caught by the wolf at last, and that Ragnarök was unfolding outside the cellar.

Snorri whined again, louder, and she hushed him again, but his whine turned into a wail. She clasped a hand over his mouth, hushed him, but he squirmed so she nearly dropped him.

"No, no, no! Hush! They'll hear!" she hissed, but he only cried louder. Holding him firmly, she sang Mother's lullaby in his ear.

Sleep, love, the sun has set.

Hear the breeze, ocean waves,

Close your eyes...

The words of Mother's lullaby eluded her memory. Astrid bit her lip.

Rest on me... feel...

Astrid hummed the rest of the line and swallowed. She forced the last line past the growing lump in her throat.

Sleep till dawning light.

It wasn't working. Wasn't there some strong mead in the cellar? It would keep him quiet until dawn, if she could find it.

Holding squirming Snorri firmly against herself with one arm, she groped with the other for the clay jug of mead. Where had Mother put it? Against the wall? Between the crates? Snorri slipped from her arm and plopped onto the ground, crying even louder. She snatched him up and covered his mouth again. When he'd quieted back to a whine, she groped again for the mead. There was a crate, a sack, two sacks, another crate—the jug! She put Snorri down. With both hands free, she untied a cord and removed the leather cover. An alcoholic smell drifted from the jug. Thank goodness Mother insisted she dress! She kept a cloth in the bag on her belt.

"Here, Snorri," she said, folding the cloth and dipping a corner in the mead. Snorri's cries stopped when he took it, and he sucked loudly.

Astrid licked her lips, realizing she too was thirsty. Using the inside heel of her shoe as a ladle, she drank. Warmth spread into her arms and down her legs, and she felt fully awake.

Snorri started crying again, so she soaked the cloth and handed it back to him. She did this several times, and he was soon fast asleep against her chest.

How long would they need to stay here? Days? A month? Then what about light? The cellar was dim at best in broad daylight, and she had no way to light the lamp. If only she kept a flint and steel in her pocket! It was never necessary until now. A flint and steel wouldn't be in her house—or what was left of it—but might be found in one of the village longhouses. Danes would be about and, if she was found... She shook her head. Nothing would be resolved by thinking about that.

Nighttime was her best chance, instead of waiting for the sun to rise. First, she'd draw water, then go search for the flint and steel.

She laid Snorri on the ground, tucked his blanket more firmly around him, and kissed his button nose. He whined in his sleep. She hated leaving him there, but she couldn't risk getting caught because of a noise he made. Here in the cellar, he'd be safe. She caressed his downy hair, then climbed up the ladder.

At the top, she eased the door open. Blessed silence and darkness met her, and no Danes. There was no moon, but she didn't have long: already the eastern sky was a shade lighter than the west. She touched her Mjolnir pendant and prayed that Thor would keep her safe.

She crawled up and out and put a fist to her mouth. Her longhouse was nothing but a black ruin, roofless, with pieces of charred wall scattered around it. Nothing could have survived. Yet, she crept toward it and peered through a gap in the wall. Without light, everything was black.

Shuddering, she straightened and reminded herself she couldn't waste any precious time. She ran to the well, drew water, and cut the bucket from its rope with her belt knife.

After placing it at the bottom of the cellar ladder, she turned toward the village. Most of the nearby houses were blackened splinters, but some had been spared. The hair on the back of her neck rose as she tiptoed to the nearest untouched house. It was too quiet. She looked over her shoulder and all around, but saw nothing besides longhouses. The burned ones looked like the legendary Undead Warriors, like black, crumpled skeletons.

She shivered and crept around the longhouse, searching for a crack, a window, something to look through.

Finally, she found a crack in a side wall and put her eye to it. A fire was burning low in the central fire pit, illuminating huddled figures. Danes. She leapt from her crack, then looked again. They slept on the floor, covering every space possible; there was no curtained-off room. Seven Danes could be in there.

But if they used the house, there must be supplies inside.

In the back corner of the house were more huddled figures. There was a moan, a whimper, and a hush. A mother wrapped her arms around three children, sheltering them.

Some of her people still lived! For a moment, Astrid's hopes rose, then sank again. She couldn't help them beyond bringing them to the cellar, if they even reached it in the first place, and they couldn't possibly get past the Danes without waking them.

She rounded the building and pushed lightly on the door. It creaked, groaned lightly, and swung open. Cold swept over her as the opening door revealed the rough figures. This was foolhardy. None stirred, however, and the one nearest her snored like a grindstone.

The family in the corner stirred. Slowly, the mother stood and beckoned her.

What else was there to do? She lifted her foot and stepped over the threshold into the house. No one moved. Good. She lifted her skirts high and stepped between Danes. Each passing moment dragged. Had it only been a moment before that she stood outside?

At last, she reached the mother, who caught her by the arms and took her to their corner. Astrid crouched among them.

"Is it you, Astrid, daughter of Arnold?" the woman whispered in her ear.

"Yes, it is I, Kona. Is your husband here?"

The woman shook her head and put her lips up to Astrid's ear. Her voice shook. "I do not expect to see him again."

Tears came to Astrid's eyes.

"What brings you here, mær?" asked the woman.

"Snorri and I are hiding, but we need supplies."

"What do you need?"

She couldn't ask for anything from this woman, who had three children and herself to protect and care for.

"I can get whatever you need," the woman persisted.

"No," said Astrid. "I do not want to make trouble for you. Do you have a flint and steel?"

"At the fire. The Danes used it. Take it."

"Thank you. What will you do now?"

The woman sighed and caressed the hair of her youngest child, who snuggled against her. "Escape, I hope, by a boat from the shipyard."

Hope returned and rose high. "Meet me there tomorrow night, before the sky lightens, and we can all go together. Better yet, come with me now."

The mother shook her head. "I cannot. Two of my children are not sturdy on their feet yet, and I have suffered an injured knee. If the gods are kind, I will meet you tomorrow night. Now, go before the men awaken. The gods be with you."

"And—" Astrid stopped short. Where were the gods in this? If the gods were there, and they looked down on her with favor— "may they be with you, too."

She rose and began the harrowing walk to the fire pit and then out the door. Lifting her skirts to her knees and holding her breath, she picked her way to the fire pit.

Only a sliver of smoke now rose from the coals. On the other side was a flint and a stone, lying side by side on the stones encircling the pit, but they lay out of reach. Rather than going around, however, Astrid stepped up on the wall of stones and dropped her skirts to hold her arms out for balance. She kept her eyes on the stones before her, placing one foot in front of the other as light as she could and glancing toward the flint and steel.

Once at the other side, Astrid stooped and picked up the flint and steel; both were cold and heavy in her hand. Then she turned and stepped back to where she'd started. Lifting her skirt with one hand, she jumped down and listened. Not a sound. It shouldn't be this easy. The hairs on the back of her neck rose at the weight of a stare. She whirled. None but the huddled family and the sleeping men around her were in sight. But the latter could be faking. *The door. Get to the door.*

Astrid poked the flint and steel into her belt pouch and held her skirts up. She followed the foot-wide path to the door. Halfway there, she stepped on a sleeve just as the man moved. She stumbled and fell over the legs of another man.

The room was awake in an instant. Shadowy figures lunged toward her with yells, and she ducked under the reaching hands and fled out the door. Shouts followed her.

"Get her!"

Her feet pounded on the packed dirt road, and her breath caught in her throat. She gasped and skidded around a corner. The footsteps of the men were right behind her.

Two figures jumped out in front of her. With a cry, Astrid threw herself away and ran toward the woods. Undergrowth crashed. Branches tore at her face and hair. On and on she ran, down one hill and up the next, around corners and between bushes, while the men gained on her. She spotted a ditch and, with the last of her strength, dove into it. Pain shot up her shoulder, but she scrambled behind the shelter of an ancient oak and curled up in its root flares. Spreading branches of a bush sprang up over her, and she prayed it hid her from sight. Her heart pounded in her ears.

Footsteps crashed past her and halted. There was whispering. Footsteps started up again, measured and slow, rounding the tree and pacing along the ditch, stopping occasionally and replaced by bushes rustling. One stepped right in front of her. His jerkin swished, a black shadow. His big hands fisted as he turned, stooped, searching, and one rested on his sword hilt. Astrid shrank into herself and dropped her eyes as the Dane's gaze traveled over her. Gooseflesh rose on her arms.

The Dane straightened with a grunt and joined his companion. Together they left, the sound of every step shaking her like the sea's stormy surf. A few minutes later, the other men came through, all around the tree where she hid.

When the heavy footsteps had gone, she let out a breath. Sobs welled from deep in her chest; she squeezed her arms around her chest and let them come.

The longer she cried, the heavier she felt. She lay on her side in the cold dirt and let her sobs convulse her—this must be what it was like to be a rat in the jaws of a dog.

Her questions, her attempts to make sense of the Christian God; she'd been a fool. It was her unfaithfulness that had brought wrath upon her people. Oh, Sven, if only he had known what it would lead to! Yet it wasn't him, as shaken as he was, but herself—herself who had no reason to doubt, and still doubted. Herself, who internally fought against her fate even though she'd submitted to it externally.

Stripped of family, friends, and home, abandoned by the gods, there was no life left for her here. But for Snorri's sake, and for the mother and children's sakes, they had to leave.

Her sobs were now hiccups, and she was sticky and shivering. Setting her jaw, she pushed herself up where she sat panting, then used a branch to rise to her feet. She staggered against the tree trunk behind her and rubbed graininess from her eyes.

As long as the boats hadn't been discovered, the others had a chance.

Chapter 5

Much to Astrid's joy, the shipyard hadn't been disturbed, owing to its secluded location on the island's eastern side, away from the village. Everything was still how the workers had left it: two newly finished longboats pulled up on the sandy shore, a box of tools near the second. Another longboat, a færing with two pairs of oars, floated in the sheltered water for a leak test. It would have been inspected that day if the Danes hadn't attacked.

A boathouse stood to the left, and inside she found several new tar buckets which she filled at a nearby stream and stowed in the faering, and a few hemp bags which she tucked under her arm.

The glare of sunlight startled her from her work. Closing the boathouse door behind her, she ran up the narrow dirt path but cut through the woods before it reached the village. At the edge of the wood, she slowed, stepping silently toward a broad old tree. No one was in sight, thank goodness! But why the prickle in her arms? She glanced behind and around her; nothing. Blowing out a breath, she made a run for the cellar.

Flinging onto the ground, she lifted the door and slid in. The door fell and plunged her into the darkness; she slipped and tumbled down the ladder. Her foot struck an object, and there was a clatter. When she sat up, her hand brushed water. She recoiled. Water?

"Oh, no no no..."

The water bucket. She'd knocked over the water bucket.

She scrambled up and groped for the lamp. Her hands shook so they could hardly handle the flint and steel she struck at the wick. Sparks scattered and merely sizzled when landing on it.

"Come on," she growled, taking a cloth from her belt pouch. She tore off a corner and struck on that, and finally the spark caught and burned, spreading to the lamp, which she took up.

Already the water was soaking into the ground, little puddles steadily shrinking. Frantically, she dropped to her knees and scooped as much as possible back into the bucket, but could only save a mouthful. There was nothing to do but draw more. With a sigh, she leaned against the wall, buried her head in her arms, and tried to ignore how her tongue, already dry from the fresh stream water, stuck to the roof of her mouth.

A tiny hand pressed against her updrawn knee, and another tapped her arms. She raised her head. Snorri had managed to pull himself up and stood wobbling back and forth. His brilliant blue eyes stared at her.

Astrid held out her arms, choking, "Come here, Snorri."

But he turned, plopped to the ground, and crawled away. She snatched him up and hugged him to her chest. He let out a howl.

"Hush! Snorri, quiet! See? Quiet." She held a finger to her lips. Snorri copied her, then squirmed and fussed. Holding him tight, she hummed softly, hoping the familiar lullaby would calm him. It didn't. His fussing continued. She wanted to shake him, but that wouldn't do any good.

She took what was left of the cloth, soaked it in mead again, and gave it to him to suck. Instantly, he was quiet. Quickly setting him down, she pried the lid off a Skyr barrel, took off her shoe, winced, and dipped the heel in. He drank it eagerly and fussed for more. She fed him until he wouldn't eat any more and instead began to crawl around the cellar, cooing and gurgling as he went.

Sighing, she drank some skyr and sat back to watch him, listening for footsteps from above. It was only a matter of time before they were found, the cellar being out in the open as it was. And whether hungry or content, what a noise Snorri made! She must risk taking him to the færing, where it was less likely for them to be discovered. Besides, they'd be ready for the mother and children to arrive.

She stirred and called softly to him. He didn't answer, so she rose and found him attempting to hide behind a sack of onions. Taking him by the hand, she led him to the mead jug and gave him just enough to make his eyes droop. He fell asleep against her chest. Now that he was asleep, she filled the two sacks she'd brought from the shipyard and tied them off with cord from the onions. When this was done, she tried to rouse him, but he would not stir. He was fast asleep.

After a drink, she peeked outside to make sure no one was around, held Snorri with one hand and a sack of food with the other, and left the cellar. She fled along the path, not daring to look back, although gooseflesh rose on her arms and hair rose on the back of her neck. It felt as if a force of Danes were hiding in the woods, waiting for her to fall into their trap.

She made it safely to the shipyard and stowed Snorri and the sack on board. He stirred a little, whined, and his cheeks flushed, but it could only be the result of the mead. Conscience pricked. She was loath to leave him, but the other sack must be brought—and the mead. It might be needed.

She tore herself away and ran down the path again, pausing breathlessly at the edge of the wood. The empty field around the black heap of her home was empty; down in the village, people were moving about, and it could not be long before they came here.

Crossing the field quietly, she came to the cellar and stopped. Chills slithered down her spine. Two distinct voices came from the open cellar, and they were talking about her.

"Someone hasn't been gone long, leaving the lamp burning like that. Shut the door. Let him think his hiding place is safe."

"He was no man! Look, a woman's boot...two of them. With the state of one, no wonder she left them behind," with a laugh. The ladder creaked, and Astrid threw herself on the ground to avoid being seen. The door shut and, with her ear pressed against the dirt, she heard them start talking again in muffled tones, but it didn't matter what they said. She must be far away before they come out.

She got up and ran for the woods. There, she grabbed the trunk of a tree and crouched beside it just as the cellar door opened. The two men came out, looked around, and separated. They searched in and around the buildings and, after a brief exchange, headed toward where she hid. Her heart hammered in her ears. She crammed into the shallow dip in the dirt and waited to be found. Leaves had fallen quickly, and the half-naked branches couldn't hide her from searching eyes.

Where were they? Enough time had passed for them to be upon her. Shaking, she lifted her head ever so slightly and glanced at the field. The two men were talking with several others, who must have detained them.

Slowly, she stood. Every noise sounded like thunderclaps. Looking over her shoulder one last time, she fled, not by the path but through the densest part of the wood, to the shipyard.

When she reached the stream near the shipyard, she collapsed and splashed ice water on her face. Her hands shook so much, she could hardly control them.

There she rested until most of the trembling in her legs had stopped, then walked through the stream and to the shipyard.

Astrid slumped against the boat's side, exhausted so much for the rest of the food and the mead. There might be time to get them later.

Snorri's blanket rustled. Shaking herself, she went to him, but he didn't start screaming as he would have done earlier. His cheeks burned red, and sweat dotted his forehead. Her stomach turned. She picked him up and unwrapped his blanket; heat radiated from him, and he was drenched in sweat. His breath rasped, and his eyelids drooped.

"Oh, Snorri!"

From then until late morning, she never left his side, bathing him and keeping him cool. There was no need now to keep him quiet, but oh, if only she had the mead! Mother always gave them some when they were ill. Around midday, he could keep nothing down. Water and food came right back up. Astrid tried her best to keep him and herself clean and to feed him as much as possible, hoping something would stay down. Time and time again, she wished for the herbs that once hung for the rafters, for Mother's knowledge, and for the village's medicine woman. By mid-afternoon, Snorri was limp and no longer whining.

The sun was beginning to set in a blood-red sky, and black clouds scarred the brilliant hue. Astrid held Snorri gently in her arms, coaxing him to drink, but could not get through his delirium. His lower lip drooped like a wilted twinflower, his face and hands were pale, and his eyelids were translucent.

She held him closer and leaned fully against the side of the boat. Might as well let him rest. And although she was no longer hungry or thirsty, a telltale pounding headache told her otherwise. To eat now was impossible, with Snorri's hand gripping her finger and the aching lump in her throat, but she'd eat when he was well.

Stroking his cheek, she whispered, "Come on, Snorri. Open your mouth for me." As with many other attempts, this one was not answered.

The boat, the beach were silent. Birds hadn't sung since the Danes came, and the waves lapping against the boat were so calm they scarcely made a sound. Unlike moving in the cellar where every sound echoed, her movements were silent, too. All was still as if holding its breath.

Rocks jutting from the water beside a jagged cliff were more exposed now, and a ring of damp encircled them. The tide was going out.

Stirring again, she called to him. Again, no response, but this time he was as still as the village. She shivered and clung to him. His fingers were turning purple. How cold they were! She smoothed a whisp of hair from his forehead and pulled her hand back with a cry. He was cold. His lips were purpling now.

"Snorri! Snorri!" She pinched his cold little ears and cold little cheeks, yet still he remained motionless. Then she shook him, crying his name. His eyelids didn't flutter, his lips didn't twitch, his hand didn't tighten; it loosened. Pressing her ear against his chest, she closed her eyes. There must be a sound. There must! But nothing, nothing but stillness.

His name died on her lips. Slowly, she pressed him to her chest and rocked him. The ache in her chest, arms, and legs hurt more than anything ever had, but she couldn't cry to relieve it. No tears would come, only stinging in her eyes and an aching lump in her throat.

Darkness fell. Astrid lifted her head, breathless and shaking, and looked around at the shadowy faering, blue beach, and black wood hemming it in. Snorri must be buried before the mother and children come.

She ran her fingers over the little face, over the feathery white-blonde hair. Mother had entrusted him to her, and she had failed. Tears came at the thought, slowly at first, then fast. Burying her head in the blanket, she let them come until they wouldn't come anymore, and they left her weak and shaking violently. She couldn't move, but somehow she must.

Not knowing how she did it, she climbed from the boat and knelt by the water.

After gently washing him, she put his old clothes back on and took him to the boathouse. There she placed him in a crate, set it on her hip, and carried a shovel on her shoulder. A suitable place was found in the woods, and she dug deep and wide enough to fit the crate inside. Kneeling by the crate, she laid him on his blanket, arranged his hands on his little chest, and placed her bracelets and two of her necklaces with him. She lowered the crate into the hole and looked at him for a long while. Then, shaking herself, set her lips and placed the lid on top, blocking him from sight forever.

The last of the dirt was packed on, and she collapsed against a tree. The wood was spinning. She slid down. The trees seemed to be closing in, pressing all around, hurling accusations. She hadn't done all she could; she could have kept him from dying, her unbelief led to all this. Shielding her head, she curled up as small as she could. The air was suffocating.

A longing to flee welled in her chest. Astrid clutched her hair and suppressed a scream. She wasn't needed anymore. What would it matter if she were killed?

She scrambled up and ran, but tripped on a root and fell. Rolling onto her back, she drew in long breaths of cold night air and wiped the damp grittiness from her face. Instinctively, she reached out to her side and laid her palm on the grass. The touch jolted her. Sven wasn't beside her. He never would be again. How often as children they'd snuck outside to watch the stars or walk in the woods! Not anymore.

She brushed her sleeve across her eyes and sat up, shaking away the bout of dizziness that had overcome her. The boats. Flee.

What life did she have?

To leave her home, the place her family had fallen, where Snorri was buried, her hill. Her body twitched. The mother and children should arrive any moment, but she couldn't leave without going to her hill one last time.

The fields around her home were empty. Far down in the village were several huge fires, their light and smoke reaching as far as the fields, staining them red and tingling her nose. She ran over the bare ground.

Familiar bushes met her with leafy arms open wide, and the path, knowing where she wanted to go, led her quickly up the hill and to the tree. Around its rough trunk, she wrapped her arms, hugging it tight, although it scratched her face. Its wood was warm, somehow, and it took away some of the cold in her limbs.

The first time she'd come here, Father had taken her up the hill and showed her the tree, the ocean, the sky, and the woods around her.

"I came here as a boy, Astrid, whenever things weighed on my mind," Father'd said with a sober smile. His gaze left the rolling waves and rested on her. He held her tight. "Now I'm showing you. And remember that, no matter what, I'll always be here for you. Your mother, Sven, and I will never leave you."

That was the first time, and this was the last. She didn't want to leave. If the Danes found her here and cast her over the cliff, so be it. This was where she wanted to be.

But Sven would never come. Neither would Father. When she went back down, she wouldn't see Mother or Snorri or Swanhild—or even Isar.

Her arms fell from around the tree trunk and hung limp at her sides. Beside the tree, the grass was still trodden down from where she and Sven had sat the day the Danes came.

She bit her lip and spun away. The path seemed to have steepened. She skittered down it, catching branches and bushes to steady herself, and all at once the wood opened up to the village, her village. She shielded her eyes from the black ruins and ran blindly to the boats.

The wood was so quiet, every move she made created more noise than a rush of deer. Astrid glanced over her shoulder, but no one followed her. The hair on the back of her neck rose, and she shivered.

At the shipyard, Astrid called softly for her mother and children. Her voice echoed back to her and faded away. She called again, and the same echo answered. She peered in the dim half-moon light at the boats, the boathouses, and the surrounding foliage. All at once, she felt dreadfully alone. Something did not feel right.

Maybe they were too far to hear her. She went to the entrance of the first boathouse and called. Not a sound, not even her echo. Where were they? It was past the agreed-upon time. She couldn't wait much longer, or she might be discovered.

She boarded the faering and hid herself, too miserable to drink or eat and too tired to care. There, she waited until the faintest change in the eastern sky warned of the coming of day, and still they hadn't come. That was when she remembered Hulskuldr's words:

"Gather the villagers and keep them under guard. We will hold a feast to Odin!"

War feasts included sacrifices.

With a heavy heart, she jumped into the icy water, hardly feeling the cold of the water swirling around her. She slipped the loop off the post that kept the longboat in place and scrambled aboard again.

The faering drifted ever so slowly, gnawing at the last cord of her sanity. But it finally reached the open sea, where the waves rocked it back and forth and the current swept it north, away from the island.

She scanned the assortment of ropes tied taut to hooks on the boat's sides, tracing each one to what it held. At last, she came to one of the sail ropes and worked at the hard knot, breaking several fingernails in the struggle. The rope suddenly shot from her grasp, and half the sail fell. She ran to the other side and undid the other. The sail caught the breeze and billowed out full and proud. The boat shot forward, knocking her against the side.

Some time passed, and a ray of light sprang over the boat and covered everything in gold. She looked back with shaded eyes and scanned the horizon. A lump rose in her throat when she spotted her island, a black speck on the edge of the sea. As she reached out her hand, it sank out of sight. She lowered her hand and stared at the horizon. Her heart plunged into the very pit of her stomach, and the ache pulsed and thudded in her empty chest. Astrid pressed a fist to her chest and turned away from where her island had been.

Chapter 6

The sun rose quickly on the fifth day at sea. Astrid pulled herself into the mast's shade to hide her burnt skin from the sun, curled up on her side and lay her head on her arm. Her vision swam. She closed her eyes and tried to ignore the pounding headache and shaking chills so she could sleep again.

Her body must need food again, but she couldn't rouse herself from the deck. What was the point? The gods had abandoned her. Drowning was preferable to the slow death of fever, dehydration, and starvation awaiting her— the water buckets having been knocked over two days before and her throat too swollen to swallow—but the several times she'd stared at the taunting waves, she couldn't throw herself overboard. Why? Was it the thought of cowardice? Of fearing the horrid life she had left when the monk hadn't?

How could life change so much? Not two weeks ago, Sven had shown her the longboats' progress. She could see him now, standing beside her, smiling broadly, the wind tossing his hair from his shoulders. Her eyes burned, but she could no longer cry.

Hunger, thirst, cursed dreams plaguing her sleep—this was her punishment, as if losing family and home weren't enough. This was not much better than being sacrificed to Odin by her enemies. At least then, the end would have come sooner.

She reached for the knife on her belt and drew it out. Its blade reflected the red, dying light into her eyes as she turned it and ran her fingertip along its edge. Her finger tingled.

Sitting against the mast, she took the knife in both hands and pointed the blade toward her chest. A shiver ran through her. Closing her eyes, she readied herself for the blow. Her arms shook so the knife wobbled. Energy surged and, with a groan, she cast the knife as far away as her shaking arms allowed and then collapsed against the mast, energy gone.

Storm clouds gathered overhead, thickening and darkening to coal black above the horizon where land must be, where her boat could run aground and be saved from the ocean. But if the storm came beforehand, it wouldn't matter if land appeared afterwards. The ocean would swallow her up, what with her vague knowledge of seafaring and inability to control a boat in a storm, especially a boat as small as the færing, and especially in her state.

She shivered. No saga told what happened to one who dies abandoned. That person certainly wouldn't enter Valhalla, and possibly not even Helheim. Wandering the earth as a spirit, without rest, was most likely her fate. A shiver ran down her spine at the thought. If the wandering was anything like this, it was more than she could bear. Her only chance was to survive, but she couldn't do it alone. Who would help her? If she called on her gods, they wouldn't help. What about the Christian God? She hadn't doubted Him; at least, not like she'd doubted the others.

"Please, God of the Christians, help me," she croaked. Her voice was barely above a whisper, but if He could hear, He might take pity. She huddled against the mast as cold, stinging salt wind whipped her face.

Distant thunderclaps rumbled. The clouds in the west raced across the sky and grew, towering, building, blackening. Lightning flashed, and thunder answered with a bang. The wind picked up and stiffened the mast. The sail snapped and filled, and the boat shot forward, up, up a wave and down, down, down the other side. Water dropped on her cheek, on the back of her neck, then the clouds broke open.

She opened her mouth and let the rain fall in. It trickled down her throat and, though it burned, it soothed and cooled. Eagerly, she opened her mouth for more, changed her mind, and sucked water from her sleeve, which gave more than catching it. Already she was soaked like a rag in a well and shaking from the wet and cold. She squinted. The other side of the boat was a mere shadow through the curtains of rain, but she rose to her knees and crawled to it with the hope that it was dryer there.

The faering was thrown sideways. She tumbled across the deck and hit a bench. A wave crashed over her, pouring water down her throat and up her nostrils. Spluttering, she wriggled between two benches and braced herself as the next wave descended, water rushing around her. A deafening crack split the air; the mast tore from the boat and hit the side, taking part of it away and letting the ocean in. Choking, she wedged herself further under the bench.

Only a fool would be out during such a storm. No one grieved the death of a fool.

It burned.

Groaning, Astrid shielded her face from the hot blinding light, then lay unmoving on her back. There were cries of birds and the roar of waves, her nose tingled with the smells of salt and fresh vegetation. Her arm tired, so despite the burning light, she laid it down again, and her hand scraped against something cold and gritty. She forced her heavy eyelids open.

The sky was its normal blue, and cloudless, and on one side of her, the last remnants of a golden sunrise colored the horizon. It was the strong sunlight that burnt so. It colored the ocean which was now calm as a woodland pool and cast a long, black shadow on the sand behind the longboat which lay two strides away, hardly recognizable as the boat in which she'd left her island. On the other side of her was a deep green wood of thick and lush grass and tall and old trees.

Water rolled over her, up to her hips, but it wasn't cold as it was during the storm. The unbearable heat burning her up inside and out was all she could feel; it was like swallowing fire and being in fire. But judging from the effort it took simply to move her head, she couldn't hide in the black shadow of the longboat.

She closed her eyes again. She was on a beach, probably on an island. Unless the storm had driven her too far south, this must be one of the islands west of Cooray that Father always mentioned with that bitter tone in his voice. There must be people. Would they be kind, or brutal like the Danes? No matter, they wouldn't find her in time. Whatever the case, the Christian God had answered and rescued her from the ocean. She thanked Him silently.

Above the rolling waves and crying birds, carried downwind, were voices that gradually grew louder. She waited, ears pounding, body shivering, unable to move. The voices grew louder until three were distinct: two boys and a girl. They were talking in conversational tones, coming nearer, then her ears rang and couldn't hear anymore. When the ringing had passed, there was the gritting of sand and panting like after a run, whispering and swish of cloth. A touch made her pulse skitter. The voices spoke a little louder now.

"Yes, she's alive." A boy's voice.

"Poor thing." The girl's.

"I say! We should've brought the water pouch. That would have brought her around." The other boy.

With all her strength, she forced her eyelids up. Gray-blue eyes in a brown face stared into her own, their kindness warming her chest.

"Bertha, Haakon," said the boy, "do you have anything to carry water with? I do not." A pause, then the boy addressed her. "Are there any besides you?"

Astrid parted her lips and could barely utter, "No." The boy leaned close to catch it.

"Strange," said Haakon, the other boy.

"Haakon," Bertha scolded. Then she said, "Eric, we can take her to Mother: she'll know what to do."

"Right." Eric turned his gray-blue eyes back on Astrid. "We're taking you to the village." Before she could respond, he put his arms under her and his clothing, scented with the salty ocean air, brushed her cheek. He stood and carefully laid her head against his shoulder.

"You got her?" asked Haakon.

"Yes, thanks."

Astrid was carried for what felt like forever before the shift-shift of sand changed to pad-pad of wood and the murmur of a crowded place, like a wharf, grew as loud as the sea. Carts rumbled by, chickens clucked, children squealed at play, a blacksmith's sledgehammer thrummed, conversations hummed, the pad-pad of wood vanished like they now walked on hard-packed dirt.

A shadow blocked the sun from Astrid's face and the walking motion rocked her gently. For the first time in weeks, memories that had haunted her at sea kept their distance. There was laughter, loud and merry. Sven always laughed like that. There was the door creaking to let Father in, and the melody of Mother's lullaby. It cleared, and she could almost hear the words. She half-expected Mother' hands in her hair, tender and caressing. There they were now, cool against her hot face.

"Fredissa, we found her on the beach," said Eric, his voice thrumming in his chest against Astrid's ear.

"She was by a boat wrecked by the storm last night," added Haakon.

"Bring her in, Eric," said a woman's voice. "Bertha, ready the extra room for her, and Haakon, fetch some water."

The walking motion started again, for it had stopped at some point, and suddenly the air was cool and warm at the same time and the light dimmed.

The next several days were a blur haunted by memories of cries and darkness and metallic smells.

They plagued her dreams but fled when she awoke, often waking to find Fredissa at her side and holding her hand tight as if trying to keep away the dreams.

Finally the fog lifted, and Astrid awoke with the fever gone and some strength back. For the first time, she could see everything clearly. She was in a longhouse room, on a rumpled bed, wearing only a linen underdress (a serk). Light peeked through a slit in the patterned curtains enclosing the room on three sides, and outside it, pots and pans gritted over coals in the fire pit.

Remembering how terrible she'd felt when she came, she lay still for a moment. Her face no longer burned, though it was tender. Her body was weak and ached with what must be hundreds of bruises from being tossed on the ship.

Slowly she sat up and swung her legs out of bed. Light and room swirled, and she felt herself falling. Holding her head with one hand and gripping the bed with the other, she leaned forward to help the dizziness pass.

When the worst was over, she sat up straight again. By the amount of light coming in, and the still-sleepy sounds of movement, it was morning, and breakfast was being made. At home, she'd always helped, but here? Did they expect her to stay in her room or come out and help?

The impulse to cry arose, and she hid her face in her hands and clenched her jaw. They must not hear her cry. She didn't want sympathy; they couldn't understand. They still had their home and family, and what did she have? While the nightmares had lasted, she'd held onto the hope that this was all but a dream and everything would go back to the way they were when she came to herself, but that hope was gone. The nightmares were real. And far away, her home island was destitute, her own longhouse gone, her people dead.

She tipped her head back and looked up at the rafters, and a faint shaft of light floated above her. She turned around. In the wall, at the foot of the bed, was a small square window. With a burning desire to know about her new surroundings, she crawled across the bed to it, lifted away the latch, and eased the window open.

It was a small village. Short longhouses nestled together, and behind each one was a garden plot. The roads were narrow and straight as a rod. To the right of the village were empty fields, and behind the fields was a wood.

She sighed, laid her chin on her arms, and watched the people pass by on the street. A horn blew faintly, and the people dropped their work. One man, dark-haired and walking with a bold, sauntering gait, headed straight for the house. The door creaked open and groaned shut.

"Erlin, just in time for the meal!" Fredissa said happily.

The man chuckled. "How is my pretty wife today?"

"Better with you here," with a laugh.

What was said next, Astrid couldn't hear, for the door opened again, and then came the voices of the three young people who'd found her. Stools scraped over the hard dirt floor.

The curtain opened. Fredissa slipped into the room and knelt beside her. She laid a cool hand against her forehead and smiled.

"It is good to see you up. How do you feel?"

Astrid turned to the window as the memories returned. She took a deep breath and said with a shaky laugh, "I feel like I've been run over by a cart! I hurt all over."

Fredissa nodded. "The storm was rough on you. How is your throat? And your sunburn?"

"Only a little sore now. My skin's peeling like old paint, but it feels better. How long have I been here?"

"Five days."

That many? It had seemed like one long, never-ending night.

"Would you like to join us for the midday meal?"

Astrid hesitated. Nothing sounded more intimidating at that moment than being watched by people she didn't know. However, she didn't want to be alone with the memories so near, and the thought of food caused her stomach to rumble with hunger. Reluctantly, she nodded.

Gently, Fredissa helped her up and pushed the curtain back for her. Astrid had to lean on her arm as she walked to the table, taking small steps. There were four people at the table, three of whom she recognized from the beach, one a man who must be Erlin, and they were watching her. She dropped her gaze and slid into a high-backed chair.

"Heil, mær," greeted Erlin.

Astrid started and stared blankly at him. Silver strands highlighted his black locks, and a white, jagged scar ran down his tan cheek and into his beard. Finally, she found her voice. "Thank—thank you," she stammered, glancing to the side. One of the boys, who sat near the end of the table, grinned at her. Astrid dropped her head and turned to her food.

Everyone else had boiled meat, bread with honey, and other foods her stomach couldn't handle yet. Her mouth watered, but she stirred a few chopped berries from her plate into her skyr. When she went to spoon the skyr into her mouth with her shaking hands, some dribbled onto the side of the bowl. Glancing around, she scraped it off with her finger and enjoyed the tingling sour taste of the milk cheese.

"How's the new boat, Eric?" Erlin asked a sandy-haired young man.

The young man looked up from his plate, and Astrid got a view of his face. Tan and boyish, with traces of a beard on his chin. If it weren't for that, Eric would have looked like a boy. And gray-blue eyes. She could have recognized those eyes anywhere. Eric was the young man who'd first helped her.

"Well, so far," he answered. "It's a seaworthy karvi, handles the wind and waves without much management."

"That is good to hear."

Fredissa spoke up from the other side of the table. "Erlin, could you pass the meat this way?"

Erlin did so and asked, with a glance at the dark-haired girl beside Eric, "And your plan is to start fishing independently on it, correct?"

"Yes. I have several other men who will fish with me, and we're currently working on the nets."

"Excellent, excellent. It sounds as though you'll soon be fishing on your own. It's a good trade, and I wish you well. Just what a man needs to support a family."

Bertha, the girl beside Eric, blushed. Eric briefly dropped his gaze.

"That's what I hope," he said softly. Astrid's throat and stomach tightened with unease, and she picked at the remaining berries.

The other boy, who must be Haakon, reached for a bowl, and his sleeve caught on his cup. With one swift, wildcat movement, Erlin grabbed the cup before it spilled. Crimson rose on Haakon's neck.

"I happened to speak with your father today," Erlin continued, with a warning glance at Haakon, who reached again for the bowl, this time moving the cup aside first. Erlin shook his head, but a twinkle was in his eyes. He turned his attention back to Eric. "He mentioned the annual trading voyage and discussed possibly buying a few of my first, saying he hoped to reach more villages next year."

Eric shook himself, straightened, and glanced at Bertha. "Yes. We'll try some new wharves near Kaupang and some others down south. It'll take us longer, about a month, but we've saved up for it. Father is excited."

"A month is a long time to leave your longboat unattended."

"A trusted friend of Father's has agreed to care for it. If it were larger, I would have liked to sail it on the voyage. It is my most prized possession, and now I understand the urge of our fathers to ride the sea more than ever."

Erlin lifted his half-empty cup. "I, too, feel that urge at times, although not as much as you, since you work on the sea and I do not. If we went a-viking, I have no doubt you'd be the greatest voyager of them all."

"I would if duty called," Eric said quietly, looking down.

Silence fell. No one made a sound or movement, except Haakon, who began to squirm. It took all Astrid had not to do the same.

"Eric's taken us to see the boat, Father," Bertha said. "It's a beautiful karvi."

A smile lifted the brows that naturally settled over Erlin's eyes. "Is that where you went yesterday morning?"

Bertha flicked a deep brown braid over her shoulder. "Oh, yes, and we had a wonderful time. We also went to the beach like we did last week."

"Praise Odin, you did," Fredissa murmured, with a glance at Astrid. She straightened to look into Astrid's bowl. It was empty. "How was it?"

"Very good, Kona."

"Are you still hungry?"

Her eyes flickered to the empty plates of the others. "Not anymore."

There was another moment of silence, during which Erlin fixed his gaze on her, eyebrows down, mouth stern, arms folded. She slid down in her chair with her heartbeat hammering in her ears, unable to look away. Then he nodded to himself, as if pleased by what he saw, and asked:

"What is your name? Where are you from?"

All eyes were fixed on her, and she slid down more. The memories overtook her, choking, overwhelming. She wrapped her arms around her middle and made herself as small as possible.

"Not now, please," she whispered. Her temples pulsed as heat crept into her face. If only everyone would stop looking at her.

Erlin's face softened. "Just your name, then."

A lump in her throat kept her from speaking. She swallowed hard and cleared her throat. "Astrid."

"Astrid, could you tell us about yourself?"

The attack… drifting on the ocean… Snorri's wails… Father's sword… the screams, the stench, her burning home. It was too much to tell. She shook her head and wished the floor would swallow her up.

Fredissa stood and put her hands on Astrid's shoulders. Astrid startled and started to pull away, then forced herself to relax.

"She needs more rest, Erlin. Give her more time," said Fredissa.

Erlin sighed, nodded, and lifted his hand in consent. Fredissa helped Astrid to her feet and took her back to the other room, where Astrid sank onto the bed.

When the curtain fell and hid her from everyone, and the conversation began again, Astrid slid off the bed and curled up against the floor below the window. She tucked her knees against her chest, lay her forehead on them, and surrendered to the deep weight settling over her.

Chapter 7

Several days later, as Eric passed by the longhouse on the way to his own, he couldn't resist stopping to knock on the open doorway.

"Come in!"

He walked in, and Fredissa greeted him with a smile, but she was preoccupied. She took a bundle of herbs from a full basket on the table and hung it on a nail in a rafter. "Heil, Eric. How is your father?"

"Heil, Fredissa. He's doing well." He glanced toward the curtain sectioning off the room where the shipwrecked girl was staying. She should've been outside where the sunlight could heal her; Fredissa, like the mother she was, would have seen to that. He lowered his voice. "Is she still not talking?"

Fredissa shook her head and took up another bundle. "Her grief is deep."

Bertha entered like a sunbeam in a longboat galley, a large basket of herbs on her arm. Her face, at least, showed no trace of worry. Her lips parted in a full smile as she set the basket beside her mother's. "Hello, Eric. If you wait a bit, we can go to the beach.

I'm almost done here, and I'm sure Haakon can come."

"I can't stay long," Eric answered quickly. "Father sent me to fetch a coil of line from home." An idea came to mind. "Fredissa, would a walk on the beach help bring the girl around?"

Fredissa blinked, thought, and shrugged. "She may not want to go. It's been a battle to bring her out for meals. Anyway, she's still very weak. Going to the beach would be too much for her." She emptied the basket on the floor and worked with Bertha on the other.

Eric hesitated. He should be going; in fact, he shouldn't have stopped. But the girl's pinched face had haunted him ever since he'd seen her at the wreck. She couldn't be much younger than himself, yet she had the hunted look of a glassy-eyed deer in a snare. What had she gone through?

"I'd better go," he said, shifting toward the door, but not without one last look at the curtained room. Father would be angry if he didn't return when he ought.

Fredissa smiled and waved him on. "Send Harald my greetings."

"I will." With a nod to Bertha, he left.

***

Astrid pulled the blanket tighter around her shoulders, sighed, and relaxed against the wall. She felt heavy, as if some force was pulling her to the ground. It was a relief to give in to it and let the now-familiar grief wash over her. Her strength was returning, albeit slowly, but it was exhausting as of yet to fight against the oppressive numbness. It was now six days since she awoke in the longhouse. Six days should have been enough time.

She listened to the sizzling and popping of frying meat coming from the main room. It was almost time for the midday meal, and she dreaded it. Three times a day, she was taken out to the open to eat under the stares of strangers, when all she wanted to do was hide. To protect herself. It was greatly preferable to eat alone, but that was no longer an option. Fredissa simply came in, said "time to eat", and helped her to the table without any further explanation.

Three meals a day. This family must be well off. Erlin was likely a jarl, the chief of the island. Or a thane.

She shivered as the word reminded her of Isar. How would life have been if Cooray hadn't been attacked?

She blinked as moisture gathered in her eyes and startled when the curtain to her room was drawn aside. Fredissa peeked in, then knelt beside her.

"Why don't you sit outside for a bit?"

Astrid stared. "Wha—"

"Food isn't ready yet," Fredissa went on, "and fresh air would do you good. It'll help you regain your strength quicker."

"Well..."

It was the last thing she wanted to do, but Fredissa didn't give her time to say so. She helped her up and brought her out of the room. There, Bertha took Fredissa's place, and Astrid leaned on her arm as they stepped to the door.

Outside, the sunlight was blinding. Fresh air rushed into her lungs with a deep breath. Energy coursed through her, and the weight lifted a little as if she'd left it inside. When her eyes adjusted, she saw Eric and Haakon standing a short distance from her, giving her room. For the first time in weeks, warmth thawed the icy interior she'd built inside. Tears threatened again.

"Let's go sit over there," said Bertha, nodding toward the side of the house. Astrid let her take her around the house and to the back, where a thick patch of grass grew. Uncommon in a village, but there it was.

She sank onto the sun-heated grass and leaned against the rough wooden wall. Bertha sat beside her, and the boys stood to one side, visibly uncertain, like young Sven when he was in trouble. Astrid found it easy to smile at them, somehow. They slowly drew near, Haakon first, with Eric following, and sat across from her.

"Feel better?" Bertha asked softly. Her voice was soft like the finest linen.

Astrid again breathed in the sweet early autumn air. "A little." Then she found the courage to ask something that had bothered her off and on. "Do you... Do the Danes bother you here?"

The others exchanged glances confusedly, and Eric answered slowly, "The only Danes we see are traders, but we've heard nothing of them in a long time."

Astrid let herself relax against the wall and watched puffy clouds sail by in the brilliant blue sky. Lowering her eyes, she looked around at the village visible from where she sat. The house was near the edge of the village, and the houses were spaced out more here. Downhill, however, they nestled closer, and the road narrowed. At the furthest place downhill was the wharf. To the left of the wharf must be the beach she was wrecked on.

"What's the name of this island?" she asked.

"Trygvey," Haakon said, sitting up suddenly. Astrid shied, but he went on. "We should show you around sometime. It's a big place, and the village is just a small part of it, not much to see there. Just the Tingstead, the wharf, the houses, the blacksmith and carpenter sheds. The wood is more interesting. You can never tell what you'll find. Of course, there are wild animals and such, and our pigs forage in there; well, not anymore. They're all harvested, except for the spring pigs. Besides that, there are trails all through the woods that the other hunters and I follow. Beyond that, there's a beach—" He stopped as suddenly as he started, blushed, and slumped, looking around sheepishly. "Too much," he mumbled.

Astrid inclined her head to hide a smile.

"Food's on the table!" Fredissa called.

Bertha stood and held out her hand, which Astrid took. At the doorway, she stopped as if she had come up against a physical barrier. Across the threshold was the dim interior, the set table, the fire pit, and the curtained rooms beyond that. Weight settled on her again with the intent of pulling her to the ground, and she shrank away from the darkness.

Bertha drew her back, and Haakon and Eric went in ahead of them. Bertha didn't urge her in any form; she merely stood by her side. Astrid threw back her shoulders and crossed the threshold into the house.

When the meal was finished and everyone sat in silence as if in anticipation, Erlin looked her over briefly. She waited with dread for the usual question, sitting up straight to brace herself for it. This time, she was ready.

The question came. "Can you tell us about yourself now?"

She looked up at Erlin. There was kindness in his face. Drawing a breath, she said slowly, "I am Astrid, daughter of the late Jarl Arnold of Cooray."

Erlin's brows furrowed. "Late?"

She swallowed and murmured, "Danes attacked our island."

Fredissa leaned forward. "What of the rest of your family?"

Choking back tears, Astrid tried to control her voice. "They were killed in the attack. I hid in our cellar with my baby brother until he died of illness." She was thankful she'd cried out most of her sorrow. Everyone watched her so closely that she would have been ashamed to cry.

"How did you escape?"

"In one of our faerings." A lump rose in Astrid's throat, and she bit her lip and lowered her face. "I sailed for five days."

"How long were you without provisions?"

Astrid's temple began to pound. She pressed a hand to it. The days had bled into each other, so there was no way to know exactly. The storm had lasted a day, or was it two?

"I don't know."

Everyone was silent. Astrid hung her head to hide her watering eyes.

"I am sorry for your loss," Erlin said finally. "You will stay here until your fate is decided."

Astrid looked up. His kind appearance had changed completely: Lines creased his forehead, and he frowned, deep in thought.

"I do not want to burden you," she faltered, twisting her kirtle around her fingers.

"You won't be a burden to us at all. We know the plight you are in. Have you anywhere to go?"

"No... jarl."

Erlin stood and left without another word.

Chapter 8

Erlin paused outside his brother Karsfien's carpenter shed and tapped his knuckles on the door.

"Come in," Karsfien called.

Erlin pushed the door open and walked inside. The smell of fresh wood greeted him from a stack of cut planks against the back wall. Wood shavings crunched under his boots, and particles of dust tickled his nose. At a table surrounded by three chairs, Karsfien, a bronzed man with clear-cut features, was bent over a piece of wood he was whittling. Scattered at his elbow were several chisels, a knife, and a sharpening block. A window built in the wall was open, flooding light into the otherwise dark room. The scene, as it did every time, reminded Erlin of all the times his own father had worked like that, in that very carpenter's shed.

Karsfien looked up, gave his crooked grin, and pushed out a chair with his foot.

"Welcome, brother," he said.

"Hello, Karsfien," said Erlin, seating himself and placing his folded arms on the table. He watched Karsfien as he went back to work. "What is that?"

"A Hnefatafl warrior." The board game piece was half a palm in length, and rough carvings of features suggested a warrior holding a shield. "Just six more after this, then I'll dye the defenders." He glanced at him and lifted a brow.

Erlin smiled faintly. "I can't fool you."

Nodding, Karsfien grunted. "Something come up?"

Erlin looked out the window, gathered his thoughts, and leaned forward. "I learned the shipwrecked girl's name is Astrid, the daughter of Jarl Arnold of Cooray."

"Jarl Arnold's a good man," continuing to whittle.

"She says he was killed not a month ago."

Karsfien stopped and stared.

"Danes attacked Cooray. Astrid was the only one of her family to escape."

With a frown, Karsfien exchanged his knife for a chisel and worked on deepening the carvings. "Why do you come to me, then?"

"As my Thane, you have a say in the decisions I make. This girl has no home, and I feel it is our duty to give her one. The Ting is coming up in a few days. Shall I bring it up during the meeting?"

Karsfien shrugged. "Perhaps."

Sighing, Erlin rubbed the bridge of his nose. "Surely you can tell me more than that."

"You're my older brother. If you say we address it during the Ting, so be it. The girl—Astrid, did you say? —cannot stay at your home forever."

"You know what happened between our islands in the past. If this isn't handled right, our people could accuse me of betrayal or another wild treachery. They'll have me killed or exiled."

"Then assert your authority. Gently, Erlin, but do assert it. I have—" Karsfien stopped short and was suddenly absorbed in his game piece.

Erlin's spine chilled. "You've what?"

Karsfien glanced at the open window, leaned forward, and dropped his voice to a whisper. "I've felt a sense of unease. It's built up slowly over the past weeks, and I feel it only occasionally. I've tried to pinpoint who brings that sense around, but so far have been unsuccessful. The groups of people I'm around are too varied."

Weight dropped in Erlin's chest, and he groaned. "I thought I felt it, but hoped it was only imaginary. Do you think this has anything to do with the Christian, Samuel?"

Karsfien shrugged. "It could. His arrival corresponded with the scanty harvests."

Erlin sighed and ran his fingers through his hair, muttering, "By the gods, her arrival couldn't have been more badly timed." He took the piece Karsfien set down and turned it over in his hands. Hnefltefl was a game with the goal to corner the jarl, a game he'd often enjoyed. Now he felt like he was living it. Quietly accepting Astrid into the village would buy him time, but such an action sounded too much like secrecy. No, this was a matter to be publicized. Besides, it could reveal his adversaries. There was no reason to let a revolt be organized.

He set the game piece down and stood. "I'll bring it up at the Ting. Keep your eyes and ears alert, will you?"

Karsfien rose and clasped Erlin's hand. "Will do. By Thor, I hope nothing goes wrong."

***

The next day, Astrid awoke greatly improved. As she stood, she found most of her strength had returned. She washed in the bowl of water left in her room and came to breakfast by herself. Fredissa smiled when she saw this and allowed Eric, Haakon, and Bertha to give her a tour of the village.

"But not a long one," she said as they left. "She must recover her strength slowly."

Eric threaded Astrid's hand through the crook of his arm and supported her as they walked. Feeling the support of his arm gave her a sense of security and brought back the day he'd carried her. Haakon strolled alongside with a huge grin on his face. Bertha ran out in front, turning back with her bright smile to tell Astrid about the sights they passed. The three led Astrid between houses and around corners until they stood in front of the Tingstead and its sacrificial pit, and she gazed at it in awe.

It was a tall, longhouse with a curving roof that dipped close to the ground on the sides. On the front were sacred carvings of sea serpents, dragons, Mjolnir, and the ravens of Odin, Huginn and Munnin.

The entrance was made of huge double doors with loop handles. Vine carvings laced the hardwood of the doors, and in the center was Yggdrasil, the World Tree.

Bertha stopped at the entrance of the Tingstead and slipped through the doors, returning with a metal horn. It was set with previous stones, and its rim was edged with sea serpents winding around and around in perfect infinity swirls. Pride shone in Bertha's eyes as she held the horn toward Astrid.

Astrid reached out and touched its cold side. "It's beautiful," she breathed.

Haakon winked. "Yes, an article of superior craftsmanship." He took it from his sister and raised it to his lips. "If you listen, it sounds just as well as it looks."

The muscles in Eric's arm tensed, and Bertha snatched the horn back. "Don't you dare! You know what Father'd do if he heard you blew it to show off."

Haakon shrugged. "Whatever you say, sister."

Bertha continued to glare at him.

"He's teasing," said Eric, with something between a chuckle and a moan. His muscles relaxed.

Although alarmed at Haakon's lack of respect for the obviously sacred horn, Astrid let herself smile.

Bertha shot him a look and melted into a laugh, shaking her head. "He always does things that vex me."

"I know you too well." Haakon grinned.

Bertha made a face and disappeared inside the Tingstead again. When she returned, her face was clear as a summer morning. "We use the horn to signal morning, noon, and evening, so the people are used to hearing it, in case of an emergency. It's a tradition passed down from the founders of Trygvey. The meeting hall and the horn are the jewels of the island." Her voice dipped. "Besides the treasury, but only Father and Olaf have seen that."

Before Astrid could ask about the treasury, Eric cleared his throat. "Let's show you some other things."

"Like what?"

"How about the fields?"

"You know she won't be impressed with that," said Haakon. "She's probably seen fields grander than ours."

"How can you be sure of that?" Astrid said, with a laugh at Bertha and Haakon. They'd just exchanged grimaces, and Bertha dealt him with a light cuff on the arm. Astrid felt the weight of a gaze on her and, looking up, locked eyes with Eric. His eyes were warm, too warm. She looked down in confusion and sudden embarrassment.

"Come on!" called Haakon, strolling out in front.

Astrid took Eric's arm and turned to follow Haakon, but noticed a man watching them. He wore simple clothing and carried a small crate. What stood out about him was his short hair, cut above the shoulders and braid-less, and his observant, mellow expression. He smiled at Astrid, nodded, and left.

"Are you alright, Astrid?"

"Who is he?" She blinked and glanced at Bertha.

"Oh, no one in particular," said Bertha, shuffling her feet and avoiding eye contact. "Just a man who came not long ago. His name is Samuel. Some say he's a strange one."

"Why?"

"He believes different, in the Christian God."

"Is he a monk?"

Bertha gave a strange sideways look and shrugged. "He lives like everyone else, if that's what you mean." She walked away, picking up her skipping gait after a few steps.

Fluttering inside with curiosity, Astrid glanced back at where the man had been and wished they could go after him. However, Eric and Haakon had to return to work. Bertha took Astrid back to the longhouse, where Astrid slept all afternoon. She awoke just in time for the meal, which was unusually quiet. Erlin was lost in his own thoughts, and his mood didn't encourage conversation.

Three days later, at the morning meal, the Ting was announced to take place the following week on Woden's Day. Much preparation was to be done; Astrid helped a little but retreated to a corner to watch when the activity overwhelmed her.

During this time, Fredissa gave her neatly folded green fabric, which was mended in several places. It was the kirtle she'd worn during the attack.

Astrid took it to her room and shook it out. It was clean and almost as good as new, unlike the smokkr she hadn't seen since her arrival at Trygvey. She removed the blue kirtle she'd been lent and pulled her own over her head. With her brooches fastened and belt tied, she felt more like herself again.

The day of the Ting arrived, and because her help wasn't needed, she was the first to ready herself. Her necklaces and brooches were shone, boots cleaned, and face, neck, and arms washed.

When it came to fixing her hair, she combed it slowly with her own comb, which had survived, save for two teeth, in her pocket during the storm. She set her comb on the bed, parted her hair down the middle, and began a braid just behind her ear. She'd put her hair up. The people would consider her a woman, and so be it. Was she not forced to stand on her own? Now, what had Mother used...

With both braids done, she peeked out from the curtain. Bertha walked by, toward her family's room in the back corner. Astrid called to her.

"Bertha, do you know if there's a blunt, curved needle around, and string? It's for my hair."

Bertha smiled and nodded. "I do. They're only in there," she said, waving toward the room. She left, then returned with the two items and handed them over. "When you're done, Mother will need the needle."

"Thank you. I'll be sure to give it back."

Another smile and nod, and Bertha skipped to the room.

Astrid retreated into her own and sat on the bed. Holding her braids around her head, she took the string and wrapped it over the braids and through the hair against the scalp. This was done all around; the string ends were tied and tucked away, and she lowered her aching arms. She felt the braids, gave her head a good shake; it would do. If only Mother had been able to show her how. Her braids were always so secure and tidy. Astrid swallowed and tugged the kirtle collar away from her throat. She shouldn't think of those things, not before the Ting.

Picking up the curved needle, she pushed her thoughts away and went in search of Bertha.

At midday, Astrid followed close behind Fredissa as they made their way to the Tingstead. Erlin, Haakon, and Bertha were just ahead. Talking, chatter, and commands came from houses they passed, as well as splashing water and clanking metal wear. A few doorways were left ajar, and inside, people scurried here and there. Movements were quick and voices lively, making her head ache.

Some families were on their way to the Tingstead as well, and their stares made her squirm.

At Tingstead, Erlin blew the horn and entered through the wide-open doors. Astrid squared her shoulders and followed, squinting in the dim light. Lamps lined the food-laden tables, and sunlight flooded through the southern-facing doorway. Although few people were inside and the lamps had recently been lit, the air was already hot and stuffy and smelled of smoke.

Fredissa sat down and gestured to the spot on the bench beside her, and Astrid scrambled to seat herself. Bertha sat on either side. Erlin and Haakon were gone.

The rumbled of voices increased as people entered the building, and the weight of their stares pulled her down. Astrid folded her arms over her stomach and stared at the table ledge, which was engraved with serpents winding over and under.

A shout, and the room hushed. She glanced up. Between the two tables stood an old man holding a metal cup in his hands, and he lifted it above his head.

"To Freya, who heard our pleas and graciously met our needs this harvest. May she bless us with abundance in years to come." Lowering the cup to chest height, he poured wine from it onto the ground in an offering. Drops splattered on his gray leg wraps and tan trousers like blood.

A cheer resounded, and the feast began.

Metal and wooden plates, bowls, spoons, and knives clanked as food was served and passed down the long tables. Sweet, sour, and savory scents swirled in tendrils around her with every dish she passed on. Broiled fish, fried ham, honey cakes, raspberry mead, stewed cabbage and carrots, sun-dried fruits, fried beets, and still more. She yearned to taste everything, but her stomach was still sensitive as of yet. So she served herself only skyr, bread, fried beets, and ventured to try a little pork, and contented herself with watching the others vicariously.

Her plate was soon empty, but to eat more could send her stomach into a revolt. So, she folded her arms on the table and observed the people. No one paid her attention. She used this liberty to her advantage and watched everyone unashamedly. At the end of the opposite table was a cluster of boys, which included Haakon and Eric; they yelled and hooted louder than the conversing of everyone else.

A little way from them, occasionally looking their way, were several men and women, gray and bent with age. One kept his eyes half-closed in a spiteful squint, and his pointed, scraggly-bearded chin jutted out further than his drooping nose. His claw-like hands gripped the head of a cane. Across from him sat a woman with her faded blonde hair plaited back in a long braid and with a gray shawl wrapped around her shoulders. Deep in her wrinkled face were two sparkling blue eyes, very keen despite her age. She looked around, caught Astrid's stare, and smiled. Blushing, Astrid dropped her eyes.

A man walked up behind her. She shrank back when he towered over her, but he nodded, and his mouth widened in a smile that crinkled his eyes.

"Time to start the cases," the man said to Erlin.

Erlin nodded, then turned to Astrid. "This is my brother, Karlsfien. He's the lawman."

Astrid tipped her head back to look into Karlsfien's face. "Greetings, Thane Karlsfien."

"Greetings, Mær. You are welcomed here."

His words brought warmth into a cold place in Astrid's chest that she didn't know had formed. She blinked away moisture from her eyes and whispered, "Thank you." He bowed his head ever so slightly and walked away.

When Karsfien reached his seat, he raised his hand, and the room hushed. Then he cleared his throat and began to recite the whole law, his powerful voice echoing through the hall for some time before he stopped and sat down.

After a moment of silence, a man stood up and presented his case, a matter of property. Erlin stood and answered him, referencing the law. Several others spoke up, and they discussed the question further before sitting.

This process was repeated several times, then came a silence longer than the first. All the cases had been presented except one.

Erlin cleared his throat and stood. Cold settled in Astrid's stomach as his gaze briefly fell on her. Astrid glanced at Bertha, and the warm glow of the lamps highlighted Bertha's encouraging smile. Astrid forced a smile in return, fighting against the trembling in her face and the flutter in her stomach. Her legs trembled so violently that she hoped she wouldn't need to stand. She gripped the edge of the table.

Erlin spoke. "A fortnight ago, my son and daughter and Eric Haraldsson found Astrid of Cooray, the daughter of Jarl Arnold, on the beach."

A few judging stares fell on her. Astrid shrank against Fredissa. "A group of Danes, led by Jarl Holskuldr, took over her island and killed the villagers. She escaped alone by boat, and a storm drove her onto our shore."

The silence turned menacing, and several men and women glared at her. Astrid choked and swallowed, straightened and threw back her shoulders. The serpents on the table were branding themselves on her fingers.

"Karls," Erlin continued, "You have heard her plight. She has no kin and no home. She will join us as a villager, but she needs someone to care for her. What say you?" He looked around the room.

No one stirred, and her stomach quivered. Many scowled, and others smirked. The rest showed no emotion. They were blank as an uncarved runestone.

Erlin's voice rose. "Why do you hesitate? If no one takes her in, I will."

A man near the doors stood. "The Cooray people are untrustworthy."

Another said, "She is a foreigner and the daughter of a jarl. She could not possibly learn to work here."

Another, after his wife whispered in his ear, said, "The gods will be angry at us for receiving a Coorayan. She will bring bad luck on us all."

Erlin stiffened. "What if she is a Coorayan? That doesn't matter, for we are all flesh and blood. The gods will not be angry. This girl believes as we do, and Baldor will count this as a good deed. He will bless our island, not curse it. As to the untrustworthiness of her people, I had known Jarl Arnold for a few years, and he was an honorable and straightforward man. Why wouldn't his daughter be the same?"

A low, guttural, masculine voice rose from a corner. "Do you not remember what happened between our islands? How the Coorayans dealt treacherously with us and destroyed us when we rebuked them?"

Astrid bit her lip and grasped her pendant.

Accusations rained on her like a shower of arrows, and she winced at each one.

"She could be lying. A spy comes to take over the island; that's what she is."

"We've been at peace for years, but allowing this girl to live with us will change that. She will bring chaos to our island."

Erlin interrupted, holding up his hand. "I know there were problems with Cooray in the past, but this has nothing to do with it. It happened before Astrid's time. And how could she bring misfortune upon us?" His voice became gruff and low, like a growl. "She's a girl, not a god. How is she any different than us? We all came from the man and woman Odin and his brothers made from the two logs. We are all people, brethren, relatives living in various places. We are like a family that fights among itself. Taking Astrid in would be like taking in one of our own. You detest doing so because Loki is deceiving you into thinking it will cause us harm. Your reasons are like stubble. She couldn't take over the island if she tried!"

"What about the Christian you let on the island? He's not one of us, and look. The crops have struggled since he came!"

There was silence, and Erlin trembled visibly, but not with fear. His brows were drawn low over his eyes, which flashed in the torchlight. His body was stiff as a rod, his fists were white, and he clenched his jaw until Astrid feared he'd crack his teeth.

His voice was quiet with rage and sent shivers down Astrid's spine. "I am your jarl, karls. It is my responsibility to see to the well-being of the island,

and anyone who goes against me goes against Odin himself and will be punished."

Karsfien rose in Erlin's defense, stared the villagers down, and recited from the law what was to be done with traitors.

Several people stirred uneasily. For the first time, Astrid noticed the man she'd seen earlier—Samuel—sitting by himself at the other table. His face was sorrowful. He closed his eyes briefly, inhaled, and stood.

"Jarl, if I may."

Erlin blew out a breath. "Speak."

"You let a Christian speak at our Ting?" came a shout.

"Silence," growled Karsfien.

Erlin nodded to Samuel.

"Karls of Trygvey," said the Christian, spreading out his arms, "hear me. My God takes delight in those who seek justice, love mercy, and comfort the orphaned and widowed. He has promised to bless those who obey His commandments." The room stirred, but he held up his hand. "Please hear me. He tells us to respect and obey authority because he instituted them to lead mankind. I beg you to heed your jarl."

After more silence, the squinting old man rose, leaning heavily on his staff. "The night before the storm, I had a dream. In my dream, I was standing on the eastern beach looking toward the horizon, searching for the sunrise. From the horizon rose black clouds that covered the sky and brought rain down on us, destroying half our crops. Riding on the waves of the storm were servants of Hel. They landed on the island and brought plague that killed a third of our people. Next came a shower of hail which broke our houses and boats, and lightning from Thor kindled a fire that the rain could not quench. The smoke of the fire went up long after the storm had ended and rolled away."

Astrid shivered. There was only one way the villagers would interpret the dream.

"What is your interpretation?" Erlin asked between clenched teeth.

"My interpretation, Jarl, is that the girl beside you has come with the curses of Hel and Loki upon her to bring calamity on us. Consider this well and save us from what will befall us."

"And how would I do that?"

"Send her away in peace, so as not to turn the anger of the gods upon us."

Erlin studied the man and lowered his head. Confusion surrounded him like a cloud, and she shrank from it. The insight given by the gods through a dream could not be denied. If Erlin dismissed it, the villages would consider him a traitor.

Astrid shivered. Cursed by Hel and Loki... had they cursed her when she doubted? Weight dropped in her stomach, and she felt sick. Holding back a sob, she wrapped her arms around her middle. If her curse had brought the destruction of her people, what would it bring to Trygvey? There was no place for her here.

A warm arm wrapped around her and held her tight. Fredissa pressed her cheek against Astrid's. "Erlin..."

He looked at her with an expression of anguish that Astrid had only seen once before on a man.

"Mother Fredda," Fredissa prodded.

Erlin took a shuddering breath and called, "Herfrida, you have the gift of interpretation and discernment. What do you say?"

The elderly woman with faded blonde hair rose and drew her gray shawl around her shoulders. Leaning on her staff, she walked down the length of the table and stopped beside Astrid. With one worked hand, she lifted Astrid's chin and looked into her face. Herfrida's eyes glazed over, and the wrinkles around them deepened. Astrid met her gaze even as her stomach quivered. The woman smiled and let her go, and looked around the room.

"This girl has not the curse of Hel on her. She is just as she said, in need."

Astrid let out a breath she didn't realize she'd been holding and felt the weight lift from her stomach.

The old man stood. "What of the dream?"

"Your dream is valid, Bikki, but I do not interpret it as you. Here is the wisdom given to me: hard times will befall the island, but some time in the future. Not as soon as you made it out, but it will come. And when it comes, it will be akin to the destruction Vingi the Traitor of Cooray dealt upon us in its severity. Whether or not the girl will be involved in any way, I do not know, but I know it will not befall us because of her. Jarl Erlin has reason.

It is our responsibility to help others, and I will do my share by taking the girl under my care."

Erlin relaxed a little. "Are you certain, Herfrida?"

"Yes, jarl."

"May the gods bless you. The Ting is dismissed."

Restrained voices broke free like waves before a storm. Everyone talked at once, growling, grumbling, hissing. They rose and flooded from the building. They'd return in the morning for more festivity, if any could be had after tonight.

Astrid pulled herself to her feet. The room swirled. Her shoulder was patted, words buzzed her eardrums, and body heat surrounded her. She needed to breathe, but the room's stale air was suffocating. Herfrida was speaking with Erlin, Fredissa, and Bertha, and Haakon was missing. From the other side of the table, Eric caught her gaze. He gave her a compassionate look that asked, "Are you alright?" Nodding, Astrid swallowed and slipped away.

Outside, cool night air hit her face, and she sucked it in. Over and over. The people around her jostled her and tugged her on, so Astrid pulled away and flattened herself against the Tingstead's front wall, well away from the door.

Eric sidled up beside her. "I'm sorry."

"Please." The word cut like whiplash. Astrid winced. "Please, give me a moment."

Her tone didn't seem to bother him. He looked around solemnly, then nodded. "I'll be inside." He left.

At last, she was alone. She closed her eyes and let the darkness wrap around her like a cloak. Through the silence came the call of the ocean, luring her.

Astrid stepped forward and stopped short. Tight whispers came from the shadow concealing the side wall of the Tingstead. There were two voices, both low, one gravelly and the other sharp.

"What about it now? I told you something would come up."

"It's your fault. I told you to get it sooner, but you skulked too long. Now we'll never find him alone. He'll be with that girl and that Christian all the time."

"I say we get rid of her and put an end to it all," the gravelly voice growled. "What foolishness has this island come to now?"

Astrid pressed her hand to her mouth and choked back a sob. Using the full moon as her guide, she stumbled through the empty streets and found her way to the beach.

The moon was rising just behind her, casting a pale shadow in front of her. The sand glowed white, the water was black, and the crashing waves were lined with spraying white sparks.

"You're the only friend I have left," she whispered to the ocean.

Wind whipped her hair in her face and stole her breath. It slithered up her sleeves and caught her skirt, blowing it out to the side. If she spread out her arms, she could have flown if she weren't so heavy. Weight had settled over her again, pulling her shoulders and sinking her heart into her stomach.

She squinted to see the line where sky met water. Her island lay beyond it—her home. Where Father, Sven, and Isar had died in battle. Mother and Swanhild... what happened to them? And Snorri... A lump rose in Astrid's throat and choked her. She drew herself upright, shut her eyes and breathed a vow.

One day, she'd return to her island. Holskuldr's deeds would not, *must* not, go unpunished forever.

As the sole survivor of her family, it was her responsibility to avenge their blood.

A warm hand rested on her shoulder. Bertha stood behind her. "We wondered where you went," she murmured. "Are you coming?"

Astrid nodded and let her eyes roam over the waves rolling on the sand, the moonlit foam, and the ocean beyond. "I won't forget you," she whispered to her island.

Chapter 9

"So. Would you like to do the washing or the drying?"

Astrid started brooding over the Ting. She'd replayed it in her dreams the night before and in her waking that morning. With a sigh, she left the bench running along the wall. Bertha stood beside a pot of water with a drying cloth in hand.

"Whatever you prefer, Bertha."

Her friend grinned and tilted her head. "No, what would you prefer?"

Astrid tossed her hands. "I don't know."

"Then you can do the washing. The water's warm, and it'll feel good. Give the dishes a good scrubbing with this." Bertha handed her a small, coarse cloth and pulled a low stool over to the pot, gesturing to it.

Despite the mental itch caused by the Ting, Astrid had to smile at Bertha's nonchalance, which could make the most mundane chore a delight. She sat down, rolled up her sleeves, and plunged her hands into the hot water. Oh, it felt good! She swished around before taking a wooden platter from the stack of dirty dishes beside her, wetting the coarse cloth, and started scrubbing.

Bertha plopped on a stool across from her. "It's nice, isn't it? I like washing the morning meal things; as long as nothing breaks, it's quiet and a good time to think. Sometimes it's dull to do it alone, so when I get to do it with someone like you, it's a lot more fun."

Astrid rinsed the platter and handed it to her. Dipping a bowl in the water, she asked, "What is Herfrida like?"

Bertha dried the platter slowly. "She's the only healer on Trygvey, and Gudrid is her apprentice. She goes by 'Mother Fredda', out of habit. I don't remember a time she was called anything besides that."

"Jarl Erlin addressed her by 'Herfrida' last night."

"The Ting is a formal setting."

The motherly look paired with the gentle upturning of Astrid's face was fresh in her memory. 'Mother' suited the healer.

"What's her family like?"

"She has none."

"Oh."

The hot water had reached an unpleasant temperature between warm and cold. Astrid sped through the rest of the dishes.

No wonder Mother Fredda's sympathy was so comforting: they were the same, without family. But Mother Fredda had no alleged curse or dream hanging over her head, was highly respected and had an occupation. Work to distract from haunting memories. Did she have them, too?

Bertha laid a hand on Astrid's shoulder. "You needn't be afraid of her. She's the kindest woman I know, besides Mother."

Astrid attempted a smile. "Thank you." Suddenly, she realized she was afraid. Erlin's longhouse was the only place she felt remotely safe. In Mother Fredda's, there would be no privacy, no way to retreat from judging eyes. A healer's home was always busy with villagers coming and going. There was always work to be done and people to be seen. She shivered at the thought.

There was a knock on the door. Bertha flicked the towel over her shoulder and opened it.

"Come in, Mother Fredda," she said.

"Thank you, child." The woman with faded blonde hair and a gray shawl entered the room and immediately met Astrid's stare.

Astrid cleared her throat, said "Good morning, Kona," and turned her full attention on the dishes, trembling as the healer's feet padded over the hard-packed floor.

Bertha took the cloth and dish from her hand and whispered, "I'll finish these."

Astrid really trembled now. Hoping they couldn't hear her heart pounding, she stood before Mother Fredda, who rested on Bertha's stool.

The healer looked her over not unkindly, and the wrinkles deepened around her eyes. "How do you feel, Astrid?"

"Well, Kona."

"You didn't sleep last night, did you?"

Sighing, Astrid shook her head slowly. If she were to live with her, she might as well be honest from the start. Something about her made Astrid think Mother Fredda wouldn't stand for untruthfulness. "No, Kona, I did not."

The healer shook her head. "Never mind what the others say, child. I know you speak the truth."

She brightened. "I have a cozy room waiting for you in my home. And call me Mother Fredda."

"Thank you for taking me in, Mother Fredda," said Astrid, twisting her fingers together and swallowing against a lump in her throat. "I'll try to work hard and help you."

"I know you will." Mother Fredda rose. "Are you ready? Good. Let us go now. Where's your mother, Bertha?"

Bertha dried a wooden bowl and set it aside. "Out in the garden, I think. Should I get her?"

"Only send her a greeting from me, please. I must return home."

"Sæl, then."

"May the gods bless you and this household," returned Mother Fredda. She gathered her shawl around herself and started towards the door. Astrid hesitated.

Bertha squeezed her hand. "Go on. I'll come by as soon as I can."

"Thank you," Astrid gasped and ran to catch up with Mother Fredda.

All the way to Mother Fredda's longhouse, Astrid walked closely behind her to avoid the stares of those who greeted Mother Fredda. Some merely glanced, others stared with contempt, and still others ignored her completely, which, for some reason, hurt more than the others. Being the topic of discussion and being branded a curse-bearer didn't help Astrid's first impression on the villagers. She released a breath of relief when Mother Fredda stopped in front of a tidy longhouse and opened the door.

Inside was a square table, polished with age, with four stools standing around it. On the left wall were large shelves full of jars, bags, and pots, and beside the shelves were more stools and a chair. In the center of the room, tendrils of smoke drifted from the fire pit's hot coals. To the right were two bedrooms curtained off with simple, plain brown fabric.

"This is my home, Astrid," Mother Fredda said, shutting the door behind them.

Astrid looked and paused at the shelves. The bags were closed except for one or two, and they were nearly overflowing with crushed dried herbs. Partially dried plants hung from the rafters beside the shelves. Her eyes moved to the curtained rooms. One of them would be hers.

A pain tightened her chest as memories of her old home rose before her. The new one felt incomplete without Father's sword and axes hanging on the wall, Sven's knife lying on the table, and Mother's loom in the corner.

Turning away, Astrid swallowed and took a breath. Her eyes met Mother Fredda's. The healer was watching her quietly.

"Does it suit you, child?"

"It does. And I will work all I can not to be a burden to you."

The corners of Mother Fredda's sensitive mouth tipped up a little, and she answered, "You are not a burden." She motioned toward the curtained spaces. "I fixed your bedroom there, in the corner room. Ask for anything you might need."

"Thank you, Mother Fredda."

Astrid stepped around the fire and walked toward her room. Whisps of chamomile, yarrow, and mint followed her like Valkyries. Pushing the thick curtain aside, she stepped in. The left-hand corner had a bed covered with green and yellow quilts against the wall, and a short table was beside it. A fox fur hung on the back wall beside the bed, and another covered the middle of the floor. On the other side of the back wall were two hooks and a shuttered window.

Astrid released the window's cold metal latch. The shutters swung open. Mother Fredda's cabin was near the edge of the village, on the wharf side, but thatched roofs hid the ocean from sight. This didn't stop the cool ocean breeze from blowing in. It played with the loose hair around her face and tickled her cheek. She closed her eyes, inhaled the sweet salty scent, and listened to the soft rush of the waves rolling on the shore. With the sound of the ocean just outside her window, she couldn't be lonely here.

Reluctantly, she closed the window and stepped away. A rekindled strength lifted her head as she slipped into the main room, and her steps were lighter than they had been since the attack.

Mother Fredda was bent over the fire pit, holding dry, crushed leaves against the smoldering coals, and blowing. An aroma like steeping tincture rose as the leaves smoked, and the rest of Astrid's worry faded. The healer's longhouse somehow felt like home.

A finger of flame came to life, and Mother Fredda placed straw around it before looking up. The smile on her face was tender, like Mother's when she cupped a hand under Astrid's chin to draw her forward and kiss her forehead. Instinctively, Astrid leaned forward, then swayed back with a blush.

"The room is beautiful," she whispered.

"I'm glad you like it, child," Mother Fredda said softly, eyes glassy and thin lips quivering.

She turned fully toward Astrid, and they stood still, holding one another's gaze. They weren't benefactor and orphan, but two women who'd both experienced loss. Both are yet feeling the pain. Both are alone in the world. Astrid choked back a cry from a pang in her chest and pressed the back of her hand to her mouth. A shadow fell over Mother Fredda, making her look more wrinkled and gray, as if her soul had seen and experienced more sorrow than was possible for her bodily age. She needed her. They needed each other.

Forgetting her discomfort, Astrid threw her arms around Mother Fredda.

"You're not alone," she whispered through her tears. "I will try hard to be like a daughter to you."

Mother Fredda hugged her tight. Astrid inhaled the scent of herbs that clung to the soft kirtle pressed against her cheek and listened to the healer's heartbeat quicken. Warmth filled her chest, and the ache that lived there for several weeks vanished.

"The gods bless you, child." Mother Fredda held her close. A shudder ran through her, and she let Astrid go with a smile. "We'd better get busy."

Not long afterwards, work began in earnest. Villagers came to Mother Fredda, and she tended their ills and wounds, blessed their children and chanted over their amulets and pendants, and sent them on their way. At midday, the apprentice Gudrid returned from the woods with a basket of herbs, and eager children flooded inside for the honey cakes kept for them. Mother Fredda never spoke sharply, never turned anyone from her open door, and always had a smile for everyone.

Astrid scrambled to keep up with her tasks, which kept her mind off the judgmental glares from the villagers. Now in the garden, now bagging dried herbs at the table, now stirring the several steaming pots of herbs over the fire. She cleaned, mended, lent a hand whenever needed, and searched the shelves until her eyes hurt. Between every few tasks, Astrid dropped onto a stool to catch her breath and marveled at how Mother Fredda kept on working without any signs of fatigue.

After the children left the longhouse, Mother Fredda gathered her shawl around herself, picked up a basket, and headed to the wharf, taking Astrid with her. Astrid felt like hiding in the folds of Mother Fredda's skirts like a child, but she lifted her head and squared her shoulders. She didn't look anywhere but straight ahead when they walked, and over the ocean when they stopped. The villagers mustn't see her fear.

"This might be your color, Astrid."

Astrid tore her attention from the ocean. Mother Fredda was holding out a folded cloth the color of early spring ferns.

"It's pretty," Astrid said. "What's it for?"

"A new smoker for you."

"I'd like that..."

Mother Fredda turned to the merchant. "This, please." She took out a few pieces of silver from the pouch that hung on her belt.

Astrid's hand fluttered to her chest. The brooches were worth the most, but she couldn't bear to part with those. She felt a cool bead. What about a necklace? Two that had survived the storm: one she'd strung together with beads Father and the merchant Wulfstan gave her; the other had the

Mjolnir pendant. Slowly, she took off the first and held it out.

"Please, let me pay."

Mother Fredda looked at her in surprise. "Child, it isn't necessary."

"No, really, let me." Swallowing sudden tears, she addressed the merchant. "Would this be enough?"

The merchant took the necklace, turned it in his hands, and grunted. "Yes, Kona." He tucked the necklace into his money pouch. A childhood of laughter and friendship went with it.

Astrid turned away and fought to keep herself under control, but it wasn't necessary, for Mother Fredda was moving to another merchant and beckoned Astrid.

***

In the Tingstead, Erlin sauntered around the tables, looking at Karls from the corner of his eye. After much thought, he'd decided the Ting would be the best time to start looking for the men stirring the villagers against him. So he studied each face carefully while trying not to be noticed. No scowls, no confidential conversations. Good so far.

He turned and went down another table slowly, taking his time. He let his body sway in his natural swaggering saunter, trying to act nonchalant. The last thing he wanted was for the traitors to know he was looking for them.

A man met his eye for an instant, then leaned toward his companion, who glanced at Erlin and whispered. The back of Erlin's skull tingled.

He stopped when he reached them and raised his hand. "Greetings, friends."

"Jarl."

They stood. The first person who'd met his eye was a tall, muscular man with a long blonde beard. A scar ran across his neck. The other was shorter and stockier, with shifty black eyes, and his light brown beard was braided at the end. He licked his lips as if they were dry and glanced around.

"May we talk to you privately, Jarl?" asked the tall man. "Perhaps behind the building?"

Erlin eyed them closely, and they met his stare openly, almost challengingly. One lifted his chin, and the other angled his body away. Erlin rested a hand on his knife handle.

"Can it be said here? I have some others I must speak to and would rather not leave the building lest something distract me."

The two men glanced at each other and shrugged, but Erlin thought he saw the flicker of a scowl on the shorter man's face.

The taller man leaned in, towering over Erlin. His sour breath fanned against Erlin's neck.

"We've heard rumors, Jarl, that opposition toward the girl from Cooray is growing. Some say you wish harm on the island, and others go as far as to say you plan to draw the Danes to this island."

Erlin's fingers tightened around his knife, and he forced a slow exhale. "I thank you for your concern, Karls. Now, if you'll excuse me, I must go. The gods be with you."

He tried to step away, but the shorter man hemmed him in from behind.

"We are warning you, Jarl. Trouble will not stay hidden for long."

Without another word, the men left the building.

Erlin inhaled until his lungs burned. He relaxed as he let the air out and peeled his hand from his knife. The hilt left red imprints on his palm.

Footsteps approached him. Erlin tensed and whirled, only to be gripped by the shoulders by Karlsfien.

"Easy, brother." His face was grave.

"Did you see?"

"Yes." Karlsfien took his hands off Erlin's shoulders and crossed his arms.

"Do you think they're responsible?"

"A good chance. But there's more."

Erlin set his jaw.

"I was walking home last night when someone blocked my path. I couldn't tell who it was, since he was in the shadows, but he said, 'Tell Erlin to guard his actions carefully. They are coming for him.' He vanished before I could stop him."

Erlin's spine prickled. "You know what this sounds like."

Karlsfien nodded. "A revolt." He looked around and nodded toward the doors. "We should talk in secret, not in here."

As Erlin started to follow, several Karls gathered near him. A man in front spoke for the group.

"Jarl, unless Astrid of Cooray's loyalty is confirmed, we will not consider her a villager. Remember the dream."

"Yes, yes, I've heard this before. Remember what Mother Fredda said. But not right now, Karls. We'll discuss this another time. I have work to attend to."

***

That night, Astrid stared at the rafters, too awake to sleep, although she was more exhausted than ever before. There was potential in her new life, even though it would be hard. The villagers would make it as hard as they could; that was certain.

Dreams or no, noble deeds gain favor. She'd do something at the first opportunity. Baldor would--no, he wouldn't help her. The gods still abandoned her. But not the Christian God. He'd answered her in the storm and brought her to the island. Her doubts hadn't turned Him away. Would he help her again? She knew nothing of the Christian ceremonies or offerings or anything that would oblige Him to help her. Was living like the monks the only way to please Him? What had the monk told Sven...

"My son, even now, search your heart. It is dead. But my God can make it alive again."

Was that it? Did she have a dead heart? What did that mean, anyway?

Frustrated, she wriggled and squirmed under the covers and ended up facing the window. The moon floated effortlessly in the black midnight sky, suspended by nothing. Its silver beams were like the pathways of the gods.

"God of the Christians, if you're listening," she whispered, "I need to know. Do you care for me, abandoned as I am? I can't go on like this... alone... Before, I had Thor and Freya and others, but now..." Her words trembled, and her throat ached.

Then, barely audible, whispered a voice: *"Fear not. I am here."* As soon as it spoke, peace overflowed her, and she slept soundly the rest of the night.

The next afternoon, during the midday break, there was a knock. Astrid looked up from sweeping the floor. In the doorway stood Eric, Haakon, and Bertha.

"Hello, Astrid," said Bertha, running up to her. "Would you like to come with us? We have something to show you."

Astrid looked at Mother Fredda, who turned from rummaging in an herb basket on the shelf.

"Go on, child," she said, rubbing a stray silver hair from her forehead with her wrist. "You've done a lot today. The work can wait."

"Thank you, Mother Fredda." With a final sweep, Astrid brushed her pile outside and laid the broom against the wall. Bertha grabbed her hand and led her out. Eric and Haakon followed them.

"Where are we going?" asked Astrid.

"You'll see," Bertha sang with a laugh. "Here's a clue. Look what Haakon's carrying."

Haakon held up his hand. In it was a lamp, unlit.

Astrid thought for a moment. "Somewhere dark? Like... an abandoned building?"

Bertha merely pursed her lips and shrugged.

They came to the edge of the woods behind the village, and here Eric took the lead. Nearest the village, the woods were thin and without underbrush, but within a few paces, they thickened and narrowed the trail. On either side, underbrush grew tall and wide, snagging at Astrid's kirtle if she wasn't careful to hold it back.

Down the trail they went. No one spoke, for talking would feel like a disturbance to the full silence of the wood. A faint breeze stirred red, gold, and green leaves overhead, and grass and underbrush hissed against their woolen clothes. Occasionally, there was the muffled snap of a dry branch under their leather soles, and the musty smell of fallen leaves stirred about them. Gray tree trunks stood all around them, some strong, sweet-smelling pine, the rest a mix of ash, alder, and others. Bare birch trees flashed white, gold, and bright green among the grays, browns, and reds. Here and there, a full shaft of light broke through the thick foliage, lighting the leaves and branches with a golden glow.

Ahead, gray flashed, and Eric looked over his shoulder. "Almost there."

A moment later, they came to a stop in front of a gray wall of rock, over which grew a thick mass of vines. Eric and Haakon knelt together, and Haakon took out a flint and steel. He struck a spark on the lamp's wick so quickly, Astrid blushed to remember her fumbled attempts in the cellar.

Eric held up the lamp, and Haakon sprang to his feet and pulled the vines aside. Underneath was a black hole in the rock. Eric and Haakon went in first; Bertha took Astrid's hand and followed after.

Into the black hole they went. After a few steps, Astrid realized it was actually a tunnel. Daylight dimmed as they went around a corner, then vanished altogether. The only light came from the lamp in the front, held high, orange flame tinging the gray rock walls and ceiling and coloring the slips of Astrid's white serk hanging below her kirtle sleeve cuffs.

The tunnel twisted and turned, then suddenly came to an end. Astrid stepped into a large, cavernous room that opened to the ocean with a boat-sized opening. Water lapped against the rocky ground. Light poured through the water opening and the few cracks in the ceiling above. Half a dozen boats lined the side of the cavern, out of the water.

"This is incredible!" Astrid whispered. Her voice echoed softly.

Haakon nodded and chuckled, and it sounded as if a whole band of laughing children were just outside on the ocean. "But there's more." He looked at Eric and winked, then went to the boats. Swinging over one's side, he jumped in.

Bertha let go of Astrid's hand. "Father asked Haakon and me to check if one of the boat's new tar was dry. It'll only take a moment." She went after her brother.

"Astrid," Eric called softly.

Standing on a fallen slab of rock beside a small, doorway-like opening, he beckoned her. Through the opening, light was shining. He set the lamp on the rock and offered his hand, which she took somewhat shyly.

He helped her up the rock and through the opening, and they came into another large room, only without water. The ground was cleared of debris. On the other side of the room was a larger opening, through which the sunlight shone bright and green.

"This is the cave we go to during emergencies, like when the island is under attack," Eric said quietly, his voice echoing. "We haven't done it since my father's early days, when the island was attacked and the villagers had to flee here. Only by a stroke of luck did they defeat the enemies and keep Trygvey as their home."

Gently, he led her through the second room and to the outdoors, where they stood in a grassy clearing surrounded by a ring of trees. Astrid withdrew her hand, clasped it in her other, and looked around.

The clearing was shaded, yet well lit, and the lives of the people who'd come there over the years seemed to have seeped into the ground, making it sacred. The sweet perfumes of late-summer ground flowers stirred as she stepped forward. A marking on a tree caught her eye, and she softly ran her fingers over the rough mark. The Helm of Awe, a symbol of protection against enemies. Astrid's fingers fluttered to the last necklace she had, to the one given her by her parents, to the Mjolnir pendant.

"Halloo, there," called Haakon, swinging his arms freely, entering the circle. Bertha skipped up from behind. "Should we go down to the beach?"

The change in mood was so sudden, Astrid couldn't speak. She was grateful, then, when Eric shrugged and said:

"Why not? There's time."

So they went down a faint trail and came upon the beach. Here, they took off their boots and strolled barefoot along the sandy shore, watching the waves roll up and down the white sand. The rolling waves washing over Astrid's feet were gentle, almost caressing.

Several times, Astrid felt the weight of a stare, but only once did she catch Eric looking down at her. He quickly turned away.

"Astrid," Bertha said suddenly, "what was your island like?"

Astrid sighed and looked over the ocean. Scores of memories flooded her mind like water in tidepools when the ocean rushed in. "It's... hard to explain."

Bertha slipped her hand into hers, murmuring, "I'm sorry, I shouldn't have asked."

"I don't mind, but—I can't figure out where to start."

"Well," said Haakon, "what did you like to do most? Did you have lots of time to yourself?"

Astrid laughed. "Time to myself? When I was a child, because Father was training Sven to be a jarl and Mother had house thralls, I was on my own. That is, when she wasn't trying to teach me how to care for a household. My friends and I ran wild, playing hide-and-seek in the woods and wading through the water."

Bertha squeezed Astrid's hand and chuckled, "Sounds like us, doesn't it, Haakon?"

"When my friends weren't around," Astrid continued, "I went out on my own, exploring caves, climbing up to the highest point on the island—which holds a breathtaking view! —and sitting on the beach, quietly watching the sky and sea."

Haakon chuckled this time. "Sounds more like Eric, now."

Eric shook his head, grinning, and asked, "What about the wintertime?"

"Oh! We built snow forts and had snowball fights. Sven made a great team leader. My family and friends recited old sagas by the fire. Father told the best ones. Sven played hnefatafl and went ice skating with me. I—" she choked. She'd never do those things with him again. She took a breath. "I liked skating best."

"I love to skate!" cried Bertha, eyes shining and arm swinging. "Every year when the lake freezes, we hold competitions. You'll love it!"

Astrid forced a laugh. "I doubt I'd win very many."

"More than me," Eric offered.

"Yeah. You can't skate a stroke!" laughed Haakon, slapping his friend's back. Eric blushed and grinned.

To keep her mind off the past, Astrid said, "I could teach you how."

Eric looked her in the eye with an expression in his own that brought heat to her cheeks. "Thank you. I'd appreciate that."

Astrid didn't know where to look. She turned to Haakon. "Can you skate?"

"Sure can," he boasted. "Better than I can climb. I fell off a cliff once."

Eric laughed outright, and Bertha shook a finger at her brother. "Haakon, don't be ridiculous."

"But it's true! A few years ago, I was sitting on a cliffside when I saw a tree with wild apples on it. I wanted to eat some, so I reached out as far as I could. I fell headfirst into the stream below. Luckily, it was deep there, and I can swim like an otter."

"Oh, Haakon!" Bertha scolded. "What would Father say? How it would have frightened Mother!"

"The strange thing is, I've never fallen from a tree." A twinkle danced in his eyes. He winked at Eric, who faked a scowl.

Astrid laughed along but couldn't distract from the pang in her chest. Bertha, Haakon, and Eric's camaraderie made her miss her family more than ever. Her throat constricted and her vision blurred. In panic, she blinked hard and breathed deep. Bertha looked her way and raised her eyebrows in a compassionate question, but Astrid plastered on a grin and shook her head.

After the evening meal, Astrid stepped into the street for a breath of fresh air. Inside the turf-house was hot and smoky from the fire used to cook dinner and the body heat of all the people who'd come and gone. Outside, the air was cooling as the sun sank toward its setting.

"Astrid!"

Bertha ran up to her, white and breathless, holding out her hands. Astrid caught and held them tight. They were cold.

"Have you seen Haakon?" Bertha asked, trembling from head to foot.

"No. Why?"

"He went to find Father. Father is missing. He was with the hunters in the woods. Haakon ran off even after I told him it could be too dangerous. Eric went to find him, but he hasn't returned. Oh, Astrid! I'm so scared!"

"It's all right," Astrid said, thinking quickly. "We will go and find them. Come on!" She pulled

Bertha toward the woods. "Where do the men usually hunt?"

"Everywhere! Who knows where Haakon and Father are right now?"

"Think, Bertha, think! Where did they start?"

They paused at the edge of the village, and Bertha stared at the ground as if the answer lay right beneath the packed dirt. Then she looked up and glanced over the woods.

"Over there," she cried, pointing to the woods to the right. Astrid took her hand and they ran together.

As they neared the woods, Eric appeared, sprinting up the hill. "Haakon isn't here," he said. "I was going to look for him in the woods."

"We were, too," Astrid panted. "Come! We may be wasting precious time!"

Chapter 10

Twilight settled in the foggy woods as the sun sank below the horizon. Astrid squinted through the dusk, searching the charcoal-black leaves and tree trunks. They had to be out there somewhere. Every sense, every instinct was heightened, tense, ready for anything. She saw every movement and picked up the quietest sound, from shifting clothing to Bertha's stifled breathing. Just ahead, Eric was choosing his steps wisely, making almost no noise in the dense underbrush on either side of the thin hunting trail. Bertha followed close behind Astrid. And although she didn't know why, they talked very little and very quietly and tried to move as silently as possible, as though they, and the wood itself, were holding their breath.

"How far does the wood go?" Astrid whispered.

Eric paused and half-turned to answer, "Over most of the island. Only the village is inhabited. The rest is untamed. Keep your eyes and ears open."

Astrid nodded. She'd already been doing that.

A light fog drifted through the foliage, further darkening the faint hunting trail before them. The half-moon rose slowly, and its weak silver beams filtered through the thick canopy, so only a faint glow made it through and illuminated the fog that was steadily thickening. The air tasted wet and stale.

Eric held up his hand and froze in his tracks. The girls did the same. In the still silence, Astrid heard talking, very quiet, somewhere ahead to the right. Perhaps it was an effect of the thickening fog, but her heartbeat quickened. The others must have heard it, too, for Eric started forward again, keeping to the path but facing the voice. Gradually, it increased to a murmur.

Eric's hands rose to his face, and he called out a loud halloo that made Astrid jump. The call was promptly answered, though it didn't sound like anyone Astrid knew. Fog does strange things to sounds.

But Eric turned again and said, "It's Haakon."

He plunged into the woods now, and Astrid struggled to keep up. Using yells to keep them on track, they soon stumbled into a hollow and almost landed on Haakon and Erlin lying crumpled against the ridge of black dirt.

"I'm so glad you're here," said Haakon, rising slowly. It wasn't the fog after all. Haakon's voice was so worn and thin it wasn't recognizable. "He needs help, but I dared not leave him."

Astrid squinted. Dark blood glistened on Erlin's face and matted on his clothes. His breath came slowly and painfully, and he lay limp against the ridge. She recoiled.

"What happened?"

"I don't know." Haakon's shoulders slumped. "I found him lying over there, bleeding and half dead. He must have lain there for a while, wounded. And I didn't know! I didn't know!" Haakon's voice broke, and he raised a hand to his temple.

Bertha caught his arm. "Haakon, you're hurt!" His eye was black, and a bloodied cloth was wrapped around his arm.

Eric unwrapped the cloth, and Haakon hissed through his teeth as the air hit his skin. Underneath the cloth was a long, deep gash. "How did this happen?" Eric asked, looking closely at the wound.

"I don't rightly know," Haakon answered faintly, wincing as Eric's fingers felt along his arm. "I ran into some men. They were hiding in the bushes or something."

"And they attacked you?"

"I don't know why..." He swayed.

Eric steadied him. "You can tell us later. Are there any more wounds?"

Haakon nodded but didn't move to show them.

While Bertha held her brother steady, Eric crouched beside Erlin. Astrid joined him on her knees and glanced over Erlin. Hesitating, she took his wrist and felt for a pulse as Mother Fredda would have done.

"It's low," she murmured with a shiver.

Eric pressed his lips together and peeled the blood-stiffened collar of Erlin's jerkin, revealing deep gashes. They looked like they'd been given by the claws of some animal. However, his blackened eye, busted lip, gashes on his arms and jerkin, could only have been from a man. Or several.

Erlin opened his eyes and shifted. He groaned and squinted through his good eye. "Not safe here," he croaked, but Eric held up a hand.

"Lie still, jarl," said Eric. "We will get help."

Erlin sighed and closed his eyes briefly. When he opened them, they moved to Haakon, and he whispered his son's name.

"He is also wounded," Eric said, laying a hand on Erlin's arm, "but we will get help for both of you."

Erlin sighed again and seemed to drift into unconsciousness. His body sank against the dirt cliffside behind him.

Eric scowled at the ground and ran his hand through his hair. He was so close, Astrid could feel the anguish pulsing from him, and it made her feel jittery. She coiled away and wished there was some way to help him.

"What are we to do?" asked Bertha, helping Haakon to the ground. He made no protest as he lay on his back against the ridge.

Eric pressed his fingers to his forehead. "Both of them have been attacked; there's no doubt about that. Both by men and beast. Neither can walk back to the village, even if—"

"I can," Haakon whispered, coughing, "if you help me."

"Poor Haakon," Bertha crooned, stroking his hair. "You can't even stand."

Sighing, Eric shook his head. "We would need to leave someone behind."

"We will need to, anyway," said Astrid. "Either you go alone, leaving me and Bertha with them, or you take one of us and leave the other."

War waged visibly in his face. "I could stay behind."

"But I don't remember the way back," whispered Bertha. She clutched Haakon's hand. Eric turned back to Astrid.

She bit her lip and looked into the swirling fog. They'd followed that trail before they heard Haakon. But how far and in what direction the trail lay, there was no way to tell. If they were all back on Cooray, it would be different. She could have found her way back easily. She shook her head. "I don't remember, either. We'll have to take a risk and let you go on alone."

Eric pinned her with a look. "What if that is a risk I am not willing to take?"

"We can't sit here all night!"

Eric remained silent.

"If Father can walk," said Haakon, his chest heaving, "we both can be brought to the village. I need only a shoulder to lean on."

"Hush!' said Bertha. "Don't be foolish."

"Warriors have walked from battles with worse," Haakon muttered. Bertha put a finger to his lips to quiet him, then covered her face.

Eric stirred and released a breath he must have held all that time; it was so tight. His gaze traveled over Erlin and Haakon, over Bertha, and lingered on Astrid. Her heartbeat thrummed in her ears.

"I'm going alone," he said. Then he shifted, removed something from his belt, and placed cold, rough leather in Astrid's hand. "Take this. You might need it."

She held it up and rotated it to catch what little light she could. A wooden handle stuck out of the leather, and the faint glow of metal was on the end. Eric's knife. She held it out to him and shook her head. "I already have one."

He pushed it away, toward her. "Mine is made for heavier work than yours. Take it." He scrambled to his feet before she could protest further, and stood still for a moment, clenching his fists. "I'll be back."

She nodded, biting her lip hard as the gravity of their situation came crashing down on her. Stinging nausea crept up her throat.

Eric glanced over his shoulder and looked over them again. "Keep the knife handy and always keep a lookout." He shifted his weight and looked like he'd say more, but suddenly turned and ran out of sight, fog swirling behind him.

Bertha squeaked and sidled closer to Haakon, whose hand she squeezed tight.

"It's alright," Astrid said, more to convince herself than her friend, "he'll be back soon."

But with Eric gone, the woods no longer felt remotely safe. Her heart quaked. Willing it to still, she leaned against the foot of the ridge. With her back against the dirt, she couldn't imagine things creeping behind her.

Instead, they could leap onto her.

She jerked her head up. Only swirling fog met her eye. She was overreacting. Taking a settling breath, she looked over at Erlin and Haakon. They were both breathing, and Haakon was conscious.

Astrid rubbed her temple, trying to think of what to do next. She got up and crouched beside Haakon.

"Does your father have any significant wounds?"

Haakon nodded slowly. "I stopped the bleeding."

"What about you?"

He hesitated.

"Haakon."

Sucking a breath through his teeth, he nodded again.

"Where?"

He touched his side. Astrid slowly lifted his jerkin, afraid of what she might see, and revealed a gaping hole from which blood ran in rivulets down his side with every breath he took. She seized her belt pouch and searched for the cloth scraps she sometimes saved there when sewing.

"Haakon!" Bertha shrieked. "Why didn't you tell us?"

Thank Thor! There were a few cloth scraps in there. Astrid balled them up and pressed the wound with it. Haakon writhed and cried out.

"Didn't want to worry you," he forced between his teeth.

"It's better for us to worry than for you to die," Astrid said as the cloth warmed with his blood. She looked from Haakon's face to Bertha's, and there was no mistaking the fear in the latter. She shivered. "Bertha, make sure your father is warm."

Bertha gave a terse nod and turned to Erlin. She touched his hand, then unclasped her brooches with shaking hands and laid them aside. With jerking motions, she removed her smokkr and spread it over him with a kiss on his forehead.

Far away, a wolf howled. Its cry ricocheted in the fog, sending chills down Astrid's spine. Bertha scrambled to her side. She locked eyes with her, questions etched on her face.

"We'll be fine," Astrid whispered. She adjusted her hold on the cloth and glanced at Haakon's face. His eyes were closed, and beads of sweat dotted his gray face. His pulse thrummed through the cloth. Bertha stifled a cry.

"He's only unconscious," Astrid assured her. Bertha let out a sigh.

Slowly, Astrid removed pressure from the wound while watching for any signs of bleeding. Seeing none, she cupped Bertha's shoulder and prodded her to the ridge again. Bertha's cold, trembling body pressed close.

Astrid's eyes burned, and her head ached, her hands were wrinkly, and her nose wrinkled at metallic blood and cold sweat. Where was Eric? Fatigue begged for rest, but she denied it. With Erlin and Haakon wounded and Bertha near hysterics, it was up to her to protect them from anyone or anything that might try to harm them. She gripped the leather knife sheath.

The fog was lifting, although the damp, musty taste did not lessen. Black outlines of tree trunks and bush clumps appeared and took form, and what little light the moon offered finally reached the ground. It brought depth to the gray world around them. It ran along the ground, alighted on the tops of leaves, and showed the place where the ridge rounded into a sloping hillside that was eventually blocked by a black oak.

One shadow on the ridge didn't make sense: a round, void-like shadow. Astrid crawled toward it and reached out, but her hand went into it. A hole. She drew back and joined Bertha, who looked at her anxiously. Astrid shook her head. Erlin had claw marks along his chest and cheek, claw marks that could have only come from a large animal. The ridge hole's size matched the animal's easily.

Nails dug into her arm, and Bertha let out a faint squeak. She inclined her head a little to the right.

Slowly, Astrid pulled off the knife's sheath and held the weapon in front of her. None of the shadows moved, yet she had a growing feeling they were being watched. Leaves rustled with the absence of wind, raising gooseflesh on her arms. Another rustle came, very near the first, and a shadow flickered to the left.

Two men stepped simultaneously out of the shadows, weapons drawn.

Astrid swallowed and forced her voice to stay steady. "What do you want?"

The men looked at each other.

Astrid pointed the knife toward them and stood as tall as she could. "Do not hurt them. You've done enough."

"It's only those two," muttered one man to another. He raised his axe, and they both rushed forward together.

Astrid found herself beside Bertha in her scramble to stand in front of Erlin and Haakon. Bertha held a thick branch in her hand and looked like a child caught in an adult's game.

The next moment was a whirlwind of metal, skin, cloth, and hair mixed in a blur. The smell of blood and sweat filled her nostrils as she dodged and thrust one thing after another. Bertha was caught around the neck by one man and was kicking wildly. Air left Astrid as she was rammed against the ridge. A man's face was merely inches from her own, and he'd caught hold of her hand, which held Eric's knife.

Astrid filled her lungs and let it out as the loudest scream she could. Her ears rang and her throat felt as if it'd split. Her captor reeled back, and she lashed out at his neck. The blade met skin, and she almost dropped it in her horror. The man's hands flew to her neck at the same time as another man lunged toward her. Bertha was free and ducking under outstretched hands. Somehow, Erlin was up and leaning against the wall with his own knife drawn.

Astrid let loose another scream just before she was knocked down, and a hand pressed over her mouth. If there was anything in the hole, rousing it was the only chance they had.

Eric's knife was torn from her grasp and held to her throat. The man holding her down scowled and spat in her face, blocking her hands from reaching him.

"Filthy foreigner!" he hissed. His sour breath was nauseating.

A low growl shut out all other noise, and the ground rumbled. The man scrambled up and yelled, brandishing the knife. Others did the same. When Astrid turned her head, she saw why: beady eyes glowed in the hole, and a big black paw with long, yellow claws was visible. Astrid couldn't move.

With a roar, the bear charged forward. She tried to scramble back, but was too late. A paw came down on her chest as the bear ran past. Cracking like dry branches and fiery pain filled her ears. She rolled onto her side and pushed herself up.

The bear was charging at the attackers, scattering them. They did not leave. One ran along the ridge toward Erlin, who'd dropped to the ground, but the bear drove him away and, without warning, charged. It swept down several and clawed at them with the intention of tearing them to shreds. Along the ridge, Erlin, Haakon, and Bertha lay perfectly still and unnoticed by the animal.

Through her blinding pain, Astrid crawled toward them. Her vision blurred and her hands shook, then gave way. Dirt ground into her face. She forced her pounding head up and saw Bertha extend her hand; she kept it in sight as she summoned all her strength to raise herself back up to crawl, fighting to reach her. The bear bore down on her. A scream tore from her lips as its claws seared through her back like a hot knife. The bear still clawed, but she only felt the impact of its weight. Then it stopped, and there were new shouts. Tender hands brushed her cheek, and the scent of the sea filled her nostrils.

Her eyelids were heavy. Summoning all her strength, Astrid slowly opened them. A blurry face above her focused. Mother Fredda.

"There, child. No, don't try to speak. Just open your mouth for me."

Astrid obeyed. Her face strained as she opened her mouth. Warm broth trickled down her throat. As it hit her stomach, her body awakened and was hungry—ravenous. She opened her mouth for more. After a few more spoonfuls, Mother Fredda put the broth aside.

"That's enough for now," she said. "Rest, and I will be back soon."

Astrid's eyes followed Mother Fredda to the curtain. When it had flapped closed, Astrid looked around. She was in her own room, in Mother Fredda's cabin. There was a stool beside her bed. The window was closed. She wished it were open so she could listen to the ocean and watch the sky. Why was the window closed? She always opened it before going to sleep.

Then she remembered: the bear attack. The pain that had felt like fire.

Besides the numb, empty feeling in her head, there was a pounding pain that she couldn't tell where it came from. With her left hand, she felt her arm. Yes, there was a bandage where the bear had cut her. There was nothing around her chest, but it hurt when she breathed. The cracking she heard must have been her ribs breaking. She shuddered. Nothing covered her face, but her fingers brushed the scabs that ran over her cheekbone and forehead. One ran over her eyebrow, touched her eyelid, and stopped halfway down her face.

Worn with the effort, she fell asleep.

When she awoke, Mother Fredda was at her side. Astrid was fed again and allowed to speak a little. The strain in her face made it difficult to talk.

"The bear attack. What happened—Erlin and Haakon?"

Mother Fredda settled down on the stool, caressed Astrid's hair, and explained.

Erlin and a few other hunters separated from the others, but they turned against him and attacked him. They would have killed him if they hadn't disturbed a bear that rushed at them and scared the other men away. The bear population had been reduced over the years by hunting, but a few yet remained on the island. Erlin fought the bear off, but not before it wounded him further.

Shortly afterwards, Haakon left to find him and came across three men in hiding. One attacked him as they ran away, wounding him and knocking him unconscious. Haakon didn't wake until the sun set. Although wounded himself, he went and found Erlin.

While the bear attacked Astrid, help came—and just in time. The men threw spears and shot arrows at it just as it brought its paw down on her and so drew its attention away. They killed it and carried the wounded back to the village, where Mother Fredda tended their wounds. Two of Haakon's were knife stabs. Both Erlin and Astrid had had a raging fever for the last few days, but now it was gone. They would recover soon.

"When will that be, Mother Fredda?" Astrid croaked.

"Patience, child. It will be soon enough." She brushed Astrid's hair from her forehead.

"What was injured?"

Mother Fredda hesitated. "Several of your ribs are broken straight through, and many more are cracked. The worst is over now, child. Now we must wait."

Astrid sighed, staring up at the rafters. "And Haakon?"

Again, Mother Fredda hesitated, this time for longer. "One of the knife wounds hit his stomach."

Astrid sat up in her surprise but fell back with a cry as pain engulfed her. One of Mother Fredda's hands squeezed Astrid's.

"Breathe," she said. "It will pass."

Astrid did as she was told, and though the pain didn't go away completely, it did lessen.

"I learned how to handle stomach wounds a long time ago," Mother Fredda went on. "The lesson stuck with me all these years, and I've done it before. If the gods are kind, Haakon will recover." She patted Astrid's hand, then rose. "Rest now. I'll be back soon."

Between snatches of sleep, Astrid lay on her bed, thinking. She had her window opened, but she could only see the clear blue sky with an occasional cloud floating by. The sound of the ocean seemed to have grown fainter, for she could only occasionally hear it if she lay still and listened hard.

Many times she grew impatient and tried to rise, but the searing pain didn't let her. Her head had quickly cleared, and the dull ache had sharpened to a knife point. Every breath brought a wave of it shooting from her head to her feet. It was always there, even though Gudrid gave her an herbal drink to help.

Over the next two days, Bertha, Fredissa, and Eric came to visit. Astrid was always relieved when they came, for they distracted her from the pain, and being alone brought all the memories of the Danes rushing back.

The most frequent visitor was Eric. During the weeks leading to Astrid's full recovery, he came with every chance he had, usually three times a day. His first visit was the morning after Astrid regained consciousness.

She was staring up at the ceiling, mentally counting the rafters to keep her mind off the pain. It was worse than the day before, and she could hardly concentrate on anything else. There was only biting fire: in her lungs, in her head, in her bones, as relentless and sickening as a berserker's knife, stabbing again and again. No mercy, no rest.

The conversations outside her room could not divert her attention, for they were muffled and always concerned with various injuries, illnesses, and anxieties. She'd had enough of that. Nevertheless, when someone tapped on the doorpost, she strained to listen.

"How is she, Mother Fredda?" It was Eric.

"Awake, but in much pain. Why don't you go and see if you can amuse her?"

"I'll see what I can do."

Steps crossed the floor, and Eric pushed the curtain aside. He smiled and sat down. His voice was low, as if not to worsen her condition. "Is there anything I could talk about that would help?"

Astrid gave the slightest nod. "Anything."

Eric sat silently for a moment, then began. He told the story of Trygvey, which had been established by Erlin's grandfather, Heithrek the Bold. An ambitious young man who'd already won honor in many battles, Heithrek left his home in Kaupang with the vision to settle his own village. He sailed away with three ships and came to an island, which he conquered and named Trygvey. He built his longhouse, the Tingstead, and the wharf, then sent one of the boats back to Kaupang with the news of his success. Eight boats of people returned: men, women, families, warriors, craftsmen, fishermen, and traders. Eric's great-grandfather was one of these.

"The trade of fishing was passed down the line," said Eric, "and when I came of age, that's what I learned. As a child, I accompanied my father, but my participation was limited when I was younger." He chuckled. "I was always in someone's way. Father often left me to play on the wharf while he worked, and eventually let me aboard and taught me the tricks of the trade. He owns a fishing boat and hires men to help him, and now I work alongside him since I am considered a man. I'm almost ready to go out on my own." His voice sank even lower here, and he looked out the window.

Astrid found that the pain had subsided a little as she concentrated on Eric's words. She inhaled a little deeper, then bit back a cry as fire shot through her chest. Fingers touched her clenched fist. Eric leaned toward her, but his face was blurred.

"I'm—alright," she assured him, forcing herself to relax. She blinked the haze away.

The curtain was pushed aside, and Mother Fredda peeked around it. The lines on her forehead were deeper than usual. Was it because of the lighting?

"Try to speak some, child. It's good for your lungs. I'll bring you more of the herbal drink soon."

"Thank you," Astrid whispered. When Mother Fredda left, she continued between tight breaths, "I heard at Erlin's that you're—going—a trip, next year."

Eric nodded. "It's been the tradition for the fishermen in my family to go back to Kaupang as a trading voyage every summer. We take traders from Trygvey with us."

Astrid tried to respond, but couldn't because of a sudden breathlessness.

Eric's hand slipped from hers, and he stood. "I'd better go, but I'll be back later today. Rest, and maybe you can tell me about Cooray."

Astrid's hand was cold. She laid it across her stomach. Recovering her breath, she gasped, "I will."

During the times Astrid was alone, she could not shake off the memories haunting her thoughts. Her mind would turn as on its own back to the day of the attack on her island, back to the last time she'd seen her mother, back to the day Snorri died. She could feel his cold hands in her own, see the translucent eyelids with the soft blond eyelashes and the drooping rosebud lips.

Astrid wiped the tears away and tried to think of her favorite songs, but the only songs that came to mind were of loss and vengeance. One stanza refused to leave:

All alone am I now

As in holt is the aspen;

As the fir-tree of boughs,

So of kin am I bare;

As bare of things longed for

As the willow of leaves

When the bough-breaking wind

The warm day ends.

When those words came to mind, Astrid would set her jaw and turn toward the window. She'd recall Eric's last visit and try to replace forbidden memories with ones more pleasant.

He always came when she needed him most, as if he'd been called to her side. Sometimes he did all the talking, sometimes she was well enough for it to be an even conversation. Other times, he simply held her hand while she waited for a wave of pain to pass.

They spoke of histories and traditions, of life experiences and desires, of favorite things and least favorite things. Within days, she knew almost as much about him as she did her closest childhood friends.

She learned his mother died when he was a child, and that Fredissa had nursed him until he was two years old. His early childhood was spent partially with Fredissa, Haakon, and Bertha, and partially with his father. As Eric grew older, he took on more responsibilities at home and was raised by his severe father. No dawdling, whether real or imagined, was allowed. Any disobedience, however small, was punished by a switch across the back of his legs, no exception. His father hardly showed any regard toward him, so Eric leaned into Fredissa's motherly nature for comfort and support. How different from Astrid's own pampered upbringing!

Healing was slow and frustrating. Even after two weeks, Astrid could sit up in bed without pain for only a moment and could still not do much. A few days later, she could complete tasks on a stool and walk around a little. But always she was driven by pain back to her bed.

During one of her rests, lying in bed with memories flooding her mind again, Eric came. Confident, light steps crossed the cabin to her room and a cheerful voice called through the curtain:

"Astrid, are you in there?"

"Yes," wearily.

"Would you like me to come in?"

"Please."

The curtain opened slightly, and Eric peeked around it. Astrid smiled, and he entered. The memories no longer bothered her.

Eric sat on the edge of the stool beside her bed and smiled warmly, but something was amiss with his eyes. They roved over the room without hardly meeting hers. And when they did, he colored and looked away.

"Eric..."

"That was the bravest thing I ever saw, Astrid," he interrupted hastily, his voice strained. "You put the jarl's life above your own." His eyes met hers for a moment; excited, nervous, eager, uncertain. He looked away.

"Thank you, Eric. But—"

"Astrid," he said, "I…uh…" he looked around wildly, as if at a loss for words.

Astrid was more puzzled by the moment. "Is anything wrong?"

"No, nothing's wrong." Eric laughed, but it had no mirth in it. He clasped his hands together and his thumbs worked, rubbing over, under, over, under. He laughed again, weaker this time. "Nothing's wrong."

Something *was* wrong. He's never appeared unsure of himself, let alone the way he was now. Had something happened? Her chest burned with fear. What could shake him like this?

Eric's voice disturbed her thoughts. "I—I-I will come again tomorrow. I… I just remembered I have some—some work to do."

He stood, mumbled a farewell, spun around, and reached the door in one stride.

When he'd gone, Astrid sank onto her pillow. She was sure he hadn't any work to do. There was something he couldn't force himself to say, though he wanted to tell her. What had gotten into him, she couldn't figure out. He was always so calm and steady. But that morning was different: he was at a loss for words.

The next day, Mother Fredda awakened Astrid for the morning meal and said before leaving, "I want you to get up a little more today. It will help you keep up your strength."

When Astrid had eaten, she swung her legs over the side of the bed and gasped as pain encircled her chest. Biting her lip, she pulled herself to her feet and steadied herself with the stool. Dizziness came and went.

Slowly, Astrid shuffled to a hook where her kirtle hung. She slipped the kirtle over her head. Once her brooches had been fastened on, she moved the curtain and pushed it aside.

There were two women in the cabin. One was seated in a chair and holding an infant, and the other stood nearby. Mother Fredda was examining the infant, and Gudrid was stirring a bubbling pot of herbs. When Mother Fredda saw Astrid, she finished her inspections and pulled out a stool at the table for her.

"Sit here, child," she said, laying a hand on Astrid's shoulder.

"Is there anything I can do?"

Mother Fredda glanced at the women, then nodded. She went to the shelves and took down several bags and a small pouch. Setting them on the table, she said, "Can you put a scoop of each in this pouch?"

"Yes, Mother Fredda."

Astrid opened the bags and carefully began to transfer the herbs to the pouch with her hands. The stares of the women amplified the pain in her chest. Astrid blinked away tears and clenched her jaw, forcing herself to breathe slowly. She could not let them see how much it hurt simply to move.

Out of the corner of her eye, Astrid saw Mother Fredda leave the cabin, probably to go pick fresh herbs from her garden out back for the woman with the baby, and Gudrid take up a basket and leave, also. The other women stayed, whispering to each other. Astrid could only catch a sentence here and there.

"How poorly she looks."

"…remember what they said?"

"How could she spin such tales… and about her own family?"

"It could be a cover-up… a spy… we can't know if it's true."

"Just ask the traders. They told me Cooray's in bad shape."

"…can't trust them…"

Mother Fredda returned, and the conversation ended. Astrid turned her back to the women and cringed.

The women left, and Mother Fredda cupped Astrid's face in her hands, looking into it. Astrid tried to smile but felt it wobble.

"Is something wrong, child?"

"I'm tired, that's all."

Mother Fredda kissed Astrid's forehead and left to greet the boy who had walked in. Astrid swallowed hard and went back to her task. The distrust was worse. She could have died protecting the jarl. If giving up her life was not enough to convince these people, what was?

Chapter 11

Astrid was preparing the evening meal in the early summer when Erlin entered Mother Fredda's longhouse. A white scar remained on his cheek, contrasting with his bronzed skin. The sight of it made Astrid's ribs ache, although she'd seen it often that winter and spring.

Putting down the spoon she used to stir bubbling sauce, she bowed her head. "Greetings, jarl."

"Heil Astrid, heil Mother Fredda," Erlin returned, nodding in turn to Astrid and to Mother Fredda, who was using the momentary lull between visitors to harvest her herbs. She worked in a corner, taking down dried herbs from their strings and gently stripping off the leaves and storing them in bags.

Erlin turned back to Astrid. "I see you are doing well."

"Yes. And you?"

The edge of the jarl's mouth tipped in a grim smile. "I'm well enough."

"Have you found the attackers yet?"

"No. They are still hiding. Where they could have spent the winter, I do not know, but from what I heard, they are still on the island. I am thankful they haven't caused more trouble." He inhaled deeply. "I'm leading another search party today, so I must be going. The Ting starts in two days. I'll see you then." He uncrossed his arms and nodded to Mother Fredda.

Astrid ignored the boiling pot and twisted the edge of her smokkr around her finger. "Jarl, the villagers... they still distrust me. Is there anything I should do?"

"Nothing will change their minds at this point. They're swayed by those men and the belief that you will bring bad luck on the island." Here, Erlin stopped abruptly and scowled at the floor. Mother Fredda looked up from her work.

Astrid's stomach twisted into knots. She kept her eyes on the floor, too, not daring to look at Erlin's face. He doubted her, too. The fear returned that she really was cursed, and the attack and the revolt were because of her. Mother Fredda could've been mistaken, in spite of her discerning ability, and she really was cursed.

A sting on her hand made her jump. The pot was spitting and boiling over. Astrid snatched up the spoon and stirred, scraping the bottom of the pot. The broth churned, and the food at the bottom stuck so badly she couldn't free it with the spoon. She gave a pleading look to Mother Fredda. Usually, the latter smiled or chuckled at this problem, but her face was expressionless as she moved to help.

Mother Fredda took the pot off the fire, set it on the stones, and scrubbed with the spoon. With a frown, she took another spoon and used the flat edge of the handle. After a moment, she grunted and put the pot back. Without a word, she went back to her corner.

Astrid slowly set the spoon back on the stones, then turned to face Erlin, fearful. He still stared at the floor. "Jarl, what do you believe?"

He raised his head, swept a hand over his eyes, and sighed. "Let's say, I only hope I'm doing right." He shook himself. "The men will be waiting. Good day, Astrid, Mother Fredda."

He proceeded out the door, his frame stiff and his usual leisurely swagger replaced by a quick stride. As he passed through the door, Astrid looked after him with a cold, sick feeling in her stomach. She'd been able to ignore the villagers' attitude toward her for the most part, though the only times she could forget altogether were when she was with Eric. Erlin's concern brought it all back. Even *he* didn't know what to think.

Astrid faced the pot and stirred, rubbing her forehead with her wrist and wishing that doing so could wipe away the problems coming to mind again. Mother Fredda silently left with a basket on her hip to pick more herbs from the garden, and Astrid was alone. She curled her fingers hard around the spoon. If those men were never found and justice meted out, she'd never forgive them, not after all the conflict they'd caused.

Neither could she forget what Holskuldr and his Danes had done.

She tried humming a song to distract her mind. She recalled words, stirring in time to the rhythm, and eventually sang aloud.

I counsel thee, Stray-Singer, accept my counsels,

They will be thy boon if thou obey'st them,

They will work thy weal if thou sin'st them:

Be not a shoemaker nor yet a shaft maker

Save for thyself alone:

Let the shoe be misshapen, or crooked the shaft,

And a curse on thy head will be called.

Upon hearing footsteps in the doorway, she hushed with a strangled squeak and hoped Mother Fredda hadn't heard.

"Don't stop, that was lovely."

She whirled at the boyish voice. Eric stood in the doorway with a smile upturning his lips. His hair was tousled from the ocean breeze, and his light blue eyes contrasted with his brown face, the image of health and excitement.

Astrid's cheeks tingled as heat surged into them, and she turned toward the pot again to hide her face. "Oh! Eric! I thought you were Mother Fredda." Black, burnt bits floated in the sauce, and the cabbage was turning soggy, but she stirred anyway, watching the spoon circle around and around.

"Mother Fredda isn't here?" Eric asked.

"She's in the garden. Do you need her?"

When Eric did not answer, Astrid looked up. Eric's face flushed, and his eyes were glassy. He crossed the room in two strides and stopped short in front of her, trembling.

"No, Astrid," he began, his eyes darting around the room. His face twitched, and his arms hung stiffly at his sides. Shaking himself, he looked at her again. Grabbing Astrid's hand, he blurted, "I need *you*. I…I love you, Astrid. Before, I couldn't tell you, but I am now. I can't stand it any longer; I need to know!" He inhaled sharply and held her gaze. The shaking of his hands traveled up Astrid's arm.

A shot of dizziness left Astrid giddy. Her heart hammered with the warmth building in her chest, beating in time to the butterflies in her middle. All she had loved before was gone. How could she love again? Eric's visits brought her joy, meeting his eyes caused her knees to weaken, but was that love?

Astrid tried to answer, but only a squeak came out. Swallowing, she tried again. "What about Bertha? I thought you—"

"That's what our parents wanted. Neither of us cared, for there was no one else. Until you came. *I want you.*"

"What about your father? Jarl Erlin and Fredissa? They'll be disappointed."

Eric's smile vanished, and he clutched her hand to his chest. His heartbeat thrummed against it, and she tried in vain to free herself gently. "Fredissa will understand," he said, "and I'll make the others understand, too. Nothing can stop us if we're together."

"Eric… I… I don't know… I don't care for you that way. You're my friend, and that is all."

Eric looked as though he'd been hit by Thor's Hammer. He dropped her hand and stared in blank surprise. Pain shot through Astrid's chest. Eric's eyes were wide and glassy and blank, as if he looked straight through her, his once rosy cheeks were pale, and his mouth hung open.

He swallowed several times before whispering, "But I thought…" His voice was weak.

"I'm sorry, Eric," she whispered, tears stinging her eyes. "I don't love you that way, but you're one of my dearest friends."

Eric stared at her in silence, then slowly turned on his heel and walked away.

Trembling all over, Astrid collapsed on the nearest stool and hid her face in her hands. She felt like she had murdered her friend. How could she help it? She was certain, confident, she didn't love him. Even still, when she closed her eyes, she saw the horrible look that had been on his face, as if the very purpose of life had been snatched away from him, and wished she could blot it from memory. She tried to breathe steadily, but an inhale caught and a sob escaped.

The pressure of a hand settled on her shoulder. She jumped and straightened. Mother Fredda looked down at her, her own eyes sad. "Don't take this to heart," she said gently. "The villagers will accept you eventually. Carry on as you've done before."

Astrid couldn't tell Mother Fredda the real cause of her tears. She wiped her sleeve across her eyes, and Mother Fredda pressed her to her side. One of her worked hands caressed her hair.

Astrid squeezed her eyes shut and swallowed hard several times. She breathed in, letting air fill every part of her lungs, and let it out slowly. She sat up. "Thank you."

Mother Fredda glanced at the pot of vegetable stew. "Is it done?"

"Yes."

Mother Fredda went to the shelves and took down two bowls. She filled one and handed it to Astrid. With trembling hands, Astrid took it and stood, locking her knees to keep them from shaking. The table was only a few steps away. Somehow, she managed to set the bowl on the table and cross the room to where the spoons were kept.

Keep it together. Focus on something else, like the Ting. Holding the Ting could be the best thing they'd done yet, but it could also be the worst. What if it incited the men to act more than they already had? Her first sight of Erlin's wounds was still engraved on her mind. Her own injuries, and Haakon's—his especially. Those men were hitting to kill, and could do something akin to it again, or worse, if they wanted. Erlin would need to be extremely careful.

Unbidden, something Father said once came back. Astrid was only four years old at the time and had been tricked by a couple of older boys in the village. They took her new doll away and ran off, jeering. Her little legs couldn't keep up. She remembered crying, and Father picking her up and holding her in his arms. His red beard tickled her ear.

"Some people cannot be trusted, Astrid," he said. "They are full of malice and want to hurt others. Stay away from them, but don't fear them. I won't let them hurt you."

Astrid set the spoons on the table and took a breath. Tears were too close.

Much to her relief, a figure filled the doorway. A young man with red hair stood there. He smiled broadly. "I'm looking for Jarl Erlin. I volunteered to go with the search party, but couldn't find him anywhere. Someone said he was here."

Mother Fredda placed the second bowl on the table. "He left some time ago. The search party already went out." She turned to Astrid. "This is Hake the Hunter. Have you met him yet?"

"No, Mother Fredda." Astrid looked Hake over. He wore hunting clothes that had wet patches of sweat. His face was smeared with dirt, and his hands also were dirty, but the kindness in his face was genuine; when he smiled, the corners of his eyes crinkled delightfully, and the smile spread to the rest of his face.

"I am sorry to hear about your accident and the way the villagers have treated you." His gravelly voice was gentle. "I don't think your gods have cursed you. The others are too quick to believe a dream."

Astrid's eyebrows puckered. "Don't you believe in the gods, too?"

Hake shrugged. "I'm from Ireland. I don't believe the same way you do."

"Do you believe in the Christian God, then?"

Hake stiffened but smiled anyway; it was a patronizing smile. "Of course not." He glanced over his shoulder and called, "I'll be right there." He lifted his hand in farewell. "Excuse me." With a spring in his step, he strode away. Mother Fredda closed the door behind him.

Astrid grabbed the bread from where it was warming on the firepit stones. "He's nice, isn't he, Mother Fredda?"

Mother Fredda sat on her stool and picked up her spoon. "He's improved greatly of late, for certain. When he first came, he was against everyone and everything."

Astrid slipped onto her stool and blew on a spoonful of broth. A muscle in her leg twitched, and she tapped her toes on the floor impatiently. It wasn't fair that he was accepted and she was not. "When did he come here?"

"About ten years ago, as a lad. He was taken as a thrall during a raid. Last year, he bought his freedom and started working as a hunter. He's one of the best on the island, as if to make up for all the trouble he caused during his first years here." Mother Fredda broke off a piece of bread and handed the loaf to Astrid. It was still warm and crackled cheerfully as Astrid broke off her piece.

"A troublemaker, he is," Mother Fredda continued. "Used to stir his peers against his master, until he was punished severely enough to understand such behavior wouldn't be tolerated."

"How come the villagers accept him?" Astrid couldn't keep a bitter tone from her voice.

"He came during a prosperous time here, so no one connected him to the decline in crops." Mother Fredda's voice dipped to a whisper as Gudrid entered the longhouse to join the meal. "If anyone bears the curse of Hel, it would be him."

Astrid squirmed. Hake was the first villager besides her friends to show any kindness. She dipped her spoon into the sauce. Its burnt taste and bits of overcooked vegetables made her gag, but Mother Fredda and Gudrid calmly ate it as if nothing was wrong with it.

When the table had been cleared and Gudrid had left on an errand, another knock sounded on the doorway.

"Greetings, Samuel," Mother Fredda called.

In walked Samuel, the Christian, carrying a basket of food. "Greetings, Mother Fredda."

A smile flashed across the woman's face. "It's good of you to bring this."

Samuel set the basket on the table and spread out its contents. "My pleasure, Kona."

The basket contained ground vegetables, cheese, and lots of meat. Samuel's movements were swift and smooth, and a peculiar air surrounded him in which Astrid found herself relaxed. Mother Fredda also relaxed, and the creases in her forehead smoothed away. With confident and kind eyes, Samuel looked over the room and met Astrid's gaze. Astrid blushed and looked quickly away.

"Are you the girl from Cooray, mær?"

Astrid twisted her fingers together. "I am."

"What they say isn't true, you know," softly.

Astrid looked up, and breath fled. Close up, Samuel resembled Sven, with his eyes kinked up slightly as he smiled, and his eyebrows arched a little in compassion as Sven's did.

"How do you know?" Astrid stuttered.

"My God is forgiving and compassionate and wants everyone to be His people, and for Himself to be their God."

Astrid's fingers touched the cold metal of the Thor's Hammer pendant. "But… what about the other gods?"

Samuel glanced at the floor, then looked her in the eye. "There is no God besides mine. He is the God of gods, and He made everything."

Sven's description of the monk came back to Astrid. The same boldness was in Samuel, too. What about this God made him like that?

Then poor Snorri came to mind, and anger replaced curiosity.

"If He made everything, what about the people who destroy and kill?" Her voice rose. She fought to control it and her trembling mouth at the same time. "Why did He make pain and… loss… and—" She choked.

Samuel's eyes glazed over. He spoke softly. "He didn't. He made everything perfect, without any of that. No pain, no suffering, no death. The first people, Adam and Eve, were able to walk with God. Then they chose to disobey God, and their action brought evil into the world. With it came death and suffering. But—"

"And God let it stay that way?" Astrid snapped.

"Astrid!" Mother Fredda scolded. "Do not speak that way to him."

Astrid glanced at Mother Fredda and snatched up a small basket. "I'm harvesting the herbs." Her voice trembled from restrained anger, and her hand shook so hard she could hardly hold the basket. She let the door slam behind her, and the boards around it rattled a retort. Astrid stuck her tongue out at them and marched to the garden.

The blanket wasn't helping. Astrid kicked it off her legs and turned so she could look out the window. Moonlight shone through it and fell across her bed.

The moon… freedom. Astrid slipped out of bed, grabbed a cloak, and left the cabin.

As she stepped into the refreshing night air, the sound of waves beating against the rocky shore whispered in the wind. They seemed to call to her and, before she knew it, she was running toward it, all caution forgotten. Once there, she slipped off her boots and walked in the cold, gritty sand, letting her shoulders sag and head droop.

The waves stumbled lazily onto the beach, creating a monotonous, soothing sound. A ways from the shore, water sprayed over jutting rocks. How had the boat missed them the day she came? The full moon threw its silvery beams across the water and lit up her surroundings. Astrid stared up at it, remembering the voice that had spoken to her before: *"Fear not. I am here."* Who'd spoken to her? A spirit? One of the gods? But Samuel said there was only one God. If that was true, he let it happen. Was it her own mind, then? No, wait! There it was again, speaking as if a person whispered in her ear.

"Peace be with you. I will never leave or forsake you."

Her arms prickled. She whirled. No one was in sight, but there was a presence she couldn't explain. "How can I know?" she whispered.

"I will keep my word, for I cannot lie. Nor do I change."

The voice faded, and panic clawed up Astrid's throat. "Please! Is what Samuel said true?"

"You know, yet you deny it."

A sob escaped, and Astrid tasted salt. She hid her face in her hands. How could something so horrible be true? A God all-powerful, but let bad things happen?

"It can't be!" she cried, grabbing her hair. "It can't!" But no voice answered but the voice of the wind wailing between the rocks lining the shore.

Bushes rustled behind her. Astrid stiffened and wiped tears from her face. She turned around and faced the black undergrowth of the woods. Although she couldn't see anything, she could feel it—eyes boring into her. Almost silently, a man emerged from the woods and walked up to her. In the silver light, his skin was white and black shadows were cast under his eyes and cheekbones.

"Astrid."

The gravelly voice sent prickles down her arm. Then she recognized him by his hunting attire. "Hake?"

"Yes, it's me. I know how to take your island back."

A jolt turned her cold, and she coiled away from him. Her breath caught. "What? How?"

"There is a man named Olaf who guards the treasury. I heard him talking to Erlin about it, and the wealth stored in there is unbelievable."

"What do they use it for? Don't the Karls store their own money in their homes?"

"It's a backup in case the island falls into hard times. Anyway, if we get our hands on it, we could gather an army from my homeland and throw off your enemy. Then you can rule where you were raised, and I could return home. What say you? It's simple: just get the keys, gather the treasures, store them in a boat, and sail away. Are you with me?"

Memories flashed by: Mother's smile, Sven's carefree laugh, Father's twinkling eyes. Bloodcurdling screams, charred bodies streaked with white and sticky red mud. Her stomach twisted, and she shut her eyes. She forced down the rising energy surging through her again.

"It would be—everything—to throw off my enemies, but…"

"But?"

"We would be stealing." Astrid nearly choked on the words. Giving in would undo everything she'd done to secure the villagers' trust, and she couldn't deny the pricks her conscience gave her. "These people rely on their treasury. If we take it, they'd be in danger."

"Nah! They have more than enough. Wouldn't miss anything. Get the key for me. Erlin keeps it in his money pouch."

"I…"

"Just get the key and meet me here tomorrow night. That is all you must do. Deal?"

Her mind spun like a whirlpool, sucking down, down, down—was honesty worth the cost of leaving her family unavenged? She could see Mother's face as she saw it last, white and drawn, and lips pressed firm. *"Keep him safe."*

"I just don't know…"

Hake's eyes softened, and his mouth upturned in a sympathetic smile. "I know. You think we'd be stealing. Erlin keeps the treasury for another reason: for good things, like raising an army. He would approve. And imagine all the people you'd help. Your family's blood is unavenged, crying for justice. Mother, father, brothers, sisters, friends, all killed by the Danes. You can give it to them, but not alone. Such an action would be foolhardy. Give me men to lead, and I will lead them myself into battle against your enemy! The Danes ruined your life—they must pay." In a low voice, he added, "I should know."

Mother's voice seemed to whisper in her ear, as she had done so many times in the past. *"Steady, love, steady."* Astrid clutched her middle and her heart pounded in her temples. She shivered, suddenly freezing in the cold night air. "Are you certain Erlin would approve?"

"By the gods, I assure you there is nothing wrong. We won't tell him, because he doesn't need one more thing to worry about. Men have been stirring up against him, as you know, and it weighs heavily on his mind right now. We wouldn't take all the treasury, of course, just enough to get you on your feet. And believe me, even a small portion would be more than you could gather yourself. This is all it takes. By this time tomorrow, you'll be sailing away to your island to save it from the Danes."

There seemed to be no harm in what Hake said. Earnestness permeated his voice. He wouldn't do anything to bring harm to the island. If it weren't for the look on his face… She needed more time to think, time he wouldn't give her. His eyes penetrated her, searching, pressing. When she met them, he seemed to melt away. Instead of Hake, she saw the amber yellow of Holskuldr's eyes and the pale line of his mouth. Pressure built in her chest, and she clenched her fist until her nails drove into her palms. Astrid closed her eyes and tried to block out Hake's face.

"Well?"

The blackened, crumbling walls of her home; the lonely grave in the woods. Vengeance. Justice, Hake had said. She couldn't do anything before, but now...

She exhaled. "I'll come tomorrow night."

Hake's eyes glittered as he turned on his heel and disappeared into the woods.

Chapter 12

"Astrid! Astrid! Wake up. Are you ill?" Mother Fredda called through the curtain.

Astrid jumped up and out of bed so fast that she fell to the floor in pain. She eased onto her bed and held her breath until the pain passed, all the while silently scolding herself.

"I'm fine. Why do you ask?"

"You slept past the horn."

"I did?" She carefully stood on her wobbly legs, dressed quickly, and left her room just as Mother Fredda put the last few things on the table. Astrid was afraid she'd have something to say about how she answered Samuel, but Mother Fredda greeted her with a smile.

"Good morning. Here is water for you."

"Thank you." She scrubbed her face, neck, and arms, poured the water on the garden when she'd finished, and placed the water bowl on a shelf.

"Did you sleep well?"

"No…" Astrid slipped into her place at the table. "I don't think I went to sleep for a while." For all she knew, she could've been at the beach for half the night.

The lines in Mother Fredda's forehead deepened. "What was bothering you, child?"

Astrid sighed and picked at her porridge with her spoon. "About…" She hesitated. "About what Samuel said. How could something so horrible be true? A God who creates bad people and lets them do bad things, yet is somehow still good?"

"Are our gods any different?" Mother Fredda said drily.

Astrid opened her mouth, then shut it. Then said, "A voice told me last night that what he said was true."

Mother Fredda's head snapped up. "A voice? Was it your guardian spirit?" Fear laced her words. Seeing one's guardian spirit often meant death.

"No, I don't think so. But it spoke to me, whether in my head or in my ear, I do not know. It also said 'I' and 'myself'. Is the voice a person, Mother Fredda?"

"I…" The woman studied Astrid's face. "I don't know, child. Did it give you any instructions?"

"You know, yet you deny it." Astrid shivered. "No."

Mother Fredda looked at her again, then focused on her food. "Listen for it, child, and do what it tells you. When gods or spirits call, that is what we must do."

"Yes, Mother Fredda."

As they put the dishes away, the first group of Karls came to visit. As usual, they eyed Astrid with suspicion while talking to Mother Fredda. Astrid turned her back to them and washed the dishes, trying to shake off the familiar burn in her chest.

The morning passed slowly, made agonizingly so by each remembrance of Hake's offer. The more she pictured it, the more apparent his greedy look, patronizing tone, and sneaking manner became. He was no friend of Erlin. Throughout the morning, these thoughts so consumed her that she tripped over stones, knocked over bags, left food to burn, struggled to talk with Bertha when her friend visited, and was made aware of accidents by a rebuke from Mother Fredda.

She didn't remember being so torn before. It was as if two people lived inside her. One side wished to have nothing to do with Hake, rather than do harm to the village where she'd found a measure of comfort and promise of new life. Agreeing and bringing the key to him, if she could obtain it in the first place, would only create hurt and harm; the mere thought sickened her. The other side tingled her fingertips with a deep desire to bring justice to her family. For his ruthless murders, Holskuldr and his men deserved death. With each time she relived the horrible night in the cellar, the desire deepened.

When a dish had been broken because of her lack of attention, Mother Fredda pinned her with a stare and asked, "Are you alright?"

Astrid trembled and picked up the remaining fragments of the clay bowl. "Yes," she said slowly.

Mother Fredda didn't move. "I have never seen you like this, not even after the Ting."

Astrid squeezed her hands together and forced herself to look Mother Fredda in the eye. "I'm sorry I've been a hindrance to you today. I... there is..." she dropped her gaze. "It's nothing," she mumbled.

Sighing, Mother Fredda inclined her head and waved toward the door. "Very well. The garden needs to be weeded, and I trust you are familiar with the various plants. Take care to only remove the weeds."

"Yes, Mother Fredda. I'll be careful."

She fled the house and went around the back to the garden, where she shook herself. "Focus, Astrid, focus!" She rubbed her temple, squatted by a garden bed, and went to work.

Not long afterwards, a strange weight and uneasiness came over her. She looked up and started, for Hake was leaning his elbows against the fence. He raised an eyebrow, but she made no answer and went back to work. Her breathing seemed far too loud, and every movement too jerky, so she forced herself to move slowly. She curled her fingers around weed stems right above the dirt and, while pulling steadily, wiggled them in a circle until they tore up.

"Did you get it?" Hake's gravelly whisper grated. Astrid pressed her lips together and ignored him.

His voice rose a little. "Did you?"

Heat tingled her cheeks, but she didn't look up. Hake shifted. Glancing toward the longhouse, he leapt the fence and stood over her, body bristling. "I said, did you? Or are you too coward to try?" The hint of a sneer tinted his words.

She made her face as firm and stern as possible and sat back on her heels to meet his eyes. Energy radiated from them, and they were wild like an excited dog. She spoke low but clearly.

"No."

He stood, unmoving, a muscle in his neck twitching. Deliberately, she grabbed the next weed and yanked it out. When she looked up again, he was gone. The pounding in her ears quieted, and she released the air burning her chest. It was over.

But was rejection enough? Was it wrong not to act against him?

"That is going well."

Astrid started and looked behind her with a jerk. Mother Fredda stood there, leaning on her staff.

"I did not mean to frighten you, child," she said, bending to pluck up a weed.

Astrid wiped her hands clean on her smokkr and attempted a smile. It shook. "No worries. I'm not my usual self today."

Mother Fredda returned the smile warmly and laid a hand on her shoulder. "Whatever it is, I hope for your sake that it will pass. Now, I have a favor to ask of you."

"What is it?"

"I am going to the wharf. A merchant who carries supplies I need has just arrived. Could you stay here for me? The children usually arrive at midday for their honey cakes."

"Yes, Mother Fredda. Where do you keep them?"

"On the third shelf from the top, in a cloth-covered basket. Let them have as many as they want; there's plenty."

After Mother Fredda left, Astrid wiped her hands on her smokkr, went inside, located the basket and set it on the table. Then came the agonizing wait. What would the children do when they saw her? What should she say? She stood and walked over to the door. Men carrying barrels and pushing handcarts to and from the wharf crowded the street. Women holding baskets of wool, cloth, and other goods mingled with them. The Tingstead horn blew, and everyone walked home or down to the Tingstead.

Little feet pitter-pattered down the road from around the corner. Astrid quickly seated herself just as the sound stopped outside the longhouse. One, two, four heads peeked around the door. Upon seeing Astrid, they retreated. Four other heads peeked in, then disappeared. After some whispering, all together they cautiously walked in, moving in a tight herd.

"Is Mother Fredda here?" a little girl asked.

"No, but she wanted me to give you these," Astrid said, picking up the basket and removing the cloth. Seeing the biscuits, the children slowly and carefully took one and sat in pairs on the four stools. All were silent for a few minutes and watched the "foreigner" pull up another stool and sit among them.

One boy said, after a great deal of finger licking, "My brother says you are Hel, and you're here to bring bad luck on us."

Astrid did her best to hide the pang it sent to her heart. Of all things, to be likened to the goddess of the Hall of the Dead. "What do you think?" she asked, forcing a smile.

The boy thought for a moment. "I don't think you are. You're too kind to be Hel," he answered. Astrid was relieved.

"Were you really the daughter of a jarl?" a little girl asked. "With silk embroidery and silver brooches?" She eyed the brooches Astrid wore, and Astrid fought the urge to hide them.

"Yes," Astrid answered slowly, "I had all of that."

"Why did you help the Jarl?" another girl asked, stuffing the last bite of honey cake into her mouth.

"He is my friend. If your friend was in danger, would you help them?"

The girl nodded.

"What was it like drifting across the ocean?" a boy asked while helping himself to another cake.

"Wet, cold, and dark." Astrid shivered at the memory.

A child slipped from her seat and ran to her. She clasped her skinny arms around Astrid's waist, and her smile reached from her wide mouth to her big, honest blue eyes, lighting her entire face. "I believe you," the girl whispered, "and I want you to stay with us."

Remembrance of what Hake had asked rushed over Astrid. She cleared her throat. "Thank you. What is your name?"

"Thora." The girl returned to her seat.

Once the children were finished, Thora stood before Astrid with her hands clasped behind her back and said, "Thank you for the biscuits, kona."

Astrid almost laughed at the developed manners in the small girl. Her face looked to be that of a seven-year-old, but she was as small as a four-year-old. Staying sober with great difficulty, Astrid replied, "You're welcome, Thora. I hope to see you again."

"So do I. Bye!" Thora followed the other children out the door.

When they were out of sight, Astrid put the stools away and swept the floor. Every brush of the broom ate at her fraying nerves. The weight of Hake's plot pulled down on her heart until she couldn't bear to be alone. She put the broom away and escaped the confinements of the house by walking briskly down the street in search of Mother Fredda.

She found her at the wharf, bartering with a merchant, holding a basket in one hand and gesturing with the other. Astrid squeezed through the crowd and stood at her side.

Mother Fredda paused and turned toward her in surprise. "Astrid! Are the children gone?"

"Yes."

"Here, then." Mother Fredda said, handing her the basket. Astrid hadn't expected its weight and almost dropped it. "Since you're here, you can hold this for me."

"Yes, Mother Fredda." Astrid adjusted her grip on the handle but almost dropped it again as someone bumped into her. She sidled closer to Mother Fredda to keep out of the swift current of villagers.

Astrid let her attention wander. Rows and rows of crates and baskets lined the edge of the wharf. Merchants unpacked their goods and bartered with the karls. Crates were taken down, emptied, and stacked up again. Once in a while, an empty stack was knocked over, and young boys were paid to collect them from the water. They climbed in a small boat and pulled them out one by one, and handed them back.

Another trading ship docked, and more merchants unloaded their goods. Astrid watched curiously as they set up in the only visible empty spot, and KKarls stopped by to see what they offered. Erlin was one of them, but he appeared only to be welcoming them to the island.

A sudden movement caught her eye. A group of children played tag among the crates, dodging in and out and squealing in delight; Astrid held her breath and waited for them to topple into the water.

She was turning back to Mother Fredda when she froze. Crouching in the shadow of the creates, inching ever closer to Erlin, was Hake. A greedy light glinted in his eye, and he licked his lips. Astrid dared not move, fearing she would prompt him to act. Hake paused as the children ran past him. Then, with one swipe of his hand, a stack of crates went hurtling into the water, taking a child with them. The boy's scream was cut short as waves closed over his head.

Erlin's boots and bear skin cloak were off in an instant, and he dove out of sight. Astrid gasped and raced to the edge, among the first of the onlookers to arrive. Erlin had reached the boy, clasped him to his chest with one hand, and gripped a rough pillar supporting the wharf with the other.

"Hang on, Jarl," men shouted. Strong hands took the trembling, sobbing child from Erlin's arms and pulled him up. "Glad you saw that, Jarl. That was a close one. You alright?"

"Yes, the gods be praised. How's the lad?" Erlin shook wet hair from his eyes and looked around.

"He's fine. Leif's taking him home to get dry."

"Good." Erlin put his hands on his hips, suddenly looked at his belt, and frowned. He picked up his cloak, put on his boots, and looked around.

"Men, I seem to be missing my money pouch."

The onlookers backed away and searched the ground, murmuring. Astrid felt sick.

"Could it have fallen in the water, Jarl?" a merchant asked.

Erlin shook his head. "It was tied securely. The only way to remove it is—" He put a hand to his belt again and found a cut piece of twine. Astrid was dizzy.

The merchant gasped. "Looks like it was stolen!"

Erlin's face hardened as it had during the first Ting.

Astrid turned to where Hake had been, but he was gone.

"Astrid?"

She jumped and turned to see Mother Fredda beckoning her.

"Come here, child. We're going home."

With one last look at the baskets, Astrid went to her side and followed her back to the longhouse.

The next chance she got, Astrid slipped away to Erlin's cabin, where Bertha stood at the doorway and Haakon paced outside.

A smile broke over Haakon's face, and he stopped. "Good to see you, Astrid." He scowled and continued pacing. "Do you know what happened? Some scoundrel took Father's money pouch! Father's gone to look for it, but I think it's gone forever."

Astrid watched him pace, biting her lip nervously. Now that she was there, she felt sick.

Bertha rubbed her forehead, snapping, "Haakon, would you quit pacing? It's getting on my nerves."

Haakon glared.

From inside, Fredissa called, "Come inside and work on your chores, then, dear."

Sighing, Bertha turned and shook her head. "I can't bear to do anything while Father is gone. Can I stay here, please, Mother?"

"Alright, you may stay."

Bertha turned back and looked over Astrid, who glanced away too late.

"Is something wrong?"

Astrid scuffed her foot on the ground, clasped her hands behind her back, and cleared her throat. "Hake was there earlier."

"Where?"

"Did you say Hake?" demanded Haakon, his eyes widening and blazing like blue fire.

"Yes. At the wharf. He's the one who caused the accident. Does... does the Jarl keep anything in his pouch besides money? Like the treasury key?"

Bertha eyed her closely. "Yes," she said slowly. "What makes you think that?"

Astrid really felt sick now, but she swallowed it down. "He met me at the beach last night—"

"So you happened to be at the beach?"

"Haakon, let her finish!" Bertha snapped.

"I couldn't sleep," Astrid cried. "The beach has a way of helping me, so I went there. I didn't expect, or want, to meet anyone there. Hake found me. He told me that if I stole the key to the treasury, he would help me overcome the Danes. I saw him shadowing your father before the accident happened."

"Were you going to steal the key?"

"No." Conscience stabbed, but Astrid pushed it away. They didn't need to know her original response.

"Does he know that?" asked Haakon.

Astrid hesitated.

"He wouldn't have helped you," Bertha said softly. "He's a troublemaker. Instead of doing what he promised, he would have kept you as a thrall... or worse. And he would have kept the treasure for himself."

"We need to get him!" Haakon leapt forward, but the girls grabbed his arms.

"Don't be foolish." Bertha shook him. "He'll get you for sure."

Sighing, Haakon relaxed and shrugged their hands off him.

"Where would he be?" Astrid asked.

"Not the treasury," Haakon replied. "He wouldn't steal it in the daytime. People are always around."

"Hiding, maybe," Bertha suggested. "Haakon, get Father. Don't go anywhere without letting us know. Hake could be dangerous." Haakon nodded stiffly and ran behind the house.

"I should get back to Mother Fredda," said Astrid, not wanting to stay around more than necessary and shaky from telling the truth. "I left without her knowing."

"Alright. See you soon."

She started off, but Bertha called her back. Her friend was smiling tenderly, and her eyes shone.

"That was brave, telling the truth like that."

"Thank you."

Chapter 13

As Astrid hurried down the street toward Mother Fredda's longhouse, a lurking shadow between two longhouses caught her eye. Stopping, she looked closer. The shadow was none other than Hake, slipping away. She stood firm and held her fists up, ready for an encounter, but he was gone.

Should she follow him, or should she find Erlin? The latter would take too long; by the time they returned, Hake would be long gone. On the other hand, if she followed him, he might lead her to his hideout. She could then tell Erlin and the others. Maybe, she'd even find the pouch herself. Then the villagers would have no choice but to change their minds about Bikki's dream.

So she followed Hake, keeping in the shadows as he was doing, and left the village without being caught. She held up her skirts and entered the woods, taking great care lest her clothes catch and make her presence known. Soon, she was far from the village's hearing.

Her ears pricked up at the sound of voices, and Hake stepped out of sight. She crept up to the bushes and found a gap to look through.

On the other side was a small, natural clearing, where five men stood; six, including Hake.

"At last, sluggard," sneered one.

"Well?" said Hake, ignoring the insult, "anything?"

"Loki! No." A short, stocky, black-haired man growled. "If you hadn't ruined our plans, we'd have had it by now."

"My plan was for the animal to do the work so we wouldn't need to and thus get caught," Hake replied coolly.

"What?" several men yelled at once. "You didn't tell us!"

"We were to remain unidentified," said Hake, "but one of you attacked the jarl's son."

A yellow-haired man threw his hands into the air. "He stumbled upon us. I left him to die so he wouldn't tell who we are."

"That didn't work, now did it?" jeered the first man. "It left them hotter on our trail than before. They nearly found me yesterday!"

"Hide better," grunted Hake.

The first man sneered again, shaking his fist. "And what have you been doing while leaving the heavy work for us? What about your end of the deal, high and mighty? If I were to risk my neck, I'd turn you in, scoundrel."

"I'd like to see you do it," replied Hake. "I tried my best with the girl, and almost succeeded. Either she is wise beyond her years, or she was given information."

"Are you saying one of us betrayed the rest?" The black-haired man's voice rose.

Hake shrugged. "Either way, she knows too much."

"The jarl, his children, and that boy know something, too," said the man who'd been silent up to this point.

"The Coorayan is the only one who knows our plan." Hake folded his arms over his chest. "I don't expect the other to know or remember as much as she. You know where she lives. Do not take the others, they aren't worth the trouble. Is it all ready for tonight?"

The others nodded, but the first one scowled. "Where will you be? Leaving us to do it, again?"

"Meet here again, and I myself will lead you."

The others grumbled and left, bushes hissing against their clothes.

Astrid ducked low, heart pounding. Everything suddenly made sense. These were the men behind Erlin's attack; the bear was not an accident, and the wounds really were intended to kill. Hake's part in it didn't surprise her, not after his temptation to steal the key, then taking it himself. Even so, heat burned beneath her face and in her chest.

She shook herself. Someone had to know. Erlin. Get Erlin.

Once no more sounds reached her ears, she straightened—and froze. Hake was walking away, his back to her, deeper into the woods.

She started forward without hesitation, still wanting to know his hideout, but he vanished into the shadows. Startled, she stopped, and a chill tingled her spine. She was being watched. Before she could duck back into the bushes, an arm wrapped around her middle and pulled her against a firm chest, pinning her arms down. Cold metal pressed against her lower jaw and forced her head up. Breath fled, and sparks danced in front of her eyes.

"Let go," Astrid whispered, breathless. Her chest throbbed with the vibrations of her racing heart.

"Would I?" Hake snarled. The knife pressed closer to her lower jaw, and Astrid held her head higher, away from it. "Would I? You thought I could be followed without knowing," he chuckled. "I brought you here. The jarl and your friends will die. But if you don't struggle, I may spare them. Deal?" He didn't wait for an answer. The knife left, and Hake grabbed her wrists and held them behind her. He pricked the back of her neck with the knife point and pushed her forward. She almost stumbled.

"Where are we going?" Her voice trembled.

"Quiet!"

He took her deeper into the woods, where she'd gone only once before. Astrid tripped over her skirt and ripped seams several times, and each time Hake jerked her arms so hard, tingling points shot up them. Eventually, Hake pulled her to a stop in front of a wall of ivy and bushes—the cave. Hake moved the knife to her neck and let go of her arm. With his other hand, he pushed the plants to the side to reveal the black opening of the cave.

He pushed her forward. "In."

Astrid dared not disobey. Ducking into the low hole, she climbed into the tunnel.

At the water cavern, Hake pushed her against the rock wall and reached for a coil of rope by her feet.

Astrid really quaked now. Perhaps he'd take her away, and there would be no escape.

Hake shifted so his shoulder pinned her to the rock wall and grabbed her hand. Astrid struggled and pulled his hand against the rock as hard as she could. He hissed through his teeth and let go, but drove his elbow into her stomach. With a cry, she crumpled.

Her head whirled as she hugged her middle. Hake grabbed the back of her collar and lifted her, then dragged her down the shore. Her senses cleared by the time they reached a boat and reeled again when he threw her inside. Dazed and feeling sick, she could not protest when he bound her wrists and feet and stuffed her mouth with a rag that tasted like year-old grime.

Then he left, leaving her lying face-up in the bottom of the boat.

Tears trickled down her cheeks and tickled her. She wished she could wipe them away. Oh Erlin! Bertha, Haakon, Eric! They'd all be killed, and there was nothing she could do. If she'd exposed Hake's plot earlier, could this have been prevented? She'd been a fool, and again, people she loved would pay for it.

"God of the Christians," she prayed silently, "You've answered before. Help me."

***

Erlin muttered under his breath while walking home. He'd returned to the wharf with Karsfien and a few of his men, and a search was made, but nothing had come up. He dismissed them for the evening meal and started home alone.

On his way, he pictured one villager after another, judging who might be responsible, wishing he knew where his attackers had gone. The island had been searched, but nothing was found.

"Father! Father"

Erlin looked up to see Haakon running toward him, flushed and with thick eyebrows down.

"What is it?" Erlin asked gruffly. He cleared his throat.

"Astrid said Hake stole the key."

"The Hunter?"

"Yes."

Erlin grunted, and his hand settled on his knife hilt. He should have sent that freed thrall away long ago. "How does she know?"

"She saw him and said he'd wanted her to get it herself. He wants to steal the treasury."

"She didn't do it," Erlin said to himself. Aloud, "Where is she now?"

"Going back to Mother Fredda."

"Come." His pace quickened now; Haakon had to sprint to keep up, but Erlin hardly noticed.

When they reached the house, Erlin swung open the door, which banged against the wall. Fredissa and Bertha looked up in alarm from the fire pit, and the latter stared at him, her eyes wide.

"Eat without me, Fredissa. I won't be back for a while. My men and I are going to find Hake. Bertha, stay with your mother. Haakon, tell Eystein, Karsfien, and Olaf to meet me at the Tingstead and assemble my most skilled fighters."

Haakon nodded and turned to go, but almost collided with Mother Fredda, who was walking in.

"I'm sorry, Kona," he stammered, stepping back to give her space. "Are you alright?"

"No worries, child," answered Mother Fredda, smoothing her hair. "Run along." When Haakon did so, she stood in the doorway and gripped the wood. She was pale, and fear was in her eyes.

"Come in, Mother Fredda," said Erlin, holding out his hands, which she took. Hers were cold. "What has happened?"

Her voice trembled. "It's Astrid. Have you seen her?"

"No."

"She was here earlier," said Fredissa. "She stopped by and said she'd return to you."

"She hasn't," Mother Fredda cried. "It worries me. She's never run off like this. And with the villagers' suspicions..." She looked away.

Bertha whispered, "She's been gone a long time."

Erlin cleared his throat again and kept his voice calm and steady for the healer's sake, despite the worry her words brought him. "My men and I are going to find Hake, whom Astrid said stole the key. It was some plan of his for her to take it."

"If he thinks she's the only one who knows..." Mother Fredda let him go and wrapped her shawl tightly around herself. "You must find her, Erlin. I cannot imagine what Hake would do."

Erlin set his jaw. "That's what I plan to do."

***

Eric was eating the evening meal with his father when someone thundered on the door, startling them both. Throwing down his knife, Harald rose and opened the door. Haakon stumbled in, breathless.

Eric jumped to his feet. "Haakon!"

His friend held up a hand and panted, "Father calls—best warriors—to arms. Assembling at the Tingstead."

Eric handed him a cup of water, which Haakon took with a nod and drank.

"Has trouble started?" Harald asked from his room. He emerged with his sword on his side and axe in hand.

Haakon nodded. "Hake is a traitor, and Astrid is missing."

A shiver ran through Eric, and he stared at Haakon's flushed face. He clenched his fists and took a deep breath, closing his eyes briefly. As much as he'd tried to suppress his love toward her, it flamed up now, and he'd give anything to protect her and, if she was harmed, to repay what had been done.

Eric straightened and looked his father in the eye. "Father, let me go."

Harald glowered. "Erlin calls the *best* warriors, and you haven't been proven yet."

Trembling, Eric fought to keep his voice steady. "Both you and Karsfien have trained me in the sword. Please!"

"You're not coming, and that is final," Harald growled, "and that is final." He drank the last of his Skyr water.

"Let's ask my father," Haakon said quickly.

Harald grunted. "Fine. Come, then."

When they arrived at the Tingstead, Erlin readily allowed Eric to join the search, and the men spread out. It wasn't long before they were called to the woods behind the Tingstead. A man pointed to the soft dirt just outside the woods, at a pair of footprints. One was a man's, and the other, a woman's.

***

With a final tug, the rag came out of Astrid's mouth, and she could breathe easily again, no more musty, dirty smells gagging her.

Shortly after Hake left, Astrid assessed her situation. She was bound, hand and foot, with rope, and her wrists were tied to her belt; nothing in reach that she could use to remove that horrid rag. She'd tried pushing it out with her tongue, but Hake had jammed it in so well that it didn't work. Finally, she managed to pin a bit of it in her armpit and pull it out.

Somehow, without that rag, she could think better maybe because it wasn't there to distract her.

She was in a longboat with twenty rowing benches, so possibly the smallest of raiding ships, a snejkka. There would be hooks here and there along its top edge, but the wall was just high enough that she couldn't reach them with her hands. But what about her feet?

Wiggling, she rotated so she faced the boat's side, then tried to lift her feet to the top. Her ankles ground together as she moved. They would smart later, but that didn't matter now.

After much struggling, she raised her feet to a rowing bench. But no matter how hard she tried, they wouldn't reach the top. Exhausted, she sighed and closed her eyes, but all she could see was the death of her friends. She screamed with fury and grief, and the cavern echoed it back mockingly.

"God of the Christians, don't let it happen! Don't let it happen!" she cried. New strength spurred her on, and she wriggled closer to the bench until her shoulders and head alone were on the bottom of the boat, and forced her feet higher. At last! They landed on top.

Slowly, and putting them back up several times, she felt the boat's side. Her feet regained some feeling, but her head pounded with blood and exertion.

The rope around her ankle caught on a hook, and she was stuck. Letting out a screech of aggravation, she scolded, "There you go, Astrid, stupid little thing. You're a fish on a hook now." But she wiggled anyway, so much like a fish on a hook that she might have laughed about it if the circumstance wasn't so urgent. Once in a while, she stopped to press her toes together and force her ankles apart. Each time, the rope loosened the slightest bit.

"If you keep this up long enough," she said to herself, "you'll get out before that scoundrel comes back."

The light coming into the cavern was fading fast. She worked harder, although her back ached and her heel and ankles were being rubbed raw, growing more frantic the more the light left. Time was running out.

Panting, she forced the rope apart again. There was a snap, and she suddenly tumbled down. She was free! Pushing her back against the bench, she sat up and grimaced. Her feet were a bloody mess from the top of her ankles to the sides of her heels.

Her pouch was not far away. Since she could crawl now, she could get to it, open it, and cut her hands free with her knife.

Before she could do so, however, a dreaded sound sent chills down her spine. The scuffle of leather boots on bare, rocky ground. Hake had returned. He was still in the tunnel, but wouldn't be for long.

Astrid scrambled up. It was painful to stand, and her legs were cramped, but she stood and stepped onto a rowing bench. She jumped down, staggering without the ability to stabilize using her arms, and ran as quietly as she could, cutting her feet and sliding on the shifting rocky shore. In the shadows stood the entrance to the other cavern.

She'd barely reached it when Hake let out a yell. Without looking back, she plunged into the complete blackness of the two caverns and came into the clearing. Thank God the moon was up! Its rays lit the wood just enough to see by, and she bolted down a thin path.

Roots rose up and tripped her, low-hanging branches reached down to scratch her face and tear at her hair, but she kept going. A snatched glance over her shoulder showed Hake was gaining.

She jumped down a sudden incline when, *crack!* A knife embedded in a tree, only a finger's width above her head.

How far to the village? She couldn't keep this up for long. As she ran, she went in the direction of the main path to the caverns, hoping she'd make it, that she'd meet up with someone, something.

Astrid wove between trees as well as she could to avoid Hake's knife, and it cracked into a tree beside her again. His footsteps were almost silent, but she could hear he was right behind her.

As she jumped over a fallen log, her serk caught and jerked her down. She twisted, trying to tear free, but Hake was upon her.

He dealt her several stunning blows, and she lay still, unable to fight as he pressed a hand on her throat. Her swirling vision was dotted with stars.

"I see it is no good to keep you out of the way," Hake hissed. A sharp scrape sent a chill down Astrid's spine. Hake drew out his dagger and pressed it to the side of her neck. She squeezed her eyes shut and waited for him to slide her throat.

There was a sharp hiss, and the knife's pressure eased a little. Astrid risked opening her eyes.

Hake stared at the woods behind them with his eyes narrowed and lips pressed firm. His fingers trembled against Astrid's stomach, and he shifted and tensed, as if ready to flee. Silence fell so thick that it was hard to breathe. Not even her throbbing heart made a sound. And in that silence was an uneasy rustling, like a cat crouching to pounce.

A voice rang out. "If you move, Hake, you will die."

Astrid gasped with joy. The voice was Erlin's!

Hake choked her. "If you kill me, *the girl* will die. I have a knife at her throat."

There was a sharp intake of breath.

A pause, and some whispering. Hake shifted again, licked his lips, and held his knife close. His eyes darted back and forth while his head remained unmoved; the energy and hate pulsing from him turned Astrid cold, making her want to get away more than ever.

Light footsteps encircled them in the darkness, and Hake hissed, "Does she mean so little to you? Surround me, and it will be her end."

Bushes rustled behind Astrid's head, and Hake ground his teeth and pulled the knife away as if preparing to give a blow.

"Only a coward would kill a girl bound and weaponless," said Erlin, much nearer this time. "Use your knife on me."

What happened next was a blur. An arrow bit into Hake's arm, and he was torn away so violently that it left Astrid breathless and light-headed. Everything turned black. There was a scuffle and cries, shouts, and the crash of underbrush. Yells and more crashes, and the sounds faded. Astrid was turned, her fingers tingled, and her hands fell on cold dirt, and she smelled the ocean.

Light returned, and Eric's face came into focus. He put a finger to her lips when she opened her mouth to ask how he'd found her.

"Hush," he whispered. "I know what you're thinking. We found the traitors and kept search until we heard you and Hake. The others are chasing after him."

He was so close, and his grey-blue eyes and sensitive mouth so tender, that she feared he'd kiss her—and for one wild moment hoped he would. But someone came up and he turned.

"Look what I found!" Haakon held up Hake's money pouch. "It must have come up in the scuffle." He dropped to his knees, poured out the pouch's contents, and held something up that glittered blue and gray in the moonlight.

"The key!" Astrid gasped, while the boys laughed triumphantly. Eric helped her up, and she promptly felt sick. For, lying beside her, lay a man, dead, with arrows and a broken-off knife hilt scattered around him.

"He tried to get him," Eric said quietly, "but Hake got away." He turned her away gently by the shoulders with a sigh. "Let's get you home."

With the two boys' help, she arrived at the path and made her way slowly to the village. At Tingstead, Haakon left, and Eric took Astrid's arm and led her the rest of the way, insisting he seeing her safely home.

It would have been pleasant to walk with him alone, at night, with the half-moon in the sky and a cool breeze fanning her hot cheeks if they'd done it months ago, before Hake, before Eric's confession, and before the attack. In spite of the villagers' opposition, life was reasonably good then. But with all that happened just that night, she felt like she'd aged a dozen years.

"Astrid," Eric began, "do you feel the same as before?"

She shivered. "Please, not right now."

He was everything a girl could want: strong, independent, well-mannered, sincere, and good-looking, too. She'd be a fool to reject him if it weren't for her inability to love again. She was positive—convinced—she didn't love him. Then why did she feel so safe around him? And why the strange flutter in her chest? During the weeks following his proposal, he'd avoided her, and she hadn't spoken to him until tonight how she missed his conversations! It was impossible to ask them back, because he'd expect her to say what she couldn't. Her actions might bring him around again—at least, she hoped—but he wouldn't forget the bitter truth.

She neared Mother Fredda's longhouse with a heavy heart.

Lamplight streamed through the open doorway of the longhouse, and Mother Fredda's shadow stood within it.

Sighing, Astrid pulled Eric to a stop and looked up. The expectant look on his face pained her, and she said quickly, "Thank you for seeing me home."

The eagerness left, and he nodded. "I'm glad you're well. Do you want me to bring you to the door?"

"I can go myself," she choked, slipping her arm from his grasp. "Good night."

"Good night."

She expected him to leave, but he didn't. He hesitated and glanced toward the open door, and when he looked back at her, his gaze dipped to her lips, and his hands twitched. Her temple pounded. But his shoulders bent ever so slightly, and he turned on his heel, dirt grinding. Then he left.

Astrid raised a shaking hand to her lips as she watched him disappear into the shadows, wanting to call him back, to tell him what he wanted to hear, but couldn't.

"Astrid! Oh, the gods be praised!" Mother Fredda ran up, wrapped the herb-scented shawl around her, and led her inside. When Astrid's wounds had been attended to, they went to bed. Astrid didn't sleep that night.

At noon the next day, the Tingstead horn sounded, and Haakon came to tell Astrid she was wanted at the Ting. She went hesitatingly and was seated beside Erlin on one side and Haakon and Eric on the other. When five prisoners were brought in, Erlin explained the situation to the villagers, starting from unease all the way to last night, and concluded by saying all men had been found but for Hake, who eluded them and escaped by boat from the caverns. Next, he told Astrid to make her case against them, and she told it as well as she could remember, even the detail about Hake's offer. A murmur rippled through the gathered crowd, but few of the faces frowned. They nodded approvingly, yet thoughtfully.

The five men were charged and sentenced to death, and the Ting ended.

The Tingstead horn sounded again, and everyone gathered back at the Tingstead. The traitors had been put under severe interrogation, and the black-haired man, who claimed to have been pulled into the plot against his will, told all, and Karsfien related the story.

It began with the unrest caused by Samuel the Christian moving to the island, and Hake, who assuredly chafed against his thralldom, encouraged several men in it. The unrest slowly built until the six of them grew to hate Erlin and vowed to mete out the gods' punishment on him. They planned to kill Erlin and blame Samuel, then Astrid showed up, and Erlin was busier than ever, and not so easily drawn away. That was when Hake suggested taking the treasury with them; for, why only kill Erlin when they could also take the island's riches? The attack was planned, but they weren't told about Hake's idea of using the bear as a cover-up. They'd grown increasingly tired of Hake's disappearances and working alone, and suspected he was only using them for himself. He hadn't told them he stole the money pouch. They'd planned to raid Erlin's house the very night they were captured.

When Karsfien finished, Erlin announced the traitors' means of death, all the most severe except for the black-haired man. Samuel tried to interfere.

"With all respect, Jarl, is it necessary to execute them in such a horrible way? My God shows mercy even on his enemies, in that He doesn't give them what they deserve in this life. They are fully punished in the afterlife. If I may be so bold, the way you propose is inhumane."

But Erlin ignored him, saying this is the way it was always done. By the jarl's set jaw, flint-hard eyes, and tight posture, Astrid knew he would not be persuaded.

Nor was he. The traitors were taken outside to the sacrificial fire pit in front of the Tingstead, and the villagers followed, crowding around and yelling. Astrid stayed inside with a few others who didn't want to see the execution.

Only when the bodies had been taken away did she step outside. The crowd was dispersing quietly now, and those who passed by her nodded. Some even smiled. And the air seemed clearer somehow, like when a longhouse is aired out after winter.

After about a week, she realized why. The suspicion was gone. Though still a little cautious, the villagers were at least respectful of her. They greeted her at the wharf when she accompanied Mother Fredda, and some even held short conversations with her. Possible friendships were started with her nearest neighbors and the people who regularly came to see Mother Fredda.

However, not everyone had changed their minds, Bikki in particular. When she met him on the road, the old man gathered his cloak around himself and made a sign of protection against evil spirits. There were also plenty of frowns and cutting looks, but Astrid paid them no mind.

Now that the villagers had mostly accepted her, Astrid could freely help Mother Fredda. She gave out medicine, bartered at the wharf, and ran errands.

One day, Mother Fredda surprised her by pulling out an old loom and setting it up in the empty back corner, saying cloth could be sold for extra income. Astrid's throat ached when she saw the loom sitting there. Mother should be working at it. Drawing a breath, Astrid sat down on the rickety stool and took up a ball of yarn.

Whenever she had the time, she wove as well as she could. A large stash of yarn had accumulated, both from payments and from Samuel's donations, so she had plenty to work with, which was a blessing. Since she hadn't dedicated much time to weaving at home, she struggled to the point of despair. Mother had preferred to do the weaving herself, and because Astrid had excused herself whenever the topic of weaving came up, she never learned to do it well.

She was staring at the tangled warp and weft, pressing her hand to her temple and biting her lip, when Bertha came in.

"Can I help you?" Bertha asked, laying her hands on the loom. With skilful hands, she untangled the yarn.

"I just can't get it to work," Astrid muttered, giving the loom a kick.

"Weaving's fun, once you get used to it." Bertha clicked her tongue and cut away a nest of impossible knots with her belt knife. "If you come tomorrow, we can practice on my loom."

Astrid sighed and watched her friend set the loom in order. She was dangerously close to tears from thinking of her mother, and forced a laugh. "Thank you. I'm a perfect idiot at it."

Bertha's laugh was genuine, and hearing it made Astrid feel better. "You should have seen me when I first started," said her friend. "I was far worse than this. Just come over tomorrow, and you'll see how much fun it can be."

Astrid hoped she was right.

Chapter 14

"There, it's all done."

In the Jarl's cabin, Astrid held up her first successful yard of cloth. It had taken many days to learn to use the loom, and she regretted getting out of the few lessons Mother had offered. Looking over Bertha's work, Astrid felt very inexperienced, for her friend wove patterns and created cloth even the king of Sweden would wear.

Bertha jumped up from her work with a smile on her face. "It's lovely, Astrid!" She fingered the fabric and held it up to the light. "We'll take it to the wharf, and I'll show you how to sell it." Grabbing a basket, Bertha danced to the door and beckoned. Astrid followed with a laugh, holding her cloth tightly against her chest.

Bertha seemed to know who to go to. She ignored the calls of other merchants and pushed through the surging crowds to a man with a large display of goods. The man looked up, and the bushy red moustache of his beard lifted.

"What do you have today?" he asked.

Astrid surrendered her cloth, and Bertha held it forward, flipping a corner of the fabric with an expert hand.

"Woollen cloth, freshly woven. The dye won't fade quickly, and the fabric is two-stranded, so it won't easily tear..."

This was familiar. Astrid let her mind wander and looked around at the Karls rushing one way, some another, and many bartering with the merchants. Some had furs for sale, rich ones that looked like the cape Father had given her years ago. Jewellery, skins, knives and axes, boots, crockery, meats, herbs, fish. Out on the water were the fishing boats, finishing up their catch for the morning. Astrid shaded her eyes and scanned them. Eric was on one of those boats somewhere.

Frowning, Astrid scanned them again. They were too far away for her to recognize any of the men on board, but she watched for the glint of sun on sandy blonde hair.

"Here, Astrid."

She jumped and turned. Bertha had stepped away from the merchant's booth and was holding out a small piece of silver. "It's not much, but he took it."

"Thank you." Astrid tucked the silver into her money pouch and glanced back toward the ocean.

"What are you looking for?"

"Eric's boat." Still no sign of him. Maybe they were around the island, and it blocked her view.

"Don't you know? He's leaving for the trading voyage today."

Astrid turned toward Bertha. Her friend's head tilted slightly, and her eyebrows were scrunched.

"No, I didn't. We haven't spoken since—" Astrid bit her lip. Blowing out a breath, she asked, "When is he leaving?"

Bertha's head tilted to the other side, like a woman inspecting pottery for sale. "Early this morning. He came by yesterday evening to say goodbye, since he wouldn't have time this morning."

Astrid spun around and searched the line of boats tied at the wharf. Near the end was a knarr, a cargo boat, with a swarm of people in and around it. Had she caught a glimpse of him? With a glance at Bertha, Astrid picked up her skirts and ran toward the boat. She squeezed between karls, dodged stacks of crates, and ducked under boards carried on someone's shoulder.

The boat was just ahead now, its sail towering above the crowd. The boat began to move. Astrid caught her breath as she pressed between two karls and found herself at the edge of the wharf. Already the boat had drifted several strides away, and men sat at the oars, lifting them. The sail dropped. Near the stern was Eric, standing tall, with the wind curling through his hair. His eyes were closed, and he breathed deep.

"Eric!" His name broke from Astrid's lips, and she caught her hand back as it reached out.

Eric opened his eyes and looked at her, pressing his mouth into a line and leaning toward her, and a smile broke across his face. He waved. Swallowing, Astrid lifted her hand up but couldn't make herself wave back. When Eric turned away, Astrid let her arm drop.

Weeks passed. Although she had fun weaving and trading at the wharf, Astrid often found herself stealing a glance toward the sea, searching for the boat that would bring Eric home.

Near the end of the summer, several karls came to Mother Fredda sick with an unusual illness. They complained of fevers, severe body aches, and nausea. What made it unusual were the lumps on their necks behind their jaw and near their armpits. Mother Fredda's face settled as she inspected them, but there was little she could do. The herbs only helped with the aches, fever, and nausea; the lumps continued to grow.

Astrid did all she could to help as Mother Fredda rushed from one house to another and attended the sick who were no longer able to come to her cabin. Astrid bagged herbs, cooked and cleaned, stoked the fire early in the morning and banked it at night.

Four days after the first case of the illness, a child died. Mother Fredda was absent the whole day, and when she returned that night, she was bent and gray and looked twenty years older. Astrid set a bowl of skause, expertly made now, before her, but Mother Fredda took no notice. She went past her and slipped into her room. Every time Astrid awoke during the night, she heard Mother Fredda chanting desperately over her medicine and begging the gods to hear her.

The next morning, Mother Fredda left before Astrid had awakened. There were two more deaths that day, and several more people were sick. The illness had spread to one of Karl's lungs, and his family had fevers. Almost every case after that included some form of lung complaints, and no lumps. Astrid was relieved, for anything sounded better than the lumps that could open up in oozing sores that made her stomach churn.

A few days later, while Astrid was at the wharf, a boat landed at the wharf and goods were unloaded. Astrid absently poked silver into her pouch as she watched, grateful for something to keep her mind off the illness and Mother Fredda. Several sailors formed a line and passed the crates and barrels from the ship onto the weather-beaten wood of the wharf, while a stocky, severe man stood by and supervised. His voice boomed as he gave orders.

One of the sailors, a youth, jumped onto the wharf and approached the man, and the sun glinted off the youth's sandy hair. It was Eric, taller and tanner than ever. He and the man exchanged words, and the man shouted orders before turning to leave. Eric followed him.

Astrid forgot she was supposed to be trading for herbs and ran toward them.

"Eric! It's good to see you!"

Eric flashed her a grin. But before Astrid could reach him, the severe man speared her with a stare.

"Not now, mær. Be gone."

"But—"

"I said, be gone. Come, Eric." The man went on his way, with Eric following, leaving Astrid behind.

Astrid, with angry tears in her eyes, stomped her foot and returned to Mother Fredda's turf-house.

It wasn't until that evening that she heard that the man was Eric's father, Harald, and that they brought news of a plague. It was spreading like a flood because many merchants went from island to island, including Trygvey, bringing the plague with them. When this news got around, most of the villagers stayed at home as much as possible, for fear of catching it. This slowed the illness, but it couldn't be stopped. New cases were reported daily, and already over a dozen new plots had been added to the graveyard.

Men and women, young and old, couldn't escape it, and it was most dangerous to the children and the elderly. All who were around it fell ill, and few survived. Thus far, Mother Fredda alone didn't catch it when exposed. She was in good health for her old age, but would it be enough?

Shivering, Astrid picked up the broom and swept loose bits of dirt out of the longhouse. It would be a cellar if the plague lasted much longer, on account of the many times she'd swept, for after a week of remaining inside at Mother Fredda's orders, everything had been done. Blankets, curtains, and clothing had been mended, washed, and neatly folded away; the garden was weedless, well-watered, and harvested a little. Four new cloths were folded beside the loom. Pots and pans were scrubbed, and there would be no lack of firewood for months to come.

When the house had been swept, she squatted by the fire and poked at it, watching sparks fly up and white-hot coals throb. Wood squeaked; she looked at the door. Nothing. Mother Fredda was gone for far too long, and she'd looked tired that morning from chanting and praying late into the night. Had she slept at all? Astrid hadn't.

The door creaked open, and Mother Fredda entered, shawl wrapped around slumped shoulders, lines deepened on her face, mouth downturned at the corners. She walked slowly as if carrying a heavy bundle and took her basket to the shelves, where she loaded it with bags of herbs.

Trembling and suddenly cold, Astrid laid down the poker, hurried to Mother Fredda's side, and gently took the basket from her. How heavy it was!

"You're doing so much," she whispered, the lump in her throat quivering. "Can't I help a little? Carry your baskets, go to the wharfs, something?"

Mother Fredda gave a weary sigh, replaced a bag on the shelf, and shook her head. The purple smudges under her eyes sent shivers through Astrid's stomach. "No, child. I'm not doing everything alone."

"You hardly let Gudrid help. I'm stuck here, by myself. There must be something I can do besides cleaning and cooking. You're wearing yourself out."

"Now, child, I am accustomed to this work. There have been outbreaks before, and I was the only healer then. If it puts you at ease at all, remember the few karls who still come here, saving my trip to them."

Astrid couldn't keep her voice from trembling. "It doesn't make much of a difference."

Shaking her head again, Mother Fredda faced her and took Astrid's other hand. "You help more than you know. Never have I seen this cabin so clean, and your cooking has improved."

Astrid forced a chuckle, but it sounded more like a moan. The accumulated days of solitude had driven her to experiment with preparing food, which Mother Fredda and Gudrid always ate without a murmur, no matter how badly it turned out.

Mother Fredda hesitated, then said, "With ill Karl coming every day, I worry you will catch it."

Cold washed over Astrid. "But I'm very careful. I stay away when they come—"

"Wherever the sick are, there it spreads. There is no escaping it. I wish that you would stay in your room. None but you enters that part of the cabin, so it is safe."

"But, Mother Fredda!"

"Astrid, please." She cupped her hands around Astrid's face. "At least until the worst has passed."

Astrid stared into her eyes. They were glassy, and purple stained the skin underneath. Mother Fredda didn't need to worry about her, too. She swallowed. "I will."

Mother Fredda kissed her forehead and let her go. She paused, looking over Astrid with tear-brimmed eyes, before picking up her basket. Slowly, she moved toward the door and, once in the doorway, turned back.

"Remember, stay in your room. For me, Astrid. Do it for me." And she was gone.

For a moment, Astrid stared out at the clear blue sky and the woods of turning leaves settled just beyond the village. Crisp autumn air twirling her hair, cool grass beneath her feet. Waterfalls of light warming her head, her shoulders. Strong fingers lacing through hers. All could be hers if she only stepped outside.

Astrid spun away and faced her room. Where had the light gone? Shadows enshrouded the curtains and swallowed the corners of the cabin. More like a ship galley than a cabin.

Before entering her room, Astrid grabbed the two games Mother Fredda owned. She tossed the games onto the bed, bounded to the window, and flung it open. Fresh air poured around her, but the sun was hidden behind low gray clouds. Astrid shivered and lifted her cloak from its hook, wrapping it around her shoulders.

She sat on her bed and looked over the games. Nine Men's Morris and hnefltefl. They were two-player games, but it was better than nothing. Maybe she could create a one-player version of both. She had plenty of time, days like rows of tangled looms. Recovering from the attack had been hard enough, but this time, no visitors, no songs, no mundane tasks to keep her mind busy. No Eric. Her breath caught how she needed him now!

The games didn't occupy her for long. Before the day was over, she sat on the edge of her bed, elbows resting on the windowsill. Mother Fredda spent all her time in other people's cabins, so Astrid couldn't listen to her voice, in the evenings when Mother Fredda was home, often as not someone rushed in to bring her to a sick friend or loved one. So, Astrid didn't even have her footsteps to listen to. Gudrid came by two times a day to cook, but that didn't last long, either.

Her friends—how were they? Bertha, Eric, Haakon... The best friends she had. If they were sick, there was no way to find out until it was too late. Mother Fredda wouldn't stand for her to leave the cabin.

Leave the cabin. That's all she wanted to do. Leave the walls that suffocated her, stole the light, hemmed her in. Astrid glanced over her shoulder, cringed, and stared out the window again. The wood lay beyond the village, orange, yellow, gray, and green in its fall colors. Fallen leaves would be on the ground, crisp and dry, waiting to crunch under her feet. And the wind, a cool, refreshing breeze, a welcome change to the stuffy, smoky cabin.

Astrid glanced at the sun. It was just past noon, and neither Mother Fredda nor Gudrid would be back until evening. No one would miss her. She stood and paused with her hand on the windowsill. She glanced around her room and back to the woods. It wouldn't hurt to spend just a few minutes outside. Fresh air would do her good.

Astrid grabbed her shawl, threw it around her shoulders and slipped out of her room. The main room was lifeless and cold. The fire had died down long ago, and its coals were but lumps of white in chalky black. Skirting the fireplace, she dashed outside. Without a pause, she scurried down the street, keeping her head down and the shawl wrapped tightly.

At the edge of the village, she closed her eyes and breathed deep. No more stuffy house.

She opened her eyes and stared. At the edge of the woods, two men were shovelling dirt over a wide pit. One turned and saw her.

He paused. "Come to mourn, Kona? Stay back until we finish."

Heat flushed Astrid's face. "I have not." Then, after a pause, she asked in a low voice, "How many?"

The other man straightened. "Five more today." He continued his work, and the other did the same.

Astrid fled. Branches tore at her face and dress, and undergrowth hid the narrow path she followed. When she came to the caves, she followed the rock face around to the clearing. There, she leaned against a tree to catch her breath and looked up to see the Helm of Awe. Chest heaving, she ran her hand over the symbol, and guilt settled over her.

Could the illness be the doom foretold by Bikki's dream? Despite the work she'd done and the sacrifices she'd made, she was still cursed. There was nothing she could do to change that, but she could change its consequence. If she left, the illness would leave. But where could she go? On the other hand, if she stayed, would the doom worsen?

Her head began to pound, and she pressed a hand to her temple. Where was the Christian God in all this? He was a creator and a maker of good, but what was happening to the island was far from good. He hadn't abandoned her when the other gods did, but had He now?

"God of the Christians, for the sake of the people of Trygvey, don't let anything worse happen."

A twitch formed between her shoulder blades; she shouldn't be here, in the clearing. Go back—so soon? Her legs ached, she was still breathless, and she was shivering. It must be the run, and the shade. But why would she be so cold? Tired, perhaps. All would be well after a good rest, but she couldn't sleep here; what if she took too long? Mother Fredda or Gudrid would return and find her missing.

With a groan, she turned back. The path was longer than she remembered, and the ache in her legs traveled up her body. Her headache increased. Lack of exercise, that's what it was. She wasn't used to it anymore. If only the shiver would go away...

When the village came in sight, Astrid leaned against a tree, panting. Her lungs burned. Straightening, she smoothed her hair and composed herself. There was no reason to worry anyone.

She finally arrived at Mother Fredda's cabin and pushed at the door. So heavy! She leaned against it, and it opened, the wood on the bottom scraping the floor.

"Astrid?"

Gudrid stood inside, beside a pot hanging over the fire.

Astrid straightened and wrapped her shawl tighter around her shoulders. Her teeth chattered and her hands shook, so she clenched her jaw and tucked her hands in the folds of her shawl.

"I just went out for a walk," she said quickly, trying to slip past Gudrid.

The apprentice caught her arm. "You're on fire! How long have you been like this?"

Astrid swallowed her tears and locked her knees to keep them from shaking. "I..." Shivers wracked her. An arm wrapped around her shoulders, and a hand cupped her elbow. The floor warped up and down, throwing her off balance. Her stomach flipped, and bile crept up her throat. At the end of a narrowing black tunnel was her room. She reached for it, grasping, but the floor tilted up and blackness fell around her.

Everything hurt. Astrid lay on her back on something soft, but even that hurt. Bruises everywhere, tossed and beaten, left for dead. Pressure on her chest, hard to breathe. Her lungs vibrated and sent her into convulsive coughing. Soft light fell on her eyelids, but she didn't dare open her eyes. She was afraid of where she was, what she would see. The last thing she remembered was the clearing beside the caves. She could be anywhere now.

A hand rested on her forehead.

"The fever's left, Gudrid. She'll pull through."

Astrid opened her eyes. Above her, Mother Fredda smiled.

"Mother Fredda, what—" Coughing took hold again.

"Relax, child. You've been sick, and you need rest. Keep coughing. It'll get out the infection."

Astrid pressed a hand to her temple. The pressure was splitting her head apart. "Why am I so sore?"

"It's part of the illness. Here, take this."

Mother Fredda held a cup to Astrid's lips. The drink was hot and soothing to her raw throat.

"There now. Rest, and I will be back shortly."

She turned to leave, but Astrid whispered, "Mother Fredda?"

The old woman came back and sat on the stool beside her bed. "What is it, child?"

Astrid swallowed. "I—I left the house. I'm sorry."

Mother Fredda took her hand and squeezed it. "All is forgiven. You meant no harm, but don't disobey me again. I don't want anything to happen to you." She kissed Astrid's forehead and stood. "Try to sleep."

When Mother Fredda left, Astrid glanced at her open window and closed her eyes. Confined again.

Time passed faster than Astrid would have expected, for she was occupied with sleep and the never-ending cough; however, days slowed almost to a stop when the pain in her chest faded and she was not sleeping as often. She was well after two weeks, but Mother Fredda didn't let her leave the room. The plague was spreading faster than ever, and Mother Fredda didn't want her to get it again.

"Just to the woods? I promise not to speak with anyone," Astrid pleaded from the stool by her bed when Mother Fredda came in with the evening meal.

Mother Fredda shook her head and set the plate on the bed. She was more worn than ever, like an old garment; her shoulders sagged, and her movements were slow.

"Can't I help around the cabin, then?" Astrid caught Mother Fredda's shawl as the healer turned away. "You've been handling so much. Please!"

Mother Fredda took Astrid's hands tenderly and squeezed them. "I'm only tired, child, and it's been a long day. I'll be myself tomorrow." She slipped from Astrid's grasp and left the room.

The next day, around noon, Astrid sat at the window and stared outside. Clouds rolled by, one like a ship, another like a bead, another like a dragon. Earlier, she'd seen some resembling a wave, a beard, a lump of skyr, a coil of rope. Astrid growled and sat back, rubbing her forehead. There had to be something she could do instead of rotting away. A scream had been building in her chest, and it was dangerously close to her throat.

Astrid swallowed and turned to her unfinished game of nine men's morris on the floor. The same pieces, the same cloth board. She'd be well into old age before she'd ever want to play it again.

Someone crossed the house with soft steps. They belonged to Mother Fredda, but how slowly they moved! There were Gudrid's quick, tapping ones, coming through the doorway and catching up to Mother Fredda.

Astrid bit her lip and moved a game piece, then scooped up the pieces and poked them back in their bag with a wry smile. There was no losing when playing alone.

Her ears pricked up when Gudrid spoke. "You really should rest, Mother Fredda." By the sound of her voice, she was somewhere near the fire. Wood was tapped as it was arranged in the fireplace. "You can't go on in your state. I can handle this."

A cough and a sigh and, "Very well, Gudrid." Slow footsteps dragged past Astrid's room.

She went cold. It couldn't be. Mother Fredda was always the one caring for others. Astrid moved to the curtain, but hesitated. With Gudrid inside, she couldn't leave her room without being seen. Groaning, Astrid sat on the floor beside her bed and drew her knees to her chest.

Gudrid remained in the cabin for some time, cooking. Every few minutes, a villager interrupted her, and she stopped and tended to his needs. It was well past time for the noon meal when she finally came in with a plate of food. Astrid took it, set it aside, and listened. Listened to the coughs coming from Mother Fredda's room, listened to Gudrid's movements.

The pent-up scream made her muscles twitch, so it was agonizing to sit still. She pressed her nails into her palm, paced back and forth, and sat down again. Then she jumped up, paced some more, and stopped and cocked her head, tapping her foot impatiently. Would Gudrid ever go away? Astrid's hands flew to her head, where they tore at her hair. When she pulled her hands away, they were tangled with strands of hair. She shook them off and paced again. Gudrid walked past, to Mother Fredda's room, and said something too low to hear.

Astrid stood by the curtain, one hand up, and waited. When Gudrid passed by, Astrid drew the curtain aside. "Is Mother Fredda ill?"

Gudrid jumped, and a hand flew to her heart. Her face was pale. "Stay in your room, Astrid."

Astrid nearly stomped her foot. Her voice rose. "Is she ill?"

"Yes, but stay out of there."

"I've already had it."

"You could catch it again."

"You go in there."

"It's my duty!" Gudrid pinched the bridge of her nose. "Forgive me. Just stay in your room."

Astrid's throat ached. "No, forgive me. I've been in here for weeks and can't stand it any longer! Can't you give me something to do?" She clamped her hands to her head, let out a breath, and dropped them to her sides. The scream sank into her chest, which tightened. "I'm sorry, Gudrid. I can't take it anymore."

Gudrid stared, then went to the other side of the cabin. She returned with a pile of bags, a needle, and thread. "You can mend these if you want. There's nothing else you can help with."

Astrid took the offered articles and hugged them to her chest to keep herself from flinging her arms around Gudrid. "Thank you."

By evening, she'd completed the bags and some other mending Gudrid had found, and was back on the floor, leaning against her bed. She picked at her food, unable to eat with the pit in her stomach.

Gudrid was called away again, and Astrid stood. She pushed through the curtain and paused outside Mother Fredda's room. The coughing had worsened throughout the day until it weakened and deepened. Right now, it was silent.

Slowly, Astrid pushed the curtain aside and looked in. Lying on the bed, white and fragile, was Mother Fredda, her ragged breathing barely audible. Her eyes were closed and her breath was regular, as in sleep. Astrid ran to the bedside, but two strong hands grabbed her.

"Astrid, don't! She is very ill, and you could catch it."

She looked up into the weary, pale face of Gudrid. "But I already had it!"

"You could get it again."

Astrid nodded slowly and let out a breath, and Gudrid released her. She knelt by Mother Fredda's bed and fought the impulse to hold her close and keep her from slipping away.

"How bad is she?"

Gudrid shook her head. "I'm afraid she can't hold on much longer."

A sob escaped Astrid's lips, and she buried her head in the covers. "This can't be! She can't be sick!"

Gudrid knelt beside her. "Keep your hope alive. She may pull through. The best way you can help is by not getting ill yourself."

"But what about you?"

"I have no other choice but to continue as I have before."

Astrid stood. Stealing one last look at Mother Fredda, she slipped from the room.

As the day progressed, she all but lost her appetite and spent all her time pacing back and forth. There was nothing she could do: nothing to take away the ache in her chest, the lump in her throat, the fist around her stomach. She heard every cough, every breath, that came from Mother Fredda's room. When her hands weren't pulling her hair, her thumbs worked over the inside of her fingers, back and forth, back and forth, while she chewed her lip raw.

As if the torment of uncertainty was not enough, guilt wouldn't leave. *She* caused this. Every family on Trygvey was experiencing this, and it was her fault. And there was nothing she could do about that, either.

Shortly after taking away Astrid's cold evening meal, Gudrid returned, her bleary eyes looking out over the dark smudges on her white, weary face. "Mother Fredda wants to see you."

Astrid sat up so quickly that the sturdy old bed creaked in protest. She searched for any sign of hope in Gudrid's face but found none. "Has she improved?"

Gudrid gave a deep sigh through her cracked lips. She blinked twice, hard. Her voice sank in her chest.

"She will not be improving. But she wants to see you. Prepare yourself, however... she's changed."

Astrid gripped the side of the bed as a crippling wave rushed over her. With an effort, she pushed to her feet and dragged herself to the curtain, which Gudrid pushed aside, and crept to the silent room beside hers. She entered it alone.

Mother Fredda was a mere shadow in the lamp-lit corner. Darkness claimed all but what the weak light could touch—the creased forehead, the parted lips, the translucent hand lying motionless by her side. Despite the warm glow, her color was ashen. Rough, strangled breathing twisted a knot in Astrid's throat. She found herself at the bedside, where she slowly knelt and took the limp hand.

Astrid forced the words past her numb lips. "I'm here."

Mother Fredda's eyelids fluttered open, and she focused her sunken eyes on Astrid's face. She lifted her other hand and stroked her cheek. "Child.... you must learn to live on your own."

Astrid's eyes misted. She clutched Mother Fredda's hand. "Don't!" she croaked.

"You won't be alone.... not long. Eric is fond of you."

Of all things, Astrid felt herself blushing. "How did you—"

A faint smile crossed Mother Fredda's face. "I know the signs."

She couldn't tell her how matters really stood between them. Not now. "I won't be alone. You are going to fight through this, and everything will be right again, just as it was before."

"Oh, child. I can't." Mother Fredda closed her eyes and took several shallow breaths, fighting to breathe. "All wasn't right.... what of the voice?"

"Please, not right now."

"Must. Samuel tells the truth."

Astrid licked salt from her lips. She sniffed and struggled to blink away her tears. She couldn't meet Mother Fredda's gaze. "I—"

"Look."

She did so and found conviction in her face.

"It is true. You know it," said Mother Fredda, staring steadily into her eyes.

A deep breath didn't keep her hoarse voice from breaking. "If it were, there would be hope," she whispered.

The faintest of smiles lifted the corners of Mother Fredda's lips. "I... I have hope." She closed her eyes again.

Astrid waited for her to catch her breath and continue, but she did not. Fear shot through her. "Mother Fredda?" Astrid whispered through stiff lips. She pressed Mother Fredda's worked hand to her chest and leaned over her. "Say something!"

Gudrid came up from behind and pushed her aside. Still clutching the limp hand, Astrid watched Gudrid press her ear to Mother Fredda's chest and squeeze her eyes shut in concentration, which melted into something deeper. Her eyes glazed over as she straightened. She need not utter a sound; the words etched on her face were enough.

"Come, Astrid," she said quietly, prying Mother Fredda's hand from her.

Astrid swayed as if struck, then launched forward. Ducking under Gudrid's arms, she threw herself on Mother Fredda's body.

Gudrid laid a hand on her shoulder. "Come."

"No!" She held on as tightly as she could. "You can't take her from me."

"She already has been!" Golden beads ran down the apprentice's cheeks. She raised a hand to her face, and the shadow cast by the lamp hid it from sight. "I've lost her, too."

Choking, Astrid grabbed Gudrid's other hand, which hung limp. "Stay here with me, then."

Gudrid sighed, shaking her head, and extracted her hand. "I have a life she left me to, with the burden of caring for those who depended on her. I can't let them down. You cannot either."

Trembling, Astrid laid her hand on Mother Fredda's chest. Then, tucking her hand into the folds of her kirtle, she kissed the cold forehead and allowed Gudrid to lead her from the room. The curtain fell into place behind them.

Chapter 15

"Astrid, you need to eat."

Astrid shook her head, and her body swayed on the old stool by her window.

Gudrid sighed, took up the cold food, and left the room, every crunch and scrape of dirt beneath her boots sending shudders through Astrid's middle. To scream, to cry out. That was all she wanted. But it was trapped deep inside, churning, curdling.

Figures moved on the street, and she traced their blurred movements. It was now several days since Mother Fredda's death, and Astrid's appetite had left; she hardly ate or drank anything. And even though Gudrid said Astrid could go outside, she refused. She couldn't leave her room without Mother Fredda. It was wrong, terribly wrong, to keep going without her.

A blurry figure moved between her and the window, blocking the light, and warm, skinny arms flung around her. A warm tingle swept down Astrid's spine and into her limbs, and she felt alive again. Eyes focusing, she looked down at the little girl in her room, squeezing her tight.

"Thora? Why are you here?" Astrid asked, running her fingers through the little girl's soft hair.

With a final squeeze, Thora stepped back. "People are leaving their homes. Oh, you look awful!" Thora clasped her hands together, and her big eyes widened until they seemed to swallow up her other features.

"How long—" Astrid's voice scraped her ears. She winced. "How long has it been since Mother Fredda... since she left?"

Thora, still clasping her hands, answered, "Three days."

Energy shot through Astrid like a bolt of lightning at the realization. "That long?" Panic swept over Thora's little face. Astrid calmed herself and said quickly, "I haven't eaten much lately; that's why I do not look like myself. Would you like to eat with me?"

Thora nodded.

Astrid pulled herself up and winced at the pricks of pain that shot up her legs as her joints creaked like an old door. She shuffled away from the window but froze at the sight of the curtain. Flexing her clammy hands, she shifted, but couldn't make herself push the curtain aside. Glancing at her, Thora moved the curtain and beckoned. Astrid ducked through and took a deep breath in the silent, dark main room. Gudrid was out, and the door was shut, and it appeared as though no one lived there.

Feeling the weight of a gaze, Astrid turned and smiled at Thora, more to assure herself than the girl, and started to scrounge the kitchen. Her limbs loosened up during the search, and she moved freely by the time she set a very stale day-old loaf, two bowls of skyr, and a piece of sun-dried pork on the table.

After the meal, Astrid stepped outside for the first time in ages. All the leaves had fallen from the trees, exposing the majestic spruce and pine and the silky white birches. The wind had a cool clip in it, and the sea churned as stormheads piled on the horizon. Snow crunched beneath her feet, her breath fogged, and Karls wore extra layers of clothes. She shivered in the cold and rubbed her arms.

Before she could go inside for her cloak, a voice called her name.

"Astrid!"

She whirled. Bertha and Haakon were running toward her, the former blinking hard and holding her arms open.

"Bertha! Haakon!" Her friends caught her in an embrace, swinging around and around. Their foreheads pressed together, and the sky above them spun. A lock of Bertha's hair tickled Astrid's cheek.

"Oh, Astrid, I'm so happy you're okay!" Bertha hugged her once more.

"I am, thanks to Thora," Astrid said, squeezing the child's shoulders. Thora looked up at her and smiled.

Astrid took a deep breath and realized she was shivering. She rubbed her arms. Her two friends grinned at each other and at her. Only two? "Where is Eric?" she asked.

The brother and sister looked at each other, and Bertha paled. Astrid stared, confused, then it dawned on her. Her fingers turned to ice. "Is he sick?"

Bertha laid a hand on her shoulder. "Astrid—"

Astrid jerked away. "Why didn't you tell me?" Her world was whirling. She could not lose him. Not after the distance that had grown between them. When was the last time they'd spoken? Bertha caught her hand, but Astrid shook her away and ran down the road to his house, ignoring the shouts following her.

Why? Why Eric? Pictures of his smile flashed before her eyes, and she could almost feel the firm grip of his hand. Her chest swelled, and tears blurred her vision.

His turf-house stood before her. Breathless, she hurried to the door and rapped on it. Harald opened it, blinking in the sunlight, and fixed his glazed eyes on Astrid. His face hardened.

"What is it?" His voice was rough like cracked wood.

"I need to see Eric."

Harald drew himself up, and his tall frame filled the doorway. "Begone, mær. This is no place for you."

Her chest tightened. She clenched her hands and held them to her chest to keep the pressure from escaping. "I'll not leave until I see him, unless you take me away yourself. Only for a moment, please!"

Harald grunted and swung the door open. He pointed a thick forefinger across the room to the curtained room on the other side. Trembling from head to toe, Astrid smoothed her wind-torn hair and ducked past him. Her boots tapped the packed dirt floor, each step grating her nerves. Time slowed, dragging her through ages before she reached the curtain and pushed it aside with tingling fingertips.

Eric lay in bed, white and limp, eyes closed, and chest moving slow and shallow like Mother Fredda. Astrid fell at the bedside.

"Eric! Eric!" she cried softly as she grabbed his hand. "Don't leave me!" Tears fell on the limp, worked hand. The warm light in her chest melted away the pressure, and Astrid bit her lip. Her family's death didn't steal love from her. She could love again—if it wasn't too late.

"Eric, I want you to know that I love you." Her voice broke, and she lay her head on the bed beside him. Astrid rested there for a moment, then slowly raised herself up. As she stood, Eric opened his eyes and fixed them on her.

"It's good to know, Astrid," he answered in a husky, weak voice. He coughed violently.

Astrid fell back onto her knees and took his hand in hers. "I wish I had realized it sooner."

One corner of Eric's mouth curved upward. "At least I know. Not too late..." His eyes closed, and he coughed hard, curling up and pressing his free hand to his side. Astrid shied but kept hold of his hand. When the coughing fit left, Eric drifted into feverish sleep. Astrid rose and left the room, shutting the door softly behind her.

Harald was sitting in front of the fire, staring into the flames. She tried to slip past him, but he said without turning, "Mær, come talk to me."

Astrid sat down on the stool beside him, the very one Eric probably used.

Harald slowly rubbed his hands close to the fire. Every muscle in his body was tense, like the man Eric had described him to be: intense, severe. But Harald was like a weather-beaten boat washed on shore. The hardness had left him.

"Mær, you've been around Eric. I've seen you with him and Jarl Erlin's children. But even they didn't stand up to me as you did. I like gumption." Astrid dropped her eyes even though he didn't look up at her. "Shortly after you came, before the traitors were found, he acted strange. I told him it was high time to marry, and he mentioned you. I refused. He seemed to accept it, but something was different." He gave Astrid a hard, scrutinizing glance. "Why are you here?"

She started, and words fled. "Why, Karl, you—uh—wanted me to—"

"Tyr! No. What made you come?" He turned to her, and this time the glance was a stare.

Astrid looked down at her hands clenched in her lap. This man was the last one to whom she'd express herself, but here she was, without choice. She took a breath. "I heard he was sick, and... I had to see him if but for the last time."

Harald stared at her in silence. "You love him, then?"

Heat engulfed her face. She swallowed. "Yes, Karl."

Harald turned back to the fire, and his hands hung between his legs. "I'd give anything for my son's healing. Please the gods, if Eric is well, I will not stand in your way."

The Tingstead horn blew, and Astrid jumped. Harald didn't seem to hear it. When the echoes of the blast had long died, he shook himself and stood. Astrid scrambled to her feet and stepped away from the chair so she wouldn't trip over it. Her knees shook so she could hardly stand.

"I should go," Astrid stuttered. Harald nodded, and she got away as quickly as possible.

After so many days of isolation and boredom, life felt out of place. Astrid returned to the wharf after weaving a basket full of cloth, shyly glancing at Karl's passing her. They were just as friendly as they had been before the plague, despite her fears the misfortune would make them reconsider their interpretation of the dream, and many stopped to greet her. She talked with them for a moment, then politely excused herself because of the soft heat creeping into her cheeks.

She was one of them.

Trading at the wharf was freeing. With a basket of cloth hooked on one arm, she brought it to the merchants to barter, enjoying the process, though her heart often panged. Every day she'd watched Mother Fredda do the same, her friendly, patient voice contrasting with the surrounding shouts, her worked hands gesturing toward the merchandise. Astrid learned all she knew from her and whispered gratefulness to her with each roll of cloth she sold.

Astrid's favorite time of day was when all work and trading were finished and she could sit by Eric's side. Though he was weak, Eric was often attentive to the sagas she recounted and the old songs she sang. She bathed his forehead with a cold, wet cloth when he was feverish, and held his hand when he was asleep or unconscious. Before leaving for the night, she would bend and kiss his cheek, a prayer to all the gods she could think of on her lips. He held on remarkably well so far. If only the gods would give him the strength to hold on until he got well.

However, after two days, he began to succumb to the illness. His body weakened further, and seeing him alert was a rare sight. Astrid's visits lengthened until she spent all her time by his side, from midday until dark, holding his hand firmly. If she could keep him alive by physical touch, she'd do it.

Her visits overlapped with Gudrid's, and Astrid watched nervously, hands clammy and heart pounding, as the medicine woman examined him. Astrid felt as if her heart stopped when Gudrid stood, shook her head, and turned to Harald.

"Only the gods can save him now. I have done all I can."

A strangling sound came from Harald's corner.

With a departing pat on Astrid's shoulder, Gudrid said, "Astrid, you need to get out more. Do me a favor and trade every day before coming here."

"But—"

"I know. But trading doesn't take long. You need fresh air. I don't want you to come down with it again."

Astrid relented with something like a sigh of relief. Putting her hand to her temple, she turned and left. The past few days, she'd skipped working and trading and focused all her energy on nursing Eric. She gave up praying to the gods again as he worsened—they still didn't hear—and started to believe the Christian God had done the same. The weight of responsibility shifted on her, rounding her shoulders, but she was with the one she loved and must be with him until the bitter end.

She arrived at the wharf with her basket on her arm and managed to trade several cloths for a good price. Now she could go back. She turned and pushed against the crowd, but it carried her along in a stiff current. By the time she broke away, she had traveled down the wharf to where a newly arrived boat was being unloaded. She glanced toward it and shied away when she met Samuel face-to-face. With a tight nod, she strode away. She didn't need anything else to add to her cares, especially thoughts about the Christian God.

A voice calling her name pulled her attention back. Astrid looked over her shoulder to see Samuel pushing through the crowd toward her. Astrid quickened her gait and reached the road, but he caught up and matched her pace.

"Could I have a word with you?" he asked.

Astrid kept her head up and kept her eyes on the road in front of her. "No, you may not."

Samuel dropped back a little, then caught up. "I've thought much about our conversation about my God."

"What about it?" Astrid snapped.

"I see you're looking for some truth to hold onto, something to anchor you in the storms of life. The gods, Odin and Thor and the rest, don't satisfy you. My God will satisfy you, but not until you understand Him."

Astrid stopped and faced Samuel. She glared up into his face and nearly choked at the rage rising up in her. "Understand? What else is there to know? A God who created everything and who lets evil run wild isn't a God worth following. If He were powerful enough to create everything, He has enough power to control evil. But he doesn't. What kind of God is that?" She tasted salt. Her voice shook, but she pushed through it. "My family has been killed. My younger brother died before my eyes. I come here, thrown in the middle of an uprising. Plague comes and kills Mother Fredda. Someone I love is at death's door. What kind of God allows that? He's worse than all the gods. I'd rather believe in Thor, who actually helps us when it comes to mind, if we aren't cursed." Her last sentence was a lie, but she said it anyway to discourage him. She clutched her seething middle, and her chest heaved with caught breaths. Heat flashed through her, and she ground her teeth.

Samuel had listened to her outburst in calm silence, looking back into her eyes. Now he stood just as silently as before, still watching her, calm as ever. He crossed his arms. A muscle in his neck tightened.

"Well?" Astrid demanded, stamping her foot and practically screaming. "Say something!"

Samuel continued to stay silent, and Astrid waited for him to speak, dreading whatever he'd say, yet yearning to hear it. Slowly, the heat left, as did her rage, and it left her tired and weak. Sobs rose in her throat, and in spite of her efforts, she began to cry. She hid her face in her hands and wished herself far away. Yet, somehow, she couldn't leave. If there was any truth in this man, she needed it now, more than ever. The weight of responsibility and grief was too much to bear.

Her sobs died down to hiccupping whimpers by the time he spoke, quiet and kind.

"You've been through much, Astrid. I have, too. We both know the pain of heartbreak and defeat, the grief of loss." His arms uncrossed and hung at his sides. "But my experience was different from yours because of one thing. My God was with me through it all. He is not the all-powerful tyrant you believe him to be. Not long ago, He came to earth in the form of a man and conquered sin and death for us. He let himself be tortured and killed for our sakes so that we would no longer be controlled by evil. This God-man, Christ, sits as king of the world in Heaven, the place of all perfect spiritual beings. He can be your king, Astrid, and give you strength and endurance if you only submit yourself to Him and trust what He did for you. He loves you and me and promises never to leave us. Unlike your gods, He always answers our prayers, never changes, and has prepared a place for all of us to go to after death."

Although ashamed of her tears, Astrid looked up. Samuel was still watching her, but something about him had changed. Either he'd changed, or she just noticed it, but compassion was in his eyes. His words, "he promises never to leave us," brought back what the Voice had said:

"Peace be with you. I will never leave or forsake you."

Could the Christian God be the Voice?

"What did your God do about what happened at the beginning of the world, with the two people?"

"Adam and Eve? That's why Christ conquered sin and death. It no longer has a hold on us if we accept Christ as our lord and King. He did it because He loves us and wants us to be with Him."

"What happens to us without him?"

"We go to a place worse than the underworld where your goddess Hel reigns."

Astrid shuddered. "But, if God loves us, why does He let bad things happen? And, do you believe our gods are real?"

Samuel thought for a moment. "No one can be certain why God lets certain things happen, but we can be confident it's for good. He uses it to bring us to Himself, to strengthen our faith, and to work in wonderful ways that show His power and goodness. Even when we cannot understand, we can be confident because God is good, He never changes, and He hates evil, death, disease, and pain. As for your gods... I believe they are not real. My God told

His people not to have any other gods besides Him, because He alone deserves our worship."

Astrid looked down at her feet. All the times the gods hadn't answered. All the times she'd been alone. It was because they were a lie. Only when she called on the Voice or the Christian God was she answered.

She asked tentatively, "Are you a monk?"

A line formed between Samuel's eyebrows, which lowered slightly. "No. I don't believe God wants us to separate from the world. After all, He said His people are the light of the world. How can we be the light of the world if we're hiding away from it? There are exceptions, but most stay separate."

"Then... do you agree with their view of religion?"

"What would that be, from what you see?"

Astrid adjusted her hold on her basket. "That religion is just a bunch of good works, prayers, and such."

Samuel stared at the ground, thinking. He said slowly, "Those things are important, but it's more than that. Christianity isn't just a religion or set of duties. It's my life." His voice dipped. "Knowing Christ changed everything."

Astrid studied the dark brown of her worn leather boots and the contrast with the light, packed dirt street. A life submitted to the Christian God contrasts with the life before. So the religion did change people. How could it not, if what Samuel said about God was true, that God was as real as he made Him out to be?

Samuel put out his hand. "May I take your basket? I'll walk you to wherever you're going."

"I'm only going home," said Astrid, but she gave up the basket anyway. She was jittery all over, and the basket pulled her down.

As she walked beside Samuel, she stole shy glances up at him. What he said was like ointment on a wound. It soothed and healed. She was seen and loved by a God who never changed; she was no longer alone.

But at the door to Mother Fredda's turf-house, weight settled on her again. This new knowledge couldn't change Eric's destiny. Her shoulders stooped, and she sighed as she took the basket. She attempted a smile and blinked hard. "Thank you."

Samuel didn't move. "You mentioned a friend who's close to death. Do not be afraid, Astrid. Do you believe in my God?"

With tears forming in her eyes, she nodded.

"Then pray. He hears, and He cares. I will pray as well."

"Does God really answer prayer?"

Samuel settled his eyes on her, and the confidence in them found her heart. "He does, Astrid. We only need to believe it, and He will give us what we ask. Pray to him. He will hear you. He may heal your friend, but if not, He is still good."

Somehow, these words also comforted. Astrid nodded, and Samuel left.

Chapter 16

Every day for the next couple of days, Astrid prayed over Eric before starting the rest of her day. She hid Samuel's words in her heart, repeating them to herself whenever fear crept in. It was like a new weapon against a brutal enemy.

Gudrid expressed surprise at each visit. No one survived the plague this long, she said. This gave Astrid hope, and she spent more and more time with Eric until she neglected going to the wharf and homework was in danger of being forgotten. Her finished fabric was piled in a corner of her house and collected dust, and the new hole in her kirtle sleeve was ignored.

Bertha came to Mother Fredda's longhouse and planted herself in front of Astrid, who was sweeping furiously so she could be with Eric. "Can you come to the wharf with me today?" Bertha asked. "You're not earning anything, and staying inside will make you listless. Already you've grown pale."

Astrid gave her floor a final sweep and leaned the broom against the wall. Her gaze flickered to the door, then back to Bertha, who watched her expectantly. "I can't, Bertha, I need to..."

"Eric can wait. You must keep up some regularity in your life. Trust in God, as you say you do."

Another glance at the door. Astrid squirmed under the searching stare. Finally, she sighed. "Fine, but real fast." She snatched up a basket and stuffed some fabric in it, puffing dust into the air. Sneezing and eyes watering, she backed into her room to grab her cloak with the conviction that her home needed more care than she was giving it. When she returned to Bertha, her friend was smiling. Astrid forced the corners of her mouth to lift. "Let's go."

Bertha nodded and put an arm around Astrid's shoulder. Astrid nuzzled Bertha's shoulder in a silent thank-you, realizing how much she'd missed Mother Fredda's touch and embrace. Thus, they went down the road to the wharf, where they pushed their way, single file, through the swarming crowd to the first merchant they could find who wasn't surrounded.

"Have you wares to sell?" the man asked, sizing them up.

Astrid stepped forward and set her basket on a crate. Taking the top fabric, she unfolded it and let the merchant inspect her work.

"Finely woven with wool," she said, "and will not tear easily. It is double-stranded to add strength and set tightly together. Yet it lays well, and would make excellent jerkin cloth."

The merchant felt it between his fingers and peered closely. He looked up. "How much are you asking for it?"

Astrid named her price, and the man's mouth screwed into a mocking grin. He objected, and Astrid named a lower price. He inspected another cloth, then turned to his own wares.

"I'll take two in exchange for some of my own things. They come from Cooray, which is east of here."

Astrid's body chilled. Her voice came quieter than she intended. "How does the island fare?"

The merchant shook his head as he dove into his crate and spread items on top of each other. "Very poorly. The Danes wiped them off the island in a bloody war, and Jarl Holskuldr has set up his own meeting hall there."

"Are all the people dead?"

"Oh, no. A few survived. Danes live there mostly, and they make life hard for the people of Cooray. But, Holskuldr has brought more trade to the island, and that was how I was able to pick up these." He spread a handful of silver brooches on the crate. Polished stones winked in their settings. "Two per fabric," he said, waving his hands over them.

Astrid stared at the brooches, instead seeing Holskuldr's eyes, reflecting orange flame like the stones reflected the sun. She turned her head away and her stomach soured.

Words tumbled from her mouth. "I'm sorry, not today. Just silver."

Grumbling, the merchant paid her, and a customer stepped up.

Bertha touched her arm, but Astrid flicked her hand away. She fled the suffocating crowd and stopped short just outside it. Red edged her blurred vision, and she could barely force air through her tight throat. She bumped against a barrel and leaned against it. A shadow fell over her as Bertha caught up.

"He doesn't know."

Astrid spoke through clenched teeth, trying to filter out the bitter tone saturating her voice. "How could he? Yet he talked lightly. It's no laughing matter. My family was killed, my village destroyed, and that—that—son of Hel is prospering. And no one can stop him." She dug her fingernails into the barrel's splintery wood and wished it were Holskuldr.

"Samuel spoke to my family yesterday. He... he said his God is a God of love. If you believe in His God, is hating the Danes like this the right thing to do?"

"Don't bring God into this. He has nothing to do with it." Astrid turned away and pressed a hand to her temple. "I vowed to avenge my family, and I will not go back on it." She shoved herself from the barrel and tried to clear her mind with a breath. It only fed the bursting energy surging like fire. "I'm done trading. You can stay if you want." She stepped forward and let her strides lengthen, venting herself through her legs and into the ground, then stopped and looked back.

Bertha stood alone beside the barrel, watching her. Her lips were pressed together, like Mother's when vexed, and her brows were knit. Wind whipped her braids around her shoulders, and her skirts billowed around her ankles. She hugged her basket handle to her chest.

A sob caught between Astrid's lips, and she lowered her head. She went back to Bertha on shaking legs and stood before her, eyes fixed on her boots. Slowly, she looked up. Bertha looked full in her face. The gaze tugged at Astrid's chest. A lump formed in her throat, and she had to raise her voice to speak through it.

"—I'm sorry, Bertha. It's just..."

Bertha flung an arm around her and pulled her close, her smooth cheek pressing against Astrid's. "I understand. It hurts me to see you like this."

Nodding, Astrid pulled away. Wind blew ice-cold on her face. Drawing a hand over her wet cheek, she mumbled, "I need to be alone."

Bertha's arm slid from her shoulder, leaving it cold. Astrid turned away and forced her feet down the road, which lengthened with every step. She quickened her pace, but time skittered to a stop, and her steps took much longer than they should have. Pressure formed in her chest, and her vision blurred. Astrid dragged a sleeve across her eyes. Her house came into sight. She felt her way to the door and pushed it open.

The dark interior swallowed her up as she stumbled inside and dropped her basket onto the floor. She bumped into the table, and her leg smarted. The table's worn surface was smooth under her hands. Hardwood lent a feeling of security, and she leaned against it, breathing deep, and let her head drop. Memories encircled her, swords flashed around her, and in the middle of it all was the dagger-sharp image of Holskuldr.

She gripped the table. She panted and shook her head, trying to clear her mind. Her ears rang, but above it came the ever-soothing sound of the ocean. The gray wooden walls of the cabin were suffocating. Corners swallowed up the light streaming through the door. She whirled and ran.

She ran down the streets, brushing past people before they could say anything. If they did, she would explode.

Not far, now. Astrid tripped over several chickens, who protested loudly, and sprawled on the ground. She scowled, picked herself up, and kept going.

Past the wharf, past the last houses, farther from the voices of the village, then, at last, sand shifted under her feet. She stumbled toward the water lapping on the shore.

The sky was gray as smoke, and so was the water. The sand was pale yellow-gray, like an old woman's hair. Wind whipped the waves high and sent them crashing down. Foam sprayed toward the shore, reaching.

Astrid picked up a rock and threw it as hard as she could. It plunked into the water, and the ocean swallowed it up. Another wave crashed, this time so close to shore that the spray wet her face.

"You, too?" she screamed. The wind dried her lips and carried the words away.

She fell to her knees and planted her fists into the gritty sand. Tears began to flow, and sobs shook her body. She hid her face in her hands until the tears wouldn't come anymore.

Finally, the sobs ceased. Hiccupping, she brushed the hair from her face and drew her sleeve across her eyes.

A faint beam of sun broke through the clouds and fell on the water.

A little longer, and Astrid rose and turned back to the village. As she neared Eric's house, Gudrid was leaving. Astrid grabbed her sleeve.

"How is he?"

"Steadily sinking, Astrid." Gudrid's shoulders drooped. "I'm afraid he can't hold on much longer. His body's too weak."

"But..."

"I know. He's held on well so far, but he simply can't keep going." Gudrid smiled weakly, grimly, wanting to say something encouraging but couldn't find any. "I'm sorry."

Astrid couldn't respond through her tight, aching throat. Gudrid gave her shoulder a quick squeeze before slipping past and continuing down the lane.

The Creator-God didn't hear, either. But she had believed! Clung to it, to the promise that He would hear and respond. He didn't. She was forsaken once again.

Pressing a hand to her mouth, Astrid staggered to Eric's house and let herself in as she had for the last two weeks. Harald was sitting before the empty fire pit, his weathered face in his hands. Slipping past him, Astrid pushed the curtain aside and knelt by Eric's bed.

This time, she didn't pray. What was the use? God didn't hear. Didn't care. It was all fake. She wouldn't be accepted into Valhalla after all. Neither would Eric.

Astrid took Eric's hand and stared into his face. There was no going back. Things would never be the same after he died. Memories of her mother and father singing together, of laughing Sven, of the gurgling baby, of Mother Fredda, came unbidden, forbidden. She couldn't bear to lose anyone else.

Through her dull fingers, she felt Eric's pulse. So low! She leaned against the bed. Softly, the words from the passage Samuel had read to her came to mind. Ask, and it shall be given to you.

Ask.

A bitter taste crept up her throat. She had asked scores of times, only to find God didn't hear. Hope dashed to pieces.

Tears slipped down her cheeks and fell on her hand. She wiped them on her kirtle. Throwing her head back, she cried, "God, Samuel says you love me, that you care. I've tried, but I cannot believe it anymore. What do you want me to do?" Words choked. She felt like she was being strangled. She pressed Eric's hand to her lips and cradled it.

"Believe."

She looked up and blinked hard, trembling. It was the same voice that had spoken to her before.

"I make all things new."

The fingers twitched and closed over hers. A deep breath came from the bed. Astrid's eyes flew to Eric's face. The sunken eyes quivered and opened a slit. They widened and focused on her. Color crept into his hollow cheeks. The corners of his mouth upturned.

"Astrid."

His voice was small and so rough it scraped her chest. A sob racked her body, and she lay her head on the bed and cried. Eric's hand stroked her hair.

After that, Eric improved steadily. By the end of the week, he was sitting up and talking, all infection gone. The moon waned from full to new, and snow and ice melted away, and Eric was up again, gripping furniture for support. Astrid walked with him, letting him lean on her shoulder. She thought she loved him when he was ill, but now?

She glanced up at him, at his still-hollow cheeks, at the thinned blond hair falling to his shoulder. Her heart raced. Now, more than ever.

During these walks, she told him all about the Christian God and how she had prayed for his healing.

She looked up into his face. "What do you make of it?"

Eric focused on his steps, right, left, right, left, painfully slow. The pause before his answer was equally slow. "Samuel is right," he said. "The God you prayed to healed me. I am in His debt." He raised his eyes to the sky. Wind tousled his hair. "My life belongs to Him, and I pray Christ will find it acceptable to him."

His gaze dipped to hers, tender. "Do you feel differently about me than before?"

Astrid tipped her head back, a smile on her lips. She offered no words, knowing the look would be enough. Eric lowered his head. Slowly, giving her time to push away, he bent down. She met him eagerly and sealed her affections with a kiss.

Chapter 17

"They'll be suspicious of us for sure after this," said Astrid, glancing at the crowd of karls gathered on the bank of the lake and drawing her cloak around herself. It was a dismal day with gray clouds, gray water, and naked gray trees that the tiny green buds couldn't cover yet. The snow was gone, but a cold edge in the air forced everyone to bundle in cloaks and shawls.

"Why's that?" asked Eric. He stood next to her with Bertha, Haakon, Fredissa, Erlin, Harald, and others set apart from the crowd of villagers.

"They will think we've gone mad. No one goes to a lake to get dunked in the water for religious purposes."

Eric shrugged and looked unconcerned. "If they ask about it, we'll be able to explain God to them. And maybe then they'd listen."

Astrid pursed her lips and nodded, trying to act as calm as him.

"Personally, I'm glad the traitors are gone," whispered Haakon, beside her. "Who knows what trouble they'd stir up if we did this while they were still here."

Astrid nodded and focused on Samuel, who stood in front of them.

"Is everyone ready?" he asked.

There were murmurs all around Astrid, and she herself could hardly raise her voice above a whisper. The weight of stares from the Karls intensified.

"Then who'd like to come first?" Silence. Wind moaned through the bare wood, and fabric rustled with uneasy shifting. Samuel looked the gathered people in the eye, one at a time, and Astrid could hardly meet his squarely without shrinking into the thick folds of her cloak.

Eric stepped forward. "I will." Samuel smiled and led the way into the water.

It swirled around them in gray eddies and rose to their waists. A short distance from the bank, Samuel laid his hand on Eric's shoulder, and they stopped. After a few whispered words, Eric nodded and crossed his arms over his chest. Samuel moved behind him and held onto his wrists with one hand and put the other on his shoulder.

A wind blew, and Astrid drew her cloak closer around her and shivered. The water must be ice. Coming out again wouldn't be any more pleasant, with the sun hidden behind thick clouds.

Samuel raised his voice. "Our Lord Jesus Christ, before he ascended to heaven, commanded his followers to make disciples from all nations, and to baptize them as a symbol of their obedience to Christ and of the new life He gives them. I now baptize you, Eric, in the name of the Father, of the Son, and of the Holy Spirit." Samuel tilted Eric back into the water and pulled him out again.

Eric rose, shivering and wiped the water from his face. Samuel clapped him on the back; Eric returned it heartily, grinning in spite of the water rolling off him, and waded toward the bank. Erlin pulled him up by the hand as Eric climbed up from the water, then the jarl climbed down to meet Samuel.

On solid ground again, Eric grinned bigger than he had ever before. It made his mouth look absurdly wide. Astrid tried to hide a giggle in the folds of her cloak, but Eric raised a brow and his grin widened so it nearly split him asunder.

"How dare you laugh at me, you little impudence!" he teased as he shook water from his hair like a dog. Before she could respond, he kissed her. The energy passing through his touch made her heart skitter.

"Eric, I'm surprised at you."

They turned to see Haakon standing behind them, his eyes dancing, and Bertha beside him smiling and nodding. Astrid shyly pulled from Eric's soaking arms.

"Surprised at what, Haakon?"

"Now it's both of you. I would have thought you'd rebel before letting him kiss you."

Heat crept up Astrid's neck. She had been torn about how to announce her engagement to the jarl's family, especially to Bertha and the jarl himself, and felt cornered. But before she could say anything, Eric left her to help a drenched Erlin up the steep banks.

When Erlin had rubbed his hair and face with a drying cloth, had seen Astrid's hot cheeks and Haakon's mischievous grin, and asked what happened, Eric laid his hand on Astrid's shoulder and replied:

"She has agreed to marry me."

Harald grunted and crossed his arms over his broad chest, and his beard lifted. Bertha and Haakon looked at Erlin in surprise, and Fredissa went to her husband's side.

Erlin held up his hand and said, "Harald spoke to me, and I made no objection."

Bertha threw her arms around Astrid and Eric, regardless of the state of Eric's clothes. "I'm so happy for you!"

"You're not upset?" Astrid asked.

"Not at all!" Another squeeze.

"But I thought...you..."

Bertha let them go and took both of Astrid's hands. "I'm happier that you're together than I could be with him." Here she blushed and hugged Astrid again. Over her friend's shoulder, Astrid could see Erlin shaking Eric's hand and Fredissa saying something. She was relieved.

Samuel called from the water, "Is anyone coming, or should I leave?"

Bertha let her go, and laughter rippled from the people around Astrid. She unclasped her cloak and handed it to Bertha, and picked up a heavy blanket to hand to Eric.

"Do you want a blanket?"

"I'll be fine," Eric said with a grin. "I sometimes stand in the winter ocean for net fishing."

Astrid dropped the blanket with a laugh and started down the lake's slippery sides. Eric grasped her hand to steady her.

"I'm coming," Astrid called.

Cold water sent a painful jolt up her body and plastered her skirt to her legs. She gasped and struggled toward Samuel. He pulled her forward and turned her away from him, crossing her arms over her chest as he had with Eric. Then he said the same words he had before and tipped her back.

Swirling water rushed around her as she plunged down, and rushed away as she came back up. Astrid gasped and pushed her matted hair from her face. After giving Samuel a quick hug, she struggled to shore, dragging the weight of her tangling skirts. Eric had to pull her up.

When all the baptisms were done and Samuel at last scrambled onto dry land, purple and shaking violently, he spread his hands wide and said, "Praise be to God, who has brought us out from darkness and into His marvellous light!"

"Amen!" Erlin shouted. The others joined the echo reflecting off the water. Eight of them were baptized that day, and they prayed many more would follow.

*****

The next morning, Erlin made his way through the busy streets on his way to the woods, where Samuel had agreed to meet him that day. There was a nip in the air, and the cold wind cut through his layers. Erlin adjusted his fur cloak and looked up at the white sky. The clouds had covered it like a blanket for the past week, yet no snow had fallen so far. But birds flew low in the sky, skimming over the longhouses' thatched roofs. The snow wouldn't wait long.

Erlin had wanted to wait until spring to build a church building, but Samuel insisted, "A building set apart for learning and teaching the Scriptures would help greatly. There, more people could gather than in a house."

"What about the Tingstead?"

Samuel hesitated, and Erlin realized why: the Karls would associate God with their superstitious practices that Samuel hated. Doing so wouldn't give Christianity a firm foundation in the village. So, reluctantly, Erlin had consented to look for a building place for the church. Samuel wanted it to be away from the village and in the quietness of the woods, but not so far that it was an inconvenience to walk there. This, Erlin heartily agreed to. It would be easier to worship God without distractions around them.

Now, a cluster of karls passed by Erlin, who nodded and kept on his way, but one of the men stopped him.

"Jarl," he said, "what was yesterday's ritual at the lake for?"

Erlin tried not to grin. He'd anticipated questions. "It was to show our submission to the Christian God, saying He is our only God and King."

The Karls glanced at each other and eyed Erlin just as they had when Samuel first arrived. Erlin swallowed.

"Are you not loyal to the king over us?" one asked.

"I am."

A couple of men muttered under their breaths, and Erlin stiffened.

"What I mean, friends," he said, "is the Christian God is King above any other king in this world, whether the king of Sweden or Norway or Wessex, and I must be loyal to him before any other." Most of the men nodded, much to his relief.

"You also said this Christian God is your only God," said another. "What about our gods? Do you simply throw them out?"

Erlin hesitated as he caught the suspicion on their faces again. The last thing he wanted was another uprising. "Yes... Well, not exactly. I am convinced the Christian God is the true God. But He says in his book, which I have been told much about, that we are not to worship any other gods besides him."

Creases appeared on several foreheads, along with frowns all around. Erlin straightened.

"I am your jarl, friends, and I only do what I think is best for myself, my family, and my people."

A hand rested on his shoulder, and Samuel spoke from behind him. "We can discuss this more at a later time."

The Karls nodded and left.

Erlin clapped Samuel on the back. "Thank you, my friend."

A smile broke over the Saxon's face. "It's the least I can do. Now, are you ready? I've been out, and I believe I've found the perfect spot. It only needs your approval."

"Lead on, then."

Samuel took Erlin to the eastern edge of the village and walked up a shallow hill that overlooked the ocean. It was a brief walk from the village, and a deep stream flowed close by. The top of the hill was perfectly flat. Soft grass and ground ivy covered it, and only a few bushes grew in the way.

Erlin dug his toe into the dirt. It was firm. "Good foundation," he said. "There will be no need to pack it down like some places. Not much clearing will need to be done, either."

Smiling and arms akimbo, Samuel looked over the hilltop. "God must have prepared it beforehand, it's such a perfect spot. Is it big enough for a meetinghouse the size of the Tingstead?"

"Plenty," Erlin replied, walking the hilltop's perimeter. He stopped at the edge and looked over his village. His people were fearful and superstitious, two things they denied. Anyone would rather die than admit fear. Christianity would be good for them. And, hopefully, it would prevent more uprisings. Or it could lead to more.

Construction began the next day. After much persuading and discussion, Erlin and Karsfien convinced five more men to help, and together they started removing brush and cutting down trees. After the brush was cleared, the men shouldered their axes and headed to the woods.

The men shouldered axes and split into the woods in twos. Karsfien with one, Samuel with another, Erlin with Eric, and two more together. Erlin and Eric took turns hacking at thick oak and pine trunks until the trees crashed to the ground, saving the birch for when they tired. In spite of the frigid north wind that swept the first snowflakes into their eyes, sweat trickled down their necks and slipped under their clothes, and they wiped their foreheads. Erlin's trousers froze to his legs as the temperature plummeted.

Work could not continue for the next several days as a snowstorm raged over the island, but on the third day, Erlin awoke to a calm, quiet wonderland. The sun broke through the departing clouds as he and the other men returned to the worksite. They worked quickly, felling the last trees and splitting them into beams and planks, and digging holes for the main pillars. A roaring fire was constantly maintained so the men could stop to thaw their frozen hands, faces, and feet. Many times, Erlin breathed thanks that the heat of a fire could drive away the cold around it.

When the holes were completed, pillars were inserted, and earth was packed in the spaces between them. Next, planks were wedged in vertical grooves on the pillars' sides to form the walls, and a capping plank was nailed in place, making everything secure.

An interior wall frame was then placed at the far end of the building to make a room for storing scrolls and other supplies.

The cold prevented work for the next week, but when the men returned, they went to work with vigour. Erlin smiled to himself as he nailed the roof frames together, knowing the others welcomed a reason to be outdoors as much as he. The six or so months of unbearable cold outside made living in the cramped, smoky longhouses nearly unbearable, especially to the men, who are used to being outdoors all day during the warmer months. Anything to get out doors changed up the monotonous winter routine the Karls dreaded. More men joined the work as time went on, also eager to escape the confines of their crowded homes. The pace quickened, and the roof frames were completed in good time. They were then lifted into place and secured. The roof was put on, and the interior wall was completed, too. Next, the door, fire pit, tables and benches were built.

Only one task remained, but the cold wouldn't allow it. All the cracks in the building had to be sealed with daub, a concoction of clay, dirt, and straw. Because the cold came in earnest now and froze any attempts at daub, it would have to wait until the weather thawed, or until spring came.

Chapter 18

Cold stung Astrid's cheeks as she left the wharf. She'd gone out to meet the few brave merchants who came to the island, to leave her longhouse if but for a moment. This winter was harsher than any she remembered before, and the cold, snow, and ice had kept her and the other villagers indoors for a month. Even so, she didn't stay outside for long. There was not much to choose from among the merchandise, and her fingers were quickly losing all feeling.

She pulled her shawl over her head, wrapped it and her cloak snuggly around her shoulders, and walked quickly to Mother Fredda's longhouse. There she set her basket on a shelf, flung her wraps onto the back of a chair, removed her gloves, and picked up the poker with clumsy hands. Her fingers felt like wood. With difficulty, she coaxed the fire back to life and held her hands over the flames with a sigh. Tingling started in her fingertips and spread upward past her wrists, then painful throbbing. She winced as she flexed her fingers.

When she could use her hands again, she removed one of her necklaces, the one with Thor's

Hammer. The one her parents had given her. Astrid rubbed her thumb over the engraved designs, over the runes spelling her name. Biting her lip and swallowing the lump in her throat, she unstrung the necklace until she reached the pendant, which she took off and tucked into her money pouch on her belt. Then she threw on her shawl and hastened out the door without stoking the fire; it shouldn't take long.

She followed the narrow streets to the edge of the village, where a lone house stood. Beside it was a shed with smoke drifting out of a hole in the top. The door of the shed opened, and a powerfully built man came out and went to the woodpile against the shed's side. Astrid lifted her skirts just enough to run up to him without letting in too much cold air.

"Greetings, Eystein," she called, her breath fogging.

The blacksmith straightened with an armload of firewood and smiled, widening his black beard. "Greetings, Kona. What can I do for you?"

Astrid pulled the pendant out and held it up with trembling fingers. She cleared her throat. "Can you make this into a Christian cross for me?"

Eystein shifted his hold on the wood and took the pendant, so small in his big hand. With a nod, he answered, "I'll have it ready by sunset tomorrow."

"Thank you." She gave a quick smile and hurried back to her cabin, where she worked until the Tingstead horn blew.

Astrid smiled when she heard it and filled her basket with food she'd prepared. Ever since her betrothal to Eric, Harald insisted she share their meals. Doing so helped Astrid get to know Harald better. Soon, however, she learned how to read the subtle changes in his calloused expression. A slight upturn of the mouth or a crinkle of the eyes meant he was amused or delighted, but if his mouth settled in a straight line, she knew to watch her words. Silence meant brooding or anger, unless he gave a faint, rumbling chuckle.

On her way to Eric's longhouse, Astrid passed the Tingstead. Its carved doors and sturdy walls were the same, but the fire pit in front of the meeting hall was changed. The sacrificial fire pit had been removed; in its place was a new fire pit, used only for celebrations.

In the two months since the baptisms, so much had changed, and it wasn't just the Tingstead. The people themselves had changed. They bundled in cloaks, blankets, furs, and shawls to hear Samuel's short meetings in the new church building, and at first, many karls came out of curiosity or suspicion. But the more Samuel taught the book of God, the more the people listened with genuine interest. Many went away speechless, reconsidering their prejudice against the Saxon and returning to hear more.

Eventually, Samuel began translating his scrolls into the villagers' language. This was a lengthy process, so for those who wanted the book of God right away, he taught them to read the Greek scrolls. Doing so proved more challenging than anyone anticipated, but the prospect of reading the scrolls spurred them on. The reading study grew as villagers tired of table games as the dreary winter months dragged on. Such joy when Samuel finished the first chapter of Saint John's Gospel! More villagers came, first out of curiosity, then out of hunger to learn more. Learning the book of God gave them peace and joy.

Astrid inhaled the burning cold air. Peace. She reached for where the Thor's Hammer usually hung. Peace overflowed the hollow her questions made, but it didn't reach the strain that drew her eyes toward the sea.

A shadow fell across the ground, and Eric stood by her side. A smile lit up his face, and he held out his hand. "Were you waiting for me?"

Sighing, she gave him a smile and put her hand in his. "No, just thinking."

"Good things?" he asked as he led her away from the Tingstead.

She shrugged. "Mostly." As Eric opened his mouth, she continued. "Is your father home?"

Eric glanced her way. "He should be."

"Good. Hopefully, I can help prepare the meal. It pains me to see him do it. Cooking's women's work, you know."

"He's used to it." Eric pulled Astrid to a stop, caught her other hand so she couldn't turn away, and looked into her eyes. "Something's bothering you, Astrid. Why don't you tell me? Your struggles are my struggles, your pains my pains." He paused, then asked in a low voice, "Is it your family?"

Astrid stared down at the strong brown hands holding hers, like Father's when he found her alone with her tears. She blinked and looked back up. Eric's eyes were glassy as he searched her face.

"—I'm sorry, Eric," she whispered. "I've kept my thoughts to myself for so long, it's hard to share them."

"You're not alone anymore. I'm here for you in good and bad; don't you know that? We're in it together."

She dropped her eyes again, and memories of the attack ran through her mind. "You wouldn't understand."

"Not fully, but I do a little. I never knew my mother."

It wasn't the same. But could it be enough?

Eric cupped her face and turned it up. He kissed her forehead. "What is it?"

Her eyes filled at the creases forming on his forehead and at the memories still running through her mind, and inexplicable pain stabbed her. Internally writhing, she opened her mouth to explain but found herself saying, "It's nothing. It'll pass."

Eric eased back and withdrew his hands from her face, slowly nodding. Then he gently took her basket and wrapped an arm around her waist. As they started forward, he said, "Come. Father will be waiting."

The next afternoon, as Astrid was walking home from the wharf, someone called her name. She turned. It was Eystein, carrying something in his hand. When he reached her, he stopped and held it out: a small silver cross pendant.

"Here's your cross, mær. It was a joy to make."

Astrid put out her palm, and the blacksmith pressed the cold silver onto it. Delicate curves adorned the cross, and her own name was inscribed lengthwise. Astrid ran her thumb over it. "Thank you," she said, looking up. Eystein nodded, gave a good day, and left.

Astrid stood still, staring at the cross in her hand, and slowly turned and went home. There, she set her basket aside, placed the pendant on the table, and grabbed a shallow bowl from the shelves. In the bowl lay the pieces of her necklace. Pressing her lips together, she strung the necklace back together with the cross in the centre and hung the necklace in its place between her brooches.

As she put on the necklace, her shoulders rounded and a weight dropped in her chest. She grasped the cross and swallowed as a lump rose in her throat. Her eyes stung. The Thor's Hammar was gone.

With a sigh, she turned away from the table and toward the food she'd prepared earlier for the evening meal: broiled meat. Now for the bread. Astrid took out the bag of flour and set it on the table, then reached for a bowl. Her fingers instead went to her necklace and wrapped around the cross. Her chest tightened.

"Your struggles are my struggles, your pains my pains. You're not alone anymore. I'm here for you in good and bad; don't you know that? We're in it together."

A sigh vented the pressure building in her chest. She didn't have to keep everything to herself any longer. The thought both thrilled and frightened. Her eyes flickered to the door, but she turned her back to it and poured flour into the bowl.

Flour spilt onto the table. Biting her lip, Astrid scooped it into the bowl and wiped her hands on her smokkr. Her hands shook as she faced the shelves and scanned them. All the bags looked the same, and their faded labels were illegible in the faint light; squinting made her eyes hurt, and she stepped away with a scowl. The bread wouldn't be made in time at this rate.

The silver was between her fingers again, no longer cold.

She snatched her shawl from the chair she'd thrown it on and wrapped it and her cloak around her shoulders as she crossed to the door. Icy wind snatched her breath away as she plunged out of the longhouse. Wind whipped her hair around her face and forced up her skirt. She shivered and quickened her pace.

At Eric's longhouse, the fire was stoked, and no one was around. Only when she had turned away did she remember Eric telling her he'd need to spend a day fishing soon.

The talking and shouting of the wharf reached her before she saw it, a rare thing in wintertime. She shuffled her frozen feet faster past the last longhouses and shielded her face from an icy blast that hit her. In the center of the wharf was a swarming crowd pressing together, both for warmth and for items being passed around. Squeezing among the villagers, many of whom held slippery cod against themselves, she broke into the middle where Eric and his fellow fishermen, in hats and countless layers, sold cod as quickly as possible. Five brimming baskets and the eager villagers surrounded them.

Tendrils of their fogging breath swirled around them as they worked.

Now that Eric was in front of her, she twisted her fingers and fidgeted. She glanced down the wharf and back to Eric, down at her feet and back again.

At last, the baskets were emptied and the crowd dispersed. Eric straightened, face red, and saw her. A crooked, tired smile upturned his mouth. But after another look at her, a shadow fell over his face.

"Excuse me for a moment," he said to his companions. They shot a glance at Astrid and continued their work.

Eric took Astrid's hand and led her away. When they had left the wharf behind, Eric brushed hair from Astrid's face and cupped her chin, looking into her eyes. "What is it?"

She took a breath and exposed the cross, holding it between her fingers. "Do you see this?"

"Isn't it new?"

"Yes." When an amused smile passed over Eric's face, she continued, "That's not why I came. It's... you told me to share what's on my mind. My family, Eric. Holskuldr still... I can't..." Her throat hurt. She swallowed and opened her mouth, but couldn't force words beyond it. This was ridiculous.

Eric dropped his eyes and slowly took her other hand. He kept his eyes on the ground, and his brows knitted.

She tried again, and her words came out in such a croaky way that it sounded like a sick chicken. "I vowed to avenge them. And... I can't go back on it."

Eric sighed and let his arms hang. "Justice is well and good, but this sounds more like revenge."

"It is not," she snapped with a rush of heat in her face. "And you know what happens to people who don't keep their vows."

He ran his fingers through his hair. "If a vow goes against what God said in His book, you shouldn't keep it."

"Does it?"

Another sigh. "I don't know."

Seething with the effort it took to keep her voice under control, she answered, "Why bring God up when you don't know? What does He have to do with it?"

Shaking his head, he dropped his hands again. "Look, I don't want to argue with you. You came to me, and I'm trying to help you. Please." He extended a hand. The look of hurt on his face was akin to the day she'd rejected him.

She winced, and her vision blurred. Blinking, she took his hand in both her own. "I don't want to, either. I'm sorry for getting worked up that way. Let's not talk of it anymore."

Eric pulled her close, and Astrid hid her frozen, tear-stained face in his woolen tunic. There was nothing Eric could do to help, nothing to take away the ache in her chest, nothing he could say to make her feel better. She was only giving him something to worry about. And the bread would've been done by now if she'd stayed home. But, listening to their hearts merge into a soothing beat, the pain was easier to bear. How often had she let her parents comfort her like this?

"Why do you hurt yourself, Astrid?" Eric murmured. His warm breath brushed her forehead. "It wasn't your fault, you know."

"It was! It was!" Her voice cracked.

"How? One girl couldn't stand against the Danes."

She could have saved her brother from dying, she could have insisted that Mother stay with them. Things could have been different, but she couldn't tell him this.

"You need to let go," he said. "What are you holding onto? You did nothing wrong."

"What about God, then?"

"Never! Didn't Samuel say He is perfect?"

She raised her head, and her thoughts came tumbling out. "Perfect doesn't mean cruel. He didn't need to let Holskuldr kill my family. That man—"

He pressed a cold finger to her lips. "If he hadn't, you would not have met me. You wouldn't have learned about God. Good came of it, don't you see? Or is your past blinding you?"

Astrid didn't try to answer. She lay her head back on his chest and squeezed her eyes shut to keep tears from escaping. To not know Eric... but it wasn't worth the death of her family. No matter what he said, the raid was her fault, and the ache wouldn't go away unless she did something to make it right.

Eric stirred. "I should get back to work. Do you want me to walk you home?"

Astrid shook her head as he let her go, leaving her cold. She wrapped her arms around her middle. "I'll go by myself. I've kept you from work long enough."

Eric ran his forefinger along her jaw and cupped her chin. Slowly, he drew her forward and kissed her forehead. "I always have time for you, Astrid."

She stood on tiptoe and brushed her lips on his cheek as he straightened. "Thank you, Eric."

A snowflake fluttered past her eyes, and they fell thick and fast until nearby longhouses faded into white blurs.

"Sæl, Astrid," called Eric, pulling his hat down and walking away. His boots crunched in the grainy snow.

"Sæl."

Wind whipped and snow swirled. She shivered and gathered her cloak and shawl and turned her back on Eric's fading form.

***

The next day, the sun broke through the clouds. Snow began to melt and dripped off the roof, splashing into the back of Erlin's clothes if he crossed the threshold at the wrong time.

The church longhouse could be finished, and then they could meet without freezing. Excited, Erlin rounded up the men who'd helped him with the church building, and they got to work making daub. A crowd of children watched as they mixed it up, and Erlin put them to work shoving the sticky mixture between planks while the men made the last repairs. The plan worked well, though the builders had to watch out for little fingers and heads.

Erlin was standing back to think of what had to be done next when squeals of delight caught his attention. Several boys were rubbing the daub on each other's faces, and one threw a mud ball at another, who squealed. The rest noticed what was going on, and a mud battle broke out. Mud balls shot from muddy fingers, whizzing here and there, landing on the building, workers, and little warriors. Erlin ducked and dodged as he made his way back to the building, but couldn't evade a big splash on his back.

"Hey, boys!" Karsfien yelled, hurrying toward them. "This is not a battlefield. This is the building place of a church or the Christian God. Go to the stream and wash up." The only answer he received was a mud pie in the face. An explosion of laughter came from the warriors, and a roar from the workers.

Karsfien wiped grit from his eyes and grinned, winking at Erlin, who chuckled.

"Well, then," Karsfien said, walking toward the stream, "if you want to fight, let's use this so the daub isn't used up." He reached into the icy stream, pulled out a handful of mud, and threw it at the nearest boy. A stampede rushed to the stream, and mudballs once again filled the air, thick as hail. The other men, full of energy from the time they spent indoors, joined in the fun. It didn't take long before Erlin and even Samuel were in the middle of it.

*****

Ah, we shall drink

Dear draughts and lovely,

Though we have lost

Both life and lands;

Neither shall any

Sing a song of sorrow.

Humming a line of an old saga, Astrid sauntered up the path to the building site. At the edge of the woods, she turned around and looked back. The village lay a little below her on the shore, edged by the sea. Thatched roofs, grayed by the sun, huddled around the streets.

She breathed the salty air. She was accepted, finally part of the ant hill down below. But at home? No, not yet. Nothing could replace the home she'd lost.

Shuddering, she hurried up the trail. So intent was she on her destination that she didn't hear the unusual din until too late. She found herself in the middle of the mud fight, plastered with icy, watery mud that ran down her kirtle. In vain, she sheltered her face with her hands and tried to orient herself until a grip caught her arms and dragged her out of harm's way. When it was safe and she looked up, Eric's laughing eyes met hers. They were the only part of him not covered.

"Wow," she exclaimed, wiping grime from her face. "How did that happen?"

Eric laughed. "It started with a little boy rubbing mud on his face. Who knew it would get this out of hand? It's like a summer battle game." He slapped his caked jerkin, and Astrid backed away from the flying debris.

She giggled, "It'll take a lot to get you looking yourself again."

Eric grinned and looked down at himself. "I do look like something from the bottom of the lake, don't I?"

Haakon ran up, dodging dozens of mud balls, and panted, fun sparking in his eyes, "Just in time, Astrid! Boy, is this fun!" What he was about to say next, Astrid never knew, because mud hit the back of his head and he tore after his fleeing enemy.

The Tingstead horn sounded. Everyone froze simultaneously and looked in its direction, except for one boy, who took this opportunity to pie another in the face.

"Well, men," said Erlin, who was completely covered from head to toe, "we cannot return to the village as we are. We will wash in the stream and change into fresh clothes when we get there. That includes the children," he added, turning to a child standing near him. The little boy grinned, and the dried mud on his face cracked.

After a few minutes of frantic scrubbing and scowling, the wet but clean karls marched back to the village. As they entered, villagers stopped and stared. Astrid smothered a grin. No wonder they did, for the workers' clothes were disheveled, and some of them left a trickle of water behind as they walked.

When Astrid told Bertha what had happened later that day, her friend laughed until tears ran down her rosy cheeks.

"Oh, goodness!" Bertha exclaimed while wiping her eyes, "That has convinced me that we can all start having fun, no matter how old we are!"

When the Karls met the next day to continue building, Samuel gave them their instructions and concluded by saying, "And this time, no mud battles!" The men roared as they picked up their tools and went to work. Several days later, the longhouse was finished.

Next, Samuel asked the town carpenter to build chairs, a desk, and a table for the building; soon, the decorative articles began appearing in the wooden structure. Meanwhile, Samuel worked hard preparing his room and the things he would need for the classes he planned on holding.

Everything was complete, and Erlin stood in front of the church with Karsfien, looking over the sea of faces gathered on the snow-covered hilltop. Everyone at Trygvey was there, huddled in cloaks and kirtles and shawls of bright green, brilliant yellow, and bold blue, contrasting with dull browns and grays of other garments and the trees around them, whispering in hushed tones while the half-frozen stream gurgled below. The faces were happy and eager, their shining eyes taking in the church, the wood, Karsfien, and Erlin himself; in spite of the excitement, Erlin stiffened upon noticing half a dozen scowls at the back of the gathering. He shifted and glanced at Karsfien, who observed the spotted sky and spice-scented evergreens without signs of unease.

Samuel rounded the longhouse and stopped before Erlin with a nod and salute.

"Are you ready?" Erlin asked.

Samuel nodded, and Karsfien shook himself as if from deep thought to raise his hand. Whispers stopped; Erlin nodded to Samuel and watched the villagers for any unwanted signs.

Samuel cleared his throat. "I am happy to be standing in front of the completed church today." A loud cheer interrupted him, and he continued when it died away. "All praise belongs to God for the work He has done by creating this perfect spot and by letting you receive His words. So you do not forget, here's a reminder for you—" He pointed up at the space above the door where runes or tapestries were sometimes put. Here were boldly carved words in the people's language which he read aloud, "' He made us, and we are His. We are His people, the sheep of His pasture.'" Turning to the crowd, he spread his hands wide. "God's son, Jesus, came to make us God's children, His sheep. The church is now open!"

He motioned to Erlin, who turned from the smiling people with a lighter heart than he had a moment ago to grasp the big metal handle and pull the door open. The people surged forward and entered like a flood, even the scowlers, who didn't appear so adverse.

When the crowd was through, Erlin entered. Inside were four rows of tables and benches set up longways like in the Tingstead, only smaller, and a fire pit and a stool were in the very centre. Along the walls were tapestries, scrolls with large writing nailed open; a shelf on the right was filled with boxes and stacks of scrolls, and a wooden carved cross hung on the back wall. To the left of the cross was the door that led to Samuel's room.

One by one, the villagers admired the room and its articles, asked questions, and left.

Erlin was the last to leave. When the last villager was gone, he let his shoulders relax and kneaded his tight, pounding temple with relief. The villagers had received it well so far. Hopefully, life would be more peaceful after this.

Samuel came up and offered his hand, which Erlin gripped heartily.

"Exciting day, Jarl," said the Saxon.

"Yes. I believe God, and this church, will be good for them."

An amused smile twitched at the corners of Samuel's mouth, and he nodded. "I believe it already has been."

Chapter 19

Astrid would always remember clearly the first time she saw a flower poking its purple head through a patch of snow at Trygvey. In contrast to the previous spring, this one was quiet, the kind of quiet where normal life rolled on but at such a leisurely pace that she noticed everything, and each detail was more beautiful than the last.

She almost dropped her basket at a glimpse of color while closing her door. Hastily, she put down her basket and crouched by the doorframe, from where a sweet fragrance drifted and carried the promise of spring. She shivered with delight as she gently brushed away the snow and gasped. Two more flowers were below it, making their way to the surface.

Over the next weeks, warmth drove away the cold, the harsh winds gave way to gentle breezes, and the glittering snow melted away. Astrid tracked mud into her house every time she entered it, and she was constantly scrubbing away mud stains from her clothing, but even that didn't diminish her enthusiasm. Spring was in the air, and soon they'd leave winter behind.

After rain, a sudden snowstorm, and more rain that washed the last remnants away, spring officially arrived.

Even though puddles of mud splattered the ground, Astrid hurried through her morning work. When work was completed, she took in her basket bags of seed Mother Fredda had harvested and went to the garden behind the house, stopping briefly at the split rail fence to lean her elbows against it. It hadn't been long before winter that she became more familiar with the layout of the plants. But now that she stood there, the layout was muddled. How had Mother Fredda arranged everything?

Astrid closed her eyes and tried to remember. The vegetables ran along the back side of the garden. The most used herbs (chamomile, and the like) were along the gate side, and a couple of seasoning plants grew along the left. But what about the front of the garden, up against the house? No matter how Astrid tried, she couldn't remember. What if it had been an early crop, and the house sheltered the plants?

She opened the gate and crouched by the plot up against the house, where she ran her fingers lightly over the dirt. Tiny green shoots were uncovered, and she touched them tenderly before moving on to another bed and picking up a couple of seed bags.

Soon she was absorbed in her task, and all the times she'd helped Mother plant the garden came back to her. Out of all her household tasks, planting had been her favorite. She loved the gritty coldness of the dirt between her fingers and the smell of fresh earth; Mother had loved it, too. Even though she had Hjordis and other thralls, Mother insisted on planting the garden herself.

A freshly plucked daisy landed in her lap, startling Astrid out of her thoughts.

"I see you're as busy as ever. Spring suits you."

Astrid looked up at Eric leaning against the fence. He was as ruddy as ever, and the smile on his face was so tender and sweet, Astrid felt the passing urge to kiss him. She ducked her head. "Thank you," she murmured.

"Is that the way you greet your husband?" he teased.

Astrid jumped up and threw her arms around his neck. "Oh, Eric, you know I'm always happy to see you! I was only concentrating for so long."

Eric pressed her to him, then let go to look at her work. "On gardening?"

"Mmm-hmm. I've always loved planting things. Did you see the flowers by my door?"

"I did, and I know a place where you can see even more. Do you want to come?"

"Would I! Wait a moment."

Astrid scooped up her bags of seed and basket and ran around the house. She placed them on the table, snatched up her cloak and pinned it, and ran back to where Eric waited for her. He held out his hand, and she slipped her hand into his.

"I'm ready," she sang.

He laughed. "Are you sure? Just wait 'til we get there. It'll take your breath away."

"How can you be sure?" Astrid teased.

He looked at her tenderly again, and it took all Astrid's restraint to keep from standing tiptoe and kissing him.

"I went there this morning to see if it was in full bloom yet, and it took *my own* breath away."

He led her straight to the woods and up a narrow path, each step stirring a cosy, old wood smell.

Slender leaves of grass poked up on either side of the trail. Here and there in the bare brown bush grew clusters of flowers, their color popping like a sunset against storm clouds. The evergreens stood out as brightly as ever with the tips of light green on the ends of their bristly branches, and the white birches looked slimmer than she remembered. At the end of every tree branch grew tiny, fuzzy, curled leaves. Sunlight streamed through the bare canopy and reflected purple on patches of shadowed snow that refused to leave.

"It's beautiful," she breathed.

He looked back with a smile. "We're not there yet."

They walked on in silence a little longer, then he stopped, stepped behind her, and placed his hands over her eyes. Astrid's pulse skittered.

"What are you doing?" she asked, laughing.

"Surprising you. It's better when you stumble upon it suddenly."

Some time later, he whispered, "We're here."

Astrid stopped, and he removed his hands. She gasped.

They were outside the caves in the clearing encircled by tall pines bright with new growth, with a brilliant blue sky above and the sun shining down, its light reflecting each tiny blade and glowing on every satin pedal of a pink, wild apple tree in full bloom, the dazzling white daisies, purple crocuses, bright irises, yellow coltsfoot, and purple liverwort growing among the trees. Bright green grass carpeted the ground. The heavenly smell of all the blooms was almost overwhelmingly sweet.

Astrid groped for Eric's hand, and their fingers entwined. He pulled her close, and she leaned against him.

His breath brushed her cheek. "So, are you breathless?"

"Completely," she sighed. Astrid blinked away the tears blurring her eyes. One escaped, and Eric wiped it away with the side of his calloused thumb.

"Tell me, Astrid, what is it?"

Astrid laughed shakily. "It's so beautiful," she whispered. "Can we just ignore the world and stay here forever?"

Eric chuckled. "Not forever. We have work to do."

Astrid groaned. "Don't talk of work right now. I can't *think* of working right now. Look at the sky, the trees, the flowers, everything. God created this spot, and all I want to do is enjoy it."

"There will be even more flowers next week. The poppies haven't come up yet, nor have the bluebells. Then there's the flowering trees. They have little buds right now, but they'll open up in a few days."

"Can we... could we..." She hesitated.

"Yes?" Eric nuzzled her hair.

"Could we be married here, when all the flowers are out?"

"I would love nothing better, but there is a lot of preparation to be done. We will discuss it with Father tonight."

"Oh!" A sudden thought struck her. "What about the dowry? And the bride price? I have no family."

Eric shrugged. "I already mentioned it to Father, and he said not to worry. All you own will come with you, and he said you are more than a dowry to him."

Her cheeks tingled. "He has changed."

"Yes," said Eric, nodding. "I think he's finally seeing the other side of life, the side with love and enjoyment and other 'soft' things, as he calls them. I think, since Mother died, he closed himself against them to keep himself from hurting."

"Did he ever remarry?"

"No. I asked him once if he would, and he glared and told me to get back to work. Mother's death was hard on him."

Astrid's throat throbbed. "I'm sorry," she murmured. "How... what happened, if I may ask?"

Eric paused and looked down; when he spoke, his voice was a whisper. "Fever, on a trip from Kaupang. I was a month old. Fredissa nursed me until I was old enough for Father to care for me alone."

Astrid reached up and stroked his face. It was wet. Eric took her hand and pressed it to his cheek. With a breath, he said, "I didn't mean to ruin our time here. But whenever I come here in the spring, I can't help but think of Mother. And wonder what she was like. How life would have been if she'd lived."

Astrid fought to keep her own tears under control. "You didn't ruin it, Eric. You said you're here for my struggles, and I'm here for yours. Love isn't one-sided, you know."

Eric embraced her, and this time, Astrid couldn't resist. She kissed his cheek, but Eric turned his head and met her lips.

A week later, in the peak of the blooming season, Eric and Astrid were married in the clearing outside the caves. Practically the whole village was there, but out of all the bright faces around them, their friends gave Astrid the most joy. Dancing, beaming Bertha, grinning Haakon, sweet Fredissa with Erlin's arm around her shoulders, Harald with his full beard lifted in a smile. Even amid the celebration, she silently remembered her family and Mother Fredda, wishing they could have been there.

After the ceremony, the two of them were left alone to wander as they pleased, bathed in a rosy, orange sunset and then under the stars, until late at night when Eric brought her into his home.

Either Harald had stayed awake or somehow awoke right before they entered, for he was at the doorway to greet them. He held out his arm. Astrid hesitated before letting him pull her into a big hug. With his protecting arms like Father's around her, something in her chest loosened.

"Welcome home, daughter," he said, with tears in his eyes and a tender smile she'd never before seen on him.

Chapter 20

The next morning, Astrid got to work at Mother Fredda's longhouse, sorting through everything within its walls. Doing so brought her to tears at the memories of the dear old healer, which in turn brought back memories of Mother and Father, Sven and Snorri, and poor Isar, all of whom she missed but, on this day, wanted to imagine being happy for her. Did they smile down on her from where they were, or did the lack of vengeance leave them frowning? This thought she pushed away.

Medicines were given to Gunhild, unnecessary cooking ware was sold, and the money given to Harald; everything was either kept, sold, or given away, until finally the longhouse stood empty and closed up, awaiting when someone would buy it.

This task was hardly done when a new feast, one of thanksgiving, was announced. There was some curiosity and argument concerning what to do about the spring feasts, since Erlin now followed Samuel's advice on feasts—as made clear by his order of a new way to celebrate Yule that winter—and the announcement of the new feast stirred great excitement in everyone, especially in those who believed the spring feasts would be abandoned.

Astrid worked hard with Fredissa and Bertha to prepare their share of food, partially because her cooking was still not up to her own standards, and partially because Fredissa wanted to take that time to spend with her. Ever since Astrid married, Fredissa, who'd always been a mother figure for Eric, became a mother also to Astrid, instructing and guiding her in the ways of managing a household. Between Fredissa's smiles, Bertha's laughter, Haakon's teasing and food sampling, and Eric's frequent visits, that festal preparation became a memory she'd hold close in her heart.

The day of the feast, Astrid, Eric, and Harald brought their food to the Tingstead. Inside, lamps flickered and the oblong fire blazed, golden light flickering on tapestries and furs which hung on the four walls, and over the crowded food, weighing down the hardwood tables. Honey cakes, several whole pigs, fish, boiled cabbage and beets, bread, mead, skyr, stews, berries. Sweet and savory smells, soupy and meaty smells, blended in an aroma so powerful one couldn't help *but* be hungry. Samuel opened the feast with a prayer, and everyone helped themselves, going from one table to the other as necessary, grabbing whatever they desired.

Astrid groaned as Eric piled more food on her overflowing plate. "Eric, I won't be able to eat it all!"

He grinned and heaped up his own plate. "I'll just eat whatever you can't."

"I can, too," said Haakon, leaning forward to talk around Bertha sitting at Astrid's left.

Bertha laughed. "You'll have enough work to do finishing *my* food," she said, poking her brother. He gave her arm a playful cuff. Astrid laughed. She never tired of their friendly buffeting.

Eric caught her hand as she reached for her spoon. "We've gone through some difficulties this year, but it was all worth it."

Astrid smiled up at him and relished the glow of love in his eyes. He leaned forward, but she hid her face, heart surging. Now was not the time for a kiss.

He was watching her for a response. She wished she could say it *was* all worth it, but burying Snorri, Holskuldr holding Father's sword, came back. She avoided Eric's gaze. "God has blessed me in many ways, and I could never thank him enough."

Once the feast was well underway, a hearty cheer sounded as a lyre and several flutes and drums were brought out. The first Karl, who took the lyre, strummed it a few times before beginning.

I dreamed a dream last night.

of silk and fair furs,

of a pillow so deep and soft,

A peace with no disturbance.

Astrid, among many, tapped and nodded to the beat, and everyone applauded when the man finished. The lyre was passed around until it reached another willing to play it.

Young and alone on a long road,

Once I lost my way...

People leaned forward excitedly as the Havamal was sung. Everyone knew it off by heart and listened intently to catch mistakes. But none were made, and the singer got through the song perfectly. His efforts were lavishly applause, and the lyre came to Astrid.

She stared at it, feeling its weight in her hands. As if it were yesterday, she remembered the times she sat and listened to Father play on his fiddle while Mother sang; her fingers tingled and she held the lyre quietly for a moment. Bertha reached for it, to pass it on, but Astrid couldn't give it up. With a small smile, she shook her head and pushed back her chair. Carefully, she held it in position and plucked the strings. The notes vibrated her fingers.

Astrid closed her eyes to let Mother's lullaby come back. Slowly, the words emerged from her memory and built upon each other like a child's toy blocks, and a thrill chilled her from head to foot. It took no trouble to sing the words she'd often heard.

Sleep, love, the sun has set.

Hear the breeze, ocean waves,

Close your eyes, rest on me

Feel my arms 'round you,

Sleep 'til dawning light

She passed the lyre to Bertha and scooted her chair in again, heart pounding and heat prickling her cheeks.

Eric squeezed her hand and whispered as the next song began, "That was a pretty tune, love."

"It was a lullaby Mother sang." Astrid surprised herself by blinking away tears. Eric gave her a look of compassion, but she swallowed and attempted a smile. "I'm fine," she whispered. Eric nodded and put his arm around her.

Samuel had the lyre now. He tested it, a little unsure, then strummed away.

I cried to my God for help.

From his temple, he heard my voice;

My cry came before him, into his ears.

Everyone turned to watch as Samuel continued, all quiet. They'd heard those words before from the scrolls he read to them, but here in the Tingstead, they sounded different. Like they belonged there. Astrid had goosebumps.

The earth trembled and quaked,

And the foundations of the mountains shook;

They trembled because he was angry.

Smoke rose from his nostrils;

Consuming fire came from his mouth,

Burning coals blazed out of it.

He parted the heavens and came down;

Dark clouds were under his feet.

Samuel finished amid great applause, and Astrid clapped until her palms stung.

The next song was a dance, and the flute and drum joined in. Villagers leapt from their chairs and joined together in the remaining spaces of the room. The ones left at the tables clapped in time. Eric caught Astrid's eye and grinned, for she was nodding and humming, and her foot tapped as if on its own.

"Do you know this one?" he asked.

Astrid laughed and tucked her feet under the bench. "Know it! I grew up on it." It was the first dance she learned, swung around the room in Father's big, strong arms with her legs dangling. Whenever the song was played at home, she could never help but join in the dancing.

Eric jumped up and pulled her to her feet. "No time to lose, then!" Astrid slipped her hand in his, and he whirled her into the ring without hesitation.

Astrid enjoyed every moment. She ended a spin and lifted her foot for a stomp, and the floor quaked beneath her as everyone brought their feet down at once. Take the hands of the people beside her, two steps to the right, tap front and behind, clap, spin, stomp, change places, take hands again. Adrenaline pumped through her veins as the tempo increased. Eric's smile flashed by as she spun. A thrill shot down to her very fingertips.

Bang!

The large double doors of the Tingstead burst open and hit the walls, and a man ran inside. The hall fell silent, and everyone stopped in confusion. Astrid tripped and staggered a few paces, ran into someone, and regained her balance.

"Jarl Erlin! Jarl Erlin!" He collapsed to his knees at the jarl's feet. Erlin lifted him up, set him in his place, and offered a cup, which the man slowly accepted with shaking hands.

Erlin waited for him to drink before asking, "What is it, Krake?"

"Danes," Krake gasped. "Danes are in sight, with longboats ready for war. Jarl, they are heading our way!"

Chapter 21

Astrid closed her eyes. The past rose before her in a smothering fog, like it had those long days on the boat. Once again, she was awakened by the bang of the door. Light and dark swirled around her as something soft and warm was pressed into her arms. Snorri. Mother dragged at her arm, pulling her away from the light.

Deep darkness smothered her, and the stench of rotting flesh and of blood filled her nostrils. Screams, guttural laughter, war chants and battle cries, roaring flames, pounded in her ears. She wanted to clasp her hands over them, but she had to hold Snorri. He was screaming above the noise. Nothing she could do could quiet him. Glittering swords and axes flashed around her, drawing ever closer. Astrid clutched Snorri to her chest and shied away, but a force hit her and left her arms empty.

"Take care of him"

Astrid pressed a fist to her chest to keep her heart from tearing from her chest.

Arms wrapped around her, pulling her to a warm body. She stiffened, but a tender hand cradled her head. Eric. She rested her head on his chest, listening to his heart beating, but this time it sounded like war drums.

Erlin's voice cut through the down-spiral, dragging her like the tide. "How many ships did you see, Krake?"

"About thirty, all small but for the jarl's."

A shield man for each warrior, and another man to shoot arrows. Roughly sixty men per boat. Though not the biggest boats, they still threatened the island's safety. The smaller, the swift and deadlier.

"To arms, men! To arms!" cried Erlin. At his word, Karls poured out of the Tingstead.

Astrid felt Eric breaking away from her grasp. She clutched at him. "You, too?"

Eric looked down at her, blinking. "Me too," he answered, caressing her cheek.

"Then may God be with you." Astrid wrapped her arms around his neck, trying to feel his warmth one more time. Eric kissed her fervently before running out the door.

Astrid bit her lip and watched the people leaving the building. The only place for her during the battle was at home, and that's where she headed, forcing her feet forward one step at a time. Her lungs couldn't keep up with her heart, and it left her breathless and lightheaded.

This could not be happening. Any moment, she'd wake up and find it a bad dream.

Only, she knew it wasn't.

In the village, women were scurrying around, collecting food and water and a few essentials, then leaving in groups headed for the woods. They were going to the caves.

Astrid straightened and wove her way through the crowd. Go home, get food and water, and go to the caves.

On her way, she passed armed men and ran to the Tingstead. Astrid looked after them and curled her hands into fists. At home, she'd done nothing to protect her people. If these were her people now, she had to protect them. Somehow.

"One girl couldn't stand against the Danes."

She shook her head.

"You need to let go. What are you holding onto? You did nothing wrong."

Why now? There was no time for such thoughts. Pushing Eric's words away, she picked up her skirts and ran all the way to her home.

Without stopping, she slammed into the door. It hit the wall with a bang. Astrid stumbled against the wall and gasped for breath. Harald had a hunting bow somewhere, but where? Surely she'd seen one.

Astrid searched along the wall, but no bow was to be found. Hesitating, she pushed the curtain to Harald's room aside. There was the bow, on a peg in the wall. A full quiver was on the floor under it. Astrid snatched them up and ducked out of Harald's room. At the sound of someone running outside, she hid in her room.

Someone ran into the house. From the footsteps, she knew it was Eric. He stopped at the side wall, and there was the scrape of leather against wood. He must have picked up his axe. He started running out when there was a collision.

"Father!" Eric cried, breathless.

"No worries, son. Come in for a moment."

Harald and Eric entered the house, and Harald went into his room. Astrid was relieved she'd gone out in time, but she feared he'd notice the absence of his bow.

He didn't seem to, thankfully, and left his room.

Eric breathed, "It's beautiful."

Astrid couldn't believe her ears when she caught a low chuckle from Harald. "I should have given you this when you married," he said, "but it escaped my mind. This has been passed from father to son, starting with my grandfather. His father got it from a raid he led and passed it on when his son came here. I never had the occasion to use it, but now you have." Harald's voice softened. "I prefer my axe, and I know you've received training with a sword. Wield it well."

Metal rang. Astrid peeked out the curtain. Eric, facing Astrid, held a sword in his hand, and its blade flashed cold in the dim light. Carvings in the handle and cross-guard shone. Eric's face was firm, and a hint of sadness was around his mouth. He swallowed and looked up at his father, whose back was to Astrid.

"I will."

Eric put out his hand, and Harald gripped it in both his own. But that didn't seem to satisfy him. He embraced Eric, then stood tall and straight like the strict father he used to be.

"Erlin waits at the Tingstead," Harald said gruffly. Eric nodded and sheathed his sword. His fingers shook as he strapped it to the belt around his waist.

They left the house, and Astrid hid her face in her hands momentarily. With a settling breath, Astrid held up the bow and studied it. It was light and small enough for her. Holding it in her left hand, she pulled the string back with three of the calloused fingers on her right hand. She strained to reach her ear. The bow had a firm draw.

Father's voice flickered back to her. "No, Astrid. To the corner of your mouth. That's it."

A smile tugged at her lips. No matter how many times she'd been told, she always drew it to her ear.

She slung the quiver over her shoulder, and Eric's knife caught her eye. It wasn't often he left it behind. Why today? She hesitated, then picked it up. It was the same one she'd used to protect herself against the bear last year. With a shudder, she ran her finger down its long blade. Eric carried another knife in his hand, and between that and his sword, he should be fine. He wouldn't mind if she took this one.

By the time she returned to the Tingstead, the village was empty. She shivered as she turned and ran toward the beach, where the Karls would surely wait for the Danes to arrive. The village was strangely quiet, like her home after the attack. An urgency rose in her chest and forced her to hurry.

Instead of standing on the open beach, she went to the woods and crept down to where dirt smeared into sand. It wouldn't do if she were discovered because, even though women sometimes fought alongside men, no one would let her stay.

She hid behind a tree and looked out. Sure enough, there was the whole force of Trygvey standing in rows stretching down the beach like a wall barring the way to the village.

Danish boats approached, the dragons' heads on the prows glaring on them. The middle longship was the largest and the most delicately carved, with a high deck and a tent in the back. As Astrid studied the boat, she caught a glimpse of a familiar but dreaded face: Holskuld. Memories appeared before Astrid's eyes: pictures of smashed houses and mangled bodies, lying in the middle of an ash and blood-covered street. Would that happen to Trygvey? All strength and courage drained away, and she leaned against the tree.

Then she remembered what Samuel had told them about David fighting Goliath.

David was a young man who had no experience in war and yet chose to fight Goliath, a skilled soldier and a giant.

Before fighting, David said, "You come to me with sword, a spear, and a javelin, but I come to you in the name of the Lord of Hosts, the God of the armies of Israel, whom you have taunted. This day the Lord will deliver you up into my hands, and I will strike you down and remove your head from you, that all this assembly may know that the Lord does not deliver by sword or by spear; for the battle is the Lord's, and He will give you into our hands."

Warmth flooded Astrid's chest, and she raised her head. God was in control, and whatever happened was best, whether they won or lost.

Spears and swords gleaming and pale wood blinding, the Danish longboats ground to a stop in a line along the shore. An eerie battle chant arose and quickened, and the raiders beat their axes and swords on their shields simultaneously. Its tempo increased and the chant grew louder, then stopped.

The defenders of Trygvey stood silent with their weapons drawn. Astrid pressed her cheek against the tree's cool bark. Holskuldr was standing in the prow of his boat, sword and shield in hand and helmet on his head, ready to conquer another island for his own.

Not caring what might come next, she straightened, filled her lungs, and shouted, "You come to me with sword and spear, but I come to you in the name of the Lord of Hosts, and He will deliver you into my hands!"

Holskuldr lifted his head, and his men looked up at where she hid as the men of Trygvey raised a shout and bore down on them. With an answering cry, Danes leapt from their boats and met them head-on. The battle began with a thundering crash of metal and wood and hardened leather.

Hidden by the brush, Astrid held up the bow, clumsily fitted an arrow in place, and drew it back. The callouses on the inside of her fingers had softened, so the string bit into her skin as she waited for a clear target. Because no one was there to replenish her arrows, she had to shoot sparingly and only when certain of her mark. But with all the confusion, friend and foe looked awfully alike. So she waited and watched, her fingers burned, and her arms stiffened.

A warrior stopped right in front of her long enough for her to take in his savage look and wild eyes; the arrow shot away. The bow jerked. The Dane's arm was struck, and he tore the arrow away. Astrid was fitting another arrow in place when a Trygvey warrior took advantage of the Dane's distraction and engaged him, killing him.

The next few arrows hit a Dane's foot, another's shoulder, and missed another entirely, and Astrid clenched her jaw with each, determined to strike one down. Her shots didn't seem to be doing anything except giving a villager the chance to defeat an opponent. At least she hadn't hit a villager yet.

When one of her arrows hit a Dane's chest and he tore it out, staggering, scarlet flowing down his dusty leather jerkin, Astrid felt sick. Cold washed over her while she watched the Dane fight furiously, face ashen and swinging his axe wildly until falling to the ground and clutching the wound. There he struggled, rolling about, staggering, and rose on one knee, where he was struck by a villager's axe through his head, and was dead.

Astrid put down her bow and pressed a fist to her mouth to keep from losing her meal. Though she wanted to run away and forget what she'd just seen, she could not turn her eyes away from the Dane's body lying in a battered heap. He was a Dane, and yes, she'd seen the result of the raid on Cooray, and she'd watched Mother Fredda die, but they were nothing compared to this. Her own arrow killed a man; would have, if the villager hadn't come when he did. Had Father, Sven, and Isar died like this? In the swarming chaos, she caught glimpses of Erlin with Haakon by his side, Eystein and Karsfien far down the beach, and Samuel giving his all in a knot of villagers; she watched them all, waiting, cold all over, for them to fall and hoping against it.

It was as if her eyes were opened. Now she saw every struggle against fatal blows, every last writhe in a bloodied puddle, every collapse. The warriors on the beach became not villagers and Danes, but men, destined to conquer or die. War was a terrible thing, and there was nothing she could do to stop it. Was she helping, or only making things worse?

Dizzy with nausea, she collapsed against the tree and watched the battle, cold and shivering, feeling like a child: helpless, and wanting to give in to a good cry. Icy fingers crawled over her skin, and she shivered in her kirtle, unable to warm herself in any way.

She stayed until her fingers and toes were numb with cold and her stomach was a burning, churning stone. When at last she rose, a sob escaped and released her stomach. She vomited and felt worse afterwards instead of better, for she was shaky and weak and as good as blind.

She stumbled through the woods for a time and, when straightening to figure out where she was and in what direction the caves lay, she remembered the bow. It had been left behind. Groaning, she turned back.

This time her head was clearer and she wasn't so shaky, so she picked her way much more easily back to her hiding place. Halfway there, she heard voices and stopped. The voices were nearby and, though the battle raged down the hill, every word was clear. Two men spoke.

"These people are very confident, Jarl. Do you think help will come to them?"

"No, Bjorni, I think not. The shieldmaiden's words encouraged them, no doubt, but their confidence is in the Christian God."

The second man's hissing voice brought a bitter taste to her mouth. Holskuldr! She held her breath and grasped Eric's dagger; its firm handle steadied a surge of anger tightening her chest. This was the man behind all the death.

"Send some men to search for their temple," Holskuldr continued. "I saw a lone building at the top of the eastern hill when we approached. That must be it. If it is, burn it. If the Karls see the flames, they will lose their confidence."

"Yes, Jarl." The two men rose a stone's throw from her, and she froze as they left, Bjorni going one way and Holskuldr another. They did not look back. Otherwise, all would be over for her.

Once more, she was paralyzed. Holskuldr's words rang in her ears. Burn the church? The big, beautiful church that brought the villagers together, that they worked on so diligently? The labor, the commitment, the love, the scrolls and paper and ink, all would be gone. She couldn't stop the battle or keep the church from being burnt, but she could save what she could.

There was no time to find the bow and arrows. Every moment mattered, for the church would be easy to find, a mere game for navigators of the sea. Going by way of the village would take too long, so she plunged into the woods in the church's direction and fought her way forward.

When the wood thinned and ended and the church stood before her untouched, her ankles, arms, neck, and face were scratched and, in some places, bleeding; her throat was so dry it hurt to swallow. No one was in sight on the hill or on the path below, but she ran to the church's double doors and pushed them open.

The inside was still a mess from lessons the day before: blotted sheets with wobbly, meticulously copied sentences, opened scrolls, corked ink bottles, and wiped-clean quills littered the tables; rolled scrolls lay in jumbled piles on the shelves, and several fell with a muffled clatter when a breeze blew in.

She looked over the tables first, rolling up Greek scrolls and tucking them under her arm; scraps of paper with Norse letters scribbled over them were stuffed in her hands. When she could hold no more, she dumped them in a nook just inside the woods and returned and grabbed armloads of scrolls off the shelf. Most were in Greek. Where were the Norse translations? In Samuel's room?

Pulling up the hem of her kirtle to make a pocket of sorts, she tucked the scrolls inside and crossed the empty hall to Samuel's room. With a pang of guilt at her breach of privacy, she went in and immediately spotted a paper and scroll-piled desk in the back corner by a neatly made bed. Funny, he should keep that tidy and nothing else.

As of yet, she couldn't read much Greek, so she couldn't tell what was important and what wasn't, and swept everything, pens and ink bottle included, into her skirt. Goosebumps sent shivers down her arms and along the back of her neck: the Danes were near, she could sense it. She scrambled from Samuel's room, holding the hem of her kirtle tight and sprinted down the long main room, reaching the door just as a towering figure blocked the way. The Dane grabbed her shoulders in a vice-like grip, and his eyes were blue ice. She shivered but tried not to show it.

"Look what we have here, Atli," said the giant Dane in a deep, thick voice.

Behind him entered a thin man wearing chain mail and a green cloak. A smirk crossed his narrow face. "A girl?" He laughed. "What scouts does the jarl have? Let go of your kirtle!"

Astrid, seething and grinding her teeth, did not move. Atli's hand shot out, and he grabbed the hem out of her grasp and sent the items crashing to the ground. The ink bottle smashed and sprayed black ink on her skirt and on the giant Dane's leg wraps.

Atli's eyes travelled over the spilt items and went back to her. She lifted her chin, although her stomach quivered at the cold fire in his eyes and the ruthless line of his mouth.

"Did our jarl mention something of a girl, Thorvold?" he said, as if to himself.

The giant Dane grunted, and his fingers dug into her shoulders.

"Take her out and wait for me." Atli pushed past Astrid, the sword at his side hitting her legs.

Thorvold dragged her out doors and stood silently, his grip ever tightening. She held her breath and bit her tongue against the pain pulsing down her arms.

After some time, Atli returned empty-handed and stood beside her, grimly silent, but with a satisfied curl around one nostril.

There was crackling, then a red glow. Flames ate through the roof and spread until the entire building was engulfed. The roar was akin to a stormy sea, and the crackling of falling beams like a breaking mast. Wind blew the black smoke into her eyes and forced it down her throat. She coughed in spite of her efforts, while the Danes stood tall and silent.

Shadows of men gathered before a burning building flashed before her eyes, and she could almost hear one saying, "Their jarl's sword." Once again, she was lifting the door to the cellar and looking out at the proud Danes in front of her burning home. Someone was handing Holskuldr Father's sword when Atli clipped,

"Come."

Astrid was snatched back to the present, blinking in the broad daylight, surprised it wasn't black around her. Atli had turned and was walking away, and Thorvold was dragging her along. Grinding her teeth, she pulled against him and dropped all her weight to the ground so one of his hands slipped from her shoulder. She twisted and rolled, tore his other hand away, and jumped to her feet.

There was a ring of metal from behind. She whipped out her knife and turned, then felt herself falling, sparks swarming. She blinked and found herself on the ground with Thorvold's foot pressed down on her chest, and a mere handbreadth away from her face was the red-gleaming point of Atli's sword.

"You will come, thrall, or I will make you wish for death." He sheathed the sword, and Thorvold lifted her up by her collar. Gagging and lightheaded, she couldn't resist the iron grip that seized her shoulder again.

Suppressing a sob, she allowed him to take her down the hill in the direction of the longboats. The battlefield was silent, and she prayed it was only a pause in the fight to care for the wounded.

Her hands and feet went cold, and her steps wavered. Each one took her closer to meeting Holskuldr face to face, and she, the daughter of the jarl he'd killed, was at his mercy.

Dead ahead was the longboat, and Holskuldr stood in the prow, watching. Astrid flexed her fingers against her clammy palms. Her knees weakened, but as she met his yellow stare, they steadied. She would not be afraid of the man who killed her family.

"Astrid, wait! Stop!"

Astrid spun. Eric was bounding toward them, body stretched out in full exertion. She reached for him, but Thorvold pinned her against his stony chest. Atli stepped in front and drew his sword with a smart ring.

They clashed, swords out. Atli's blows were weighed and precise, forcing Eric back. Eric set his jaw and pushed hard, gaining a little ground.

Astrid watched in terror, clutching her throat. Waves of fear weakened her until her legs gave way and she collapsed. Dirt ground into her palms, and she tasted blood.

Atli towered over Eric, raining down blow after blow, pushing him back in retreat. Eric danced around him, fitting in jabs and cuts where he could, but Atli deflected his blade. Both men sized up their opponent and changed their tactics. Astrid's heart rose a little. But as Eric moved his sword to block a blow, Atli rushed in. His blade stabbed deep and returned coated in scarlet. A scream tore from Eric's throat as he dropped his sword and hit the ground. Trembling and in mute horror, Astrid watched him struggle up and Atli push him back down, hissing,

"Die in your agony." He wiped his sword on Eric's back and sheathed it, and turned to Thorvold. "Put her in the cargo boat."

Astrid's vision whirled as Thorvold grabbed her shoulders, turned her around, and dragged her toward a boat. As he threw her on the boat, she caught a glimpse of Eric staggering to his knees. Thorvold opened the door to the hold and pushed her in. Pain exploded in her back as she landed, and her head cracked against a corner. A square hole above her closed with a bang. Darkness closed in.

Chapter 22

Astrid opened her eyes, and a large, square, glowing outline of light came into focus overhead, then the faint shadows of square crates and lumpy hemp sacks piled on all sides. The place she lay was the only clear one, and even here her head lay on a sack. She was in the cargo long ship, captive.

Slowly, she sat up, rubbing her temple. Why was her head so sore? Her shoulders and arms were, too, from Thorvold's rough handling, and ached when she moved.

Closing her eyes, she recounted the events leading up to her current situation to be sure she remembered them all; with her head pounding like never before, it would be good to do. She remembered shooting from the woods, seeing the Dane fall, the overheard conversation, going to the church, something burning, then the feeling like teeth clamping onto her shoulder and pulling her along— that must have been Thorvold. But what came next was blurred. It was something awful, something that hurt as much as Snorri's death, but what was it? She thought hard, rubbed her temple, and even tried to feel how she remembered feeling, but it only left her sick.

She sat still for a moment, wondering dully what to do next, when her ears started ringing in the silence. Rubbing them, she paused. It was unusually silent. Come to think of it, the silence was strange. There ought to be others with her if this were the thrall boat. Ears sensitive from the ringing, she cupped her mouth and whispered, "Hello? Anyone there?" The words were swallowed by the crates and sacks; not an echo returned. Neither did they answer. So the Danes weren't capturing thralls after all? They'd come solely to kill and conquer?

A misty memory arose like the tide, slowly taking form. Fear. Haunting yellow-green eyes. Pain in her shoulder pulled her to a place she didn't want to go, and then a voice called her back. A young man running from out of nowhere, drawing his sword, gray-blue eyes flashing with fury and sandy hair rippling in the breeze. He fought for freedom and for love, but collapsed under another's sword. Astrid hid her face as tears welled and fell, aching with that same pang that had cut through her when he fell. And where was he now? Lying dead and cold on the beach, having died in agony, or still languishing in another thrall boat?

"Pull yourself together!" she whispered to herself, hiccupping and drying her tears. "You can't do anything about it like this."

The door above was too high to reach, but not if she stood on something. She dragged a crate over and climbed up, but not even stretching as high as she could have made her tall enough. After testing several crates, she found one that wasn't too heavy and stacked it on top of the first. This had better work. Something might be on top of the door to weigh it down, but it didn't hurt to try. She climbed up. Ah, now she could reach!

Pressing the palms of her hands flat against the wood, she eased the door open a crack. Cool, fresh, salty air flowed through, and she breathed it in eagerly. The hold air hadn't felt stifling until then, but now it was thick and reeked of old straw and damp wood.

She squinted and blinked through the bright sunlight. All she could see from that angle was the big blue sky, until someone stood in the way: a big, sturdy man with bushy red hair. He threw down an armload of weapons.

"Hey!" Astrid yelled. Her voice cracked, and she licked her dry lips. The man paid no attention to her.

"Thorvold!" He turned, and his mouth hardened. Surprised? Disgusted?

"What are you doing?" he growled.

"Where is Eric?"

"Who in the name of Thor is Eric?"

"The young man Atli...stabbed...on the wharf. Where is he?"

"What business is that of yours?"

"Where is he?" she demanded, louder.

Thorvold rolled his eyes, then glared. "We left him to die in his misery. Atli's aim was always good. Your Eric should be dead by now, unless Atli had a bad day."

Astrid's arms shook so she almost dropped the door. Her lips tingled as blood left her face, and once again tears welled, but she blinked them away.

"Why are you still there, looking at me with those big eyes?" Thorvold growled. "You think I'll let you out?" He spat. "Pray to your God to make me."

"Where are the villagers?" she asked to try to appear bolder than she was.

Thorvold spat again. "Pray for your pious villagers, too. They're scared. Religion's made them soft: can't fight anymore."

Heat flashed in Astrid's face. "The God we worship delivers His people from their enemies. Your strength and the strength of your men are nothing compared to God's."

Thorvold didn't answer, but glared at her and brought his foot down on the door. The force threw Astrid to the floor of the hold, knocking her head against the crates. Her head whirled.

"That's what I think of you and your God, rat!"

Something scraped over the deck above her, and Astrid leapt to her feet. She staggered, caught herself, and climbed up the crates again to push the door. Stuck.

She hit the door with her fists and sank onto the crates, hiding her face in her hands. A sob rose in her throat, but she choked it down as she remembered what she'd told Thorvold. God was bigger than any enemy she could face. "Oh, Father," she cried, "Let us win just this once!"

What seemed like days later, but was likely less than a quarter of the day, the floor above her scraped again. The door was flung open, and sunlight flooded the hold. Atli peered down at her.

"Stand on those crates."

Astrid obeyed, and Atli grabbed her arm and pulled her up. As she lay on deck, she rubbed her arm and breathed deeply. It was good to get fresh air into her lungs. And the sun! She would never take it for granted again.

Atli pulled her to her feet and made her disembark. There was no chance for escape, for Thorvold was there waiting and grabbed her arms before she'd steadied herself. Atli disembarked and, with one hand on his sword hilt, took hold of her and led her toward the empty village. At the end of the wharf were half a dozen men sat lazily and looked up as she and Atli approached.

"What d'you have there, Atli?"

Someone chuckled, and the others winked and grinned at each other. Astrid shrank away from them, stomach quivering, and Atli's grip tightened.

"No concern of yours," he snapped. "The Jarl sent for her."

The men exchanged glances and fell into sullen silence.

Atli took her through the wharf and to the village. The village was silent, so silent it was deafening. Astrid strained to look at the beach, where the battle had been, but already it was blocked from sight by longhouses.

She was pulled to a stop at the Tingstead, where a swarm of Danes was gathered around the fire pit, talking in harsh tones. When Atli cleared his throat, they turned and faced them, and Astrid trembled under their gazes. Holskuldr was among them. A shiver like cold water trickled down her back. Holskuldr gave her a scrutinizing look. Nothing escaped his narrow eyes.

"Let her go." His voice hissed, like a snake. Gooseflesh rose on Astrid's arms.

Atli hesitatingly uncurled his fingers, and Astrid flexed her hand to encourage the blood in her arm to circulate. It began to tingle. Astrid resisted the urge to rub her arm. She never took her eyes off Holskuldr.

He walked slowly around her in a circle, one hand on his sword. He glared at her from under thick eyebrows. "Do you know who I am?"

Astrid ground her teeth.

"Do you know what I'm here for?"

Astrid bit her lip. Undoubtedly, for the same reason that brought him to her home island.

"I was told this island has a great store of wealth. Thralls also make excellent spoil. A man told me the wealth was stored in a treasury. A girl betrayed him, he said, and she knows where it is. You are the girl, are you not?" The Dane paused, but still she didn't answer. He turned fully toward her. "Tell me, and you will be freed and your people spared."

Astrid nearly choked. The man could only be Hake. The name nearly crossed her lips, but she bit it back. She answered Holskuldr as firmly as she could. "I don't know anything about it."

Holskuldr's eyes widened for an instant, and he looked intently at her, searching, his mouth hardened as if displeased with what he saw. Something greater than fear surged, and she drew herself upright.

Holskuldr stepped toward her. "Who are you?"

"I am Astrid of Cooray, daughter of the late Jarl Arnold."

He resumed his walk, circling her. "I see your father in you." He stopped. "Where were you?"

She clenched her shaking hands.

Rage darkened the Dane's face. He grasped his sword handle, but instead of drawing it, he said, "Are you afraid?"

"No." Even after a brief moment of searching, she realized she was not afraid. Astrid lifted her chin.

"Why not?"

Astrid didn't know herself. Where fear should have been, there was a burn in her chest that engulfed anything else she may have felt. But she could not explain this to Holskuldr.

Daring to meet his eyes again, she pulled her answer from the words Samuel had taught her from the scrolls. "I do not fear those who destroy the body only, but the one who can destroy both body and soul and cast them into Hades."

The Danes standing nearby burst into guttural laughter. Holskuldr's thin, wide mouth twisted into a grin, and he chuckled. "You are doing a foolish thing, believing in this Christian God. Mark my words, Astrid of Cooray, if you depend on this God of yours, you will come to the same end as your family."

Astrid clenched her jaw. Even with her eyes open, memories of her family flashed through her mind.

"You have until sundown to decide to tell me what you know. Put her in the longhouse we decided upon."

She was grabbed by her bruised arms again and thrown into a longhouse nearest the Tingstead. She fell against the wall and sprang to her feet, and the door slammed shut.

Not caring who heard her, she finally let out the scream that had been building in her chest and pummeled the wall, wishing it were Holskuldr. He was so callous, threatening her with his snake-like voice. Only, she knew they were more than mere threats. This, as she knew it, was the end.

Dear Eric, even if he hadn't died on the wharf during the night, she'd never see him again. What about Haakon and Bertha? She hadn't seen them since the beginning of the war. Were they lying wounded somewhere? Were they dead?

How she wished they were all here! Even if they all died together, it was better than meeting the end alone. Now she was crying, for goodness' sake!

She wiped her tears away. What would they do if they were here? Eric would take her in his arms, and she'd be able to hear his heartbeat with her ear against his chest. Haakon would try to say something funny and cheer them up, and Bertha would either hug all of them or pray in her new, sweet faith.

Pray. She could do that. Samuel said it can do wonders, and she sure needed wonders right now.

"Father," she whispered, "be with them, wherever they are. Be with Eric, whatever may be happening to him. And please, Father, help me get out of here!"

Chapter 23

Erlin turned his back to the ocean water visible through the cavern opening and walked up the rocky shore to the candle-lit caves, cringing at the sound of the gravel crunching under his feet. The sound reminded him of ringing metal, guttural cries, shouts, and clamor. His people had suffered much during the battle, and he was powerless to help them.

He ducked through the low opening into the first cavern, where the wounded were. Several men lay in rows along the wall, muttering in their feverish sleep or hovering between life and death, and the rest huddled with their wives and children. The room smelled strongly of herbs and lye, mixed faintly with blood and other sickening smells. Gudrid went from one man to another, tending their wounds and instructing four other women who were doing the same.

Erlin started toward the other cavern, but his sleeve was caught, and he looked down into the half-bloodied and torn face of a man with a shattered arm.

"We did our best out there, Jarl," the man said. He was trying to give some measure of encouragement, poor Karl, and his unwavering courage was touching. Erlin grasped the man's hand and bowed over it to show his gratitude, and even forced a grim smile which the other reflected, but didn't speak. Grief was too heavy on him in that room.

Erlin passed quickly into the other cavern where the rest of his people were sheltered and joined his family beside the outer opening. Bertha scooted aside, and he lowered himself to the ground with a sigh. He leaned against the uneven, cold stone wall and closed his eyes. None spoke, and for that he was thankful. They were between a cliff and a pack of wolves—or a ridge and bloodthirsty men, as he'd found himself a year ago—and few options remained.

The hidden boats could hold them all, but where could they go? Nearly uninhabited lands were few, and anyone would be suspicious if they were flooded with two hundred wanderers. If any village could support such an increase so suddenly.

Surrendering to the Danes was not an option. They still believed in the gods who demanded blood for every successful raid. He and his people would be killed, enthralled, or worse.

Organizing an attack... foolhardy. His remaining fifty fighting men were nothing compared to the near hundred and twenty of the enemy.

"Erlin," Fredissa called softly.

He regretfully opened his eyes. Fredissa was offering him a water pouch. He took it and drank, holding the water in his mouth to relish its coolness before swallowing. Then he motioned to Haakon, who moved over, and drew Fredissa to his side. He wrapped his arm around her and held her tight, and took Bertha's hand and squeezed it. Haakon moved to sit beside Bertha, to see him more easily, no doubt. He'd been more loyal than a dog ever since the bear attack. Now, Haakon bore a black eye and a dozen cuts as a token of his loyalty. For he'd hardly left his side during the battle. Poor boy. Erlin nodded in approval, and Haakon smiled and sat straighter.

Samuel walked up, so Erlin let go of Fredissa and motioned for him to be seated. The Saxon did so and studied him briefly before speaking.

"How do you fare?"

Erlin rubbed the bridge of his nose. "As well as can be expected. I must soon decide what to do; we cannot stay here for long."

Samuel nodded. "What might you do?"

"Sail to a better life, most likely. It is the best chance we have."

Haakon opened his mouth eagerly, then shut it and settled back down again.

Smiling to himself, Erlin said to him, "What is it you would say?"

Haakon reddened but leaned forward earnestly. "To flee would admit defeat. It would bring dishonor on us."

Erlin nodded slowly. "It would, but right now, I'm willing to live with it if we escape."

"May I have a word?" asked Samuel. His face was thoughtful, but there was an excited air about him.

"Speak on," said Erlin.

"Before the battle, in response to the Danish war cry, I thought I heard a woman declaring David's words of defiance to Goliath. She declared God would give them into our hands."

Erlin groaned. "If Astrid was in battle as you said last evening, it could only have been her. I heard the voice, too, and her words stirred courage and strength within me. Where she is now, I wish I knew."

"Well, because God's name was invoked, I believe he will act. Yet, we cannot do nothing."

"So you're saying we ought to fight? Does God say anything about that in His book?"

"He is called a Warrior; His people are called to stand for truth. I believe that war with a just cause is good, such as in defence or to defeat a wicked ruler."

Erlin put his head in his hands. The decision could not be put off any longer. He raised his head and called for Karsfien, who came and stood beside Samuel. Erlin cleared his throat.

"I do not doubt the integrity of your words, Samuel, but an attack is something I simply cannot risk. Have you not heard of raid outcomes? People were slaughtered, leaders tortured, and far more horrible practices I will not mention. I witnessed one before, carried it out, in fact, and it was enough."

Samuel's steady gray eyes did not waver. "I have heard of them, although I am blessed not to have seen any."

"Samuel has a point, brother," said Karsfien. "We will be discovered at length and have no sure place to go. Does not one of our sagas say, 'Fight your foes in the field, nor be burnt in your house'?"

An itch formed between Erlin's shoulder blades. "Do you think I don't understand that?" he growled.

"Father," Haakon ventured, hesitating, "we could try. I'd rather die facing them in battle rather than being killed hiding. The same saga says, 'Better to fight and fall than to live without hope.'"

He grunted, then began rubbing his hands together in an attempt to remain calm and think straight. "Does not another say, 'A person should not agree today to what he'll regret tomorrow?" He clenched his jaw and said nothing more, for nothing else could possibly be said.

The others were silent for a moment. And then Haakon ventured to speak again.

"We have something Hulskuldr cannot beat," he said.

"And what is that?"

"We have God."

Erlin stopped rubbing his hands together and raised his head. Confidence showed in every part of Haakon: his straight posture, rolled back shoulders, and the lift of his chin. For the first time since they'd fled to the caves, Erlin felt hope, something he had long abandoned. He nodded to his son, then looked to Karsfien, who flashed a grin. Erlin chuckled to himself, stood and raised his hand. The room was silent as all eyes turned on him.

"We are assembling a surprise attack. All able-bodied men will come and fight after spies are sent out and have returned."

The din of the answering cheer made his ears ring.

***

Astrid shuddered and sighed and leaned her head against the wall. Stories of war thralls entered her mind, their terrible ends, the agony they had to endure. Outside, dozens of Danes waited, with only the command of their leader holding them back. The lack of complete victory had left them restless.

She curled up tighter and hid her forehead back on her knees. The thought of ending it came, and although a knife to the heart would be an easier way to die, she rejected it. The same urge that had told her to save the manuscripts now told her to wait.

Clenching her jaw, she looked up. The cabin was dark except for faint sunlight that forced through the gap around the door. The hazy light lit the scattered pots and pans, odd-end utensils and other items lying in a heap, and the blackened fire pit spotted with puddles that had extinguished the fire. She licked her dry lips, pulled herself to her feet, and hurried over.

Eagerly, she scooped up the water with her fingers and drank. It tasted of ashes, made her cough, and stung her sinuses, but it was cool and took the dryness from her mouth. Refreshed, she leaned back on her haunches.

Her eyes roamed around the room again, from the black back wall to the front door, then flicked again to the deep shadows swallowing up all details. Most longhouses had back doors; there was no reason why this one wouldn't.

She rose and stepped forward cautiously, feeling with her feet for anything she'd trip over. Gray outlined a bench and several stools in one corner, and an open, curtained room in the other. She felt along the splintery wooden wall until her fingertips found a crack, the edge of the door. Light shone faintly around it. Feeling along the crack, she came to the cold metal latch, lifted it, and pushed.

The door wouldn't move. She pushed again, using her full weight, yet it still refused to budge. Gritting her teeth, she threw her shoulder against it. The door rattled but stayed shut. Releasing a growling shriek, she rubbed her aching shoulder. The house was secure, all right.

Her temples pounded. Pressing her wrists to them, she exhaled slowly to relieve the pressure in her chest. There had to be some way out of here. A flood of thoughts came at once, all jumbled into a big mess, and she stomped her foot.

"This door is locked," she said aloud so as to focus on one thought at a time, "and I may not be able to open it in time. Now, how many men are outside the front?" She paced the room a few times, digging her fingernails into her palms, and took a settling breath before approaching the door. Putting her ear to it, she listened. Someone was outside muttering to himself and shuffling impatiently.

With trembling hands, she lifted the latch and eased the door open. Air brushed her face as an ocean-weathered and brown-haired Dane whirled. His bushy eyebrows lowered over his cold blue eyes.

"It's not sunset yet, if that's what you want," he growled. Outside, the shadows under the roofs were long. No one else was around.

"I'm hungry," she said loudly, standing tall and looking him in the eye. Danes hated cowards.

A smirk raised a corner of the man's mouth, revealing yellow teeth. "You should've thought of that before letting yourself get caught. Scrounge." The door slammed shut and narrowly missed her fingers.

She shook her fist at him and turned away.

After taking another drink from the fire pit, she sank onto a stool and buried her face in her arms on the table with her eyes closed. The weight settling on her shoulders was tiring, yet she could not sleep. It was like awaking from a bad dream to find the night stormy and just as miserable as the dream. She shivered and tucked her legs under the stool.

Her breath was trapped between her arms, and the table was getting hot and stuffy. She propped her chin up and breathed deep, then exhaled slowly. When she opened her eyes, she blinked mist away and leaned forward, squinting.

In the back corner, a line of light glowed ghost-like. She crept to it, half-afraid it would fade as it would in a dream, and ran her finger along it. The line was the result of a crack in the board, which bent outward because of this. The board, about a hand-breadth wide, was slipping out of its upper groove that held it in place.

The crack must have been recent since the homeowners hadn't fixed it yet, but what caused it, she could only guess. Whatever had happened, the board was broken, so it was held together only by its splinters. The one to its right bore a similar mark, although much less severe.

Trembling, she glanced at the front door. Her breath seemed to roar in her ears, and the swish of a fold of her kirtle falling sounded like the ocean's surf. She stiffened, and the back of her neck prickled.

The guard hadn't come in or made any other sign that he'd heard. She was overreacting. Slowly, she splayed her hands out on the most damaged board and pushed. It crackled, creaked, and groaned, and there was a snap. The board gave way several inches.

She paused and moved to the other, where she did the same as with the first, except this board was louder. It shrieked with splintering and creaking that was nearly deafening in the dead silence, sending off just as out warnings in her head. She obeyed them so heedlessly that she crashed into a stool and sent it clattering to the floor.

At that moment, the door slammed open and the guard entered. In three long strides, he crossed the room and stood over her, black with a white outline from the light pouring through the open doorway.

"What are you doing?" he barked.

Astrid remained silent, frozen in place, heart pounding, and tried not to look toward the boards. He dealt a sharp kick to her side, and she clutched it and gasped for air.

"Answer me, dog!" Two more kicks, then a pause. She thought hard for an answer as he raised his pointed boot toe.

"I tripped," she gasped.

"What were you doing over here? And what was that noise? I'm not deaf nor blind. Guilt is in your face." He drew out a dagger that gleamed pale silver.

"Threatening the thrall, Trym?" mocked a voice from behind him.

The guard Trym turned his back on Astrid, and she looked from between the guard's legs at the doorway where a man stood, arms crossed and smirking, with several others behind him peering in curiously.

"I'm following orders, Agnar," stormed Trym. "Mind your own affairs."

Agnar spoke deliberately. "Did he give you leave to do as you please? No. You're plotting behind our backs."

Trym thrust his knife in its sheath and grasped his sword; the other laid a hand on the axe tucked in his belt. "Are you calling me a traitor? Liar!" Trym spat. "None is more loyal to Holskuldr than I."

Agnar's brows lowered, and he frowned. "I trust what my eyes see." His voice lowered, and it sent chills up Astrid's spine. "You called me a liar to my face, and that will be repaid." Then he smirked. "Unless you're not man enough for it." Now he was obviously trying to stir Trym up by taking advantage of the guard's restlessness and anger, and by Trym's tense trembling, he was succeeding.

"So I'm a traitor and a coward, am I?" the guard roared. "Both will be repaid. I challenge you to a fight, Agnar, and you will soon know I'm neither."

"I accept," Agnar said haughtily, "and propose these terms: the victor gets both shares of the treasury and the first claim on the thrall."

"Which I accept." Trym stomped out of the building, and the other men jumped out of his way. "Someone watch the thrall!" Another man took his position in front of the longhouse and closed the door. There was yelling, silence, then talking.

Alone at last, Astrid scrambled back to the wall. Yells and metallic rings sounded outside, covering any noise she made, so she hit the boards with full force. The splintered one immediately gave way with a crash, but the other was harder. With her shoulder, she rammed it again and again, watching the door. The board cracked, creaked, groaned, and finally gave way, and she tumbled with it out of the longhouse. In spite of a shot of pain in her ankle, she fled.

Several houses away, she stopped and collapsed against a wall. Her throbbing ankle would let her run no further, but she would be safe enough. No one was in sight, the noise of the fight had faded, and she'd soon enter the wood. Hopefully, she knew the woods enough to find her way. All she had to do was go in a straight line in the direction of the caverns.

Without knowing why, she turned and looked back. The longhouses were orange from the setting sun, and, though she couldn't see them, she knew the Danish longboats would be, too. They'd all be down at the wharf, their furled sails glistening and carved bows towering. Was Holskuldr down there? Was he alone? If he were, she could end this war once and for all.

Something told her to leave, as did a prick of conscience and something Samuel had once taught. But since she didn't remember, was it really important? Putting all caution out of mind, she slipped among the longhouses down to the wharf, paused, and flattened against a shadowed wall.

There was Holskuldr's longboat, the largest of them all, the third down the row. The red eyes sparkled in the carved dragon's head. On deck stood two men: Holskuldr and another. They spoke, occasionally gesturing to the island, then the stranger left. Holskuldr ducked into a tent set up in the middle of the boat, beside the sail.

When the coast was clear, she crept to the boat and jumped lightly aboard, easily because its edge aligned with that of the wharf. Beside her lay a few axes and daggers, and to her joy, a short bow with its quiver. One arrow remained. She took up the bow and fitted the arrow on the string, then slowly stepped toward the tent. Her heart pounded in her ears, and her clammy hands shook. It took deep breaths to keep herself steady. And the closer she came, the more Samuel's teaching from God's book weighed on her. What had he said? Oh, what was it?

At the tent, she held the bow and the head of the arrow in one hand and reached out to push the tent flap away with the other, revealing the startled face of Holskuldr.

Then she remembered.

"Vengeance is mine, I will repay, says the Lord."

How blind she'd been! Why couldn't she have heeded the words when she first heard them? She hadn't wanted justice, but vengeance, just as Eric had said. And now, did she want to merely end the war, or avenge her family? She didn't know anymore.

With a gasp, she released the tent flap and scrambled away. Why hadn't she listened when instinct told her 'no'? Limb nor mind would obey her now, and stumbling, flailing, she reached for the side of the boat, but the back of her kirtle was caught, the bow and arrows that she still held were torn away, and she was spun around. Holskuldr gripped her arm more firmly than Atli or even Thorvold had done, and his sword was drawn.

"How did you escape?" he demanded.

Her mouth went dry, and her tongue wouldn't cooperate. She swallowed and searched for an answer. Remembering the words, she'd quoted from David, she answered, "God set me free."

He scowled. "So you came to preach to me? Or could you not wait 'til sundown?"

She swallowed and curled her hands into fists to hide their trembling. "I didn't come to tell you anything."

A smirk slowly widened his mouth and, by the look that came into his eyes, she knew that he knew she'd come to kill him. Yet he said nothing. Exhaling, she dropped her gaze to the wooden planks on which she stood.

"Religion's made you soft, too, Astrid of Cooray," he hissed.

The sun was now setting, and its colored light reddened the planks, like blood, and the memory of that fateful night in Cooray arose before her. No, she couldn't change the past, and it wasn't her place to fight. "God," she prayed silently, "this is your place to fight."

Holskuldr turned her around and took her all the way back to the Tingstead.

Chapter 24

When they reached Tingstead, the fight was over, and the men were silent. Holskuldr tossed Astrid to the ground; dirt and gravel pierced her palms. Feeling too faint from terror to get back up, she remained where she landed, feeling three dozen eyes on her. Heat rose in her neck.

"Where is Trym, whom I set as guard over this thrall?" Holskuld demanded. "What is the meaning of this?"

"He challenged me to a fight, jarl."

Astrid looked up. Agnar stood out from the others and, although blood was smeared across his face and forearms, he looked fearlessly at his commander. "It was a matter of honor," Agnar said, straightening. His gaze flickered to Astrid, who trembled and looked quickly down.

"Was the matter settled?" Holskuldr growled.

"It was."

There was a moment of such silence that she heard above the pounding in her ears the cracking of Holskuldr's knuckles as he clenched a fist.

"Trym," he hissed in a low voice, "your charge is before you, escaped."

Tentatively, she raised her head just enough to be able to see Trym standing before her, slouched and bleeding shoulder. His expression was unreadable despite the dread he must be feeling.

Holskuldr stepped forward with a hand on his sword. "We do not have time for proper punishment, so consider that a gift from the gods."

Everyone swarmed around Trym, and two men forced him to his knees as Holskuldr came nearer. Astrid looked away just before there was a guttural cry. Trym gave several wrenching gasps amid shouts and hideous laughter. Astrid risked a peek. They were dragging the guard's body away, and Holskuldr was cleaning his sword. The body was left hanging on a tree, and the men returned. Holskuldr put his sword away with a click.

"The thrall has refused to give information," he said, "so according to my word, I hand her over to you. Only, do not kill her; that is for me to do."

Dizzy and sick, Astrid lay frozen in place while the Danes rushed forward. She couldn't even pray.

But before the Danes reached her, there was the whistling sound of arrows that flew from the wood behind them, each hitting its target. The men scattered and ran for their shields, whipped out their weapons, and dove for shelter. The arrows ceased, and warriors charged from the woods, and her heart leapt, for they were Trygvey villagers led by Erlin. Holskuldr shouted orders above the confusion, and his men formed a shield wall, which the Trygvey men engaged and broke through. Full-fledged battle began.

Astrid still could not move even though the battle shifted toward her. She was shaking with fear, surprise, and exhaustion, and her ankle throbbed. When she gave herself up to being trampled underfoot, a young Trygvey fighter broke out of the battle, pulled her to her feet and, covering her with his shield, took her safely past the Tingstead to the woods. Only in the foliage did he stop and ease her to the ground.

Sitting on the ground, Astrid wrapped her arms around her middle and tried to catch her breath. Her head swam, and she feared she'd faint.

The fighter crouched beside her and asked, "Are you alright?"

Gasping, she could only nod. The fighter's voice was familiar, but she couldn't recognize him until he removed the helmet covering his face, and she looked at him, blinking. She opened her mouth several times before she could speak.

"Haakon!"

He grinned. "Didn't expect to see me, did you?" He became serious again. "As soon as you're able, go straight for the caves. There's a guard at each entrance, and they've been commanded to kill any Dane who comes near. Give a holler when you come near. God be with you." Putting on his helmet, he turned to leave.

"May He be with you, too," she called. He paused, bowed his head, and sprinted away with a wild yell.

Now that she was alone, she found herself sobbing ridiculously. It felt good, and she felt better afterwards. Brushing tears from her eyes, she focused on breathing deep—inhaling, filling every part of her lungs until they burned, then slowly exhaling. She remained sitting until her heart no longer pounded and her wits were pulled together. Before standing, she searched the ground on her hands and knees for a stick to lean on. The best she could find was on the short side and crooked, but it would do. Slowly, she stood, biting her lip against the pain, and the stick held her weight. Then she turned in the direction of the caves.

Progress was slow because the stick caught on bushes and vines, but soon the sound of battle faded, and she hit the trail, where travel was easier.

At long last, gray flickered among the tree trunks, and the rock wall came into view. Still a good distance from it, she stopped and called, "It is I, Astrid Arnoldsdatter of Cooray."

"Come, then," answered a voice. She did so, and just as she reached the entrance to the caves, an armed man stepped from the shadows and pulled the curtain of vines aside. She thanked him and stepped into the deep darkness. Soon she entered the first cavern, the one with the rocky shoreline and the exit to the ocean, and lowered herself onto a slab of rock with a groan. Pain was pulsing up her leg now, and she was tired.

At a squeak, she opened her eyes. Bertha and Fredissa stood side by side at the edge of the water, and Bertha's face was pale. Her eyes widened, and she broke into a run. Astrid pulled herself up to meet her.

Bertha engulfed her in an embrace and held her tight. "Astrid, oh, Astrid! I thought I'd never see you again! When Samuel told us you'd been in the first battle…" Bertha kissed her cheek and said no more.

Astrid pulled gently away when she couldn't stand up any longer. "I'm sorry, I can't…" She sank to the ground as the room wobbled. Her head was spinning, and Bertha's face blurred. She closed her eyes only to see spinning colors against a background of black.

Bertha's voice cut through the ringing in her ears. "What is it?" She held her by the shoulders.

"Nothing much, just my ankle."

"Have you had anything? Food? Water?"

"A little water." At the mention of food, her stomach felt hollow.

Something was held to her lips, and a voice like her mother's spoke. "Drink this." She obeyed—it was sour, and when it hit her stomach, she was the slightest bit less hungry. Watered-down skyr. Fredissa sat beside her and drew her close. Astrid leaned against her.

"Dear Fredissa," she murmured.

Tender hands stroked her hair. "We're glad you're safe. Here, drink more."

In a moment, Gudrid arrived with Bertha following close behind. The healer frowned at the swollen ankle, but after examining it, declared it a minor injury that would heal in a week or so, if cared for.

Astrid sighed with relief once the bandaging was done. "Thank you, Gudrid. It's good to see you."

"It's good to see you, as well," Gudrid replied with a faint smile. She rose stiffly. "Excuse me, but I have many wounded to care for."

Once Gudrid had left, Fredissa stirred. "Let's get you to the other room, Astrid. We can make you more comfortable there."

Astrid nodded wearily and laughed. "I'm so tired, I could sleep right here." Fredissa smiled but did not laugh.

With Fredissa on one side and Bertha on the other, Astrid was borne to the cavern for the wounded, where she stopped and her pulse skittered. A familiar figure, now just a shadow, lay propped up on the other side of the dim room. Eric. One of her hands flew to her throat. "Is that...?"

"He is well," Fredissa whispered in her ear, "and has been asking about you." She and Bertha helped Astrid forward and lowered her beside him.

Pressing a fist to her mouth, she took Eric's hand. His color was ashen, and his eyes were closed and sunken. Even in his sleep, his face was pinched as if in pain. Tears pressed behind her eyes, and it was hard to breathe.

"It can't be," she croaked. "I thought I saw him die."

Fredissa spoke quietly. "He'd left the caves— slipped away, in fact— in search of you despite our warnings against doing so. That night, he was found on the shore halfway to the caves. Although he remembers little of what happened after he was wounded, we've gathered that he dragged himself to where he was found. Thank God, it wasn't too late. Gudrid is a good healer."

Astrid blinked hard, murmuring, with a glance toward Gudrid bending over someone, "She learned from the best."

Calloused fingers curled around her hand and gripped it, bringing her attention back to Eric. The gray-blue eyes opened, and opened wide.

"Astrid?" Eric rasped. "Is this another dream?" He brought her hand to his mouth and kissed it.

"No." Joy bubbled up in her chest, and her lip trembled. She swallowed against the lump in her throat.

Fredissa whispered, "We'll leave you alone," and nudged Bertha, who frowned but obeyed.

When they'd left, Eric gave a faint smile and relaxed against the blanket under his head. His smile disappeared, and his grip tightened. "To see them take you…"

She shuddered. "Hush," she said hastily and brushed a lock of hair back from his forehead and bent to kiss him. "Don't think of that. We're together now." She took his other hand and forced a wobbly smile.

"But not safe yet." A troubled frown pulled at the corners of his mouth. He looked her over while rubbing a thumb over her fingers. "What happened?"

She dropped her gaze, and pain shot through her ankle. Wincing, she shook her head. The fear and anger she'd experienced clawed at her throat. She swallowed, mumbling, "Not yet."

Eric nodded and kissed her hand again.

Fredissa returned and cupped Astrid's shoulders. "Would you like to stay here?"

"May I?"

Fredissa nodded.

"Please, then."

Bertha, who'd come up silently, danced away to fetch a blanket to cushion Astrid's ankle.

***

Erlin finished off one opponent and engaged the next. Deafening confusion of shouts, rings, cries, roars, battered him; smells of his own sweat, of hot leather, of blood and of smoke were overpowering. As he fought, he avoided longhouse walls and garden fences and the bodies lying on the ground.

His opponent was down, so he hid himself in the shadow of a longhouse to survey the odds.

Not nearly as many Danes stood as before; the arrows had done their job. Fighting in the village gave his men the upper hand since they were familiar with the layout. And the sun had just set, so they couldn't go on fighting for much longer. Their only light source was fire that the Danes had set to several longhouses. The buildings blazed like giant lamps.

There was a series of cracks, and the longhouse beside him shuddered and collapsed. Sparks sprayed everywhere, burning his face and singeing his clothing and hair.

He went from that place only to be born down upon by a tall Dane. Their shields and swords clashed, and they held their swords ready. Holskuldr's yellow-green eyes glittered from inside his helmet.

Erlin advanced but was pushed back. His elbow bumped into a wall, so he stepped away and braced against Holskuldr's ramming shield. The Danish sword stabbed, Erlin blocked and pushed. Holskuldr was unbalanced for the briefest of moments, so Erlin advanced and gave a series of blows which were caught either by sword or shield.

Tripping over a body left him briefly bent and exposed. Holskuldr's sword came down and bit into Erlin's shoulder bone, and on its way back up caught on his helmet and sent it clattering behind him. The force and shock of the blow sent Erlin to his knees, but he held up his shield in time to catch a blow that hit the shield against his head and rattled through his skull. Blindly, he lurched upward, dropping his shield and switching the sword to his remaining good hand, and charged, driving Holskuldr back a few steps. His enemy was a black blur framed by piercing light from a burning longhouse, and Erlin deflected glinting metal, avoided pale wood, and aimed for the shifting dark void.

Blood tingles his nostrils. The shoulder must be bleeding. The taste of salt and grit coated his tongue; his wounded arm hung useless at his side, and the other shook with each blow it gave and received.

Holskuldr advanced again, and his shield caught on Erlin's jaw, jamming his teeth together. White stars exploded, and he brought up his sword in defense as he felt himself falling backwards and hitting the ground square on his back. The shifting black blur stood over him, and metal glinted.

Holskuldr gave a jolting, sharp cry and fell over him. Gasping, Erlin pushed him away and scrambled to his feet, reeling, prepared to fight. But when a few deep breaths cleared his head, there he saw Holskuldr, lying dead with an arrow fletching poking through the arm hole in his plate armor. Shot through the heart. If the archer could be found, he would be rewarded greatly.

Erlin ran back to where his shield and helmet lay, scooped up his helmet and placed it on his head and, with a yell, charged at a knot of fighters a stone's throw away.

As the battle waged on, the remaining Danes fought with enough ferocity for two. They dealt heavy blows, rammed shields without holding back, and put all their strength in their swings. Whether or not they'd seen their leader's fall, they fought as though they had. And when one of Erlin's men fell, the Danes hacked at him until the warrior couldn't possibly be alive. This filled Erlin with such rage that he threw himself upon the Danes he saw doing so, despite the odds. Still, the battle raged on until full darkness of night fell, and the attackers fought even more brutally. Few were left now; instead of surrendering, however, they continued to the end, many with a shattered arm or leg and gaping wounds and stuck with arrows and spear-points.

At last, the battle ended.

Erlin removed his helmet, let it fall, and dragged the back of his hand over his forehead. His men stood silently, looking at the heaps of carnage around them, some with astonishment on their faces. The light of the longhouses had long since burned low, but the piled bodies of their enemies, and some of their friends, were visible. Erlin wiped his blade on the only clean patch of sleeve and returned it to its sheath. The snap echoed like lightning in the silence. It roused the men, and they raised a mighty cheer. The shout loosened the tightness in his chest and brought strength back to him.

Then he took the horn that hung at his side and blew it, calling his men to himself. They came, slowly and weary. Many limped, and all bore one or more bloodied wounds. Thirty-two of the fifty remained, and two he sought were not counted among them.

"Karsfien and Samuel, are they among you?" he asked.

A few mumbled too quietly to be understood, and after a moment, Samuel came forward, limping and clutching his side, and gripped Erlin's hand with the faintest of smiles. But nothing was said. Erlin squeezed Samuel's hand and bowed in thanks.

He looked over his men again. "Where is Karsfien?" Several shook their heads, and a weight dropped in his stomach.

"I am here, brother," said someone to his left. Karsfien came around a corner. Despite his battered appearance—heavy breathing, many wounds, and dragging his right leg forward—he stood straight and on his face was a stern happiness. Erlin ran to meet him, embraced him with his good arm, and brought him to the rest of his men.

"We will do no more tonight," Erlin said, looking up at the cloudless sky. "Half the night yet remains, and we will return to the caves to rest. Tomorrow, all who are able will clear the bodies and burned buildings."

They filed silently down the path to the caves, where the women welcomed them. Wounds were cared for, and all those well enough removed their armor, changed their jerkins, and washed their faces, necks, and arms. Weariness overcame Erlin, and it was all he could do not to stumble around like a drunken man. Finally, when everything was cared for and he and his family lay out a mat on the ground, he lay down and fell asleep as soon as his eyes closed.

***

For the next month, life was busy for everyone. The damage was cleared away, and new longhouses were rebuilt, and now the village hardly looked as if the battles had ever taken place. But it wasn't an easy task, what with the lost lives and the wounded. Out of the seventy-four men who'd all fought, only thirty-eight remained, and the rest were yet healing. Few were the women who hadn't lost a father or brother, and who now carried the full responsibility of providing for their households. Because of this and the men's inability to work as hard or as long, food was harder to come by until the harvest was in. It was a time that tested the villagers' bonds, and happily, their bonds were strengthened. Everyone helped each other rebuild, care for households and livestock, and harvest the fields, so no one was in need.

Bikki, the old man whose dream had prodded the villagers against Astrid, tried to point out that the battles were Astrid's doing, but with Erlin, Karsfien, and Samuel silencing him and the villagers paying him no heed, his words did nothing more than make Astrid wince when she thought of them.

At the end of the month, trees started turning gold and red and brown, looking like they'd been dipped in gold or dye or bronze, and a cold breeze had returned. Astrid chopped the wood and brought it in herself to save Eric from doing so, because he was still healing.

"How I wish I could do it myself," groaned Eric, when Astrid arranged the fire and blew on it gently.

"Oh, hush," she scolded, glancing at him where he sat in their only high-backed chair. "The more you rest, the sooner you'll get back to it. You can stack the wood high as the tree behind the church; you can stand in the frozen ocean and fish for the whole night—"

Eric interrupted her with a laugh, and Astrid set a pan of fish over the brightly burning fire. Then she stood, wiped her hands on her smock, and returned to her stool by Eric's chair. He smiled as she seated herself, and she smiled back. It came naturally now, with the Danish invasion slowly fading into memory. She leaned on the arm of his chair, took a lock of his hair, and began to braid it. He sighed and closed his eyes.

"It's good to be home," he said.

She nodded and said with a chuckle, "I never taught you to skate last winter."

He opened his eyes and laughed. "It'll keep us busy this winter, once I'm well. I'm afraid you'll find me an impossible learner."

Laughing, she leaned forward and planted a kiss on his cheek. She settled back down, braided another lock, and lowered her voice. "I'm glad everything's over."

His smile faded, and he nodded slowly. He glanced at the door where Harald had gone out a moment before to help with building, and said, also in a low voice, "You never told me what happened."

Her hands faltered, and a pang went through her chest. She looked away, but Eric cupped her cheek and turned her toward him.

"You didn't go straight to the caves, did you?" he asked.

He wouldn't be denied, that was certain. Besides, she'd promised herself to confide in him more. Sighing, she clasped her hands together. "No, I didn't. I went to Holskuldr's boat instead. I wanted to kill him. To end the war, I thought, but really for vengeance. I… I was wrong." The smell of frying fish wafted by, but before she rose, Eric deterred her with a hand on her arm.

"Stay, just a moment."

Reluctantly, she obeyed, feeling like a child being confronted by its parents.

"What changed your mind?" Eric prodded, taking her hand and lacing his fingers between hers.

Astrid kept her eyes on her blue wool kirtle. "What Samuel taught us. That vengeance is only for God. It wasn't up to me to do it the way I thought best. And, I remember now the command, 'You shall not kill'. I was going about it completely wrong."

"But you see that now. Killing in battle, 'just battle' as Samuel calls it, is acceptable, but not what you were going to do. And justice is right and well, and revenge is another. If Holskuldr had been condemned and put to death by the council, that would have been right, but it isn't for us to do that." He lifted her chin just enough for her to look at him. "When you let go, God dealt with him. It is finished now."

She swallowed against the lump in her throat. "Thank you." Heat crept into her cheeks. "I guess I haven't trusted God as I should."

A smile came back to Eric's face. "You can always begin now."

Astrid couldn't help but smile back, even though her lips quivered. "I've been trying. Yet… I miss my family, now more than ever. I've tainted my memories of them."

Nodding, Eric squeezed her hand. "Do you want to see Cooray?"

Astrid blew out a breath and stared at the flickering fire and sizzling fish. "Just for a visit, if I can. To say goodbye."

"I'll do what I can."

She lifted her eyes from the fire and met his. They were gentle and full of love, plunging her deep into the ocean she'd only gotten a glimpse of before. It tugged on her chest and prickled her arms. And for a wild moment, she didn't know whether to laugh or cry. It left her breathless and wondering, if she'd known such love existed, would she have held onto things of the past the way she always had?

"If you want a visit to your island," continued Eric, "you'll get one. I understand how you feel. If my mother were not buried at sea, I would go to say goodbye."

Chapter 25

Salty summer air stung her nostrils, but it felt good. She was going home.

From the prow of Harald's knarr, his old and beloved trading boat, the whole ocean was visible to her, unobstructed until it curled into the horizon. For two years, Astrid had looked at that line from the shores of Trygvey; now, she would finally cross it to her island.

But two years was a long time, and her island had gone through so much. It would be different. Or, she would be different. She would still be at home there, wouldn't she?

She turned back for a final look at Trygvey, but it had vanished. The ocean behind them was empty; a stone sank into her stomach. There was so much to do there, so many people left behind. If she closed her eyes, she could still see Fredissa, Bertha, Haakon, and Erlin standing at the wharf and waving farewell. She'd be back in only a month or so, but an overwhelming desire to go back washed over her. Was this homesickness?

A breeze stole her breath away and whipped through her hair. Above her, the tied-up sail flapped wildly.

"Let the sail down!" Harald bellowed from the tiller.

Eric and another man leapt up from their rowing benches and grabbed the ropes hanging on either side of the sail. With a fluid motion, the sail dropped. The boat lurched forward, throwing Astrid off balance. She caught the boat's side. Eric glanced her way, leapt over a crate, and offered a hand to help her up.

"Are you alright?" he shouted above the wind.

She took his hand, and he pulled her up. She offered a smile. "Yes, thank you," she shouted back.

He put an arm around her shoulder and squeezed. "I'm excited to bring you with us, love. Kaupang is like no other place you've seen before, and I know my way around fairly well. I'll show you everything. The childhood longhouse of my grandfather's father still stands, and family members live there. You'll love it."

Her eyes moistened as Eric's words brought back images of her own childhood house, no longer standing. "That's... amazing," she choked while attempting a smile. The trip couldn't be spoiled by her own grief.

Eric frowned. "What's wrong?"

She sighed. She couldn't keep anything from him. "Cooray. I look forward to seeing it, but I also dread it. I know it *must* have changed significantly. Many of the houses were burnt down, including my own. In truth, I'm afraid of what I'll find there." She'd been looking down at Eric's boots next to hers, but now looked up into his face. "Part of me wants to sail back to Trygvey and stay there."

"It is a deer island. I couldn't ask for a better place to call home. As for your island, let's hope its changes were for the best."

She shivered, thinking again of the burnt houses, and he tightened his arm around her.

"Get a move on, Eric," Harald shouted over the noise of the wind. "It's your turn at the tiller. Now I know why wives often stay at home," he added with a wink. "Hard to keep the men at work." Several others laughed with him.

Eric gave a quick kiss and let her go. "You can join me back there if you want."

Astrid glanced at the sea in front before answering. "Thank you, but I'll stay here."

He nodded. "Just hunker down, then. It gets rough in this high wind." He turned and went around the cargo tied to the center deck.

"I will."

***

Five days later, the first rays of dawn roused Eric out of a deep sleep. He stretched lightly with a groan and sat up as slowly as possible, so as not to wake Astrid sleeping beside him, wrapped in a blanket. She murmured in her sleep. Eric kissed her cheek softly and crawled out of their makeshift canvas shelter without waking anyone. They'd worked hard the day before and would all be sore that day. Being woken suddenly after an arduous day was not pleasant and could result in a grumpy crew. No one wanted that, especially him, and especially on this day, because they might arrive at Cooray, the first stop on their voyage.

One of the crew members was faithfully manning the tiller for the last night shift. The Karl nodded in greeting as Eric sauntered forward.

"Good morning," said Eric. "How was your shift?"

"Very well," replied the Karl. "No wind, and no clouds, either. A few are now on the horizon, as you can see, but they do not forerun a squall. And by the looks of it, a wind might pick up sometime soon."

The sun rose completely over the horizon. Eric shaded his eyes against its blinding glare and looked due east. Reds and golds rose like an aurora, flickering over the ribbon-like clouds and the brightening blue. Just below the sun, sitting on the edge of the horizon, was a black speck: Cooray. Astrid would like to see this.

Eric nodded. "All good news. Do you mind keeping at the tiller a little longer? I want to show my wife this." The Karl grinned and nodded, and Eric slipped back under the canvas and crept to Astrid.

He shook her gently, whispering, "Astrid, the sun is rising."

Her long lashes fluttered as she opened her eyes, and a sleepy smile spread across her face. "Time to get up?" she murmured.

"There's something I want to show you."

With a stretch, Astrid sat up and put her blanket aside. He held out his hand, and she slipped hers into it. Even after months of marriage, his heart tripped at her touch. Together, they crept out of the shelter.

"What do you see there?" he asked, pointing.

She shaded her eyes and squinted. A moment passed, and a glow lifted her face. "Cooray! There it is!" She withdrew her hand and ran to the side of the boat, gripping the edge, her whole frame lit by the glow.

The glow passed, leaving her like the flowers that had grown limp and pale on their wedding feast tables. Eric put an arm around her shoulders, and she smiled up at him, but it was forced. Were those worry lines? Eric wrapped his arms around her. Her body was tense at first, then relaxed under his touch.

"Thank you, Eric," she breathed against his jerkin.

Eric didn't say anything, but lay his cheek on the crown of her head and ran his hand down the length of her hair. If only he could keep away the pain of her past by holding her like this. He looked out to the rapidly growing silhouette of Cooray and pressed his lips together.

***

Astrid kept out of the way while the cargo was being unloaded. She'd tried to help, but was so distracted by her own excitement that an exasperated Harald, tired of himself and the other men running into and nearly over her, brought her to a safe part of the boat and ordered her to stay put, which she meekly did, and was at first too ashamed of being a hindrance to look around her. But, gradually, she grew interested in the sights around her and saw them clearly for the first time.

The wharf, although sparse, was the same as she left it: busy and bustling, and with that same salty, wild fish smell. Beyond that, as far as she could tell, was where the changes began. The wooden planks that had extended a way into the village were now gone, and all the longhouses bordering the wharf were unfamiliar. Old houses took over from there, with a new Danish house dotted among them, and towering above on top of the hill was a proud, ornate Danish longhouse that marked where her home had been. Her throat constricted at the sight of it. She couldn't see anything else from her vantage point, but it wasn't looking good. Her home island was a stranger. Her only comfort was the absence of the burned longhouses.

Eric came and told her, in a low voice as if knowing the tangle of emotions knotted in her chest, that it was time to disembark. She followed him and, while they walked to the side of the boat where the crew was leaving, she slipped her hand into Eric's. He squeezed it.

They were the last to leave the boat. A Coorayan karl gripped Astrid's hand and helped her down.

"Steady there," he said.

Astrid stared into his face. He was familiar, but his name escaped her. When he gave her a quizzical stare and a playful wink, she shook herself and quickly looked down.

"How has the village fared?" she asked quickly.

The Karl's mouth widened in a grin. "We've fared mighty well of late. Before that, not so well. You're from Trygvey? Then you must have heard that the Danes took over about two years ago. Many of our people were killed, including the jarl and his family. The poor women and children," he said, shaking his head. "It was bad."

Astrid nodded and bit her traitorous lip.

"They left last harvest and didn't come back, those Danes. Holskuldr was going on another one of his conquests. Very few remained here, so our remaining men threw them off. A man named Gorm is Jarl now."

Warm fingers threaded between her own, and Eric said, "The Danes and Holskuldr were killed in battle on our island."

The Coorayan's face lit up. "You don't say! The others will be glad of that. We've prepared for the Danes' return, but feared what we had left wouldn't be enough." Sadness came over him again. "Jarl Arnold would be happy if he'd lived to see this day. He'd fought a losing battle when the Danes attacked."

The Karl's name suddenly came to her. She spoke through the lump in her throat and offered her hand. "Karl Wulfstan, I am Astrid Arnoldsdatter."

Wulfstan's hand engulfed her offered one, and he looked her over with wide eyes. "Little Astrid?" His whisper was hoarse. "How..."

"By God's grace I escaped... but only me," she added falteringly. Seeing Wulfstan brought back all the grief the attack had brought.

Wulfstan looked over her again, as if unable to believe she was right in front of him. "You're not so little as I remember. You didn't forget old Wulfstan?"

Her smile, albeit wobbly, returned, and she laughed softly. "How could I, dear Karl?" She turned to Eric. "He was an old family friend. He's a merchant, and used to let my friends and me explore his boat when he returned. He'd give me little tokens—beads and such."

"Who's this?"

"Oh, sorry. This is my husband, Eric Haraldsson."

Wulfstand gave a nod and a wink. "You have your hands full. My best wishes. But now, I must return to work; I can't wait all day. I'll see you around."

Before Astrid could get in another word, he'd left.

Suddenly, the whole island was before her, and she couldn't move. Through stiff lips, she mumbled, "It doesn't feel right. I'm intruding."

"But this is your old home," Eric answered. "You used to live here."

Among the strange, Danish longhouses? She shook her head. "Not anymore."

"You wanted to say goodbye, didn't you? This is your chance."

He was right. She couldn't stand there all day. With a breath, she forced a step forward and found she could move again.

Passing the first few houses would have made her hide her eyes if she were any younger. The new ones were tiny and poorly constructed, crooked and had many gaps in the walls that were sealed with daub, some even made of boards left over from burnt buildings. Here and there, an old house appeared, a token from another time that knew no sorrow, its wood untouched for the most part.

One old house caught her eye. It was the one where she'd met the mother and children. Hesitating, she knocked on the door, which was answered by an old and bent woman. Behind her in the house was a young woman, not much older than Astrid herself, carrying an infant only a month old. She came to the door, where Astrid could see her face clearly. Both women were strangers. Then she remembered the horrible command of Holskuldr's to keep thralls for a feast for Odin.

"I'm sorry," she stuttered, backing away. "I thought someone I knew lived here."

The old woman harumphed and croaked like a raven, "Small chance for that," and left.

The young woman came nearer. Her eyes were like gray drops of rain. "No harm done," she said. "Good day, and the gods be with you."

"Good day."

The door shut, and Astrid turned away and started walking again. Without realizing it, she came to where her home once stood, and paused, blinking in the sudden sunlight as a cloud rolled away. She rounded the dreaded longhouse and bent close to the ground, where the cellar would have been, and felt along the ground. Eric stood close by. Finally, her fingertips brushed a crack in the ground; she dug her fingertips into it and felt it shift. There was a creaking groan, and slowly, she lifted a square of grass. The cellar below was sooty black.

She laid the door back and, with a breath, ascended the ladder, now shaky and creaking. Eric followed close behind. They squinted in the near darkness while their eyes adjusted.

Nothing had changed. The crates, bags, and barrels stood in the same places, untouched. The nearly spent lamp still sat on a crate, and her old show was on the floor. She stooped and picked it up, and the experience flooded over her. This felt more real than any of the memories had been, and it hurt more, too. Her eyes watered, and she swallowed against her tightened throat, but couldn't ease the pain growing in her chest.

She groped for Eric, who wrapped his strong, protecting arms around her and held her tight. She buried her face in the soft folds of his salt-scented jerkin and clenched her teeth against the sobs rising up.

"I'm sorry, love," he whispered against her hair. The pain lessened.

Blinking hard, she looked up into his gray-blue eyes. "I still have you." A tear escaped, but she smiled. He wiped it away, and his throat bobbed. With a deep breath, he gave a crooked smile. "Yes. And I have you."

Heat flamed her cheeks, and she looked down.

"Where do you want to go next?" Eric asked.

More than anything, she wanted to see Snorri's grave, but hadn't a clue where it was located. She shifted her weight and looked back up. "There's one other place I don't think has changed. It's my favorite place on the island."

"The hill?"

"The hill."

The other side of Eric's mouth tipped up. "Then let's go."

They climbed out of the cellar, closed the door, and turned toward the woods. The path had grown over somewhat, yet it faithfully led them uphill and to the clearing on top where the tree waited for them at the edge of the cliff. Solitude still reigned on that hill and would do so as long as it existed. And for the first time since landing at Cooray, Astrid's shoulders lightened.

She wrapped an arm around the tree, where sunlight fell in beams around her just as they'd always done. The foliage opened up below, like a curtain, to reveal the shining ocean. "I came here whenever I wanted to get away," Astrid said with a cheek on the tree's cool, rough bark. "Problems, worries, anger, frustration, sadness. Sometimes work, too," she added, laughing. "Father showed it to me when I was a child, and soon it became Sven and mine's favorite place."

Eric nodded slowly. "The caves back home are my place, but I must admit they're nothing like this."

"And there's nothing like the caves."

Eric's sigh was one of contentment. They sat down together with their legs dangling over the edge of the cliff, and a breeze came and brushed their faces. Astrid breathed in the scents of pine and fir and fresh grass and the salty air of the sea: the unique perfume of the hilltop.

Eric breathed it in, too. "It's easy for me to believe in God here. I shouldn't wonder if He created this spot just for us and others to find Him here."

"Maybe that's why I felt peaceful here," Astrid sighed, resting her head on his shoulder.

There was a long moment of silence, during which she thought over the past two years, from the night of the attack to where they were now, and somehow, for some reason, it stopped hurting so much. Stirring, she said, "Before we go, there is one last thing I want to do for my people."

"What would that be?"

"Give them what is left in the cellar. Almost everything should still be good. They need it more than I do."

One month later, Astrid shaded her squinted eyes and scanned the busy wharf of Trygvey. As the knarr was rowed closer, she spotted Bertha and Fredissa waving among the crowd of the waiting wives and children of the karls on board. A thrill of excitement ran through Astrid as she waved back. Then, to her delight and amusement, Haakon, followed by Erlin, pushed through the crowd to join them. Haakon shouted something she couldn't understand, but she waved anyway.

"Steady, now," Harald commanded from the tiller. "Reef the sail and drift her in." The Karls did as they were told and used only the motion of their oars to drift the knarr to the wharf. With skilled strokes, they brought it to a stop, and a rope was thrown to a Karl standing on the wharf, who tied it to a post to keep the boat in place.

"Well done," said Harald, coming forward. He glanced at the sun. "Gather your goods and unload the rest, then off to the evening meal with you."

"Yes, Karl Harald," the men answered in unison. Excitement filled the air as they stored away their oars, flung the hold door open, and unloaded the boxes and bags from below.

Astrid ran to where the makeshift sleeping shelter had been and stuffed into a bag the few personal items—blankets, combs, and such—she and Eric had brought on the trip. She slung the bag's long strap over her shoulder. The traded goods were already off the boat, and the men now brought out their share, which they'd stored in bags under their rowing benches. Then, one by one, the men leapt onto the wharf, where they were engulfed by loved ones.

"Come, Astrid. Time for us to do the same." Eric appeared by her side. Together they disembarked.

How good it felt to be on solid ground again! The voyage had been a good one, but Astrid always felt in the way. With nothing to do but distribute prepared rations twice a day, she'd felt useless and bored. There was nothing for a woman to do on board a ship but sit unoccupied. It was with great relief that she left the boat.

"Sæl, Astrid! You're finally back!" Arms wrapped around her, and Bertha hugged her tight. "How was it? How were Cooray and Kaupang?"

"Delightful," Astrid laughed. Good old Bertha. She hugged her back, then let go to embrace Fredissa. "How have you been?"

"All is well, and improving." Fredissa kissed Astrid's cheek. "The rest of the harvest was bountiful, and there have been two more conversions."

"Samuel wrote down more of the Scriptures," said Haakon. "A saga about Christ, and another which is similar to the Havemal. It tells many wise sayings."

"Proverbs, you mean," said Bertha, with a twinkle in her eye and a laugh in her voice.

"Yes, that's it." Haakon rubbed the back of his neck.

"That's not all," Bertha added, lowering her voice to a loud whisper. "Haakon's *seeing someone.*"

Poor Haakon turned scarlet at the laughter that ensued.

"Is it that girl you danced with at Yule?" asked Astrid.

"Y-yes, she is. But Bertha, she's not getting anywhere."

Bertha dug her elbow into her brother's ribs, and he dealt her with a playful cuff on the arm. Astrid laughed.

"Did I miss anything?" Eric came up from behind them.

"Eric," Bertha scolded, "where have you been? Why didn't you come see us right away?"

"Your father spoke with me and Father, that's why."

Fredissa embraced Eric, then, laying a hand on his shoulder and beckoning Astrid, said, "You two must be hungry. Those rations aren't enough to keep a bird alive. Eat the evening meal with us. It's done and waiting."

"We would be delighted," said Eric. "You go on ahead. I will wait for Father." For Harald, Erlin, several of the Karls from the voyage, together with their wives and little ones, were exchanging stories and laughing heartily.

When at last Eric brought them to the longhouse, the meal was set.

"Why," said Harald when he walked in, "this is a feast. Don't tell me you went through the trouble for us."

Erlin waved his hands toward the table. "We wanted to celebrate your return from a successful trading trip."

"It was really no trouble at all," said Fredissa as they all sat down. She passed by Astrid and whispered, with a squeeze on her shoulder, "For you, dear."

The meal passed quickly, so full it was of enjoyment. The laughter, the invisible bond between them, the looks of love, all confirmed she'd come to the right conclusion—this was home. How ironic that this was where she belonged, where none of her blood family were. Yet this was her family, the close friends she'd made and who'd let her into their lives.

After the meal was over and the dishes cleaned and put away, Harald, Eric, and Astrid walked back to their own home. There, they found a fire burning in the fire pit. The house was warm and smelled of sweet pine smoke.

A chuckle rumbled in Harald's chest, and his beard lifted. "Erlin's doing, no doubt." He knelt by the fire and stoked it for the night. The sprinkles of white at his temples shone, and the fire's hot coals glowed red. He placed thick pieces of wood over the coals, and a string of smoke rose and disappeared. "Get some rest," he said, looking up. "You deserve it."

"I will," said Eric. "You do the same. Good night." He went to his and Astrid's room, pushed back the curtain, and waited for her.

Before following Eric, Astrid slowly stepped toward Harald. He looked so much like her father the night of the attack.

His eyes were soft. "Good night, daughter."

She did something she hadn't dared do before. Without hesitation, she bent and kissed his weathered cheek. He smelled like Eric, salty and fresh as the sea. "Good night, Father."

He blinked, face expressionless. When Astrid went to Eric, she looked back. Harald still watched her, but his beard had lifted again. The curtain fell.

Eric kissed Astrid and laughed softly. "He didn't expect that," he whispered. "To tell the truth, neither did I."

"He's my father, isn't he? Do you think he minded?"

Eric laughed again. "If I know him, he was delighted." He suppressed a yawn. "Let's get to bed. I could fall asleep standing up."

A wave of exhaustion hit her. Sleep would not ruin the beautiful moment. It had been a long day. She made no objection and slowly removed her outer clothes. She'd change her serk in the morning, when she wasn't so tired. With a quick combing and braiding of her hair, she climbed into bed.

She was asleep in a moment, and slept soundly until the twilight of the morning, when her eyelids fluttered open of their own accord. The waves were thundering in the distance, but from her bed, they sounded like the whispers of wool slipping across a worn, beloved tabletop. Astrid turned on her side and reached up to stroke Eric's face. He stirred, murmured, and sank into slumber again. Kissing his cheek, Astrid nestled against him.

Eric drew his arm around her and mumbled, "You alright?"

"Mmm-hmm, just listening to the ocean."

Eric yawned. "Not morning, is it?"

"No."

"You have a habit of going to the beach at night, don't you? You want to go?"

"Please, if you don't mind."

Eric slowly sat up with something like a groan. "There's nothing I'd like better."

Careful not to wake Harald, Eric and Astrid slipped outside and walked to the beach where they stood quietly, Astrid fingering her silver cross thoughtfully, until the sky lightened and the fabric of stars dimmed. Eric sighed, put his arm around Astrid's shoulders, and nodded toward the village. They'd better return before Harald awoke. After one last glance over the ocean, she let Eric take her back.